THE AVON ROMANCE

Kathleen E. Woodiwiss, Johanna Lindsey, Laurie McBain, Shirlee Busbee...these are just a few of the romance superstars that Avon Books has been proud to present in the past.

Since 1982, Avon has been continuing a different sort of romance tradition—a program that has been launching new writers of exceptional promise. Called "The Avon Romance," these books are distinguished by a ribbon motif on the front cover—in fact, you readers quickly discovered them and dubbed them "the ribbon books"!

Month after month, "The Avon Romance" has continued to deliver the best in historical romance, offering sensual, exciting stories by new writers (and some favorite repeats!) *without* the predictable characters and plots of formula romances.

"The Avon Romance." Our promise of superior, unforgettable historical romance...month after dazzling month!

JILLIAN HUNTER

HEART OF THE STORM

AVON
PUBLISHERS OF BARD, CAMELOT, DISCUS AND FLARE BOOKS

HEART OF THE STORM is an original publication of Avon Books.
This work has never before appeared in book form. This work is a
novel. Any similarity to actual persons or events is purely coincidental.

AVON BOOKS
A division of
The Hearst Corporation
1790 Broadway
New York, New York 10019

First Avon Printing, December 1985

AVON TRADEMARK REG. U. S. PAT. OFF. AND IN
OTHER COUNTRIES, MARCA REGISTRADA, HECHO EN
U. S. A.

Printed in the U. S. A.

WFH 10 9 8 7 6 5 4 3 2 1

To Jim—
my husband, my best friend, my forever love.

Acknowledgments

I would like to express my grateful appreciation to my editor, Carin Cohen, for her assistance and invaluable suggestions.

Chapter One

The heavy stable door slammed with a resounding bang that muffled the soft, triumphant laughter of the young girl leaning against it. Golden-green eyes dancing with reckless excitement, eighteen-year-old Juliana Marie Pendarvis kicked off her dainty satin pumps and sank to the floor, inhaling the sweetly mingled scents of hay, leather, and neat's-foot oil as she waited for the stitch in her side to ease. She dared not proceed with her misadventure until she was certain no one had seen her escape from the house. She listened intently for angry shouts and hurried footsteps. She heard only the erratic thumping of her own heart.

Seven minutes later she rode out into the stable yard dressed in a faded serge jerkin and filthy linen shirt, her long, firm-muscled legs encased in loose homespun breeches and scratchy woolen hose that bunched above the clumsy riding boots. That the borrowed garments she wore stank of horses and pungent male sweat bothered her but mildly; for the moment she wanted no more than to conceal the feminine curves and contours of her lissome figure. Hiding her hair had presented the greatest difficulty. It had been a struggle to get the waist-length tumble of burnished auburn waves tamed into an untidy braid and pinned under a cocked, low-brimmed felt hat whose shadows blurred the finely sculpted features of her heart-shaped face. But her efforts had paid off. So far nobody about the small country estate had as much as glanced at her askance. However, the ultimate test loomed before her in the form of her father,

1

whose unexpected appearance in the stable yard threatened to thwart her leisurely escape on one of his finest mounts.

Bull-headed old tyrant, she thought, indignant anger rising inside her at the sight of the short, barrel-chested figure limping past the water trough. *If it weren't for you, I wouldn't have to go to such preposterous extremes.*

"Evenin', sir," she mumbled, hastily lowering her eyes for fear their unusual color would betray her identity.

But she needn't have worried. Suffering from a painful attack of gout, preoccupied with thoughts of his troublesome youngest daughter, Sir Walter paid the unkempt stableboy scant attention except to note the powerful white stallion he rode.

"Bit late to be exercising Ajax, isn't it, lad?"

Juliana felt her heart lurch beneath the thin linen shirt. " 'Tis summer, sir. We've a while left before dark."

"Still, 'tis unwise to ride abroad so near dusk, when a rock or pothole could trip your mount before you know it." His watery blue eyes flickered over her with suppressed amusement. "Not to insult your manliness, son, but a spill from Ajax here could cripple a stripling like you."

The obstinate chin lifted a fraction of an inch. "But yer daughter—Miss Juliana—rides 'im all the time, sir."

A spasm of annoyance crossed Sir Walter's face, bringing into play an extensive network of deeply engraved wrinkles. "And my daughter does so in deliberate defiance of my orders, lad. That's one of the reasons she's been confined to the house tonight. If she wants to ride from now on, she'll ride sidesaddle on that gentle little mare I bought her in Penzance last spring."

Juliana might have voiced her opinion of the plodding cart horse some crafty farmer's wife had unloaded on her father had she not suddenly caught sight of her two brothers riding toward her from the paddock. Her older brother, Stephen, reached her first, his gaze narrowing as he reined in his gelding alongside Ajax. With an impatient swipe, he pushed back a lock of tawny gold hair that had fallen onto his forehead, tucking it behind his ear so that it blended into the premature grayness at his temple.

"No need to worry about young Jim, Father," he said,

assessing the situation at a glance. "Martin and I promise to keep a close eye on him."

Sir Walter frowned. "Jim? The name's familiar, but I can't say I remember the face. Let me take another look at you, lad."

To Juliana's relief, Martin, the youngest member of the family at seventeen, came to her rescue. "Jim's one of the Colruth boys, Father," he said, his thin, puckish face devoid of any deception. "We thought it a good idea to have him accompany us into the village to watch over the horses. You know how wild it'll be tonight."

"Hmph. You've a point there, I suppose," Sir Walter said. "You can wager them thieving gypsies will be about to take advantage of the confusion." A devilish chuckle sounded deep in his throat. "Just mind Jim doesn't get distracted from his duty by some pretty fortune-teller."

" 'Tisn't likely, Father," Stephen said, a slow grin softening the usual solemnity of his features. "Jim's not the least bit interested in women. He far prefers the company of horses."

The older man nodded his approval. "Well, go on, then. Enjoy yourselves. I'm sorry your sister will have to miss the fun tonight, but 'tis high time I took a firmer stand on her behavior. If it isn't too late already."

There was a moment of awkward silence during which Sir Walter raised his eyes to his daughter's bedchamber window as if he hoped to glimpse her lovely face there. But he could discern no movement behind the rose chintz curtains, no indication that she had been observing the activity in the courtyard. It hurt him more than he could ever admit to anyone, this recent rift with Juliana. Their relationship had been deteriorating for almost a month now, since the blessed departure of his eldest daughter, Evelyn. Not that he could blame the straightforward Evelyn for the upheaval her brief stay at Rosmorna had caused. She had only confronted him with the truth, what he himself had realized long ago but had not the courage to face.

He could still hear her stinging rebuke. "Don't deny it, Father! You've raised Juliana as though she were another son, a female extension of yourself. Boasting of her prowess in shooting, teaching her to trim a sail when she can't follow a simple recipe without poisoning someone, or—or handle a fan but it becomes a lethal weapon!'' That was an exaggeration, of course, but Evelyn had made her point.

The cawing of a raven in the meadow that adjoined the paddock roused Sir Walter from his unhappy reflections. Glancing up, he caught both his sons regarding him with poorly concealed disapproval. ''You think I've been unduly harsh on your sister, don't you? You'll not believe me that this is for her own good.''

Martin shifted uneasily in his saddle. ''Neither of us questions your motives, Father. But it does seem unfair to curtail her activities merely on the strength of Evelyn's advice.''

''Evelyn does get a bit carried away at times,'' Stephen added.

Sir Walter smoothed down his manicured white beard with the ball of his thumb, an unconscious gesture that indicated his growing agitation. ''Evelyn is a proper witch, Stephen, but this time she happens to be right. Juliana's a young lady—whether we've treated her as one or not—and she'll have to start behaving accordingly. That means she'll not be allowed to cavort until all hours tonight with a crowd of drunken fishermen. Now be off with you, and remember to be quiet when you come home. I'm expecting a visitor tonight, and he'll probably want to retire early.'' He stepped back to allow the three riders out of the stable yard, a note of wistfulness slipping into his voice. ''Leap through the flames once for me, Martin.''

''I will, Father,'' Martin called over his shoulder. ''Good night!''

It was June 24—Midsummer Eve—and the fresh sea breeze that rippled inland from Kenvellas Beach seemed charged with an undercurrent of magical excitement. In keeping with the ancient Druidical rite, bonfires would be built immediately after dusk on the hills and cairns bordering Mount's Bay. Long into the night there would be celebration, singing and dancing around the scattered bonfires until their flames burned down low enough for the fire-jumping ceremony, believed to purify the soul and bring a year of good luck to the participants. In nearby Penzance and the other parishes of western Cornwall, tar barrels would be lighted and sent rolling down the streets between processions of torch-bearing villagers.

Juliana held her silence until she and her brothers were halfway across the Pendarvis meadow, now thick with cowslips and buttercups and wild daffodils whose colorful heads bobbed gaily as they passed. "Imagine forbidding anyone to leave the house tonight. And all because of that meddling Evelyn. I swear I'll never speak to her again." But after a moment her feelings of resentment began to fade, and her face relaxed into an impish grin. "It's amazing how easy it was to pull this off. Papa didn't suspect a thing. I just hope none of the servants remind him that Jim went to Newlyn for his uncle's funeral. By the way, you were wonderful, Martin. He has a bright future in London as an actor, don't you think, Stephen?" she asked, referring to Martin's dream of becoming a famous player.

"Oh, God, Juliana. Don't encourage him."

Juliana's eyebrows arched at her brother's reproachful tone. "What's the matter with you, pray tell? You sound as sour as Evelyn."

"That was the first time I've really lied to Father. I didn't care for it one bit."

"Oh, that." Juliana looked amused. "Well, put it out of your mind for tonight. Think about something pleasant. Think about that cargo we're expecting from Bordeaux. We'll need to recruit every able-bodied man in the village if we're to dispose of all that cognac on schedule."

Stephen gave a short laugh that was both rueful and admiring. "You're pressing your luck, Juliana. If Father doesn't recognize you in that ridiculous masquerade by then, one of the smugglers is bound to. Anyway, on that matter he and I are in complete agreement. Free-trading is a man's profession. You're better off helping Louisa unpack tea from the oilskin bags."

Juliana resisted the temptation to point out that she'd been helping land contraband cargo for almost five years now. She enjoyed the excitement of participating in a successful run and was proud of the fact that her father was considered by the villagers as something of a public hero. Unemployment was rampant and smuggling provided work. A hard-toiling laborer or a fisherman could never afford to feed his family without the added wages he earned smuggling. Barely able to eke out a tolerable existence from his exhausted plot of land, the tenant farmer couldn't even enjoy a well-earned tot of brandy at the end of the day for the taxes he had to pay on it. Without the extra income from smuggling, many coastal villagers would undoubtedly revert to the ghastly, ancient practice of wrecking—luring ships to their destruction and plundering the wreckage while the crew members who hadn't drowned were callously left to struggle to shore.

Pushing the gruesome thought from her mind, Juliana dug her heels into Ajax's sides to catch up with Stephen. She knew she would be on hand two nights hence when the smuggling boats harbored in Kenvellas. Why spoil the evening with an argument?

"I rather fancy myself in these breeches. Your wife offered to take them in at the waist, but there wasn't time." She wrinkled her straight nose in distaste. "Too bad she didn't give this shirt a good washing."

Stephen shook his head. "I'll never understand how you talked her into acting as your accomplice. It's so unlike Louisa."

"Martin did it," Juliana said, twisting around to grin at her younger brother. "You should've heard the impassioned plea he made on my behalf. I almost wept."

Stephen smiled wryly. "No doubt."

Juliana lapsed into silence as she guided Ajax along the narrow hillside path that wound down onto the small tract of moorland that lay between Rosmorna and the village. Twilight had begun to fall, its grayish lavender haze darkening the hollows of the granite-studded hills that loomed before the three riders. Staring out across the windswept land, she remembered the blissful hours she had spent here with her brothers, playing out the adventures of King Arthur and his knights, gathering up fragrant armfuls of heather on the way home for their mother's soaps and sachets. Yet the moors held bitter memories, too, for it was here she had come to grieve when her mother died, finding unexpected strength and comfort in the changeless realm of rock and heath.

"Hurry up, Juliana," Stephen said impatiently.

Unaware she had come to a halt, Juliana urged her horse into a walk, wanting to shake off the sudden spell of melancholy. "Graham will probably faint when he sees me in these clothes," she said. "I wonder if he'll be too embarrassed to admit he knows me."

"Graham?" Stephen pulled his mount to an abrupt stop, his voice sharp with irritation. "You haven't invited that perfumed popinjay to meet us, Juliana? Damnation! I'd never have agreed to any of this had I known."

"You're teasing us, aren't you, Juliana?" Martin asked, slowing behind Stephen.

Juliana's mouth twitched with secret amusement. "No. I'm not. He's supposed to meet us in Rook Hollow. I trust neither of you will embarrass me with your bad manners." And before either brother could frame a retort, she had turned the stallion's head and set off across the moors at a restrained trot.

Stephen swore under his breath, staring after her. "What does she see in him, Martin? It can't be his personality. He has none. Is it his wealth? His title?"

Martin smiled reflectively, his sensitive hazel eyes following his sister's progress as the large white horse picked a path between the gorse and stones. "I suspect there's a little more to it than that."

"What's that supposed to mean?"

"Has it not occurred to you that Juliana spurned Graham until just recently, since her falling out with Father? She knows he detests the sight of Graham."

"Hmm. Louisa said much to the same effect the other day. Sometimes I wish we'd listened to Evelyn long ago. If we had packed Juliana off to one of those posh finishing schools in London, she'd have her choice of suitors. Certainly she wouldn't have fallen for the first powdered fop she met. And no matter what you say, I still think the idea of a viscount paying her court has gone to her head."

"Perhaps. But I'll bet she'd drop Graham in a minute if Father approved of him. This is war between them, you know."

Stephen rode on, considering. It made sense, and if anyone knew the rebellious workings of Juliana's mind, it was Martin. "Well, I suppose there's no real harm in it," he said without conviction. "So long as she doesn't carry it to the extreme and decide to elope with him just to spite Father." He nudged his horse forward. "Come along. We don't want to miss the look of horror on Viscount Avonston's face when he beholds his beloved in her breeches."

Stephen and Martin caught up with their sister on the summit of the lowest hill that slanted down into the hollow. A half-dozen or so bonfires had already been kindled in the distance, their flames leaping into the amethyst-stained horizon. Juliana slid off her horse and handed the reins to Stephen, straining her eyes through the gathering darkness.

"If he's late, we'll not wait for him," Stephen warned her.

Juliana ignored him. In the shadow of a granite outcrop she could just make out the silhouette of a lone figure crouching before the shallow stream that rushed down the hillside. About a yard away a horse stood cropping a patch of clover.

Stephen leaned forward on his saddle bow to stare down into the hollow. "Ah, we're not wearing our ivory satin cloak tonight, I see. Our hair looks a bit darker, too. Could Graham have forgotten to coat it with the usual pound of powder?"

"I'm going to sneak up on him," Juliana announced suddenly, her gold-flecked eyes twinkling. "He laughed at me when I said the hollow was haunted by a miller murdered for turning evidence against a gang of smugglers. I'll give him the fright of his life."

Martin glanced at her with apprehensive eyes. "I wouldn't, Juliana. Graham doesn't have your sense of humor."

"Graham has no sense of humor at all," Stephen interjected. "But do it anyway, Juliana. I'll hold Ajax for you."

With no petticoats to snag in a clump of bracken, no wobbly heels to cause her to stumble, Juliana had an easy time reaching the foot of the hill undetected. There she immediately ducked behind a blackthorn shrub and hunkered down on her heels to quietly observe Graham through a screen of spine-laden stems. How strange, she mused. She'd never noticed until now how powerfully broad he was in the shoulders. It had to be the heavy brown cloak.

A twig cracked beneath her foot, and she froze, holding her breath. The horse pricked its ears and turned its head to fix her with a curious stare. Juliana stared back at the muscular bay with a frown puckering her brow. Had Graham mentioned something about buying another mare? She couldn't remember. She rarely listened to his inane prattle, anyway. And what in heaven's name was the ninny doing at the stream? Admiring his reflection like Narcissus?

Above her she heard Ajax whicker softly. *Now!* she told herself. She rolled onto the balls of her feet, curling her slim frame into a bow as she prepared to pounce. She wanted desperately to laugh, knowing her brothers were watching and would appreciate her performance.

" 'Ere, mister," she called out in a rumbling Cornish dialect. "Ye've disturbed my peace."

She watched the tall figure stiffen, the dark head slowly lift. "Who is it? What do you want?"

Good Lord! thought Juliana. The silly ass is too frightened to even turn around. Oh, this is fun. " 'Tis me—Jack Westfield—the ghost of Rook 'ollow. This is my hauntin' ground yer trespassin' on. Price to pay is yer soul."

And then, with an unearthly screech that shattered the twilight stillness and a frantic waving of her arms, Juliana sprang into the air and attached herself to the back of the crouching figure, the impact of her assault rocking him forward to one knee.

"Surprise! Scared the wits out of you, didn't I, Gra—"

The name perished on her lips as she realized her dreadful mistake. "Oh, no," she whispered, feeling her heart plunge to her stomach. "Oh, *no* . . ."

Chapter Two

She caught a glimpse of a lean, angular face with a broad-bridged nose and a square-cut, clefted chin. A muscular forearm shot upward to clamp down on the nape of her neck with numbing force. Not Graham, her mind registered dazedly. This man had Graham's tall, athletic build and dark, waving hair, but there the resemblance ended. God in heaven! What must the poor fellow think of her? Before she could gather her wits to beg his forgiveness, she felt herself effortlessly hoisted into the air, then flipped over the powerful shoulders and deposited in the streambed. For a long horrible interval she was so stunned she stayed exactly as she had landed, lying flat on her back with cold, clear water bubbling over and around her; small hard pebbles dug into her shoulder blades and bruised derrière. Then as the shock began to recede, she made a feeble effort to rise, only to find herself instantly forced back down into the rushing coldness by a booted foot planted squarely on her chest.

"Not so fast, tadpole. You'll need to learn to swim before you're ready to hop about attacking unwary travelers."

The cool mocking voice slashed like lightning through Juliana's consciousness, bringing her completely to her senses. "Would you kindly remove your filthy foot from my person, and release me?" she hissed up at the shadowed face, all thoughts of apology forgotten.

"Why? To give you another chance to slit my throat and relieve me of my purse? I think not, tadpole."

"And what am I supposed to slit your throat with, idiot?" she shouted. "I have no weapons!" To prove her point she wrenched the jerkin out from beneath his foot and threw out her palms, deliberately flinging a spray of water in his face as she did. "This whole thing was a—a terrible mistake."

"I'll not argue that," he said and calmly brushed off the droplets of water that had dribbled down his chin and onto his buckskin breeches.

Juliana caught her underlip between her teeth in impotent rage. Curbing the impulse to attempt an escape, she decided her safest course would be to remain calm until her brothers arrived to rescue her. Then she could watch on with great satisfaction while this uncouth brute got the thrashing of his life. Her immediate concern, however, was to get out of the stream and onto her feet before he decided to drown her for the sport of it.

" 'Twas only a prank," she said, feigning meekness, though the unfamiliar attitude stung her fierce pride. "I thought you were a friend of mine."

He snorted rudely. "Well, thank God I am not."

Juliana glanced about in desperation, wondering what could be keeping her brothers. Couldn't they see what was happening? Dare she scream to summon them? She thought it a good idea until the man bent forward, and she noticed the pistol holster he wore strapped beneath his waistcoat. Panic flared inside her. "Lay a finger on me, and you—you'll hang for it!" she blurted out. "My father is an important man in this district!"

With the rising moon illuminating the hollow in only scattered patches, Juliana could not read the stranger's face to tell whether her threat had worked. Apparently it gave him pause; after a moment he drew his foot away.

"All right. But no tricks, mind you." He knelt then and searchingly ran his hands over her slender body, chuckling as he reached her armpits and she leaped up with a strangled cry. "Ticklish, eh?" he said, regarding her with amused gray eyes. "They say that's a bad sign in a boy."

At once conscious of her small pert breasts thrusting through the damp linen shirt, Juliana clutched the sodden jerkin together and scrambled past him onto the sloping bank. How fortunate she had not revealed herself as a woman! Who knew what perversities the beast might have attempted had he discovered her sex? Shaking with cold, fright, and frustrated rage, she straightened up to run to safety but found herself standing on suddenly boneless legs that buckled after only one step. Cursing her own helplessness, she collapsed against a boulder.

"You wouldn't last an hour in the wilderness, tadpole. You're too soft."

"Wilder—" Juliana spun around. "So you're a colonial," she spat, injecting as much contempt into the word as possible. "That explains your savage behavior."

In one fluid movement the stranger climbed the bank and crossed the short distance between them, pressing Juliana back against the mossy boulder until she could scarcely draw a breath for the disturbing nearness of him. Catching her chin between his thumb and forefinger, he forced her head to one side and scrutinized her face under a pale shaft of moonlight.

"And you're uncommonly pretty for a boy. Do your brothers share your favors?" With a jeering smile, he noted the fragile facial structure, the soft, trembling mouth and porcelain perfection of the fine-grained complexion. And those eyes. What color—He pulled his hand back abruptly, shocked and disgusted at an unexpected prickling of desire as the boy's delicately boned fingers inadvertently brushed his groin. By God, he thought with grim humor, the weeks of forced abstinence at sea had taken their toll.

Juliana's voice jerked him back to the present. "And do *you* amuse yourself with pretty young boys in the colonies?"

"Do I—?" The impudent question caught him unaware. Before he could decide whether the lad was insulting him or working up to a proposition, he detected the faint thrumming of hoofbeats beyond the hollow, the unmistakable approach of two riders.

"Your brothers," he said, his mouth tightening. "I believe 'tis time for us to part company, tadpole."

"My brothers are very protective of me," Juliana said with a sudden rush of courage, although her less sensitive ears had not yet picked up the sound of a single hoofbeat. "You'll have a hard time explaining yourself to them."

"I don't intend to try." He pivoted and hurriedly collected the tricorn hat and saddlebags he had left on the bank.

Confident now no harm would befall her, Juliana trailed after him. "Coward! What about my clothes? I'm soaked."

He slung his saddlebags over the mare, glancing back at her with a half-apologetic, half-sardonic grin. "Sorry about the ducking, tadpole. I guess we both made a mistake. I'd lend you a shirt, but I haven't time to unpack one."

Juliana glowered at him in response, looking so pathetic in the wet, ill-fitting garments that on an impulse he removed his cloak and tossed it to her. The unplanned act of charity cost him; he turned around to find his path blocked by two horsemen leading a riderless white stallion.

"Oh, Stephen!" With a cry of relief, Juliana darted forward to stand by her brother as he dismounted. "Where in God's name have you been?"

"Chasing Ajax across the moors," he answered crossly. "He broke loose and bolted when you let out that inhuman screech. You're damned lucky we caught him before he made it home."

Martin glanced around the hollow, his eyes lingering curiously on the tall, dark-haired man standing behind his sister. "What's going on here anyway? Has something happened to Graham?" He dismounted and moved to Juliana's side. "You look upset."

"Upset?" Juliana sputtered, tossing her head with an outraged glance in the stranger's direction. "Oh, no, Martin. I'm not at all upset that this man—this colonial clodhopper—threw me into the stream and tried to drown me!"

Stephen pulled away from her and, squaring his shoulders, took a step toward the stranger. "Did he, now?"

"Yes," Juliana sniffed. "Just look at me. I'm sopping wet." She cast another malicious glance at the colonial, who, to her profound disappointment, did not appear the least bit intimidated but was merely leaning back against his mare with an air of long-suffering resignation.

"Is this true, sir?" Stephen asked solemnly.

"I'm afraid there's been a misunderstanding." The mist-colored eyes shifted accusingly to Juliana. "I had but stopped to refresh myself and my horse at the stream when your brother jumped out from behind a bush and attacked me. Understand that I've spent most of my adulthood living on the frontier. I'm trained to react to potential danger without wasting precious time in hesitation.''

"We don't have Indians in Cornwall," Juliana snapped over Stephen's shoulder.

The man continued in the same infuriatingly self-righteous manner. "Assuming I'd been set upon by brigands, I simply did what was necessary to defend myself. Fortunately, neither I nor the lad got hurt.''

Stephen dropped his menacing stance, seemingly satisfied with this explanation. "Well, Jul—uh—Jim only has himself to blame, I suppose. What brings you to Cornwall, sir?''

"Personal business. Actually, I might even end up making my permanent home here.'' He extended his hand. "The name's Tremayne. Adam Tremayne.''

"Tremayne, is it? Now that's a Cornish surname for you," Martin said with a warm smile, stepping in front of Juliana to shake Adam's hand. "In fact, my father had an old friend by that name, though I doubt there's any relation. I'm Martin Pendarvis, sir. This is my older brother, Stephen. And, of course, you've already met our little prankster, Jim.''

Adam forced a polite smile, wondering if he'd heard correctly. Pendarvis? Oh, God, no. Was *this* the renowned smuggling family he was supposed to form a partnership with? Instinctively, he decided not to reveal any more of himself than necessary.

"What colony are you from, sir?'' Martin inquired, breaking into Adam's thoughts.

"Virginia, originally,'' Adam replied carefully. "However, I've been staying with friends in Boston the past four years. Before that I lived in the New York wilderness.''

Martin's eyes brightened. "I reckon you've got some good stories to tell. We ought to bring him home so that he and Father can exchange harrowing experiences, eh, Stephen?''

Juliana could not believe what was happening. She could not believe that her brothers were making no attempt whatsoever to avenge her. She could not believe that the pair of simpletons were chatting with and practically extending a social invitation to a man who had insulted and abused her!

Unable to contain her resentment, she cut rudely into their conversation. "Why don't you ask Mr. Tremayne to call in a fortnight for tea and a game of whist? No doubt I shall be dead of pneumonia by then and won't have to endure his company."

Stephen glanced back at her and sighed. "It looks as though we've no choice but to take you home."

"I'm not going home!"

Adam bent forward to pick up the cloak she'd refused. "Are you sure you won't take this, lad? 'Twill keep you warm until you're home."

"I am not going home," she said between her chattering teeth.

Stephen flushed. "I'll not be held responsible if you take sick." And under his breath he added, "You really are behaving quite stupidly, Juliana."

That did it for Juliana. She snatched Ajax's reins out of Martin's hand, swept them over the horse's head, and mounted unassisted with a lithe-limbed grace that drew Adam's head up in admiration—and surprise.

"Molly Upmon's cottage is but a quarter-mile from here. She'll loan me something to wear until these clothes dry."

"But what about Graham?" Martin asked.

Juliana scowled into the darkness. "The devil take Graham. He can find his own way into the village."

Martin remounted his horse, and Stephen swung onto his gelding with another heavy sigh. "I'm getting too old for this sort of nonsense. I should have stayed home by the fire with Louisa." He nodded to Adam. "Accept my apologies for Jim, sir. I trust if we meet again, 'twill be under more favorable circumstances." He tightened the reins to wheel his mount, then hesitated. "Would you like an escort into the village, Mr. Tremayne? We'll take you by a shortcut. 'Tis wise to avoid the main roads on a night like this."

Adam turned away from his horse. "Thank you, no. As a matter of fact, I'm headed in the opposite direction."

Adam watched the three riders disappear into the moon-dappled shadows of the hollow, the disgruntled Jim leading the way. What a peculiar family, he thought. He was glad he'd chosen to keep his destination a secret. If the mis-

matched threesome weren't closely related to his old friend
Sir Walter, he might have gotten himself and the Pendarvis
family into trouble by revealing the reasons for his visit to
Kenvellas. He could just picture the hotheaded young Jim
running to the authorities with the information that Adam
had come to Cornwall to forge a link in a notorious smuggling ring.

On the other hand, if the three were indeed immediate
members of Sir Walter's family, Adam would merely excuse his reticence as a precautionary measure. Stephen and
Martin seemed levelheaded enough to understand. But as for
little Jim . . . He vaulted into his saddle and coaxed the
mare onto the slanting hillside path, smiling to himself as he
imagined the shock the lad would have when he was introduced to Sir Walter's long-awaited guest from America.

Chapter Three

"Oh, Father, you're not sitting alone in the dark again. How positively morbid. One would think you were a mole."

"Stop fussing and come over here by the window, Louisa. Leave the damned candlestick on the table. Now then. Do you reckon they've lit more bonfires this year?"

The plumpish brown-eyed young woman came behind her father-in-law's armchair and gazed obediently out the window at the glowing landscape. "I think so, Father."

Sir Walter dropped back onto the chair with a grunt of satisfaction. "Festival fires, Louisa. We consider ourselves a Christian people, and yet once a year we pay tribute to Baal exactly as our pagan Celtic ancestors did centuries ago."

"I loathed Midsummer Eve when I was a child," Louisa murmured, her eyes dark with memory. "My cousin made me run through the flames once, and my skirts caught fire. I had to walk home in my shift with everyone laughing at me. 'Twas horrid."

"Juliana always loved the fire-jumping best," Sir Walter said quietly. "Used to come home with her petticoats singed and her hair smelling of smoke. Caught her with ale on her breath more than once, too." He turned away from the window and glanced at the attractively spread table in the corner, the crystal goblets glinting in the candlelight. "You mentioned to her we was having a special supper, didn't you?"

"Yes, Father, I did. She said she'd come down later if she wanted anything."

The shaggy white eyebrows drew together into a troubled frown. "Told her we was going to play cards afterward, did you?"

"Yes, but I really wouldn't expect her down tonight. She was complaining of a—a sick headache." Uneasy in the lie, she moved to the sideboard and there made a great pretense of rearranging the bowl of roses she had cut that afternoon.

"Juliana has never had a headache in her life," Sir Walter said dryly.

"Perhaps it's the weather, then. I felt quite unwell myself earlier. This heat . . ."

Sir Walter leaned forward on his walking cane and stared at the flustered young woman until at last she turned around and faced his accusing gaze. "So even you have turned against me, Louisa."

The thought of having hurt her father-in-law's feelings filled Louisa with so much guilt and remorse, she would probably have broken down and confessed everything had he not given a sudden excited shout.

"The door!" He banged his cane down on the floor with a powerful thwack that rattled the silverware on the table. "Someone's knocking at the front door, girl!"

"Well, all right, Father. No need to work yourself into a state. Audrey or Mrs. Sennen will see your guest into the—" She fell silent as the door behind her opened, and the housekeeper ushered in a big chestnut-haired man in a dusty traveling cloak and mud-caked top boots.

"Adam! By God, it has been an age, hasn't it?" Sir Walter raised himself out of his chair and hobbled to the door, keen affection masking the pain in his voice.

"Almost six years now," Adam said, clasping the dry, outstretched hand.

"That all?" Sir Walter laughed ruefully. "Feels more like sixty, boy." He drew Adam into the room. "Adam, this is my daughter-in-law Louisa, the only member of the family with the patience to keep a cantankerous old man company. I fear I take terrible advantage of her. You'll meet the others later."

Adam bowed politely. "A pleasure, ma'am."

Louisa's cheeks dimpled with a timid smile. "You'll want a hot meal right away. I'll run after Mrs. Sennen and ask her to start dishing out."

Sir Walter caught her arm as she started for the door. "Be a good girl, and try to coax Juliana out of her room," he said softly. "I've a feeling she and Adam will take to each other right off."

The moment Louisa left, Sir Walter limped to the sideboard and poured out two glasses of brandy. "Calvados," he said, handing Adam a glass. "You'll never lack for the best in our business, Adam."

As they stood together sipping the potent Norman brandy in appreciative silence, Adam had an opportunity to study his host in the candlelight. At a glance it seemed age had only improved Sir Walter's appearance. His trim beard and full head of pure white hair lent him a dignified facade, an air of gentility that contrasted with his gruff manner and uneducated speech. Although stouter than he had been during his military career, he held himself erect and still cut an impressive figure, the absence of his left arm barely noticeable in his handsomely tailored broadcloth suit. Yet after a time it occurred to Adam that the ruddy complexion might not be an indication of good health but of quite the opposite. And why the shortness of breath after taking only a few steps?

"You've been ill, sir?"

"A twinge now and then, but nothing serious. Except this bloody gout." Sir Walter sank down onto the armchair, grimacing as he propped his bandaged foot on the three-legged stool before him. "Hard to believe one's big toe could cause such agony. I've often wished them Indians had taken it off with my arm."

Adam smiled. "You're as bad as my father."

"William has the gout now, too, does he? Well, well. That makes me feel better. How is he otherwise?"

"He was well enough the last time I saw him."

"Which was when?"

"About two years ago. He's busy with his plantation and the Governor's Council. These are challenging times for Virginia. And you know my father. Always has to have a say in everything." Adam took the chair adjacent to Sir Walter as he continued. "Frankly, I've been too busy with the shipyard to venture far from Boston. I never really intended to become that involved in the business, but it didn't seem fair to leave my partner with all the work."

Sir Walter stared at Adam, his direct gaze signaling the end of polite conversation. "I was hoping you and William would have worked out your differences by now, but I can tell by your tone it isn't so. And don't give me that look. You're breaking your mother's heart, the pair of you." The weathered face softened perceptibly. "I'm disappointed you couldn't talk Katherine into coming for a visit. Half of the old Helston boys still fancy themselves in love with her. I know your Uncle Logan was. He never forgave her for running off with his brother, but he loved her until the end."

Adam sat forward, frowning. "Then you were with him when he died?"

"No. We'd met about a month before. I knew then that he had the cancer, but I'd no idea it would take him so fast."

Adam did not speak for a moment. What an enigma Logan Tremayne had been, the uncle he knew only from eavesdropping on private conversations and studying family portraits. Why would he bequeath his estate and whatever money he had possessed to the youngest child of the brother he bitterly resented? Had he felt a strange kinship with Adam? Was it because he'd had no children of his own? To be sure he had been an eccentric, converting to Catholicism at the age of thirty, moving from his hometown of Helston to live like a monk in a lonely seacoast house while running a smuggling business on the side.

"Can you honestly state, Sir Walter, that you did not try to influence him on my behalf?"

"Indeed, I did not."

"There is a codicil to this will which requires I live at Mentreath for one full year before it becomes mine," Adam went on. "You had nothing to do with that either, I suppose." At the other man's silence, he nodded. "I'd guessed as much."

A sly smile tugged at the corners of Sir Walter's mouth. "Well, you could hardly expect to head the southwestern operation from the colonies, Adam. In all the years he and I worked together, Logan found precious few men he could trust in his absence. I rely heavily on my sons. Pity you've no relatives left in Cornwall." He paused to drain his glass. "What about this valet you mentioned in your letter, the strapping young Scot you rescued from prison? Has he tried to run away yet?"

Adam grinned. "He's been a free man for over a year.

'Twas against his better judgment that I left him behind at Mentreath.''

"Well, the boys and I will teach you all you'll need to know about smuggling," Sir Walter promised. "It's a way of life around here, a necessity."

Adam became quiet as he absorbed Sir Walter's words. He was only beginning to realize how crucial smuggling was to the Cornish people. From the day he'd arrived in Cornwall, he'd been appalled at the evidence of poverty he'd encountered—large families, broken in spirit and bordering on starvation, crowded into dilapidated one-room cottages. A rural laborer had to work for a fortnight to bring home enough money to buy a bushel of grain, while his wife and children dug turnips and plowed the fields so that they could afford kindling. At the mercy of bad harvests and economic fluctuations, many relied on parish assistance to survive, and many simply did not survive at all. Was the lure of smuggling really so difficult to understand?

When Louisa reappeared to announce the imminent arrival of supper, the two men were discussing the property Adam had inherited, specifically Mentreath, an Elizabethan manor house with surrounding acreage on the desolate Lizard Peninsula.

"There's some surprisingly good farming soil farther north, Adam," Sir Walter said as he rose stiffly and made his way to the table. "I think you'll be pleased with your tenants. They're an independent lot. Louisa, it looks as if Mrs. Sennen has really outdone herself tonight. Juliana will have to fight me for these lobsters."

Louisa slowly unfolded her napkin, her eyes fixed on her lap. "Juliana isn't coming down, Father. She . . . she's gone to bed, and asked not to be disturbed again."

Sir Walter's mouth thinned. "Then we'll eat without her. I'm not about to beg for the pleasure of my own daughter's company."

Adam lowered his gaze, pretending interest in the rosy slabs of roast beef that Audrey, the maidservant, was heaping on his plate. Past experience had taught him not to pass judgment on a person he had not met. However, from what he'd gathered about Miss Juliana Pendarvis, he considered himself fortunate to have their introduction postponed. He'd met enough petulant young ladies in Boston to last a lifetime.

After supper Louisa retreated into a corner and sat quietly stitching on a sampler. Behind her the four sash windows were open to the light evening breeze which carried on it the delicate scents of woodbine and damask roses from the garden. Sir Walter had settled back into his armchair with another glass of brandy after Adam admitted he was too tired to play cards.

"That's his third glass this evening," Louisa said, darting Adam a glance. "He's not supposed to drink anything stronger than barley water. The doctor would be cross."

Sir Walter took another sip of brandy, a flicker of defiance in his eyes. "Tomorrow I'll take you around Rosmorna and show you our fleet, Adam. The word's already been spread that you and I fought in the wars together. You should be accepted for your Cornish blood if not on the strength of your uncle's reputation. You'll meet the rest of the family at breakfast. Stephen and Martin won't be home before we're abed. I'm embarrassed that my daughter hadn't the simple courtesy to come down to introduce herself. Has nothing to do with you, of course. She and I have had a great falling out."

Stephen and *Martin?* Not just cousins or nephews then, but Sir Walter's sons! The amusing incident at the hollow flashed through Adam's tired mind, but on impulse he decided not to mention it. The old man clearly had enough to worry about with his daughter, and the fact that little Jim's name hadn't cropped up in the conversation yet indicated that perhaps the lad was also a sore spot with his father. Why upset Sir Walter unnecessarily?

He lifted his shoulders in an unconcerned shrug. " 'Tis a relief to discover that mine is not the only family with its personal conflicts." He felt a sudden stirring of pity for the older man. "I wouldn't worry. You're bound to make it up sooner or later."

"Hmph. I'm not so sure, Adam. The girl doesn't understand why she must conduct herself in a certain manner, and I can offer no better explanation than that society demands it. God knows I meant to raise her proper. I spared no expense in hiring tutors to educate her. Brought in a governess all the way from Paris once, too, but there's a limit to what money can buy."

Adam leaned back in his chair, his eyes contemplative. "She's a tomboy, I take it?"

"Yes," said Sir Walter.

"No, she isn't!" said Louisa, and both men glanced over at her, startled by the vehemence in her voice. "Juliana is *not* a tomboy," she continued, her tone gentler now, though two spots of color had risen to her cheeks. "She loves jewelry and perfume and pretty clothes just as much as I do. She's a far more graceful dancer than I am, too. She never misses an assembly."

"Or a wrestling match," Sir Walter added, smiling in spite of himself.

"Has she many suitors?" Adam asked, his curiosity piqued.

"She's scorned the few I thought well enough to encourage," Sir Walter replied. "In fact, the only man—if you can call 'im that—she's shown any real fondness for is a young Bodmin aristocrat whose family has mining interests in northern Cornwall and properties here in the southwest. An insincere little jackanapes. I hated him on sight."

Louisa rose from her chair. "Oh, Graham's not so bad," she said, brushing loose threads from her skirt with a distracted frown. "Anyway, I'm sure Mr. Tremayne would rather get some rest than discuss our problems. 'Tis well past two."

Sir Walter pulled out his enamel-inlaid pocket timepiece. "So it is. Come on then, Adam. Louisa will light the way with one of them candles she's so fond of burning. There's a portrait of Juliana in the hallway outside your room. Girl inherited her mother's looks but nothing of her docile nature."

Adam got to his feet, thinking he would have to find something flattering to say about this Juliana even if she had the face of a gargoyle and the figure of a Viking warrior. The old man obviously doted on her.

Halfway up the staircase Sir Walter clutched the handrail and stopped to catch his breath. "Bloody thing gets steeper every day," he muttered.

"You've gotten out of shape, Sir Walter. Too much drink and not enough—"

"You've not remarried, Adam?"

The gray eyes became guarded, "No, sir."

There was a pause. "That's a mistake, boy. And I speak from experience. I should have taken another wife if only to guide Juliana into womanhood. Ten years without a mother was too long." He turned and resumed the ascent to the second-floor landing, his footsteps slow and heavy. "Nothing to be done about it now, I guess. Best I can hope to do is find her a decent husband."

"Graham, I *must* go inside now. If my father should happen into my room for any reason and discover that the lump under the counterpane isn't me . . ."

It was warm and dark inside Ajax's stall, so dark, in fact, that Juliana did not realize Graham had crept up behind her until he slid his arms around her waist and lowered his mouth to her neck. "You're still angry with me for being late, aren't you?" he whispered, nuzzling her ear. "I told you it wasn't my fault. I couldn't very well not make an appearance at Aunt Henrietta's birthday soiree. Especially not when my parents were traveling all the way down from Bodmin."

"Especially not when your luck was holding out at the gaming table, you mean," she countered. "And stop doing that to my ear. Your mustache tickles horribly."

With a resigned sigh, Graham, third Viscount Avonston and only son of the Earl of Wynherne, lifted his head and allowed Juliana to wriggle out of his arms. Blast the minx! If she were any of his other love interests, he could easily smother her protests with a kiss or some meaningless declaration of his undying affection. But that was the problem. Juliana was so completely unlike the simpering, well-bred misses he associated with in Bodmin that he hadn't the faintest idea how he should handle her. And, oh, how very desperately he wanted to learn! Since the evening he'd met her last year at a Michaelmas ball in St. Ives, he had been wooing and pursuing her with the feverish intention of making her his mistress. Yet so far she had managed to keep him at bay and, to his frustration, her sexual aloofness had only heightened his desire for her, his determination to possess her. Recently he had even contemplated marrying her. As a last resort, of course. His parents would be mortified if he married the daughter of a lowly knight, an inconsequential country squire of common lineage and no connections at court.

"I had too much at stake in that game to leave for the sake of an absurd heathen ritual," he said reproachfully. "Besides, you could have come with me if you'd chosen to. You know Venetia thinks you're great fun."

Juliana burst into an unrestrained peal of laughter. "Your cousin is one thing, Graham, but what about your mother, *madame la comtesse?* She disapproves of me as it is. Imagine what an ado she'd have made had I appeared before her in these clothes. The silly old goose would've taken an apoplectic fit."

Graham pursed his lips in sullen annoyance. Juliana did have the most indelicate way of expressing herself. And he wasn't the tiniest bit amused by the disrespect she showed for his mother. In fact, her impertinence was the first in a series of undesirable traits he would demand she change after they were married. She would have to become socially presentable if she wanted to be his viscountess. She would have to learn to obey him in *all* matters. A pleasurable flush of anticipation spread through him as he imagined how he would break her spirit and tame her into submission.

"Well, Graham?" Her voice was challenging, dampening his ardor. "No defense for Mama tonight?"

"Give her time, Juliana. She'll come round once she gets used to you. Be polite if we meet her at the fair tomorrow. Wear a nice frock." He dared to brush the underside of her breast with his fingertips. "You are still coming with me, aren't you?"

"Oh, I suppose so. Call for me around noon." And before he could reach out to detain her, she had slipped outside and was stealing across the stable yard, a slender wraith vanishing into the swirling mist, eluding him again as she had done so many times in the past.

Juliana drew a relieved breath to have gained her freedom. Oh, she enjoyed Graham's company most of the time. Carefree and frivolous, with an ample purse to indulge his expensive taste, he proved a refreshing contrast to the unsophisticated young locals who had attempted to court her. But tonight his amorous mood had made her feel uneasy, more annoyed than aroused. Besides, foremost on her mind was the matter of sneaking back into her bedroom. . . .

For a disquieting moment she thought she detected a faint thread of candlelight showing through an upstairs window. Only my imagination, she decided, and continued on her way, undaunted. At the kitchen door she paused to remove her boots and thick woolen hose. In an effort to avoid apprehension, she had done a thorough job of trampling Mrs.

Sennen's herb garden, and tomorrow morning her brothers would probably receive an undeserved lecture from the elderly housekeeper. The thought pleased her immensely.

The latch lifted with a long-drawn-out creak that she feared would awaken the entire household. She let a minute elapse and then proceeded into the kitchen, grateful for the glowing embers in the fireplace that enabled her to avoid stumbling over the copper coal scuttle someone had carelessly left in the middle of the floor.

She passed through the entrance hall, peering into the parlor with a shiver of relief. Nothing woke up Papa once he had gone to bed. Congratulating herself on her successful evening out, she tiptoed into the parlor and went to the sideboard to reward herself with a hastily downed glass of port. On the way out, she stopped to study her reflection in the beveled pier glass that hung above the mantelpiece. She really did look a fright. Somehow, in the course of the night's events, she had lost not only her brothers, but also Jim's felt cap and the silver bodkins that had secured her braids. Her hair had come loose and was spilling down her back in a rippling cascade; with a disgusted scowl she bent forward to disentangle a leaf she had picked up during her race through the woods with Graham.

She had just started up the staircase when she heard low murmuring voices drifting from the hallway leading to her bedchamber. She shrank against the banister, the painful thudding of her heart filling her chest. Louisa! No mistaking that soft, childlike laughter. But there was another voice, too, a deep, rich baritone that Juliana knew instantly did not belong to her father, although it sounded vaguely familiar.

Prudish little Louisa carrying on with a man in the hallway? But who? A servant? Impossible! It could only be Stephen, drunk perhaps. She chided herself for not thinking to check the other stalls for his horse. Yes, of course it was Stephen. Hadn't he been complaining that he wished he'd stayed with his wife?

She hurried up the staircase, boots slung over her shoulder, a tolerant smile hovering on her lips. Louisa and Stephen were undoubtedly waiting up to make sure she returned home safely. The dear, dull, predictable fools. One day they would worry themselves right into the grave.

Chapter Four

"Well, Adam, did I exaggerate? Wouldn't dream I could sire such a lovely creature, would you?" Sir Walter leaned forward on his walking cane so that he could observe Adam's reaction as Louisa brought the candle closer to the portrait.

Adam caught his breath; the polite compliments he had been prepared to utter suddenly seemed so inadequate that for an embarrassing moment he found himself at a loss for words.

"Exquisite, isn't she?" Louisa said, smiling faintly at his sudden disconcertment.

Adam nodded, struggling to regain his composure. "Exquisite . . ." Oh, yes, that was the only word to describe the delicately etched face with its haunting gold-green eyes and framing masses of bronze-highlighted hair that tumbled in luxuriant waves over the rounded white shoulders. He blinked as a memory stirred in the recesses of his mind. No . . . 'twas a trick of the candlelight, the combination of brandy and travel fatigue. Impossible to forget a face like that . . .

"Tell me, Louisa, how old was—"

"Juliana!" Sir Walter's hoarse cry of shock cut Adam off in mid-sentence. "I pray to God that this does not mean what I fear it does!"

Louisa spun around and gasped, her face ashen and startled in the wavering light of the candle she held. "Oh, Juliana," she whispered, her free hand flying to her mouth.

Adam drew his eyes away from the portrait and focused them on the slim-hipped young woman standing in the darkened window alcove. Her head was bowed, the penitent face partially hidden behind a curtain of glorious auburn hair. Obviously she had been attempting to sneak back into her room when her father caught her. He stole a concerned look at Sir

27

Walter, who had flushed a dark, unbecoming shade of purple and who looked furious enough to strangle the daughter he had moments before spoken of with such irrepressible pride. It was an embarrassing situation for all involved, and Adam felt compelled to prevent it from erupting into an ugly scene.

"We—ah—we were just admiring your portrait, Juliana," he said in a pleasant conversational tone, as if it were perfectly normal for a young gentlewoman dressed in boys' clothing to be apprehended sneaking back into her bedroom in the dead of night. "Your father has every right to be proud."

Juliana's head lifted, the deep timbre of his voice sending a shiver jolting up her spine. No . . . it couldn't possibly be. . . . "You!" she burst out, staring at the lean, sunbronzed face in stunned disbelief.

Adam's eyes widened, traveling swiftly up the slender white ankles and loose breeches before settling on the astonished young face. "Tadpole?" he whispered incredulously.

Juliana could feel the blood draining from her face. Her father looked fit to flay her as it was. If she were one of the boys, he'd have taken his cane to her right then and there. How would he react if he learned what had happened in the hollow? And this man, this uncivilized foreigner, what was he doing in their house?

Fortunately, Sir Walter was too caught up in his own anger to question the cryptic exchange between Adam and his daughter. "Go to your room, girl," he said wearily. "This is neither the time nor the place to discuss the matter. Suffice it to say I am heartsick at what you've done this night." He looked a decade older than his sixty-two years as he turned his attention back to Adam. "I hope you'll not have to witness any other shameful family scenes during your stay with us, Adam. Sorry to have put you through such an unpleasant evening."

Adam bade everyone good night and from his doorway watched the tall, graceful figure of Juliana disappear down the hallway and into her room. Unpleasant? He turned his head for a final glimpse of her portrait, disappointed he could see so little in the moonlight, remembering the tempting softness of her mouth, the promise of unawakened sensuality in her gold-flecked eyes. No, it had not been an unpleasant evening, he thought. On the contrary. It was probably the most enjoyable one he had spent in years.

Chapter Five

Juliana dreaded the thought of having to go downstairs and face her father. A nasty row was inevitable. The supercilious Mr. Tremayne had no doubt recounted every humiliating detail of their encounter in the hollow by now, she thought bitterly. To add to her troubles, she had awakened with a stomachache from drinking Molly Upmon's home-brewed blackstrap cider last night. Damn! She should have told Graham to call for her earlier so that she would have an excuse to escape the house before her father arose. But it was only nine o'clock, and Audrey, a dim-witted girl with a fondness for gossip, had just brought word that Sir Walter expected everyone in the parlor for breakfast in a half hour.

She expelled a sigh and seated herself at the dressing table, carefully spreading out her silver lace-trimmed petticoats. After an hour's deliberation, she'd decided to wear a midnight-blue watered silk gown with a snug-fitting sculptured velvet bodice. Actually, it was the only gown she owned with a décolletage modest enough to pass Lady Wynherne's inspection. On her bed sat a wide-brimmed gray felt hat embellished with a band of silk forget-me-nots. Excluding a possible meeting with the countess, she at least had a pleasant afternoon to look forward to.

"I won't need gloves today, Audrey. I'd only lose them at the fair, or stain them eating those strawberries they sell on the quay."

"Yer dad says you ain't goin' nowhere today, miss," Audrey said matter-of-factly. "I heard 'im tell Mrs. Sennen you was stayin' in to entertain that 'andsome lieutenant."

Juliana reached for her hairbrush. "We'll see about that.

Now, do hush and help me with my hair. I washed it this morning and 'tis impossibly wavy.''

She left the bedchamber almost twenty minutes later, her hair arranged in a loose plaited chignon. Although outwardly composed, she was so worried about the forthcoming confrontation with her father that she failed to notice the tall, broad-shouldered man standing at the top of the staircase until she'd walked straight into him. A big, suntanned hand reached out and grasped her elbow, steadying her as she jumped in surprise and swayed sideways toward the staircase.

"You really should be more careful, Miss Pendarvis," a rich, amused voice chided her. "You've a disturbing habit of charging innocent gentlemen."

Juliana lifted her chin and answered Adam Tremayne's good-natured grin with a cold, unblinking stare. "And you have an inflated opinion of yourself, Mr. Tremayne," she retorted, increasingly conscious of the pressure of his fingers on her skin. " 'Gentleman' is the last word I'd use to describe you."

Adam quirked an eyebrow. "You may be right at that, Miss Pendarvis," he said after a thoughtful pause. "No gentleman would dream of attempting what I am about to do." And before Juliana realized what he intended, he had slipped his arm around her waist and was drawing her backward into the privacy of the window alcove.

Juliana was so taken aback by the boldness of his action that when at last she recovered from her astonishment and began to struggle, she could not save herself. "You can't . . ." she protested breathlessly. "Oh, you wouldn't dare!"

But by then his other hand had stolen upward and curled around the nape of her neck, cradling her head so that she could not twist away from him. His face loomed briefly over hers, the firm masculine lips parting slightly as they descended, then captured hers in a kiss that sent streaks of wildfire flashing through her veins. Vaguely she felt the resistance leaving her body, leaving her defenseless against the artful persuasion of his tongue as it pressed between her teeth and slid into her mouth. *Fight!* the urgent voice of her conscience commanded. Yet something more powerful within her resisted. Something wild and alien to the Juliana she knew had already surrendered to the sensual magic of this man. Then dimly, as if rousing from a dream, she realized the arm around her waist had slackened, realized the demanding mouth had relinquished hers. Her eyes lifted to Adam's face. Still, she did not move, could not move out of the circle of his embrace. Only as her heartbeat resumed its normal rhythm did she regain mastery of her errant senses and wrench herself free.

"I'm certain my father did not mean his hospitality to include ravishing me!" she hissed.

To her surprise, Adam's face did not show the smugness she expected, but rather a genuine bewilderment that could have reflected her own jumbled emotions at that moment. "I'm not quite sure what came over me just now, Juliana," he said slowly. "But I apologize for it, and though I can't explain why it happened, I do know it has nothing to do with your father. Perhaps I wanted to prove to myself I haven't developed a sudden penchant for pretty stableboys. Surely you can forgive a moment of weakness." He reached out his forefinger to coax back a tendril of hair that had fallen across her cheek, smiling as she swore at him and pulled away. "You're a bewitching young woman, Juliana. 'Tis fortunate for us both you're also selfish and hot-tempered, or I might be in danger of falling in love with you. And that, believe me, would mean trouble all around."

"Well, you needn't worry your arrogant head for one minute," she snapped, her emotions running riot again. "I assure you that the sentiment would never be reciprocated."

Adam's smile broadened, revealing even white teeth that flashed boldly against the bronze darkness of his skin. "Don't you find me attractive, Juliana? Most women do."

Juliana's lips curled into an insulting sneer as she subjected him to a dispassionate head-to-toe inspection. He exuded an aura of restrained power, a feeling of gentle strength that suggested that here stood a man who could only be pushed so far. He seemed younger today, in the sunlight filtering through the narrow sash window, than he had last night. He wore his thick chestnut-brown hair pulled back into a queue and tied with a black velvet ribbon. His angular face was closely shaven, his cheekbones broad, the mist-gray eyes watching her from beneath a high, intelligent forehead. His ruffled cream linen shirt and burgundy superfine coat with its quilted black satin waistcoat and matching breeches were craftfully tailored, expensive if not as fashionable as the clothes Graham wore. And, yes, he *was* attractive, but she'd be damned before confessing she thought him so.

"The sort of women you associate with would probably find any man between the age of seventeen to seventy attractive so long as he had a few coins in his purse," she said sourly, making to move past him.

He grasped her wrist before she took the second step. "That doesn't answer my question, Juliana. Do you—?"

"Juliana! Mr. Tremayne!" Louisa was calling to them from the foot of the staircase. "Hurry up, you two! Breakfast is getting cold!"

Reluctantly, Adam released Juliana's wrist. "We'll continue this discussion later. After breakfast, perhaps?"

"I wouldn't count on it, Mr. Tremayne. I have plans for the afternoon, and you, most assuredly, are not part of them."

Adam followed slowly in Juliana's wake, mulling over his wayward conduct. What *had* come over him? True, the girl was the essence of feminine enchantment. True, the delicate scent of her sweet young flesh teased his nostrils and stirred violent longing inside him. But he was no longer a callow youth who allowed desire to cloud his judgment. Perhaps he was overtired. He hadn't slept well last night, his body weary, his mind troubled. For all he respected and felt a genuine affection for his host, the reunion with Sir Walter had been more difficult than expected, reawakening memories within him of a time he had spent years trying to forget.

He had been born twenty-seven years ago, Adam Randall Tremayne, the youngest of three children whose parents had left their native Cornwall to make their fortune in the colonies. Within thirty years William Tremayne had become one of the most prosperous planters in Tidewater Virginia, serving as a county magistrate and eventually on the Governor's Council. His eldest son, Edgar, seemed destined to meet similar success; at thirty-two he was a representative in the House of Burgesses and the owner of a modest plantation.

Although Adam had no interest in tobacco or politics, his father decided he would become either a planter or a London-educated lawyer who could provide the Virginia Assembly with the professional legal council needed to challenge the Brit-

ish Parliament. To this end Adam sailed across the Atlantic to
the Inns of Court, from which he was expelled for dueling a
year later and was sent home in disgrace.

Will Tremayne had been furious. "Hot-blooded young
rakehell! Ruining a brilliant career for some flighty whore
who probably can't even remember your name!" had been
his greeting on the wharves. And, during that seemingly
endless ride home, he'd continued, "Well, boy, I've no
choice now but to apprentice you to your brother as an over-
seer. Maybe associating with slaves will make you aspire to
a nobler life-style."

But all Adam learned from his stint on Edgar's estate was
that he was not suited to be a plantation master. Naturally,
Will was disappointed. In fact, everything about Adam and
what he wanted from life disappointed Will with the exception of Miss Lucy Spencer, the genteel daughter of a prominent Williamsburg surgeon. As a bride Lucy would bring
not only a large dowry, but also a background of refinement
that might temper Adam's reckless nature. When Adam and
Lucy announced their engagement, Will and Kate Tremayne
lavished blessings upon them with heartfelt relief—a relief
that dissolved into horror a month after the wedding when
Adam broke the news he'd acquired a small land grant on
the New York frontier. Another ambitious young couple had
already invited him and Lucy to share their crude but spa-
cious log cabin that doubled as a store and trading post on
the Mohawk River.

Those first months of playing the trader housewife were
pleasant for Lucy. Then she found herself pregnant, and with
the discomforts her condition caused, she began to yearn for
the life she'd so impulsively forsaken. Adam and Tom Wyeth
often spent days at a time deep in the Canadian wilderness.
Alone with only another woman for company and protection,
Lucy felt isolated and vulnerable, especially at night when she
would awaken to hear the drunken singing of the Iroquois in the
encroaching woodlands. Her fears were justified; panic was
sweeping the northwestern frontiers of the British colonies as
reports mounted of Indian raids and atrocities, of families
butchered and homes burned.

By the time Adam returned for the winter, Lucy could no
longer control her fear and resentment. She hated this life!

She hated the customers who arrived in the middle of the night: the poachers and trappers in clumping boots, the backwoods German immigrants, the dirty Indians with their pelts, and the French-Canadian renegades with their whores. But, above all, she hated her husband, and she wanted to go home.

Adam's heart tightened at the memory of how he and Lucy had spent their last Christmas together, fighting, realizing too late their marriage had been a mistake. He agreed she should return to Virginia, but in winter the waterways were frozen, the roads piled with snowdrifts. Only after Lucy, in hysterics, threatened to kill herself and the two-week-old Anne did Adam finally consent to take them to nearby Fort William Henry, where Lucy could work as a hospital nurse until after the spring thaw.

Recently arrived at the fort seeking recruits for his Rangers was the infamous Captain Robert Rogers. Adam had heard of the Rangers, of course, but had no idea he was about to enlist as a scout for that company of hard-drinking regulars engaged to spy on and harass small patrols of Indians and Frenchmen. With his hunting and tracking experience, he was, in fact, an ideal candidate.

"Volunteer if you want to," Lucy told him. "Go fight the heathens and let 'em boil you alive. I don't care."

On January 17, 1757, Adam set out for the French garrisons on Lake Champlain. Detained by a series of spying missions, he was unable to return by spring as he had promised, and Lucy was too petrified of the wilderness to travel alone. He never saw her or Anne again. In August of that year, the Marquis de Montcalm laid seige to Fort Willian Henry. Under his command but not his control were eighteen hundred bloodthirsty Indians. The first victims of the massacre were those in the hospital tents. Lucy and her daughter died under the hatchet of an Abnaki, a Roman Catholic Indian of the Penobscot Mission.

Adam stirred, feeling Juliana's eyes on his face as she threw him a haughty glance over her shoulder before vanishing into the parlor. Suddenly the ugly shadows of his past seemed to disappear as though touched by a brilliant shaft of sunlight. Standing alone in the doorway to compose himself, he felt the frown easing from his brow. Juliana. What an enticing diversion she was turning out to be. With a slow, puzzled smile, he entered the room.

Juliana was still trembling inside when she walked into the parlor and quietly took her place at the table. She pretended not to notice that Adam had followed and was seating himself beside her. *Three other empty places at the table, and he has to choose me as his victim,* she thought indignantly. Then, through the thick layers of her gown and petticoats, she felt his kneecap nudge hers as he leaned forward to readjust his coattails. It might have been an accident; indeed, it was *her* knee that protruded, but the disturbingly pleasant tingle which danced up her thigh dissuaded her from granting him the benefit of the doubt.

I'll not give the ill-bred lout the satisfaction of knowing he's upset me, she decided. And deliberately thrusting him from her mind, she picked up her napkin and spread it across her lap, glancing at the thickset figure at the head of the table.

"Good morning, Papa."

Sir Walter looked up in surprise, hesitating for a moment before he responded.

"Good morning, Juliana," he said. "Pretty frock you're wearing. Remind me to save you more of that French silk."

"Thank you, Papa. I'd like that."

Relief swept through Juliana. If her father wasn't going to punish her for last night's mischief, she certainly wouldn't risk renewing his anger by asking why. Whether his forgiving mood was due to Adam's presence or to the intervention of Louisa, the family peacemaker, she couldn't guess. She only knew she was grateful, and also suddenly ravenous, having eaten nothing since yesterday afternoon. She reached eagerly for the platter of sticky yeast buns on the table, gasping to feel her fingers close around the hand Adam had extended moments before.

"There you go again, Miss Pendarvis," he said under his breath.

She snatched her hand back to her lap, hazarding a glance around the table to see if anyone had overheard the teasing remark. Stephen and Martin were so engrossed in eating, she doubted they even realized she had come downstairs. Louisa was concentrating on pouring Sir Walter's coffee.

Her father caught her eye and smiled. "What are you two whispering about?"

"Juliana was offering me a bun," Adam said innocently.

Louisa moved behind Adam's chair, filling his porcelain cup with hot black coffee at his nod of assent. "There's more food on the sideboard, Adam. Ham, sausage, herring, poached eggs, and toast. The custard pudding is made from fresh cream. Hand me your plate."

"Your housekeeper sets a tempting table, ma'am."

Louisa loaded his plate and set it down before him with a sigh. "Far too tempting. And Father wonders why he suffers from gout."

While Adam consumed his meal with uninhibited relish, Juliana found her appetite waning after only a few sips of piping Hyson tea. It's his fault, she thought, surreptitiously studying Adam from the corner of her eye. Perversely, she allowed herself to relive their meeting in the hallway. No wonder she had no appetite! She could still feel the disturbing pressure of his body against hers, the gentle persistence of his tongue as it had plundered the vulnerable interior of her mouth and skillfully aroused her senses.

"Oh, damn!" She banged her teacup down on the saucer.

"Bite your tongue, Juliana?"

"No, Martin. I burned it. This tea is scalding."

"Eat something while it cools," Sir Walter advised her. "You haven't touched that ham. Your own fault if you caught a cold last night." His eyes went to Adam. "Girl usually eats like a horse. Feel her forehead, Adam. She looks a bit flushed to me."

"Oh, honestly, Papa!" Juliana tried to draw away from the hand Adam had lifted to her forehead, but it was impossible to do so without creating a fuss.

"Hmm." Adam frowned and bent over her chair, his tapered brown fingers cool against her skin. "She does feel warm, sir." His eyes locked with Juliana's. "I wonder why."

The implication in his tone, in his eyes, rekindled her anger like a spark to straw. The man was insufferable! Did he actually believe he had only to kiss her once and she would turn into some lovesick little twit whose temperature rose every time he looked her way? Surely he wasn't so egotistical as to assume he was the first man she had ever kissed!

"Maybe Mr. Tremayne has an Indian remedy for whatever ails you," Martin said. "He brought Father a foul-smelling concoction for his gout."

She gritted her teeth. "There's nothing wrong with me, Martin. I wish everyone would go on with breakfast, and let me alone to do the same."

The conversation shifted to various topics as the meal continued. Sir Walter expressed his anxiety over the future of the colonies. Did Adam feel that the breach between Parliament and the colonial government was widening? Stephen wanted to know if Adam's recent shipbuilding venture had proved lucrative. Was there still money to be made running rum and sugar from the West Indies? Was it true the Bostonian portsmen and customs officers were as corrupt as their British counterparts? This led to a lively discussion about the differences between smuggling in the colonies and in Cornwall. Adam's smuggling experience in the North American wilderness would be useful, but he admitted he had a lot to learn. The two women sat quietly sipping tea and did not contribute to the conversation, Louisa because she had been taught it was unladylike to offer an unsolicited opinion, Juliana because she was disgusted with her whole family for treating Adam as though he were royalty. And Martin, her confidant, her staunchest ally through thick and thin, was the worst traitor of them all.

"I should've thought last night to associate you with the Lieutenant Tremayne of the Rangers we've heard so much about," he was saying, too excited to catch the warning look Juliana threw him. "For months after his return, Father drew crowds to the house with his talk of how you and he fought the redskins. I'll bet you've collected a string of scalps since those days, Mr. Tremayne. Didn't bring any with you, did you?"

"Martin, please!" exclaimed Louisa. "That's hardly a suitable mealtime topic."

"What about this recent Indian uprising along the western borders? Did you really turn down a captaincy in the New York Independents so that you could come to Cornwall?"

"Finish your food, boy," Sir Walter interjected, frowning at his youngest son.

Stephen leaned back in his chair, chuckling. "Come on, Adam. Tell him a good Indian story with lots of grisly details. We won't have a moment's peace around here until you do."

Juliana glanced at the ormolu clock on the mantelpiece. Eleven-thirty. Thank heavens! Only a half hour now before Graham came to the rescue. She decided to make an effort to be congenial until then. It would please Papa, and she desperately wanted to accompany him to the beach tomorrow night.

"Oh, do tell us of your adventures, Mr. Tremayne," she said in her sweetest voice. "I'm sure you've led a fascinating past."

Adam shot her a measuring glance. "Your interest is flattering, Miss Pendarvis, but I would not risk offending your sensibilities with some of the gruesome scenes I've witnessed."

Sir Walter nodded. "Wouldn't want Louisa to lose her breakfast on us. You know what a weak stomach she has."

Juliana lowered her eyes in acquiescence, though not before intercepting the grateful look Adam sent her father. *I wonder what it is in Mr. Tremayne's past he does not care to discuss,* she thought shrewdly. Could he have murdered someone? She wouldn't be surprised, considering the way he had treated her.

"Later perhaps," she heard him tell Martin. "Before I leave, I promise to recount how your father saved my life and lost his arm as a result."

"How about tonight, Mr. Tremayne?" Martin asked him immediately, leaning across the table, his lace jabot brushing his plate of half-eaten eggs. "After the women have gone to bed."

"Well . . . if your father has no objections . . ."

Martin slumped back in his chair, elated. "He saved you from getting scalped, didn't he? Juliana and I once saw a man at a show in London who'd been scalped and lived to tell of it. For a shilling he'd pull off his wig and let you feel his head."

Louisa rose abruptly, her palms pressed flat against the table. "You'll have to excuse us now, Mr. Tremayne. Stephen has offered to take me into Penzance for the day, and we'll never make it home before dark unless we leave soon. Martin, you'd better hurry if you want to ride with us.''

Noon came and went, and Juliana was still in the parlor with Adam and her father, halfheartedly serving them the fresh coffee and biscuits Audrey had brought after clearing the table.

''More coffee, Papa?'' she inquired, stifling a yawn.

''Better not. Time we was heading into the village. I want Adam to get a good look around in the daylight. Juliana, as charming as you are in that frock, I fear you'll ruin it riding. Hurry upstairs and change.''

''I can't go with you today, Papa. Graham and his cousin Venetia are taking me into Penzance for the fair.'' Juliana was suddenly conscious of Adam's eyes on her face. ''In fact, that sounds like Venetia's coach in the courtyard now.'' She slid off her chair and ran across the room to the window. ''It is. I'll fetch my hat and cloak.''

She made it halfway out the door before her father called her back into the room. '' 'Tisn't often I ask anything of you, girl, but when I do, I expect you to obey me. You're not going into Penzance today. Is that clear? Run outside and tell your fancy friends we've a guest.''

''Why, I'll do no such thing! I promised Graham just last night that I'd go. The countess will probably ask me to dine with them. Besides, he and Venetia came miles out of their way to pick me up. I couldn't possibly be so rude.''

''Last night?'' Sir Walter struggled out of his chair. ''So that's who you was off with. God Almighty! Are you stupid, girl? Do you think your prissy viscount would encourage you to sneak around behind my back if he gave a damn about you?'' He turned to Adam, the veins in his thick neck throbbing into prominence. ''You know the sort, Adam. Won't have nothing to do with a girl once he's ruined her reputation. Another maidenhead to his credit, and he's off!''

Juliana began backing away from the table. ''I don't have to stand here and listen to your vile accusations. I know what I did last night was wrong, but you make it sound so sordid . . . as if Graham had—had seduced—''

Sir Walter was at the door before she could finish, his stocky body trembling with rage. ''If he did, it's the last taste of pleasure he'll ever have!'' he shouted. ''I'll see that strutting donkey never touches you again, if I have to geld him myself!''

Juliana whirled in desperation. "Adam, please, you have to stop him. He's bound to do something foolish."

"Well, I—I'd rather not interfere."

"Oh, please!"

Together they hurried through the hallway and emerged into the courtyard just as Graham was stepping down from the lacquered coach. As usual he presented a picture of dandified elegance, dressed in a hip-length rose brocade coat which he wore open to display a flowered waistcoat and pearl-buttoned silk shirt. His slender legs were sheathed in tight-fitting gray satin breeches and stylish black silk stockings. His chiseled aristocratic features were coated with rouge and rice powder, and his heavy-lidded opaque blue eyes gazed out upon the world with practiced disdain. When he caught sight of Sir Walter hobbling toward him, he glanced back into the coach with a malicious smile, whispering something behind his slim gloved fingers that elicited a ripple of subdued laughter from his two companions.

"Good afternoon, Sir Walter," he said smoothly, not bothering to conceal his own amusement as he turned to face the older man. "Sorry we're late. My cousin takes hours to dress, you know. Is Juliana ready? Ah, sink me if that isn't the adorable chit coming now." He inclined his head to Sir Walter in a gesture of dismissal and, turning away, began to stroll toward Juliana.

"You have less than two minutes to get back into that coach and off my land."

Graham stopped and pivoted slowly on his high-heeled pumps. "Sir?"

"You heard me. I don't want to catch you sniffing around my daughter again. She can do far better for herself in Kenvellas."

Graham's pinkened lips curved into an unpleasant smile. "How so? By marrying a country bumpkin like you, and hoping he'll get knighted for losing one of his limbs in the king's service? Juliana's lucky she has any friends at all considering what an ignorant old toad she has for a father."

"Why you—you preening little turd!" Sir Walter swung

with all the force of his unleashed rage, his gnarled fist sinking into the center of Graham's diaphragm.

"Papa, don't!" Juliana cried out, stopping cold in her footsteps. Oh, God, how could he do this? Didn't he care that he would make her the laughingstock of the entire county? Her cheeks flaming with shame, humiliation immobilizing her, she stood beside Adam and watched helplessly until she felt him suddenly break away from her to interrupt the fight.

"Hold this," he snapped, tearing off his coat and thrusting it at her. "And don't move from here unless you want to cause more trouble."

Graham had doubled over, emitting a low grunt of pain and surprise. As he straightened up, he raised his left arm to deflect the next blow and simultaneously threw a vicious punch that caught the elderly knight on the side of the temple. Sir Walter reeled, cursing in frustration as he felt a restraining hand on his shoulder and looked up into Adam's worried face.

"Leave off, Adam," he said, his voice hoarse with exertion. "This is my—"

"That's enough, Sir Walter," Adam broke in gently. "You've made your point." He turned his head and raked Graham with a distasteful glance. "I think you ought to leave."

Graham flushed and lifted a hand to straighten his wig. "And I think you ought to mind your own bloody business." He cocked his head impatiently to see around Adam, who topped him by half a head. "Juliana! Are you coming or not?"

"Yes . . . yes, Graham, I am!" She dropped the coat and ran forward to follow him to the coach, passing Adam and her father without even a glance of acknowledgment. "Graham, I'm so sorry—"

He cut her off brusquely. "It wasn't your fault. Look, perhaps it's better if you don't come today." With a frown he caught her hand in his and drew her behind the opened door of the coach, motioning the footman to stand beside them as a precaution. "I'll be leaving for London at the end of the week. When I come back we'll be married—with or without our parents' permission."

"Oh, Graham, I don't know . . ."

"I do." He bent his head and quickly kissed her cheek. "I should be back sometime in late August or early September. You can always stay with Venetia until then if the situation here becomes unbearable." He paused a moment, his frown deepening. "That dark-haired man, Juliana. I've not seen him around here before. Who is he?"

Juliana glanced back over her shoulder at Adam, feeling a queer prickle of pleasure to find him staring at her intently. "No one of any consequence. He and my father fought together in the colonies."

"Well, see that you stay away from him. I don't like the way he's looking at you."

Juliana stepped backward to allow him around the door and into the coach. She sensed Venetia and her male escort peering at her through the window, but she could not bring herself to meet their pitying gazes. The coach turned smartly, and through tear-blurred eyes she watched it rattle off down the drive. Ungovernable anger welled inside her. Dashing away tears with the back of her hand, she turned and strode up to her father.

"I hate you for this," she said softly. "I wouldn't blame him if he never spoke to me again. You're crude and boorish and narrow-minded, and I h-hate you!" She gave a broken sob, picked up her skirts, and began running back to the house.

"Juliana!"

She flew up the stairs, stumbling as her heel caught in her petticoats, and reached out a hand to push open the door. Let him call me until he's blue in the face! she thought savagely. There's nothing can be said to make up for the humiliation he caused me. I'll never forgive him . . . never, never. . . .

"*Juliana!* For Christ's sake, help me!"

Adam, she thought dimly. It was Adam who was calling her, and something in the urgency of his voice penetrated the white-hot core of her fury. With her shoulder pressed to the door she hesitated and then slowly turned around, her eyes widening in horror as she realized what had happened. Her father had crumpled to the ground, gray-faced, his fist crushed to his chest. Adam was kneeling beside him.

Chapter Six

As far back as Juliana could remember, the Pendarvis family had faithfully observed one fundamental rule of behavior: In times of crisis, put aside all differences and forget all quarrels, no matter how long-standing. In the hour that followed her father's attack, Juliana's concern for his life obliterated her fury. She could not even find it in herself to resent Adam for his dictatorial handling of the situation. But it was late evening, and the family had gathered in Sir Walter's bedchamber before she realized she was actually grateful to him. She was sitting at her father's bedside, her refined features pinched with worry as Adam quietly explained to Stephen what the doctor had told him.

"Dr. Wendron thinks your father is suffering from an underlying heart infirmity. He mentioned a recently recognized condition called angina pectoris."

Sir Walter raised his head from the pillow. "Indigestion. Wasn't nothing but a case of wind from those eggs this morning." He looked so fit, had recovered so swiftly, that everyone was tempted to believe him.

Adam continued with a wan smile. "He gave your father an infusion of the purple foxglove, to be safe, and said he'd bring some heart pills on his next visit. We're to apply a mustard poultice to his breast if he complains of pain. The doctor also prescribed a small glass of rosemary wine, to be taken upon arising and retiring."

"Hear that, Louisa?" Sir Walter chortled. "I'm to have wine."

Stephen frowned. "I don't know about all this heart nonsense. He's had these attacks before and come to no harm."

"So did Uncle George," Martin said softly. "Remember what happened to him."

Louisa bent and patted Sir Walter's hand. "You have a nice rest while I help Mrs. Sennen with supper. Perhaps Mr. Tremayne will entertain everyone downstairs with his horrid Indian stories before we eat."

Juliana dropped a light kiss on her father's forehead and slipped out of the room before the others. Head bowed, she walked restlessly down the darkened hallway, aware of a pressing need to be alone with her troubled thoughts. Today was the first time Graham had ever come right out and asked her to marry him, and his proposal had forced her to confront a host of conflicting emotions she might otherwise have never acknowledged. She was more than a little dazzled at the prospect of life as a viscountess—what girl wouldn't be?—but could she conform to the countless rules of deportment and limitations on her freedom that it would entail? She was fond of Graham, for all his foppish airs, but did she love him? Even as she searched her heart for an answer, the image of another man's face rose in her mind, and she had to summon all her self-control to banish it . . . to suppress the tumultuous feelings the thought of its owner aroused inside her.

I'm overwrought, she told herself consolingly, *so worried about Papa I couldn't possibly make a rational decision tonight.* Perhaps a long walk in the evening air would clear her mind. At any rate, she needed to get out of this house, away from Adam. . . .

At the bottom of the staircase she suddenly remembered she'd left her shawl in the parlor. The door was ajar, and as she walked toward it, she could hear faint snatches of conversation carrying into the hallway.

" 'Twas in the summer of fifty-eight, wasn't it, Adam?"

That was Stephen's voice. She wavered outside the door, reluctant to enter or make her presence known. So far no one had brought up Graham's name in regard to her father's attack, and she was certainly in no frame of mind now to defend him if they did. Yet against her will she felt herself being drawn into the room. Adam had begun talking. She refused to look at him.

"I'd been sent from Fort Edward with a unit of sixty

Rangers to intercept a party of French bushfighters that were ambushing our supply wagons on the Lyman Road.'' He faltered slightly, his eyes following Juliana across the room to the worn velvet settee, not leaving her even as he continued. ''En route to Lake Champlain we met a detachment of British regulars under your father's command—he was Major Walter Pendarvis then. I recognized him instantly. He took longer to remember me, of course. I was only ten the one time he visited my parents in Virginia.''

Martin sat forward with avid interest on his face. ''He said your men weren't allowed to talk during marches, and that you forbade them fires at night.''

Adam nodded. ''Unfortunately, we began to relax caution on the afternoon an express brought us word that the raiders had escaped back to the French fort.''

''Which they hadn't,'' Stephen added knowingly.

''No,'' Adam said. ''They hadn't. Just before dawn the next day we were attacked. Much later I discovered that our three guards had gotten drunk on spruce beer during the night and wandered off into the woods to have a—'' He broke off, conscious of Juliana. ''Well, you know. . . .''

''A pissing contest,'' Martin supplied.

Adam smiled ruefully at the memory. ''I remember opening my eyes and seeing a naked Caughnawaga raise his tomahawk above my head. When I realized I wasn't dreaming, I jumped up and rammed my musket into his belly, but it misfired. Before I could call for help, there were two more of them on me, forcing me back down onto the ground so that the first could cleave my skull. I guess it was then I heard the gunfire and screams all around me. I thought I was dead when your father rushed up and shot the bastard's leering face off. Unfortunately, he swung his tomahawk down on your father's shoulder as he fell. By then our men had the situation under control and the attack party was fleeing into the forest. We lost twelve Rangers and almost thirty regulars.'' He paused, his mind still in the past. ''If you'd seen how badly mutilated the bodies of our three guards were, you'd understand why I will forever be indebted to your father.''

Juliana left the parlor while Adam was still talking. She had heard this story many times before, but tonight it had taken on new meaning. Tonight one of its major characters had become real to her, so real, in fact, that it seemed as though he had always been part of her life, a dark figure waiting in the shadows of her destiny.

Without conscious thought to destination, she walked through the meadow, a round yellow moon lighting her path, the hem of her gown brushing the dewy foxtail grass and clinging wetly to her ankles. The fine evening mist felt good against her face, and she filled her lungs with calming draughts of air that was fragrant with the summer scents of honeysuckle and freshly mown clover. Around her the world was still. She spread her shawl over the low stone wall that enclosed the meadow and leaned against it on her fore-arms, tilting her head back so that she could count the stars.

"Would you mind some company?"

She swirled around, her heart leaping into her throat at the sight of Adam standing before her. How long he had been there she could not guess. It was almost as though he had materialized out of her secret thoughts.

"I'm afraid I'm not up to another verbal duel just yet, Mr. Tremayne."

"Nor am I, as a matter of fact," he replied, his eyes glistening like quicksilver in the moonlight. "Actually, I came after you because I feared I might have said something that upset you."

It took Juliana a moment to realize he was referring to his recitation of the Indian attack and not their clash that morning. "No." She shook her head and quickly turned around, her eyes raised to the star-encrusted heavens. "I don't share Louisa's squeamishness. Another of my unladylike traits, I guess."

"Another of your traits I find enchanting," he said quietly, and moved a step closer to her. "Juliana . . ."

She closed her eyes, praying that he would touch her, terrified that she would crumble if he did. It had been an emotionally exhausting day, and now, at its close, she felt dangerously vulnerable, unable . . . unwilling to fight the strange new sensual yearnings he had awakened within her.

"I meant to thank you for everything you did today." She began chattering to break the silence, to break the powerful current between them. "I would never have gotten Papa into bed without your help, Adam. He's thick-skulled, but he seems to listen to you.''

The next step Adam took brought him so near Juliana, she could feel the heat radiating from his body. "I care about him, too, Juliana." He placed a hand on her shoulder and gently turned her around. "I care about both of you.''

Juliana went into his arms with a low moan of surrender, all coherent thought lost to the reckless urgings of her body. How could she fight what she did not understand? What weapon could she use against the melting sweetness she experienced at the first touch of his mouth on hers? Her lips parted under the demanding pressure of his kiss, and as the tip of his tongue slid inside her mouth, she felt herself float away, cast adrift on a dark sea of exquisite sensations. Slowly she became aware of a liquid warmth suffusing her body, building in her abdomen and flowing through her veins until she was clinging to Adam in trembling abandon. Then suddenly she felt his hand caressing the fullness of her breasts through her gown, the tender peaks springing erect beneath his skillful fingers. Bewildered by her body's ardent response, she uttered a soft cry of protest and pressed her palms against his chest to force him away from her. She did not trust herself to speak.

"Juliana," he murmured hoarsely. "Oh, God, Juliana, I never meant for this to happen." He pulled back slightly and cupped her delicate face in his hands, staring down into her frightened eyes with the burning intensity of his passion. "Try to forgive me. Try to forget this happened.''

"But—but why?" she asked him in a voice so low and husky it came as a shock to her ears.

"Juliana," he began gently, "you are very sweet and beautiful, and I want you more than I've ever wanted anything in my life,''—he pressed his thumb to her lips to stem the question forming on them—"but you're also young and inexperienced, and your father is a man I deeply respect and would not hurt for the world." He forced a nonchalance into his tone he did not feel. "You deserve so much better than me."

She stared up at him with defiance flaming in her eyes. "Shouldn't I be the judge of that?''

Adam could not think of an immediate retort. What had

happened? How had this headstrong young woman gotten under his skin in only two days without his realizing it? God, the rich irony of it all! Sir Walter's own daughter, his favorite child. Without question he had to fight it, had to close his heart against her for her sake as well as his own.

"There are many things about me you don't know," he said at last. "I am not always an easy man to get along with. My own family will attest to that. I've led a disreputable past even by your father's liberal standards. I was wrong to take advantage of your innocence. Thank God it went no further than this." He drew his hands back to his sides as if he felt he no longer had the right to touch her. "Perhaps it would make you feel better if I promised it won't happen again."

Juliana felt as though she had been slapped. Oh, she was innocent, all right. As green and gullible as a village milkmaid! Why else would she have fallen into his arms so eagerly? And to think she'd read an avowal of love in his kiss! Just because it had jolted her to the depths of her very soul didn't mean that he'd felt anything stronger than a casual stirring of lust. She should have kept to her first impression of him. He was heartless and unprincipled, and she could only offer the upsetting events of the day as an excuse for her own disgraceful conduct tonight. Harder to excuse—or to understand—was the unbearable hurt constricting her heart, the sudden humiliating urge to burst into tears. And just as she feared she would indeed break down, pride surged through her and took control.

"You're right, of course," she said with cool composure, leaning back against the wall. "This has been a most distressing day, and neither of us is behaving in a normal fashion." She summoned a self-reproachful laugh, hoping he would not detect its hollow ring. "Why else would a woman who'd just gotten engaged indulge in a playful flirtation with another man, a stranger at that?"

Adam's dark, rough-hewn face did not mirror any amusement. "What in blazes are you talking about?"

"Graham asked me to marry him this afternoon. I'd planned to announce our engagement at supper, but I doubt the news would be well received after what happened between him and my father." She arched her shoulders in a wistful shrug. "I might never be able to announce it at all. Graham and I will probably have to elope and hope to be forgiven afterward."

Adam shook his head disbelievingly. "You can't be serious. A man like that would make your life miserable. The moment you were married, he'd start trying to change you. He isn't worth one minute of the heartbreak he'd cause you and your family."

"Graham happens to be a viscount, Mr. Tremayne," she snapped. "I'd never lack for anything again in my life."

"Except happiness," Adam said with brutal honesty. "And the freedom to be the sweet wild spirit you are right now. And what about love, Juliana? I haven't heard you once mention the most important reason for any marriage. Do you love Graham?"

"Of course." She turned her face away, her voice quavering, uncertain. "Of course I do."

"I don't believe you," he said, his voice harsh. "How could you? How could you love a man who wears ribbons in his hair, and who's probably gambled away more money in this past year than Stephen and Martin will make in their lives?"

"Well, what if he has? He can certainly afford to. And just because he follows the latest fashions and enjoys a highly popular pastime doesn't mean he won't be good to me." She turned her head sharply. "Be careful, Mr. Tremayne. You're beginning to sound jealous."

"Maybe I am." His eyes were hooded, their expression unreadable. "But that's beside the point. You still haven't convinced me that you love him."

Scorn tightened Juliana's delicate features. "Why should I? It's enough that he and I know it."

"You're a liar, Juliana," he said softly. "A lovely but unpracticed liar. If you truly loved your viscount, you would have left with him today. No power on earth could have held you back. What you want, you take, and no one or nothing can stand in your path. That's the sort of person you are."

She raised her chin. "What a fascinating analysis of my character. May I ask on what basis it was formed?"

"On the basis that I see myself in you, as strange as that may sound. I also see you about to make the same mistake I

made years ago. Marry a man who accepts you and your
family for what you are. Marry a man who loves you *because* of what you are, not despite it.''

No man had ever spoken to Juliana before on such an intimate level—except perhaps her brother Martin—and certainly no one had ever presented her with such an accurate
assessment of her own temperament. It had an unwelcome,
upsetting effect upon her self-possession.

"But I do love Graham,'' she murmured, and the slight
tremor in her voice betrayed her innermost doubts.

"Liar!'' Without warning Adam reached out and hauled
her into his arms, his left hand pressed to the base of her
spine so that her slender body was molded to the lean hardness of his. "Has Graham ever made you feel like this?'' He
brought his mouth down on hers in a kiss that made the
world explode and dissolve into blackness behind her fluttering eyelids. "Have you allowed him the opportunity to
even try?'' he whispered against her lips.

As his mouth traveled down her throat, searing her
creamy flesh with quick, feverish kisses, Juliana pushed
against him with all her strength, and, gaining her freedom,
staggered back against the wall, her heart pounding violently, her lips still parted and trembling. "You
promised—''

Adam's exultant laughter interrupted her. "I knew it!
You've never let him touch you, have you?''

"You know nothing!'' she said furiously.

"Despite what your father believes, you're as pure as the
day you were born, Juliana,'' he continued, staring at her
with a satisfied smile. "In fact, I suspect a great deal of Graham's infatuation with you lies in wanting what he can't—''

The slap Juliana dealt him came as a shock to both of
them, ringing discordantly through the stillness of the night.
"Oh!'' She pressed her hand to her mouth, the palm still
stinging, almost as hot as her face. She half expected him to
slap her in return, as Stephen and Martin would have done
. . . as the small inner voice of her conscience whispered
she deserved.

But, to her amazement, he merely lifted a hand to his
cheek and lightly touched the livid imprint of her fingers.
"The truth hurts, doesn't it?'' he said, smiling ruefully.

"But better to suffer a little pain now than to ruin your whole life with one childish act of defiance."

"It's my life to ruin," she said, forcing the words past the lump of inexplicable emotion that had risen in her throat.

Adam's smile faded. "So it is. And in less than a fortnight, I shall be out of it, and you'll be free to do exactly as you please."

"You flatter yourself if you think your presence will have any influence over my behavior, Mr. Tremayne. If I do not announce my engagement before you leave, it will only be out of concern for my father."

"Juliana—"

"Louisa will have supper ready by now. Perhaps you'll be kind enough to inform everyone I've gone straight to bed. Strangely enough, I've lost my appetite." She gathered her skirts in hand and swept a wide arc around him, then stopped to deliver an irrepressible parting shot. "I suppose it's useless to hope your conscience will keep you awake tonight. I doubt you even have one."

But after she had returned to the house and sought refuge in her bedchamber, falling onto the bed before taking the trouble to undress, Juliana found that it was she who could not sleep. Her lips felt bruised and tender from Adam's kisses; her ripe young body ached and throbbed with nameless desires that brought a stain of shame to her cheeks at the erotic fantasies they engendered.

For no matter how hard she fought to deny it, no matter how desperately she struggled to expel him from her thoughts, every single one of those forbidden fantasies centered around Adam Tremayne.

Chapter Seven

Juliana and Adam did not meet again until late the following afternoon at dinner. As usual Sir Walter presided over the meal, refusing to stay in bed another minute longer, swearing that there had never been anything seriously wrong with him in the first place. Besides, he argued, he had a valuable cargo to land and begin dispatching that evening.

Stephen heard his father out with obvious annoyance. "Martin and I are perfectly capable of supervising the whole bloody operation, and well you know it. You've missed runs before. Nothing special about tonight's, is there?"

"I'm not questioning your capabilities, Stephen," Sir Walter said. "In another year you and your brother will have assumed total control, and that's as it should be." Amusement glimmered in the depths of his eyes. "I'll not get in your way tonight, if that's what you're afraid of. I only want to show Adam around so he'll have an idea of how we operate."

"But to introduce a stranger during a run," Martin said in a low voice. "You know how suspicious the men are. . . ."

Sir Walter wrinkled his forehead. "Aye. I'd meant to take him into the village yesterday."

Adam broke the silence that had descended. "Perhaps we'll have another chance before I leave. I don't want to cause any problems for you, Sir Walter. I can understand if your men are wary of outsiders."

Juliana's golden-green eyes narrowed in contemplation. The way her luck was running lately, she'd probably end up stuck in the house tonight entertaining the wretched colonial. Damn the man, anyway, she thought. Why do I have to waste my time amusing him? I want to be in on the excitement tonight. If only I could think up a way—

"I have an idea," she said suddenly, and she rushed on to reveal it before her father could interrupt her. "Mr. Tremayne and I can ride up to Medrid Bluff and watch the goods being landed from there. I could explain everything to him as it's happening."

"But that's a sheer drop to the rocks," Louisa protested, her voice fading away at the quelling look Juliana sent her.

"It's the safest place in the world," Juliana went on. "We shall be able to see almost everything, and yet not be seen ourselves."

Adam stared at her in surprise. What had brought about this sudden change of heart? Guilt over her escapade the night before last? A sense of duty to her father? Adam would have been pleased to think that his charm had won her over, but it didn't seem likely.

"You're not afraid of heights, are you, Mr. Tremayne?" she asked him, her voice softly taunting.

"Not in the least, Miss Pendarvis," he replied with a grin. "And if your father gives his permission, I would very much like to accept your offer of an escort."

The matter was settled within minutes, Sir Walter granting his reluctant approval, not unaware Juliana had turned the situation to her personal advantage. Plans were hastily reviewed over an after-course of coffee and almond trifle. Then the company dispersed, everyone hurrying upstairs to change into suitable attire except Louisa, who went on with her embroidery as though tonight were no different from any other.

Adam was leading the horses into the stable yard when Juliana appeared, slim and elegant in a fox-trimmed, forest-green velvet riding habit that enhanced her striking coloring. Politely, he moved beside her to help her onto Ajax, but she ignored him, her mouth set in a stubborn line, her eyes distant as she brushed his hand aside and swung herself gracefully into the saddle.

"I should have known not to accept your offer at its face value," he said dryly. "Squiring me around was the only way you could get out of the house tonight, I take it?"

She nodded curtly without meeting his eyes, then pulled back on the reins and wheeled her horse so sharply that Adam had to jump back to avoid being knocked down. But if Juliana was willful and fiercely proud, she also did not have it in her nature to hold a grudge, and presently she began to respond to Adam's gallant attempts at conversation as they rode abreast on the uneven road to Kenvellas Beach.

"I'm frankly curious about something, Juliana. Why did your father not wait to set out for the cove? He cannot hope to accomplish anything before dark."

"More deeds go undetected in the shadows of dusk than at night, especially in isolated villages like Kenvellas. Our smuggling boats usually slip in with the local fishing fleet after a transaction has been conducted outside territorial waters."

"But it seems so obvious. I can hardly believe you've had no trouble with the excisemen."

Juliana shrugged. "We've had a few minor run-ins with the dragoons, a lugger seized in the Channel once, but nothing serious. With barely five hundred riding revenuemen to patrol the entire English coast, there's little to worry about. The Board of Customs has enough problems regulating the larger ports without patrolling every tiny cove and harbor in Cornwall. Anyway, it's a small risk to take when so many of the villagers depend on their smuggling income to support their families. My father would stop the smuggling tomorrow if he believed it actually harmed anyone. He's a good man at heart, and believe me, if it weren't for him, a larger, possibly vicious gang would move into the district."

She was silent for a moment as she shortened the reins; they had reached the steep clifftop ascent to the bluff. "You'll want to run your operation differently in Mentreath, I'd imagine. The cove there is invisible from the high road, secluded, actually, though it's far more dangerous to navigate than ours, and you have no large fleet to rely on. I don't think your uncle made much money from smuggling, mind you."

"You've visited Mentreath?" Adam asked in some surprise.

"Once—when I was eight. 'Twas the summer before my mother died. She and Logan were close friends. I think she

was the only woman he really confided in. I know she tried
to help him get over your mother. He cried his heart out at
Mama's funeral.''

The trace of sadness in her voice was not lost on Adam.
''I should hate to think that my future home holds painful
memories for you.''

''No.'' She shook her head, a tendril of dark auburn hair
escaping the green tricornered hat to curl at the base of her
neck. ''Quite the opposite. The summer I spent there with
my mother was happy. I think of it often.''

''Then perhaps you will come to visit from time to time,''
Adam said impulsively, but when she made no reply, he did
not pursue the subject. Indeed, he thought it most likely they
would never meet again after he left Rosmorna.

At last the perilously narrow cliff-track ended, opening
into a deep pocket on the top of the sheer greenstone bluff
that looked out over the murmuring sea. Adam dismounted
first, automatically raising his arms to help Juliana down,
surprised when she leaned toward him and his hands encircled the firm uncorseted flesh of her waist. What a pity she
was the old man's daughter, he thought suddenly. How
much he would enjoy staying on here a little while longer in
the hope of winning her heart. And the realization of this astonished him, for he had lived with his loneliness for so long
now, had quietly accepted it as his lot in life, that it never
occurred to him to seek a cure for it . . . or even that one
might exist.

She moved away from him the moment he set her on the
ground, and sank to her knees on the edge of the bluff,
motioning him to sit beside her. In one hand she held aloft
her father's spyglass; with the other she was distractedly
yanking off her hat and pulling at the hair coiled on the top
of her head until the entire mass came tumbling down
around her waist in a cascade of luxuriant bronze-streaked
waves. Adam caught his breath at her pure loveliness. The
combination of the ride and the cool sea air had brought out
the delicate tinge of rose in her flawless ivory complexion.
Beneath the dark-winged brows, her eyes were
mesmerizing, reflecting the shadowed depths of the sea below with all its mysteries.

Unmindful of the enchanting picture she made, she shook

her head and glanced up at him with a puzzled smile. "Come on. What are you staring at? 'Twill be dark soon."

Wordlessly, he took the spyglass from her hand and knelt beside her. His vision was keen, and although he strained his eyes through the fading sunset shadows he spotted nothing suspicious in the fleet of incoming boats, each one laden with baskets of hake that glinted like coins as the vessels bobbed closer to shore.

"What would happen if the excisemen were waiting on shore to search the boats?" he asked thoughtfully, focusing the binoculars on the stocky one-armed figure he had just seen emerge from a cave.

"It rarely happens."

"And when it does?"

"Someone is sent up here to warn the men not to come in with the goods. They weight the kegs down with stones and moor them as near to shore as possible to be retrieved later when the beach is clear."

Behind them the two horses were cropping the sparse grassy turf, their rhythmic chewing and the harsh crying of the seabirds that circled overhead the only sounds. Finally, Adam put the spyglass down, shaking his head. "It's difficult to see anything now. What happens next?"

"Well, in bad weather the stuff would be hidden in the caves until it could be conveyed inland. These cliffside tracks turn to mud in a rain." She was lying flat on her stomach now, absently fingering a clump of white-flowered brookweed. "Tonight will be easy. 'Tis impossible to see exactly where they are, but I'd guess they had everything landed. For beach work we use sturdy carts with iron tires and dark-colored farm ponies."

Adam studied her profile, his eyes tracing the broad, unlined forehead and finely boned nose, the full lower lip and perfectly sculpted jaw. He knew he should be paying more attention to the activity on the beach below and less to this spirited young beauty, but he could not help himself. Nor did he particularly want to.

"It's kind of you to answer all my questions," he said, forcing himself to look away at last. "I confess I never expected to find a woman so knowledgeable about smuggling."

Juliana shrugged. "Smuggling has been in the family for generations. I'd have to be an utter dunce like Lou—well, I'd have to be pretty stupid not to know something about it."

"And stupid you are not," Adam said earnestly, gaining nothing for the compliment but another indifferent shrug. "However, you *are* breaking the law and cannot plead ignorance as an excuse for it."

"We should leave now," Juliana murmured.

"Consider the problems men like your father are causing this country, Juliana. The monies lost in revenues, the manpower wasted in patrolling the coast when the navy is so desperate for men that the government encourages impressment. None of this surprises you, and yet you display no regret, no qualms of conscience that your family is leading simpler folk astray with its illegal pursuits."

Juliana sat up hurriedly, a frown creasing her brow. "Of course my conscience is clear! Why shouldn't it be? My father has done more for the villagers of Kenvellas than any hundred fat-arsed members of Parliament will ever do. Besides, there'd be no need for smuggling if the government reduced our taxes—taxes that were levied to pay the debts incurred winning *your* war, I might add."

"My war?" Adam echoed.

"Your attitude really dismays me, Mr. Tremayne." She scrambled to her feet, her voice rising. "As a colonial, a former smuggler yourself, you've felt the strain of crushing taxes and unfair trade practices. I hardly expected your condemnation."

Adam's face was nonchalant. "I have several clients—Boston shipowners—who are blatant in their defiance of His Majesty's revenue acts. They make no secret of their smuggling. In fact, they consider it their duty—a symbolic gesture for independence, a stand against tyranny."

"Oh, I see," she said angrily. "It's criminal for us and patriotic for the colonials. Perhaps you ought to consider a career in politics. You certainly know how to twist facts to your benefit."

Adam stood up beside her, trying not to smile. "Calm down, Juliana. I am not such a hypocrite as to condemn a

profession I hope to again become active in. Quite the re-
verse, I agree with every word you said.''

"Then why did you let me rant—?'' She broke off with an
angry gasp. "Oh! You deliberately provoked me—you were
baiting me. You wanted me to make a fool of myself!''

"No. I only intended to play the devil's advocate. However, I have to confess I did enjoy hearing my own views de-
fended by such a lovely champion.'' He followed her to the
wind-stunted elm he had used as a tethering post for the
horses. "I'm sorry if I upset you. Won't you forgive me?''

She turned slowly, her face inscrutable. "Perhaps. If you
do me one small favor.''

"If I can.''

"You've said you're interested in every aspect of my father's operation. Ride with me to Saint Joan's in the
village—that's where he makes his contacts and collects
payments for whatever merchandise is to be delivered lo-
cally.''

"No.'' Adam's tone was firm. "Not without his express
permission. He'd have me drawn and quartered if you so
much as stubbed a toe.''

"A church—the safest place in the world! And my father
need never know we were there. We'll watch from the hillside, out of the way.''

"If anything should happen—''

Juliana dropped her eyelids and glanced at him askance, a
coquettish gesture she carried off with remarkable success
considering how ridiculous it made her feel. "What could
happen? You'll be there to protect me.''

"All right, Juliana. Don't overdo it.''

St. Joan's lay on the wooded outskirts of the village, a
small fifteenth-century church that had been used for the
concealment and pickup of contraband cargo for almost
three hundred years. In times of emergency, cases of tea
were stashed in the vestry, bolts of silk stacked in the crypts.
Of course, it helped to have an understanding clergyman
who could, if necessary, deliver a stirring sermon to a congregation forced to stand because the pews were occupied
by brandy kegs.

From their hiding place on the hillside Adam and Juliana
observed small clusters of men flitting through the shadows

of the churchyard, porters assembling in lines to deliver six-gallon casks of French cognac to the inns and public houses of neighboring villages, pack trains forming to haul bolts of silk to the market town before dawn. In the graveyard the batmen stood guard, their faces illuminated by the moonlight filtering down through the Cornish elms. Adam thought it a tight, well-run operation. Sir Walter and Stephen, their faces masked, supervised on horseback. Martin seemed to be everywhere at once.

"Those men down there," he whispered, pointing to the five nebulous figures lurking in the rectory garden. "I didn't notice them earlier. What function do they serve?"

Juliana peered down the hillside. "What men?"

"They're just moving off into the graveyard now. I thought your father said his men never carried firearms."

"They don't—"

An outraged cry erupting from the graveyard confirmed their unspoken suspicions. "Revenuers! Hell's bloody bells, wot's to do now?"

Shouts and curses rang through the air. One of the revenuers leveled his musket at a smuggler only to have it wrenched off his shoulder from behind and used as a club to strike him unconscious. Juliana saw her father ride into the center of the excitement, shouting furiously. Following closely at his horse's hooves were two of his prize mastiffs, their barking adding to the confusion.

"Goddamn, Stephen! I thought you'd taken care of this."

"I did!" Stephen shouted back, struggling to bring his mount under control as a warning shot exploded behind him. "These aren't the officers I paid off last month. Someone must've talked. What'll we do with 'em?"

Sir Walter cursed roundly, weighing the situation with a disgusted glance. Two porters had an officer disarmed and cornered on the vine-clad church porch, unmoved by his cries of, "Stop, I tell you! In the King's name—" Cudgels raised with ominous intent, a group of batmen were closing in on the two excisemen cowering behind a pony cart in the graveyard. The fifth officer, young and inexperienced, had positioned himself in the crotch of an elm tree and was threatening to shoot the first smuggler who moved.

"Well, what should we do?" Stephen asked again, impatient, sweating beneath his mask.

"Get that silly bugger out of the tree before he hurts someone," Sir Walter growled. "Then lock 'em all up in the crypt for the night. I want no bloodshed."

In the ensuing tumult, the presence and stealthy progress of two more officers on the footpath into the opposite end of the graveyard went unnoticed. Adam spotted them before Juliana, but it was she who scrambled down the slope first to alert her father.

"Oh, no, you don't!" Adam caught up with her at the foot of the hill and roughly pulled her to the ground, his arm an iron band across her midriff.

"But my father—my brothers!" she said frantically, twisting and kicking, jerking at his arm.

"And do you think it would help them if you gave their identities away, or got yourself shot?" he hissed. "Stay here, Juliana, or by God, I swear I'll knock you out and tether you to the tree with the horses. Do you understand?"

She nodded, resentment burning in her eyes, but within moments after he had released her, she was on her feet and running behind him. It never occurred to her that she might be placing herself in any danger until she passed through the gabled lych-gate and a masked figure sprang out from the shadows to grab her.

"Jesus God, Juliana! What are you doing here?"

"The graveyard, Martin," she said, sagging against him in relief. "Behind the altar tombs. Two more excisemen—"

He drew her into the darkness, his face grim. "I'll handle this. Stay out of the way."

In less than a minute he had recruited six burly villagers to surround and disarm the remaining officers. There followed a brief but violent scuffle, and from the lych-gate Juliana heard a volley of startled oaths as one of the muskets discharged in the course of changing hands. Then suddenly men were running past her, abandoning their duties to gather around the horseman who had just fallen in the graveyard.

"What—what's happened?" she called to a running figure, cold dread spreading through her, numbing her limbs.

"The old man's been shot through the 'eart!" came the hasty reply.

No one questioned Juliana's presence; no one made any attempt to prevent her from reaching her father as she pushed wildly through the crowd encircling him. Trent Lansyn, the leader of the batmen, even cleared a path for her and ordered his men to stand back a respectable distance. Once again Adam was on the scene, crouching between Stephen and Martin, who were conferring in hushed tones as they removed their father's waistcoat and gingerly examined his chest for the exact location of the wound.

Juliana pressed her hand to her mouth, afraid to move, afraid to speak. "Is he—"

Martin glanced up at her. "No, no. But he's in terrible pain. Has someone sent for the doctor?"

"Aye," Lansyn replied soberly. "I sent a man on yer father's own 'orse. Figured 'twere the quickest way."

"Where in Christ's name did the ball enter?" Stephen muttered. "I swear he clutched his chest when the musket went off, but I can't find any blood."

Sir Walter stirred and opened his eyes, moaning weakly. "Pain, oh, God, God, the pain. Something crushing my chest . . . Can't breathe . . ." His fingers plucked at Adam's sleeve. "Shot, was I, lad?"

"No, Sir Walter. I think it's your heart," Adam said, turning his head to meet Stephen's questioning look. "His body is reacting to the pain. He's gone into a cold sweat, and his pulse is weakening." He glanced around him, acknowledging Juliana with a faint scowl. "It would help if one of you could find a blanket to cover him with."

One of the porters shuffled forward. "We could load 'im into a cart and fetch 'im over to Parson Foxcombe's cottage."

Adam shook his head. "Until the doctor comes we would be wiser to keep him still."

Stephen nodded. "Go about your business as though nothing had happened. Lansyn, you'll have to return here before dawn to take care of the revenuers. Drop them off in the middle of the moors, and make sure their blindfolds are secure. There won't be another run till I've found out who betrayed us tonight."

Chapter Eight

It was the longest night of Juliana's life. Shortly after receiving a dose of laudanum-laced brandy, Sir Walter began to recover from shock and asked to be taken home. Heavily sedated, he slept on and off until early morning, when he woke complaining of thirst. Sometime during the night he had developed a fever. Dr. Wendron did not hold much hope for his survival, and this he explained to the Pendarvis family in the upstairs hallway.

"It's my opinion that a thrombus has formed in an artery and is disrupting the circulation of blood through the body. Possibly regular treatments of bloodletting could dislodge the tumor, but there are several grave complications that might arise before a cure could be effected, and 'tis to the prevention of these we must direct our attention."

"What are we to do for his fever?" Louisa asked worriedly, following him to the staircase.

"I've just administered a dose of emetic powder that should work within the hour. After his stomach has emptied, you might begin giving him vinegar baths and frequent feedings of salt-broth. I'll be back this evening. Send one of the boys after me if he takes a turn for the worse before then."

Juliana, Louisa, and Audrey spent the day in Sir Walter's room, sponging him down with cool vinegar-dampened towels and coaxing him to swallow Mrs. Sennen's lukewarm broth, a half-spoonful at a time, as though he were an infant. By late afternoon he began to rally, twice cursing Louisa for spilling broth on the bedclothes, a good sign, Juliana thought. When the doctor returned that evening, the fever had broken.

"Well, you've won the first battle, Sir Walter," he said, perching his thin frame on the edge of the bed. "Now we shall have to contend with the danger of another attack, or an inflammation of the lungs. No more smuggling runs, or the next time you and I meet in a graveyard, 'twill be for your funeral. We're not as young as we'd like to believe."

Pointedly ignoring the physician, Sir Walter struggled to raise his head and glance about the room. "Everyone's here," he muttered. "Good, good. Stephen, you've found out about last night, I trust."

"Betty Hamlyn's cousin is missing," the tawny-haired young man replied. "Dick Tendennor jilted her and thinks she wanted revenge. It won't happen again."

Sir Walter grunted, lowering his head. "Bloody females. Always at the heart of trouble." His pale blue eyes swung across the room to Juliana. "That goes for you, too, miss. Don't think I didn't know you was there last night." A sly grin gradually eased the angry tensing of his jaw. "Have to keep a tighter rein on her till she's broken, Adam. Got to teach her right off who's in control."

Hot color flooded Juliana's cheeks. "Honestly, Papa! I'm not a—a horse, and my conduct is hardly Mr. Tremayne's responsibility."

Sir Walter smiled blandly, his gaze shifting from his daughter's indignant face to Adam's openly amused one. "Juliana's husband—if I approve of 'im—will receive a handsome marriage settlement, Adam. Roughly five thousand pounds that I've netted over the years from some sound investments."

"Five thousand pounds?" Stephen repeated, disbelieving. "Why, she could have a bloody marquess for that. I wasn't aware we had that sort of money to throw around."

Sir Walter narrowed his eyes. "You boys'll get the lion's share, Stephen—my properties, the profits from the business. Surely you don't begrudge your sister a dowry. Truth be told, though, I expect Louisa deserves more than the whole damned lot of you put together."

Louisa stretched forward from her chair to rearrange Sir Walter's pillows. "He has years and years yet to worry about his will, doesn't he, doctor?"

Dr. Wendron raised his sparse eyebrows. "Well, one

never knows. Best to keep one's affairs in order, just in case.''

Sir Walter gave a weak nod of gratitude, the strain of carrying on a conversation beginning to show on his face. ''My will was drawn up years ago. Anyway, 'tis the matter of Juliana's dowry I mean to discuss. Adam, where d'you think you're off to?''

Adam glanced back over his shoulder, his right hand poised on the doorknob. ''Well, I thought . . . I mean, this is family business. I assumed you'd want some privacy.''

''I want you here,'' Sir Walter said testily, sliding up against the headboard. ''What I have to say concerns you, too. Juliana, come closer to the bed. The rest of you are to remain in the room.''

With a prickle of apprehension, Juliana crossed the room and reluctantly walked with Adam to the great oaken bedstead. Her father was studying them keenly, and the calculating gleam in his eye put her on guard. He's up to something, she thought, her spine stiffening. Her unease must have shown on her face, for as Dr. Wendron stood up to grant her room, he shot her a sharp look in which she read a disturbing message: *Your father will not live long; humor him until the end.* Her eyes filled with stinging tears that she quickly blinked away. It couldn't be true. With rest and regular medical attention, he could go on living for perhaps another decade. Yet as he began to speak, his voice so feeble she had to strain to catch his words, she vowed she would do nothing to upset him during the time he had left.

''Just the other day you told my family you were indebted to me, Adam.''

''You know how I feel,'' Adam said without hesitation. ''I'm not ashamed to admit it. You've shown me more kindness and understanding than anyone in my own family. I'm also aware you helped convince my uncle to name me his heir, whether you confess to it or not.''

''Feel you owe me, don't you, lad?''

''There is nothing I wouldn't do for you, Sir Walter. Have you a favor to ask of me?''

''Aye. I do.''

''Then name it, please. You have plenty of witnesses here

to see that it's carried out—so long as it is within my power. I give you my word.''

"Your word," Sir Walter repeated, smiling slowly. "Did everyone hear that? Adam has given his word that my final wish is to be fulfilled. I shall die at peace, after all.''

"And I shall die of curiosity if you don't tell us what this favor is,'' Martin said, looking from his father to Adam with a baffled grin.

Sir Walter let a long moment elapse before he spoke again. "Adam has just agreed to become your brother-in-law, Martin. At last the problem of finding Juliana a suitable husband has been solved.''

Chapter Nine

Shocked silence filled the room, broken by a string of varying reactions that ranged from Juliana's loud snort of disbelieving laughter to Stephen's red-faced denunciation of his father's ruse. Oddly, it was Adam who appeared the least perturbed. Louisa took the longest to recover. But when she did, she grabbed Dr. Wendron's arm and half dragged the startled man across the room, insisting she have a word alone with him.

"Could it be—is it possible the fever has affected his brains, doctor?" she whispered.

"Well, it's—"

"Nothing wrong with my head, Louisa. Nor my hearing. All the whispering in the world won't change what's been done." Sir Walter was leaning back against the pillows with a wan but triumphant smile. "A bargain's a bargain, eh, Adam? He's consented to the marriage, and that's the end of the matter."

"It certainly is not! I think I should have a say in this!" Juliana had finally collected her wits enough to challenge her father's authority, too upset to care whether she broke the vow she'd made to herself only minutes before.

"I only want what's best for you, girl."

"Then you'll be glad to hear I've decided to marry Graham," she burst out in one defiant breath. "Once he succeeds to his father's title and estates, I'll be a countess. Don't you want that for me?"

"You've let him cloud your good sense with visions of a world you don't belong in. He'll break your heart, girl.

He'll gamble and drink away every penny his father leaves him, and drag you down with him on his way.''

"I think you're wrong about Graham, Papa. He's generous to a fault."

"Aye. With his parents' money," Sir Walter said wryly. "But he'll not get a shilling from me. You'll marry Adam or go to the altar a dowerless bride."

Juliana clenched her fists to her sides. "I don't believe this. Adam doesn't love me, Papa! Don't you realize what an embarrassing position you've forced him into?"

"Love isn't my primary concern, Juliana. It usually comes with time. Besides, it might be better if Adam doesn't love you to start off with. You won't be able to twist him around your little finger as you have me and your brothers. In fact, he's the only man I know who could handle the hellion you've become since your mother died." He lifted his gaze to Adam, still standing tall and rigid, his angular face impassive as though carved from stone. "Not that I give a damn, Adam, but I suppose I have to ask: Do you love my daughter, lad?"

Adam turned his head and stared down at Juliana, his expression so cool and unreadable that when he gave his reply, she could not believe her ears. "I think so, sir."

"Why, you—you damnable fiend!" she cried, her voice rising on a hysterical note. "How dare you stand here lying to my face!"

Adam answered her outburst with a helpless shrug. "That was no lie, Juliana, however hard we both find it to accept."

"Well, I don't love you!" she sputtered. "And I refuse to become the victim of some perverse arrangement between you and my father!"

Dr. Wendron stepped in front of her. "I'm afraid I have to ask you to leave the room now, Juliana. Your father's had too much excitement as it is. In fact, I'd like everyone to join me downstairs in the parlor for a conference. Sir Walter needs rest more than anything else."

"Don't worry, Juliana," Martin whispered, slipping his arm around her waist to walk her to the door. "It won't come to anything. Father isn't himself."

Juliana nodded and followed him downstairs. Of course

Papa didn't know what he was saying. She felt ashamed of herself for letting him provoke her into a rage.

Dr. Wendron did nothing to ease her conscience.

"That was exactly the sort of scene we have to avoid," he said, frowning at her over the rims of his spectacles. "In his weakened condition the slightest upset could kill your father."

"So it really is that serious," Stephen said. "I was hoping you were trying to scare him into behaving."

Dr. Wendron took a chair by the fire, politely declining the glass of port Louisa offered him. "Too late for that, I fear. I've treated a dozen similar cases, and can only warn you to anticipate the worst."

"How long does he have?" asked Martin, taking Juliana's hand.

"It depends. A matter of days if complications develop. I would guess he has a fortnight at most. Of course, there is the remote chance that he will outlive us all. In any event, his life will be lengthened if he is kept quiet and not subjected to further excitement."

"Good God, man!" Stephen exclaimed. "Are you suggesting my sister marry someone she hardly knows in the hope of adding a few days to our father's life?"

"Speaking as a physician, no. But as a longtime family friend, I will take the liberty of suggesting she at least pretend to heed his wish."

"We'd never get away with it," Juliana said. "He'd want to know why we weren't sleeping together. He'd probably insist on watching us consummate the marriage."

A ghost of a smile flitted across Adam's face. "I've a feeling that isn't what the doctor meant, Juliana."

Wendron nodded. "You need do no more than convince him you intend to marry Mr. Tremayne. It takes three successive Sundays to publish wedding banns, does it not? Insist on a traditional ceremony with a reception held here afterward. Louisa will support you. Announce your betrothal to the village. Tell the old man these things take time to arrange." He got to his feet, covering a yawn with his palm. "The final decision is yours to make. Don't get up, Louisa. I'll see myself out."

"Goddamn." Stephen began to pace the length of the

room, relieving the thick silence with an occasional curse. Finally, he stopped before Adam's chair. "You're in this as deep as we are, Adam. Actually, you were the only one who kept his wits about him. It was admirable of you to go along with him in this madness, even professing to love Juliana when we all know you and she can barely stand the sight of each other. What's your opinion of Wendron's suggestion? Will it work?"

"It might. However, I did give your father my word." Adam's eyes drifted to Juliana. "And I intend to keep it."

"Oh, you bastard!" Juliana sprang off the settee, her anger unleashed. "At least have the decency to admit you're after that five thousand pounds!"

"The money means nothing to me."

"The hell it doesn't!" she said viciously.

"That's quite enough, Juliana." Stephen rose from his chair to guide her back to the settee. "Mr. Tremayne is to be commended for his honor. Swearing at him like a fishwife will help no one. These aren't the Dark Ages, you know. Obviously you can't be forced into a marriage you oppose." He looked back across the room, his face concerned. "Adam, may we count on your cooperation in this? It won't be easy, I grant you. Father is very shrewd. You and Juliana will have to put on quite an act to fool him."

Adam took his time forming an answer. "I suppose I have no choice."

Stephen pulled his chair into the center of the room, deliberately placing himself between Adam and his sister. "We may as well begin devising our strategy tonight. I think it's clear that you two will have to agree to an immediate truce if we hope to pull this farce off."

Chapter Ten

A fresh sea breeze dried the tears on Juliana's cheeks as she raced Ajax along the moonlit shores of Kenvellas Cove, her hair streaming out behind her like a silken banner. How could her life have changed so much in barely a week? It was as if the very foundations of her world were crumbling beneath her, and no one, not even Martin, could save her. Gently she drew back on the reins and slid down onto the sand, leaning back against the horse's heaving chest and gazing out at the sea as frothy wavelets curled and burst around her booted ankles.

It was here that her mother had drowned in a yachting accident ten years ago this November. Memories of that day remained so vivid in Juliana's mind that even now they brought hot tears to her eyes, and an aching sense of loss inside for the woman who had been the center of her universe, her guiding force, until that gray autumn afternoon when a sudden gale had capsized the Pendarvis yacht.

How much different would our lives be now if Mama and her cousin had not impulsively decided to go sailing that day? she wondered. Would I have become the lady everyone laments that I am not? Would she and I be planning my wedding together, making trips to the dressmakers in London for a stylish trousseau? Mama had loved elegant clothing. But would she have approved of Graham? Juliana secretly thought not. Marie Jeanne Pendarvis had detested snobbery, although she had once been the toast of Helston society herself, courted by a duke and a member of Parliament before losing her heart to a dashing young army officer. And Adam Tremayne . . . would her mother have deemed *him* a worthy match for her youngest daughter? The question slid covertly into Juliana's thoughts only to remain unanswered after she had given it reluctant consideration. In all probability, she and Adam would never even have crossed paths had her mother lived. Had her father not needed a channel for his grief, he would not have come out of retirement and reenlisted in the army, volunteering to serve in the colonies during the Seven Years' War. But for her mother's death, Adam Tremayne would be no more to Juliana than the son of a distant family acquaintance, and how she wished that were the case right now!

She sighed deeply, pressing her face against Ajax's pulsating sweat-streaked neck. No. It wasn't fair to blame Adam for what was happening, even if his presence was an unsettling complication in her life.

A fine drizzle began to fall, casting a gossamer web of moisture over Juliana's unbound hair and shoulders. The breeze had grown bolder, whipping the surface of the sea into small glassy waves that came tumbling onto shore. Ajax stepped back gingerly, nudging Juliana with his nose as if in protest.

"All right, boy." She laughed and grasped the pommel to remount. "I suppose we don't want to get caught in the rain."

She rode back through the village at a restrained pace, aware that the wild race along the beach had altered nothing at home but feeling better for it all the same. The groom and his two stableboys had been asleep even before she went out, and not wanting to disturb them, she brushed Ajax down herself and quietly settled him into his stall for the night. It was past midnight when she finished. Ruefully she realized she was in need of a bath herself, but would now have to wait until morning.

She crept through the hallway, pausing at the parlor door to wonder why Louisa had forgotten to put out the fire and to shut the windows before retiring. The carpet would be ruined if it rained during the night. Her mind must have been on Papa, she thought as she slipped through the crack in the door. She was still struggling to close the last window when a sudden gust of wind blew a spattering of raindrops onto the windowsill.

"Here. Let me get that. I promised Louisa I'd do it before I went to bed."

Juliana did not turn around, did not need to. She recognized that rich masculine voice by her body's uncontrollable reaction to it, the now-familiar warmth that seemed to radiate from her abdomen, the shameless leaping of her pulse. Without comment she stepped aside to allow him access to the window, noting in a surreptitious glance how the muscles of his back and shoulders strained against the finely woven threads of his full-sleeved cambric shirt.

"There. No damage done." Adam wiped his hands on his breeches and braced himself by his elbows against the sideboard. "I would have done that earlier but I fell asleep on the settee. It looks as if the civilized life has finally begun to dull my senses."

"I had no idea you were in the room," Juliana said, her voice clipped. "I'm sorry I disturbed you."

"Don't be." Adam's tone was suddenly intimate, his eyes lingering on Juliana's wind-flushed face with an unwavering concentration she found disconcerting. "To be honest, Juliana, I was waiting for you."

She paled. "Why? Has something happened to—"

"Your father is fine," he assured her gently. "Sound asleep the last time Louisa checked on him."

"Then why are you . . . ?" Instinctively she began edging away from the sideboard. "How did you know I'd gone out, anyway? Everyone was upstairs when I left."

"I watched you leave from the hallway window. Rather foolish to go out riding alone so late at night, don't you think?" He shifted his weight forward, folding his arms across his chest. "It was all I could do not to order you back into the house."

"And what stopped you?" she could not resist asking.

"Would it have done any good?"

She bit her lip to keep from smiling. "No."

"Well, there you have it," he said softly. "You see, I really do understand you, Juliana. We are alike in so many ways. Perhaps when you realize it, you'll no longer be afraid of me."

"Afraid of *you*, Adam? Why, what a fanciful notion."

"Then why are you moving away from me, Juliana? I feel like a hunter who has unwittingly cornered some rare wild creature that would destroy itself before submitting to captivity." He swung forward then and began to advance on her, one step at a time, speaking in a low, soothing voice as if he were indeed attempting to gentle her. "Don't be frightened, my sweet beauty. I don't want to hurt you."

"Perhaps—perhaps you've mistaken distaste for fear," she retorted, artfully stepping around the settee to place a barrier between them.

"I think not." He stopped within an inch of where she stood and stared down at her, an indulgent smile twitching the corners of his mouth. "You're trembling, Juliana. Do you know why?"

"It—it was cold on the beach," she lied, marveling that she could sound so cool when she felt as though she were on fire inside, burning with the wanton feelings this man had ignited. "I walked along the shore and got my skirt wet."

"Then let me pour you a glass of sherry to warm you."

"No! No, Adam, don't. I'd rather go straight to bed."

"Do it to please me, Juliana." He returned to the sideboard before she could muster another protest. "Let's make it a toast to our truce."

For months afterward Juliana would look back at this one moment and wonder why she had not seized it as an opportunity to flee the room. It would've been so easy, with Adam occupied at the sideboard, his face to the window as he concentrated on filling the crystal glasses. She could have stolen out the door and run halfway up the staircase before he even turned around. He wouldn't have chased after her. She could have escaped him. But she didn't even try.

She'd turned slightly to stare at the door, still debating an escape, when she felt Adam's hand on her shoulder. Shock waves of excitement rippled down her spine, but somehow she managed to appear unaffected by his touch, forced herself to hide the fact that she *was* frightened. Frightened and yet fascinated.

He pressed a glass into her hand, his long fingers curling around hers for an electrifying instant, then bade her sit on the settee while he turned back to the sideboard for his own glass. Numbly Juliana obeyed. Rain was beating steadily against the windowpanes, its unbroken rhythm accentuating the silence inside the house. Poised at the edge of the velvet-cushioned settee, Juliana clutched her glass and stared at the flames leaping into the chimney, knowing that whatever happened now was of her own choosing, the consequence of her improvident nature.

Suddenly Adam was standing before her, his dark face filling her vision as he urged her to her feet and proposed a toast to the truce she had reluctantly agreed to earlier in the evening. "Drink it all, Juliana," he whispered recklessly, and just as recklessly she complied, draining the glass with her head tipped back and her eyes locked daringly with his.

"There!" She waved the empty glass in the air. "Another toast, Adam?" she challenged. "Shall we drink to the health of Mrs. Sennen's cat? I could really put my heart into that one."

Adam reached behind him to set his glass on the mantelpiece, his free hand lifting to his throat to loosen his cravat. "Another night, perhaps," he said, smiling at her. "I would not want it said I got you drunk. Or vice versa."

Juliana suddenly felt emboldened, whether from drinking sherry on an empty stomach or the unexpected excitement of the moment, she could not tell. "Indeed, Mr. Tremayne, I do believe you're taking the role of being my fiancé far too seriously. Staying up until I come home, forbidding me a second glass of sherry . . ." She turned to place her glass on the card table behind her. "So much trouble to satisfy one foolish old man," she said, venting a soft sigh. "And he knows no one can refuse him anything."

"Perhaps he's not so foolish, after all."

Juliana straightened with an involuntary gasp to find that Adam had moved across the room and reached her side without her hearing him. Instinct urged her to bolt before it was too late. Determination to prove she did not fear him held her rooted to the spot.

"Mayhap, just this once," Adam continued, "you should trust him to know what's best for you."

Her lips curled scornfully. "Odd advice coming from the black sheep of his family, isn't it?"

"From one black sheep to another, I'd say it was damned sound advice."

"But you didn't always obey your father, Adam," she said, desperate to keep the conversation flowing so that she would not succumb to the seduction in his eyes. "You told me yourself that your parents disapproved of the life you've led."

Her ploy failed miserably, as she had hoped in her secret

heart that it would. Without a word he gathered her into his arms and for several moments just gazed down into the thickly lashed golden-jade eyes until she, knowing she could resist him no longer, began to tremble.

"Damn you," she whispered fiercely. "Damn you for doing this to me."

"Don't fight what was meant to be," he said, his breath a sweet warm caress on her forehead. "I tried, and it didn't work."

"Why did you have to come here?" she cried, despair deepening her voice. "Why can't I go back in time just one week and have everything the way it was? Papa and I had our differences, but life was simple. . . ."

Smiling tenderly, Adam cupped her chin in his hand and traced his thumb around the borders of her lips, pink, moist, already parted as if anticipating his kiss. "Like it or not, fate has chosen to bring us together, my spirited darling. I fully intend to find out why."

Juliana's eyes widened and then fluttered shut as Adam drew her closer to him and crushed his mouth down upon hers, stifling the small sob that had broken in her throat. Her mind began to whirl, reveling in the heady sensations his kiss evoked, the lingering sweetness of sherry on his breath, the teasing pressure of his tongue as it flicked against hers and leisurely explored the satin interior of her mouth. Slowly, unthinkingly, she raised her hands to entwine her fingers in his soft dark hair, straining her body upward, shamelessly pressing herself against the swollen core of his passion. She wanted this! She wanted to follow him down whichever pathway he would lead her, wanted to go beyond his kiss to the world of forbidden pleasures that beckoned her newly awakened senses. Graham and her family—everyone and everything—receded to the edges of her consciousness. For this one moment, only she and Adam existed, and from deep within her rose the shocking realization that he was right—this was meant to be.

As if sensing her surrender, Adam gave a victorious laugh deep in his throat and brought both his hands to her shoulders. She heard her riding jacket drop to the floor before she realized he'd removed it. She felt a rush of cool air on her skin as nimble brown fingers unbuttoned her blouse and released her small round breasts from the confines of her black lace chemise. Dear God, she thought, what would happen next? What, if anything, was *she* supposed to do? She forced herself to hold still as Adam bent his head and kissed each milk-white mound, lapping at and coaxing the soft rose tips into tingling hardness with his agile tongue, sending feverish chills streaming throughout her. Then sudden fear of the unknown gripped her, diminishing the delicious aching within her womb. For all her bravado and independent airs, Juliana was at heart an innocent inexperienced in the rituals and rudiments of lovemaking. Would he laugh at her naivete?

Suddenly Adam swung her up into his arms and carried her the few steps to the fireplace. His eyes were smoky gray, heavy-lidded with passion as he gently deposited her on the thick Oriental carpet placed before the hearth. "How lovely you are," he said hoarsely, folding to his knees beside her.

"I—I feel so untidy." She glanced away self-consciously, wishing she had a comb to untangle her hair, wondering how he could find her desirable after the wild ride on Ajax.

He smiled and leaned forward to kiss the hollow of her throat, then trailed a tantalizing path down the gentle slope of her shoulder to nibble at one firm, uptilted breast. "You smell sweet and clean, my love, of sea air and lavender soap," he murmured. He worked one hand beneath her riding skirt and petticoats, his fingers shaking as they strayed upward to caress the silken folds of flesh between her thighs. "That's it, beauty," he whispered, feeling her muscles tense and then loosen around his probing fingers. "Relax, and let me love you with my hand. Trust me not to hurt you."

She closed her eyes, pupils dilated with desire, and leaned back against the cushion he had pulled off the settee, allowing herself to be swept into the wave of pleasure building inside her until finally it crested and flooded every molecule of her being with molten sensation. She felt as though she were drowning in feeling, body and soul, the experience so intense it threatened to overwhelm her, leaving her breathless in its aftermath.

"I won't force you, Juliana." The raggedly uttered words betrayed the effort it cost Adam to keep his passion in check. Suppressing a groan, he changed his position to ease the throbbing pressure in his groin. ''We needn't rush. We needn't go any further tonight.''

Juliana opened her eyes. The potent sherry, Adam's skillful mouth and hands, and the exhausting events of the day all seemed to have conspired to lower her defenses. And yet those were only excuses, she realized uneasily. There was something about this man that touched off a deeply emotional response in her heart, something about his teasing humor and the distant sadness in his eyes that spoke directly to her soul in a language that didn't rely on words. She ached to comfort him without knowing why, to meld her being with his. She'd never met anyone like him before. Even now she found it hard to believe that a man like him really existed. Frantically, she tried to dredge up all the reasons why she disliked him, but her mind refused to cooperate, spiraling instead in wild circles. Telling herself to resist him was useless. She had no struggle left inside her, no will to deny him, no desire to turn back now that she hovered on the verge of womanhood. Helplessly capitulating to the sweeping intensity of her budding feelings, she wanted to lose herself in the rapture of his kisses, of his touch. She felt his gaze caressing her, and she smiled back at him invitingly.

That was all the encouragement Adam needed. He ached with wanting her, and the realization that he would soon possess her lovely body made him suddenly feel awkward, fumbling like a schoolboy to shed his clothes, flinging them behind him in a disorderly heap. The chance was remote that anyone would awaken at this hour and interrupt them. And if it happened—Well, he would simply hang his head and sheepishly confess that he and Juliana had been unable to resist each other. After all, he had every intention of honoring his promise to marry her, if he were allowed to. It wasn't as if he were taking her virginity to carve another notch in his belt.

Regaining his composure, he bent down to finish undressing her. The firelight's golden haze highlighted the curves and hollows of her exquisite body, the rose-tipped breasts rising proudly above her sleek belly, the soft nest of auburn curls between her thighs, and the moist, inviting crevice beneath. She was the embodiment of every fantasy he had ever woven, the flesh-and-blood realization of his young man's dreams. And she belonged to him.

As he knelt over her, he could feel the blood roaring in his ears, could feel it singing through his veins. "Your body is perfection," he whispered. "Made for mine."

Lowering his head, he kissed her again, his tongue plundering her mouth until she lay gasping beneath him. He stroked the smooth skin of her abdomen with his palm, and her nerve endings quivered as she felt him separate the dewy lips of her most sensitive place. "Yield to me, Juliana," he muttered, his fingers quickening, torturing her vulnerable flesh.

Teeth catching the edge of her underlip to repress a sob, Juliana twisted as if to escape him and the almost unbearable sweet torment he was inflicting upon her. What was this leading to? she wondered fleetingly. Would her entire life be changed afterward? She felt her heart expanding with emotions she didn't recognize, emotions that had taken root somewhere, sometime, in her consciousness, without her knowledge or consent. She didn't understand the wonderful sensations burgeoning inside her loins. She didn't understand the complex depths of her feelings toward Adam. But her heart understood, and her body answered its command. Her hips writhed in an instinctive tempo as he slid one finger in and out of the velvety recesses of her sheath to prepare her to receive him.

"Now," she begged softly, not knowing what it was she sought so desperately, but feeling she would die without it. "Oh, Adam . . . please, please . . ."

"Hold still then, sweeting," he whispered and mounted her, carefully lowering himself between her thighs. "I'll try not to hurt you. . . ."

He entered her gently, as slowly as he could. Perspiration broke out on his forehead as he fought the primitive instinct to plunge into her warm depths. Ah, God, the sweet agony of it! She was so tight, so tempting, so wildly exciting. Still, he held himself back, concentrated on bringing her as much pleasure and as little pain as possible.

Relieved to feel only vague discomfort instead of the pain she had expected, Juliana relaxed and arched her back with sensual grace. She heard Adam's answering groan, and then she felt the pulsing hardness within her respond. Craving more of him, she draped her arms around his neck and moaned softly, straining to draw him deeper inside her, willing him to fill her completely.

He was ready, mindless with wanting her. Muttering, "Forgive me, my sweet Juliana," he withdrew his shaft and thrust swiftly through the silken tissue. Hot streaks of pleasure shot through his groin as, little by little, he felt her yielding to accommodate him. He tried to be gentle, tried to remember her innocence, but he could feel his control slipping, and only by drawing on his last shreds of restraint did he manage to stave off his release.

Juliana's eyes flew open, wide with sudden shock and hurt, and instinctively she struggled to escape the next searing thrust. Yet even as she fought to expel him from her body, the pain abated, fading away until it was supplanted by an exquisite ache that his every invading stroke intensified. Without even realizing it, she was moving to his seductive rhythm, her pelvis jutting upward to answer his need, to fulfill her own. Inflamed by her response, Adam quickened the tempo of his movements and then both were swept into a whirling spiral of mindless sensation and flung out into a universe of bright, exploding stars.

Inhaling deeply to calm his erratic heartbeat, Adam collapsed onto his side, spent but exhilarated. "I'm sorry it had to hurt so much for you, Juliana," he whispered, reaching out to draw her against his chest. "And I'm sorry it had to happen here, like this, instead of in a warm comfortable bed in our own house. Believe me, I didn't plan it this way. I'd wanted to make your first time special. I had every intention of waiting until our wedding night." A wicked smile lifted the corners of his mouth. "Of course, if seducing you in the parlor was what it took to make you face your feelings, I suppose it was worth the sacrifice. Besides, you and I are too independent-minded to restrain our desires simply because polite society decrees we must."

Scarcely had Adam's words faded in the air than he felt Juliana twisting to break out of his embrace, and with a sense of deflation he wondered if he'd made an error in interpreting her response to him tonight. Concerned, he bent over her and was shocked at the anger and bewilderment on her face. I've moved too fast with her, he realized belatedly.

Her body had been ready to accept him but her heart had not. By becoming her lover, he had made it impossible to be her friend.

"Juliana, talk to me." He got to his feet, lifting her up with him. "Tell me what you're thinking. Don't close me out."

"Leave me alone!" She pulled away from him and swooped down to retrieve her clothing from the floor. "I guess you're feeling pretty smug right now, aren't you?" She darted behind the settee to dress herself, the bitter words bubbling from her lips in an unbridled torrent of emotion. "Ply the gauche country girl with sherry, whisper an endearment or two in her ear, and she falls at your feet like a—a ripe apple in an orchard! Well, I have a surprise for you, Adam Tremayne. Just because you've taken my virginity doesn't mean I'm going to agree to this preposterous marriage. I might have lost my maidenhead, but I haven't lost my mind!"

Adam reached down for his breeches, feeling vulnerable in his nakedness. "But you seemed—I assumed—"

"You assumed too much!" She slung her riding jacket over her shoulder and stepped out from behind the settee. "You must need my dowry desperately if you're willing to marry someone who despises you to get it. Did you come to Cornwall to escape creditors in Boston, Adam? Or did my father offer you a bonus if you managed to deflower me before he dies? I wouldn't put it past either of you to have staged this debasing little scene tonight."

She sat down on the settee and finished buttoning her blouse, averting her face so that he would not see the unshed tears of hurt and helpless confusion glittering in her eyes. Suddenly she was aware that the rainstorm was over, that the world outside was still and slowly recovering from the cruel bruising it had undergone. So it seemed to her that the storm of passion she'd been caught in had ended. She felt bruised inside, so incredibly vulnerable that she feared she would shatter if she remained alone with him for another moment. But she would not grant him the pleasure of knowing how deeply he'd hurt her. She would not! She rose unsteadily, only to find him blocking her path, his lean face drawn into a mask of harsh impatience.

"Goddamn it, Juliana! Stop behaving like such a child, and look at me." His arm whipped out to encircle her waist, holding her immobile against him. "You can't believe any of this was premeditated. If you must know the truth, I'm still recovering from the shock of what I promised your father this evening. It was the last thing in the world I expected him to ask of me."

"But you just couldn't bring yourself to refuse that settlement, could you?"

"No amount of money could induce me to marry a woman I didn't love, Juliana."

"Are you trying to convince me that you love me, Adam?" A smile of cold contempt tightened her mouth. "And when did this awesome revelation dawn on you? Not that first night when you almost drowned me in the stream?"

Adam could not suppress a chuckle at the recollection. "I think it was a day or so afterward, actually. I'm not sure. I do know I didn't want it to happen. I certainly hadn't come here seeking a wife. In fact, I'd rather looked forward to leading the simple bachelor life, unencumbered by emotional demands and restrictions. But what can I do? One has no control over the strange workings of the heart."

"I do," Juliana said under her breath.

"You stubborn little fool," he said softly. "This frightens you to death, doesn't it? You can control just about everyone and everything around here except the woman that Juliana is becoming. Is it really that painful for you to admit your father may know what's best for you this once? I know you want me. You proved that tonight."

Juliana clenched her teeth, pressing down on his forearm with the heel of her right hand. "If you don't release me on the count of three, I swear I'll scream."

"Go ahead," he said, a devilish gleam in his eye. "You scream like a banshee, and I'll howl like a wolf until we've awakened the entire household. We'll tell everyone it's an Indian courting ritual."

"You wouldn't dare."

Adam threw back his head and released a low, plaintive howl, which Juliana promptly smothered with her palm. "Oh, you incorrigible ass!" she hissed, but even as she glared at him, she could feel the amusement welling up within her until she finally burst out in helpless laughter.

Adam held her tightly against him, his rich baritone laughter blending with the silvery notes of hers. "And you think we are not well matched, Juliana? Can you laugh this easily with any other man of your acquaintance?"

"No—" Her laughter subsiding, Juliana pressed her hands against Adam's naked chest and leaned back to look at him. The adoration in his eyes was devastating in its intensity. "Oh, Adam, I don't understand what's happening between us. . . ."

"We're falling in love, Juliana. It's natural for you to feel bewildered, to fight against something that will change your life." He lowered his head to graze her lips with a tender kiss. "These past few days have been hard on you. You need time to sort out your feelings. We both do."

"I know how I feel, Adam."

"No. I don't think you do." He lifted his head, his face suddenly thoughtful. "I have to meet with my uncle's solicitors in Helston sometime this week. I may leave tomorrow morning if your father's condition seems stable. I'm not sure how long I'll be gone. There are papers to be signed and tenants to contact. I suggest you use my absence as an opportunity to think everything over."

She remained stubbornly silent, her face betraying none of the tempestuous feelings raging inside her.

"I ask only one thing of you, Juliana. Oblige me in this, and I'll try not to influence you again."

She granted him a resentful glance. "What?"

"Don't do anything foolish while I'm gone. Don't elope with Graham or the village wheelwright just to punish me, or your father."

"The village wheelwright already has a wife and six children," she said stiffly. "And Graham's away with the earl until September."

Smiling to himself, Adam released her from his grasp. "Then that leaves the field clear for me. You'll have decided to marry me before the summer ends, or I've seriously misjudged you. In any event, the matter is now out of my hands. I won't press you again."

Chapter Eleven

"Five thousand pounds! Why, it's vulgar. Disgusting! Father only gave Harold eight hundred for me, and it took us years to collect it. I think he's gone dotty in the head. I'll tell him so, too."

"Oh, Evelyn, you wouldn't—"

"Oh, yes, Louisa, I would. Damnation, Juliana, do hold still!"

"For heaven's sake, Evelyn," Louisa scolded, clucking her tongue. "Watch what you're doing in your temper. This gown is old. You've put a huge hole in that ruffle."

"I think I know how to lengthen a hem, Louisa."

Juliana gazed at her reflection in the mirror, listening dispiritedly to the bickering voices of the two young women kneeling below her on the carpet. Evelyn had been at Rosmorna only a week and was already running the household. Running everyone's life. Poor old Evelyn, she thought with a sudden rush of fondness as she glanced down at the russet-haired figure. She really had done her best to be a mother to the other Pendarvis children before leaving home to marry Harold Cartersford, a well-to-do Truro businessman. It wasn't her fault that she resembled Sir Walter in both character and appearance.

She gave a guilty start as she felt Evelyn's alert blue eyes on her face. "I don't know why you didn't demand a Paris-made gown, Juliana," she mumbled, pins protruding from her wide mouth like fangs. "You just weren't thinking. It would've taken ages to complete, and you'd have gotten a lovely trip into the bargain. Louisa looks as though she could use a rest."

"But I couldn't leave here now," Louisa protested.

"Of course you could," Evelyn said with a frown.
"Anyway, Mother's gown will serve for our purposes. After what Dr. Wendron said this morning, I don't expect Father will live to see Juliana wear it. And, Juliana, if you
don't stop hopping about, this lace will be attached to your
bum."

"Then let it!" Juliana cried suddenly, wrenching off the
delicate pearl-seeded Juliet cap and flinging it to the floor.
"I don't give a damn! I'm not getting married, anyway!"

She ran across the room and threw herself facedown on
the bed, closing her ears to her sister's ruthless lecturing.
Well, let her lecture! It wasn't Evelyn who faced the horrifying prospect of marriage to an arrogant stranger in less
than two weeks. For despite the hour of intimacy she and
Adam had shared the night of the storm, he was more of a
stranger to her than ever since his return from Helston four
days ago. Not that she could fault his conduct toward her.
Oh, no! He was politeness itself, inquiring after her health
each morning at breakfast, restricting his conversations to
such prudent topics as the weather or her father's condition
when by chance they met each other in the hallway. He
hadn't attempted to touch her again, although several oppor-
tune moments had arisen. In fact, he hadn't dropped a single
clue to hint their engagement was anything more than a
charitable act to appease a dying man. Perhaps he'd come to
regret his impulsive urging that they bow to her father's
wish and gamble on a life together as man and wife. Perhaps
he no longer desired her. And yet always she felt that he was
watching her, waiting for *her* to give him just one sign of encouragement. . . .

"Oh, dear. If this is a bad time, perhaps I should call
tomorrow—"

The sound of the soft, cultured voice floating from the
doorway brought Juliana's head up with a snap. "Venetia,
don't you dare leave!" She sprang off the bed to draw the
elegantly attired young woman into the room. "You're just
the person I need to see! I think I'm losing my mind."

With a faint smile to Louisa and Evelyn, Venetia settled
into a tapestried chair, smoothing out her riding skirt and
petticoats. Despite the hour ride to Rosmorna, not a single

raven-black ringlet on her head was disarrayed; not a speck
of dust marked the elbow-length gloves she tugged off with
a flourish. "I passed Dr. Wendron on my way up," she said
in a hushed voice. "He was so preoccupied he almost
knocked me down the stairs. Your father isn't—he
didn't—" She faltered and glanced around the room, relieved when Evelyn concluded the thought for her.

"Die? Not yet. But we're expecting him to any moment
now. We think he had another attack during the night but
won't admit it. Louisa found him on the floor this morning."

Venetia shook her head sympathetically. "Dear, dear.
No wonder you're so distraught, Juliana." She leaned forward suddenly, her eyes darting from her friend to the detached lace train Louisa and Evelyn were spreading out over
the floral Turkey carpet. "But that's a bridal gown!" she
exclaimed softly. "You haven't decided to go through with
this wedding?"

"Of course not!" Juliana snapped. "The gown is for my
father's benefit. He insists on my wearing it." She stood
and executed a graceless pirouette at the foot of the bed.
"It's as hopelessly old-fashioned as he is. My mother was
married in it."

Venetia's expert glance took in the detailed handicraft on
the molded lace bodice and ivory watered silk overskirt.
"It's quite lovely on you, though. All those pearls and
silver-embroidery rosebuds would cost a fortune today. It's
almost a shame you shan't be wearing it. But what if—" She
bent to pick up a glove she'd dropped, at the same time lowering her tone. "What if your father hangs on indefinitely? I
mean, there's a limit to the sacrifices one should make, even
for family. I shudder to think of your future should you actually marry that—that Indian fighter."

Juliana leaned back against the bedpost and closed her
eyes. When she opened them, it was to see Evelyn standing
before her, her face troubled, reflecting Venetia's apprehen-
sions. "She has a deuced good point. I wouldn't put it past
Father to live another decade."

With a disheartened sigh, Juliana pushed off the bedpost
and walked to the window. No matter what he had done to
her, she didn't wish her father dead. Yet what would she do

if the wedding day dawned and he was still lingering on? Would her refusal to marry Adam then trigger a fatal attack? God, what a coil! And with each passing day, she became more hopelessly enmeshed. But who could help her?

She spun around to Venetia. "Do you think Graham got my letter yet?" In desperation she'd penned a message to him in London, entrusting its delivery to Venetia.

Venetia nodded reassuringly. "He must have gotten it by now. I hand-delivered it to Lady Wynherne the morning she left for London. I told her how important it was."

Juliana groaned inwardly, feeling the last crumb of hope she'd been clinging to disintegrate. In the core of her heart, she had been depending on Graham to somehow rescue her from this predicament.

"Oh, Venetia! You know that woman detests me. Graham will never see my letter now!"

Evelyn ran over to the escritoire and snatched up a quill. "Write him another letter, Juliana! He'll make it back here before the wedding if he wants to."

"Write another if you must, Juliana," Venetia said quietly. "However, I do have another suggestion."

Juliana looked up, frowning. "Go on."

"Bribe the parson to allow you use of the church for an hour while you have an actor perform a mock ceremony. It's been done more often than you'd believe. Usually it's some scoundrel wanting the pleasures of a honeymoon without the responsibilities of matrimony afterward. I see no reason why it wouldn't work in your case. I know this marvelous retired actor in St. Ives who adores playing this sort of part."

Louisa jumped up looking horrified. "In a church? Oh, Venetia, it's the most disgraceful thing I've ever heard! It's blasphemous. It's—"

"—time to make tea, Louisa," Evelyn said crisply, pushing her sister-in-law toward the door. "I'll handle this, thank you."

Juliana was only too glad to let Evelyn approach Parson Foxcombe with Venetia's brazen scheme. She hadn't the smallest doubt that the elderly clergyman would be properly scandalized and boot them out the door. But, as Evelyn said, there was no harm in trying, and so she sat back on the faded velvet sofa and silently examined the interior of the parsonage while Evelyn argued her sister's case like a criminal lawyer at Newgate.

The tiny whitewashed cottage was charmingly untidy, dusty and cluttered, with dishes and books half-hidden beneath piles of paper that were covered with scribbled fragments of inspiration for next Sunday's service. A plump gray cat sat preening itself on the hearthstone before a cheerful fire.

"It's not as though we're asking you to actually *do* anything, parson," Evelyn pointed out. "You'll only have to leave Kenvellas for the day. Maybe you'd like to visit your niece in Treen. We'll think up an excuse. Father's in no state to question your activities."

The parson gave his three young visitors a look that indicated he despaired of their salvation. "I can't believe that you, Evelyn, of all people, are a conspirator in this heinous plot. To think that I christened you in the very church you would defile, that I encouraged your father to let you raise Juliana. If this is an example of your influence, I do not wonder that she became a—a hellion. It might indeed be her redemption to marry this gentleman your father thinks so highly of."

Evelyn narrowed her eyes. "While we're casting stones, parson, I don't suppose that was *smuggled* tea you offered us earlier, or that you still enjoy your evening glass of *smuggled* cognac before retiring. And these curtains— Valenciennes lace, aren't they? Now how on earth do you afford such luxuries on a country cleric's stipend?"

Parson Foxcombe's lips tightened. "In order to lead men along the path of righteousness, I must first gain their trust. I cannot hope to serve my congregation if I condemn its very livelihood." A concerned frown creased his forehead. "No. What you ask of me is too distasteful to contemplate. I'd like to pretend you never came here today."

But Evelyn wouldn't let the matter rest without a final try. "My dear parson, that's precisely what I suggested. Pretend you know nothing of this. Merely allow us the use of your church for an hour."

Venetia nodded. "It's done all the time."

"Not in my parish," he said gently, rising to show them out. "Do try to attend church this Sunday, girls. The sermon will be intended for your benefit."

In dismal silence the three women rode past the church-yard and spurred their horses down the hedge-enclosed lane that led to Rosmorna. Evelyn, unable to accept defeat, held herself rigid in the saddle. Juliana hadn't expected anything to come of the interview, so she wasn't overly disappointed. Besides, she still couldn't shake off the feeling that none of this was happening. Impossible—as she rode on in the waning afternoon sunlight—to imagine that in a fortnight she'd be wed to a man she scarcely knew . . . or wanted to know.

At the fork in the lane just before the Pendarvis estate, Venetia reined her mount to a halt. "It could still work, Juli-ana. You'll just have to say you've changed your mind and want a private ceremony. We'll have it in my home."

"It's no use, Venetia," Juliana said. "My father isn't stupid. He'd suspect a hoax if I decided not to be married at Saint Joan's and then brought in a strange parson to perform the ceremony. I'd just as soon be done with this deception and refuse him outright."

"Which is what you should've done in the first place," Evelyn admonished. "You've never been the least bit sub-missive before. I don't know what prompted you to start now."

Juliana said nothing. What did it matter that it had been Evelyn who'd convinced their father that she, Juliana, needed a strong-willed husband to restrain her unconven-tional inclinations?

Then minutes later, when Venetia had disappeared from view, Evelyn remarked, "If you don't have the heart to tell Father no, then what about this colonial lieutenant? He can't have much of a conscience left after the life he's led. Nor does he strike me as the type who'd let anyone dictate to him." She paused to study her sister, her lips puckered. "I wonder if in some odd way he finds you attractive. . . ."

"It's the money," Juliana said hastily, feeling her cheeks grow warm.

"Well then." Evelyn pushed a strand of hair from her forehead. "Perhaps *I* should have a talk with him."

Juliana widened her eyes. "You, Evelyn? What good would that do?"

"I could convince him that there are easier ways of obtaining five thousand pounds. Let's face facts, Juliana. Marriage to you would be living hell for any . . . normal man."

Evelyn declaring war on Adam? Just thinking of the two monumental egos engaged in a battle of cunning brought a smile to Juliana's lips, the first in days. "All right, Evelyn. If you won't let him intimidate you—"

"Intimidate me?" It had been the right remark to raise Evelyn's hackles. "That's a laugh, my girl. Wait till I get him alone."

But it wasn't until after supper three days later that Evelyn finally managed to confront Adam. Stephen and Martin had rushed off during the second course to land a cargo of snuff from Guernsey. Juliana had excused herself from the table, murmuring she had to read to her father, and Adam had taken the faint glimmer in her eye as a clue that she was party to whatever was about to happen. For two days now he had known Evelyn wanted to talk to him, and he'd skillfully evaded her before she could corner him. Tonight he had decided to satisfy his curiosity and find out what she was after.

He leaned back in his chair and sipped his brandy, waiting for her to make her move. She was not as tall as Juliana, solid and large-boned but nicely proportioned. She had a clear-skinned oval face with arresting blue eyes, and as he studied her, Adam couldn't help thinking that she'd have made an ideal wife for a colonial settler. It seemed perfectly natural that she, and not Stephen, had become head of the household in Sir Walter's stead.

The minute Audrey left the room with a trayload of dishes, Evelyn set down her glass and looked Adam straight in the eye. "I'm not one to mince words, Mr. Tremayne."

Adam almost smiled. "I didn't think you were. There's something you wish to discuss with me?"

"Juliana," she said curtly, reaching for the brandy bottle. "It can't be easy for you to suddenly find yourself engaged to a girl of my sister's remarkable temperament. My father has indeed put your friendship to the test."

Adam watched Evelyn down her second glass of brandy.

"You must be aware that no one in your family but your father actually believes this wedding will take place."

"That was my initial understanding, Mr. Tremayne. However, I think the time's come to consider the consequences of this charade should my father remain alive."

"He grows weaker by the hour."

"In body, mayhap, but not in spirit. You've only nine days left until the wedding."

Adam hesitated. Why was she baiting him? "Juliana has sworn repeatedly that she wouldn't marry me. I think we can count on her to call the ceremony off."

Evelyn cocked her head thoughtfully. "I'm not so sure. For all her faults, Juliana is exceedingly tenderhearted, especially where Father is concerned. I'm afraid you'll have to be the one to stand up to him on this."

"I do not give my word lightly."

"Of course you don't. But one has to make exceptions. Believe me, none of us would think less of you for backing out at this point. You could even leave tomorrow if it's convenient. I'll break the news to my father, say you were called away on urgent business."

"I've the distinct impression you want to be rid of me, Evelyn. Could it be you think me an unworthy match for your sister?"

Evelyn was visibly taken aback by the bluntly posed question; her features hardened. "Martin tells me that you have a controlling interest in a Boston shipyard, that you're seeking capital to expand your venture. Five thousand pounds is a goodly sum, isn't it?"

A slow enigmatic smile uptilted the corners of Adam's mouth. He'd been waiting for this. "I've recently come into an unexpected inheritance," he said softly, the smile deepening but not reaching his eyes.

"Logan Tremayne's estate," Evelyn said, drumming her fingernails on the side of her glass. "I'd heard he allowed the old cliff house to fall into shocking disrepair. Smuggling was his passion. After your mother."

"He left me sixty thousand pounds."

"Sixty—" The glass slid from Evelyn's fingers, spilling droplets of amber liquid as it rolled across the table.

"I only found out myself about a week ago. My reaction was not unlike yours."

"Then why the devil—?" A disbelieving laugh bubbled in her throat. "What fools we've all been," she said softly. "You really do want to marry Juliana."

"She is . . . exceptional," Adam mused quietly.

Evelyn laughed again. "She's that, all right." Her eyes assessed him with renewed interest. "She has a viscount keen on her, too, you know. He's heir to an earldom, to a great fortune."

"He'll be heir to nothing if he doesn't stop incurring debts on his father's credit," Adam retorted. "His reputation as a rogue is starting to spread even to Helston. While there I made a few discreet inquiries after him that only confirmed my first impression."

"Yes." Evelyn heaved a sigh, nodding thanks to Adam as he righted her glass and splashed an inch of brandy into it. "My husband tried to tell me the same thing, but I didn't want to listen. Viscount or not, he's rotten."

"Then I can count on your support, Evelyn?"

"Well, I—" She met Adam's hopeful look and smiled a trifle tipsily. "I've never had much influence on her before. And we've so little time. . . ."

"Nine days," Adam said, returning her smile.

Chapter Twelve

Only an hour left before dawn, Juliana thought, drawing away from the window with a delicate shiver as the cool mist penetrated through her thin nightgown. She'd have to hurry if she hoped to be on the road before anyone else wakened. She turned and crossed the chamber to the tall oak armoire, pulling the door open to ascertain she'd packed everything she valued. The bronze silk pelisse with the sable lining? She turned and glanced at the small red leather valise sitting on the bed. It wouldn't hold so much as another chemise. But then, Graham would probably insist on outfitting her with a new wardrobe, anyway. Certainly he'd insist she discard the serge vest and woolen breeches she intended to wear for the ride this morning.

Graham. It was due to a message from him that she was leaving home, although she had waited until last night . . . until the night before the supposed wedding to make her painful decision. She was to ride to Venetia's, and from there the two young women would take a private coach to Bath to meet Graham.

The sound of footsteps in the courtyard roused her out of her reverie. She began to dress hurriedly, shedding her nightgown and donning the unflattering garments, then securing her hair into a thick, glossy braid.

That had to be Martin outside, she thought, on his way to the stable to saddle Ajax for her. She would miss her brother terribly, would miss the unfailing comfort and support he provided. Not like that snake-in-the-grass Evelyn, who had turned against her own sister in favor of a stranger.

She went straight downstairs to the kitchen to fortify herself with a tankard of mulled cider. She couldn't eat so much as a crumb of bread even though the delectable aroma of Mrs. Sennen's late-night baking for the wedding feast still hung in the air. It was here, in this room of a thousand pleasant childhood memories, that she suddenly found herself overcome with emotion. How many times had she sat on the hearthstone and watched her mother bake pasties? How could she forget the afternoons Evelyn had tried to teach her to roll out dough only to throw up her hands and march off in disgust?

"There you are." Martin appeared in the doorway. "Ajax is ready. Be careful, won't you?"

She nodded, blinking back tears. "Did you look in on Papa? I was terrified I'd wake him."

"He's fast asleep. Don't worry, Juliana. I'll make him understand."

"I just have to see him one last time, Martin. I couldn't live with myself if I didn't. . . ."

"Hurry then. Louisa and Mrs. Sennen will be down soon to start preparing for the reception that isn't going to be."

Outside her father's bedchamber Juliana hesitated, realizing she still had the valise clutched to her side. Cautiously she propped it against the wall and turned the doorknob. Just a silent farewell. To have Papa awaken and catch her in the midst of her cowardly flight would shatter her.

She'd already stepped over the threshold before she realized that the bed was empty, that her father was sitting in a chair by the fire putting on his stockings. Her immediate reaction was to turn and flee. But it was too late for that. He'd seen her.

"Didn't recognize you at first, girl," he said. "Thought maybe you was Stephen in them breeches." He chuckled weakly. "One final act of defiance before you settle down, eh? Bet you was out riding that stallion. I trust Adam'll put a stop to that nonsense."

"Papa, what are you doing up this early? And why are you out of bed?"

"Wanted to get myself washed and dressed for your wedding. Wouldn't want me to give you away in my nightshirt, would you?"

Juliana sat down on the edge of the bed, her shoulders sagging, her eyes bright with unshed tears of frustration. "You know you're not well enough to go anywhere."

"Do you see the mate to this shoe?" he grumbled, motioning to the floor. "Blasted silly thing with a bow on it."

"It's behind your chair," she said tiredly. "No, stay where you are. I'll get it."

It's no use, she thought despairingly. Everything is working against me. Stay or leave, I'll never be able to live with myself afterward.

"Are you sure you feel well, Papa? You look rather peaked to me."

He looked ghastly, in fact, his face pallid with a bluish tinge to the lips, his black broadcloth suit hanging loosely on his shrunken frame.

"You're a fine one to talk about appearance," he jested. "Adam might have second thoughts if he caught you dressed like that."

"Adam thinks she is charming no matter what her apparel," rejoined a rich baritone voice from the doorway. "Remember that love is blind."

"Too excited to stay abed, Adam?" asked Sir Walter. "I trust we didn't wake you."

Adam strode into the room, eyeing Juliana's costume with a curious amusement she pretended to ignore. "I've been up for an hour, sir. I had a feeling you'd insist on putting in an appearance today."

"I've tried to talk him out of it, but to no avail," Juliana said. "Maybe you'll have better luck alone with him, Adam."

"Time I was up and about," Sir Walter said, panting as he pulled on his shoe.

Juliana began edging toward the door. "You'll both have to excuse me. I have so much to do this morning." If she was to leave, she had to do it while Adam was preoccupied with her father. Grab the valise and make a dash for the stables . . .

"A moment please, Juliana," Adam said, following her out into the hallway. "I won't see you again until the ceremony, and I wanted to give you this."

Juliana stared at the small jeweler's case he held out to her. "Oh, I can't accept it—"

"You must," he said gently. "I had it made to go with your gown."

What Juliana had meant was that she couldn't take the

case without putting down her valise, which so far Adam had apparently not noticed. She backed away from him. "I'm sure it's lovely. Leave it outside my door for me, Adam. I want to bathe before I dress."

"Don't you at least want to look at it?" Adam flicked open the gold clasp to reveal an Oriental pearl choker on a slender white velvet band from the center of which hung a teardrop diamond. "Let me put it on you."

"No, I—"

She could tell by his sudden silence, by the stiffening of his fingers on her skin that he'd seen the valise and understood what it meant. Pausing only a heartbeat, he finished fastening the choker around her neck and came back to face her.

"I doubt it was meant to be worn with breeches, but it's pretty on you, nonetheless." The pain and disappointment on his face belied the lighthearted words. "Perhaps you'll find a use for it some other time."

To her horror Juliana felt tears welling in her eyes. "Adam, please try to understand. I didn't want to hurt anyone. I simply can't go through with this."

He smiled sadly. "Don't apologize. It isn't your fault if I misjudged the depth of your feelings for me. I only wish I could think of a gentle way to break this to your father."

Before Juliana could find the courage to turn away, a figure emerged from a bedchamber down the hallway. With a sense of ultimate defeat, she watched Evelyn approach, hurriedly tying her wrapper.

"Shame on you, Juliana! Don't you know it's bad luck for Adam to see you before the wedding? And aren't those Stephen's old riding breeches you've got on?" She glanced up at Adam with an apologetic smile. "She will have her little joke, even on an important day like this. I'm glad you have a good sense of humor." She tried to grasp her sister's hand, but Juliana pulled away. Evelyn shook her head and began to move down the hallway, pausing outside Juliana's room to call teasingly to Adam. "I'll make sure she changes for the wedding, but after that she'll be your responsibility!"

Juliana, torn, confused, heard Adam speaking to her in a lowered voice intended for her ears alone. "We were meant to be together, Juliana. I've already made you mine."

Chapter Thirteen

"Wed during August's sultry haze, love's promise fulfilled will sweeten your days."

Juliana turned woodenly and stared down at the slightly inebriated middle-aged widow who had just approached her. "I beg your pardon, Mrs. Selwyn. What was that you said?"

"Oh, dear. I'm not sure I remember now," the woman replied, reaching out a hand to steady herself against a chair. "That port went straight to my head. I forgot your father always serves the strongest waters. Where is the old rascal anyway? Haven't seen him since the ceremony."

"He's gone upstairs to rest until dinner."

Juliana excused herself before the woman could engage her in further conversation. The small, rarely used ballroom had become so crowded that the musicians had been forced to move out into the foyer to tune their instruments and await instructions to begin playing. At the French doors to the terrace behind the foyer, Louisa and Stephen were still greeting late arrivals and ushering them inside. Vaguely, as though she were a disinterested second party, Juliana acknowledged the fresh round of congratulations and nuptial jests directed at her as she attempted a furtive escape to the garden.

A strident female voice stopped her at the door. "You're going the wrong way if you're looking for your husband."

"He's standing near the last window talking to Maria Renleigh," added a second voice. "Lord, how handsome he is, Juliana. Aren't you afraid to leave him alone with that woman?"

Juliana didn't bother to hide her annoyance as she turned to face Prudence and Penelope Hendoran, the twin sisters she had played with as a child, both spinsters now at twenty-three. "Why don't the pair of you guard him for me while I take a walk?" she suggested coolly.

Prudence sniggered behind her fan. "I'll wager you'll be more possessive of him after tonight. You are staying here, aren't you? You aren't going to let 'im whisk you off to the colonies, I do hope."

Penelope, the more serious twin, shook her head. "He has a fine old house on the Lizard. I expect Juliana will invite us down for a visit after she and her husband have settled in."

Husband. My husband. The import of the word slashed through Juliana's benumbed mind like a sword thrust. From this day forward she and that dark-haired man across the room would share a life, a house, a bed. She would bear and raise his children, and yet she had known him scarcely a month!

"It was wicked of you not to introduce him to us before the ceremony," Prudence chattered on, oblivious to Juliana's utter lack of attention. "You should've brought him to the house for tea. Of course, we always thought you'd land that viscount. Didn't jilt you for a London heiress, did he?"

"It was a lovely ceremony," Penelope said, tactfully changing the subject.

Juliana frowned. "Was it?" In truth she remembered so little of it, she half expected to wake up and discover the whole morning had been a bad dream. She glanced down at her left hand, hidden beneath a filigree of lace. Adam had been so sure of her that he'd bought her a ring, a heavy heart-shaped diamond mounted on a scrolled gold band. How could he have known that she'd go through with the wedding when she had devised such detailed plans to escape it?

"Madam, I believe everyone is waiting for us to open the first dance."

Everything around Juliana seemed to dissolve into a faraway haze. Would that voice still have the same disturbing effect on her ten years hence? "Adam, you—you startled me."

Staring up into his darkly handsome face, Juliana felt panic clutch her heart. This was the first time they had spoken to each other since their exchange of vows at St. Joan's. She didn't want to be alone with him. If the twins hadn't been obstructing her path, she'd have turned and fled through the side door.

"Juliana, everyone is waiting." As if he had guessed her thoughts, Adam grabbed her hand and drew her onto the dance floor, around which the guests were assembling. "Come along. I promise not to tread on your toes." He dropped his voice. "And try not to look as though I were leading you to the gallows."

Why shouldn't she? Juliana wondered. She flashed him a resentful look as he bowed before her and signaled the band to start. What was wrong with him anyway? Why had he wanted to marry a woman who avoided him at every opportunity? Surely he could have found a more willing victim, even among the female guests gathered here today. Undeniably he was handsome, especially so in formal attire: a tailored pewter-gray brocade suit with a gold-buttoned waistcoat and ruffled ivory silk shirt. And, too, there was the lure of his adventurous past and recent inheritance. Why then had he singled her out as his prey? she wondered as she heard the opening strains of the allemande. Did he have to ruin her life to fulfill an obligation to her father?

They began to advance toward the end of the ballroom, at one point separating to turn so that several agile hops were necessary to bring them together in the middle of the dance floor.

"I thought Louisa said you danced well," Adam commented under his breath.

Juliana caught the remark too late to summon a retort; keeping the lively three-quarter time required more concentration than she could manage. They separated again, her face flaming as she walked alone along the edge of the floor. From opposite angles, she and Adam came face to face in a square formation. By now other couples had begun to fill the dance floor, following the directions of the bride and bridegroom.

Annoyed by Adam's criticism, Juliana forced herself to finish performing the figures of the allemande without another misstep, though her feet felt leaden and she knew her movements were stilted.

Finally, the music ended, and Juliana quickly backed away from Adam, watching with boundless relief as he claimed Louisa for his next partner. Almost immediately she was besieged with requests for the next dance, all of which she declined while surreptitiously inching toward the foyer where she stood alone for several moments. She hadn't expected Adam to be such a skillful dancer, but then she knew so little about him. If he were to turn into a fire-breathing dragon at the stroke of midnight, she wouldn't be surprised.

Suddenly Martin was at her elbow, guiding her through the foyer. "Let's sneak outside for a minute. The fresh air will do you good."

Juliana complied eagerly. Every note the musicians played seemed to hammer at her temples. And the pungent scent of warm perspiring bodies had combined unpleasantly with the heavy fragrance of the white rose-and-rosemary wreaths adorning the walls. The mild summer air was like a balm on her strained nerves.

She and Martin walked as far as the blackberry arbor, where the hedges were laden with clusters of light pink blossoms. Here the only sound to disturb the midday quiet was the song of a chaffinch as it hopped about in the almond tree.

Seeing the anguish on his sister's face, Martin couldn't help asking the question that had been tormenting him all day. "Why, Juliana? We had everything planned. Why did you change your mind?"

She shrugged and looked away, staring into the distance at the rolling hillocks that encircled Rosmorna. "I don't know, Martin. I guess I'm a coward, after all. When I saw Papa struggling to dress for the wedding, and then Louisa showed m-me that exquisite trousseau she'd worked so hard to f-finish, I just couldn't—" She broke off with a small choked sob that had risen in her throat. "How c-could Papa do this to me?"

Martin placed his arm around her shoulders, his concern for her overshadowing his admiration for Adam. " 'Tisn't the end of the world, Juliana. I'll help you if you really don't want to stay with him. Maybe this is the time for me to try my luck at acting. Between the two of us, we must have enough money to live in London until I get work on the stage.''

Juliana's sobbing intensified, but even at the height of her distress, she couldn't find it in herself to destroy her brother's dreams. Life in London would do that soon enough. Gradually her tears abated, and with a meek smile she blew her nose on the handkerchief he handed her.

''Feel better?''

''A little.'' She pulled away from him and leaned back against the almond tree, her veil fluttering in the breeze. ''I'll never be able to face Graham or Venetia again.''

Martin frowned. ''Venetia will come round eventually. Graham's another matter. I can't picture him accepting rejection gracefully. But if you ask me, you're well rid of him. At least with Adam—'' He stopped cold at the look she flung him. ''Sorry. The last thing you need now is to hear me defending Adam.''

''Maybe that's just what I need.'' Juliana's eyes flashed with rekindled spirit. ''If I'm to be stuck with him for the rest of my life, I may as well try to understand what makes him so damned appealing to everyone else.''

''He's really not the monster you make him out to be,'' Martin ventured tentatively. ''He has a sharp wit.''

''Of which I am most frequently the target.''

''He's a fine-looking man,'' Martin continued. ''And at least as his wife, you'll be able to stay near home. Graham travels about constantly.''

Juliana turned her gaze to the small graystone manor house. ''Small consolation,'' she said with a resurgence of bitterness in her voice. ''I'll never feel the same about this place again.''

''You think that now, but later—'' His head swerved sharply toward the house as a thin, anguished scream rent the afternoon serenity. ''Oh, God, that sounded like—''

''Evelyn,'' Juliana concluded, gathering up her skirts to run. ''I'd know that voice in a crowd of a hundred. It came from upstairs, near Papa's bedroom—''

Propelled by the same unspeakable thought, they raced past the terrace and entered the house through the kitchen. On the way Juliana lost her veil and tore her skirts, but her darkest fear was realized when at the top of the staircase she spotted Evelyn, her face convulsed with grief.

She stumbled up the stairs, her mouth so dry she could hardly talk. "Evelyn . . ." The name emerged as a frightened whisper.

Evelyn looked up slowly. Then all at once she gave a heartwrenching sob and threw her arms around Juliana. "I j-just came upstairs to bring him a g-glass of champagne, and I f-found him in his chair. . . ."

"No." Tears of sorrow and anger rolled down Juliana's cheeks, splashing onto Evelyn's lace collar. "I want to see him."

She disentangled herself from Evelyn's arms and lifted her skirts to climb the stairs, but a hand at her shoulder stopped her and turned her around.

It was Adam. She had no idea where he'd come from, but she realized from his agonized expression that he knew what had happened. She thought, *If he orders me to stay out of my father's room, I'll push him down the stairs.* But, instead, he caught hold of her hand and stepped up beside her.

"We'll go in together."

Instinctively she recoiled, searching his face for hidden motives, but finding only her own raw grief mirrored there. Then, murmuring, "Thank you," and with her head bent and her hand resting loosely in his, she allowed him to lead the way.

Adam and Juliana left Rosmorna two hours after Sir Walter's funeral services in St. Joan's. The house had been open to receive callers since noon, smugglers and fishermen, farmers and gentry, all stopping by to offer their condolences to the bereaved family and to reminisce amongst themselves about the colorful figure whose passing had cast an indelible shadow over their lives.

"Are you positive you feel up to this, Juliana?" Adam asked as he met her in the courtyard, noting the mauve shadows under her eyes, the only hint of color against the whiteness of her face. "There's nothing I must do that can't wait another day."

She turned away from him. "If I have to sit through one more anecdote about my father, I'll go mad."

"Louisa thinks you might be more comfortable traveling by coach."

"I hate coaches. I want to breathe fresh air for a change. The scent of lilies inside the house is overpowering." Her voice was low and desperate. "Just take me away from here, Adam." She placed a hand on his arm. "Please."

He laid his hand over hers; even through the thickness of her riding gloves, her fingers felt like ice. "All right, then. We'll have to wait until Evelyn returns from the village. She went to post a letter to her husband."

"Martin will tell her good-bye for us," she said quickly, disengaging her hand. " 'Tis better that way. I know I'd say something unforgivable if I saw her now."

"Juliana, it isn't fair to blame Eve—" He fell silent at the look she gave him, a look so cold it sent a sudden chill through his soul. *Oh, God,* he thought, *it's me she blames.* "Whatever it is you're feeling, don't hold it inside," he said fiercely. "I know the price you'll pay for that composure, Juliana. Believe me, it isn't worth it."

"Would you rather I wept and beat my breasts, Adam? Is that what you want in a wife?"

"I want you as you are. I want you to share with me whatever it is you're keeping inside—anger, hurt, resentment—"

"Emptiness?" She hurled the word out like a challenge, then moved past him toward her horse. "I'll ride out to the moor and wait for you until you're ready."

"I'm ready now," he said tersely. "Have you only two saddlebags?"

She answered without even turning around to look at him. "Louisa's having the rest of my belongings sent down by coach."

Adam shrugged in helpless frustration and wheeled to mount his horse, noting with displeasure that his bride had left the courtyard without him.

Chapter Fourteen

For the present Adam had resigned himself to accepting the situation as it stood. He realized it would take time before Juliana learned to trust him. Love would come at its leisure, or not at all. He took it for granted that she'd seek the physical rewards of their relationship before the emotional. The only real hope he dared allow himself was that some of the resentment festering inside her would work its way out of her system before they reached Mentreath. In this he was to be severely disappointed. The harder he tried to reach her, the deeper she seemed to withdraw into herself.

In fact the only thing that appeared to be in his favor as they set out from Rosmorna was the weather, and that changed almost immediately after leaving Penzance, where they had stopped to dine. That in itself was a mistake. It was market day, and they had to wait ages for a poorly cooked meal only to fight their way back down the main street past screaming fisherwomen and crowded market stalls.

Then the rain began—not a cold drenching downpour but a steady veil of moisture coming off the sea that muddied the stony hillside paths and hedge-enclosed lanes they traveled. Adam had intended to push on as far as Germoe before stopping for the night, but changed his mind as they entered Marazion, the meeting place of medieval pilgrims drawn to St. Michael's Mount on the bay.

"Juliana?" It was almost twilight, and he had turned impulsively down a narrow street, keeping his eye out for a quiet inn. Now, as he glanced over his shoulder, he suddenly realized that Juliana was not behind him. Fear tightened his throat. When had he last seen her?

She was such an accomplished horsewoman it never occurred to him that she might have taken a spill. But they had argued during dinner, after he'd chided her for barely touching her pie and then downing a pint of ale.

"Is this typical of what I can expect as your wife, Adam?" she had sneered at him, impervious to the amused looks of the merchants seated opposite them. "Telling me how much to eat, how much to drink, how I should spend my grief." She'd paused then, noticing him glance about the room. "Am I embarrassing you? Would you like to tell me how and when I should speak, too? Shall I hold my tongue until you grant me permission to use it?"

Come to think of it, she hadn't spoken to him again after that. Had she run away? Would he have to endure the humiliation of returning to Rosmorna and begging permission to speak with his errant bride? "I told her not to drink on an empty stomach, Stephen," he would confess remorsefully. "Do you think you can persuade her to give me another chance?" Granted he had to make allowances for her current state of mind, but—

"Juliana!" He wheeled his horse abruptly. "Where the blazes have you been?" His eyes scanned the tall, cloaked figure, the face so alarmingly pale beneath the blue velvet hood. "Damn it, answer me! Where were you?"

Briefly her eyes met his, and in that fleeting look he read that her disappearance had been deliberate, a perverse act of retaliation for whatever wrongs she imagined he had done her. "I dropped my riding crop in the gutter." No trace of apology in her voice.

Adam clenched his jaw, forcing himself to spur his mount forward. "In future I'd appreciate it if you'd keep me alerted as to your whereabouts." He felt rather than witnessed the defiant lift of her head. "That is a request, Juliana, not an order," he added over his shoulder.

He came almost to the end of the street before halting at a nondescript little inn wedged between two shabby cottages. He glanced dubiously at the illegible wrought-iron sign swaying above his head and, sighing, gestured for Juliana to follow him into the stable yard. As he was dismounting, an ostler emerged to welcome them and stable their horses.

"A poor night to be travelin', sir. Ye'll want a room and supper, I reckon."

Adam nodded, moving past the short leather-clad figure to Ajax's side. "Do you want a bath, Juliana?" he asked, barely glancing at her as he began to unfasten her saddlebags.

She slid to the ground. "If it's no trouble."

"Of course it—" He walked around the horse until he faced her. "Juliana, are you crying?"

"No." Her voice was muffled by the white lace handkerchief she had pressed to her nose. "I think I'm catching a cold."

"I see. In that case we'd be wise to get out of this drizzle and into the warm." Fighting the desire to take her into his arms, he turned on his heel and strode through the rain-splattered yard to the inn's front entrance.

A large unsmiling woman intercepted them in the taproom, sending the bartender a questioning glance that Adam was not meant to catch but did. He straightened his shoulders. Did he and Juliana present so bedraggled an appearance that the proprietors of this wretched inn would refuse them a room? Bemused, he looked over the woman's mobcap-covered head to the common room where perhaps a dozen patrons supped.

"Can I 'elp ee, sir?" she inquired, raising her head in a useless attempt to block his view.

"Yes. A hot meal and a room for the night." He glanced around at Juliana, braced wearily against the wall. "My wife would like a bath before we sup."

"Ye'll want yer supper upstairs, away from this lot?" the proprietress inquired hopefully, jerking her head back to indicate the noisy group in the taproom.

Adam hesitated. If he had to consume another indigestible meal, he would prefer doing so in the privacy of his own room without some unwashed, loud-voiced fisherman breathing down his neck. Unfortunately then his wife would probably assume he couldn't wait to get her upstairs to rape her, as he'd resisted any attempts at lovemaking during those last solemn days at Rosmorna. Not that she had anything to worry about, he thought wryly. Fatigue, grief, irritation at her aloofness, and a feeling of mild revulsion at his surroundings had done an effective job of dampening his desire.

"Sir?" the woman repeated.

He sighed. At this point a little discomfort would be worth suffering if it helped relax Juliana. "If you don't mind, we'll eat—"

"—upstairs," Juliana finished quietly, moving past him to the rough-hewn staircase, where she paused to look back at the proprietress. "My husband and I are heavy sleepers, so you needn't worry about disturbing us during the night. In fact, 'twould be wise to have a chambermaid call us around seven in the morning. If it's not a bother . . ."

Relief seemed to soften the woman's sallow face. "No bother at all, my dear. I'll 'ave young Mary here fetch you up an 'earty breakfast to see you off. Mind you remember that, Mary," she warned the girl standing beside Juliana.

Juliana grinned. "Might I have a pot of fresh China tea on my tray, too?"

The proprietress met the bartender's startled look then released a deep appreciative chuckle. "You might at that. Now go on up with Mary, and let her 'elp you off with them damp things."

"What was that all about?" whispered a mystified Adam as he caught up with Juliana on the staircase. "I'm not a heavy sleeper. I awaken at the drop of a pin."

"Didn't you notice the sheets of tarpaulin in the carts outside?" she whispered over her shoulder. "This inn is a smugglers' drop."

"Oh." Adam felt suddenly quite annoyed at his own inability to recognize the obvious. Naturally, this was a smugglers' drop. Chances were he could have walked into any number of inns on the west Cornish coast and met a similar reception in each.

"They're expecting a cargo tonight," Juliana went on haughtily.

"Do I look like an exciseman?"

She paused, one arm resting on the banister while she subjected him to an impartial glance. "No. But your voice, and those clothes . . ." She resumed the climb to the landing, not waiting for him in the hallway.

"What's that supposed to mean?" he demanded.

"You're a foreigner." She rolled the word off her tongue

as though it left a bad taste. "You can't expect to be received with open arms."

Especially not into your arms, my lovely bride, he thought sourly.

"Is this room to yer likin', sir?" The young serving girl showed them into a large, plain room at the end of the hallway. In the darkness he could barely distinguish the outlines of a big lumpy bed, a gate-legged table, and two chairs in front of the unlit fireplace. " 'Tis the only room we 'ave wot don't overlook the alley. Sometimes that stink alone is enough to keep ye awake, not to mention the noise."

"Is the bedding clean?"

"Yes, sir," the girl replied, lowering doubt-filled eyes.

Adam nodded, watching Juliana sit down on the bottom of the bed. "I'll be in the taproom while you have your bath, Juliana. I wouldn't mind one myself if the water's still warm when you're through." He laid the saddlebags against a chair. "Can you manage without me?"

"I think so, Adam. I did bathe before we were married."

A half hour later, fortified with a pint of ale, Adam returned to the room to find Juliana sitting before a beckoning fire, brushing out her hair. In fascination his eyes followed the sweeping movements of her hand as it tugged the silver-backed brush through the inch upon inch of bronze-highlighted tresses.

She looked at him briefly, her slender hand arrested in midair. "Don't you believe in knocking?"

He unbuttoned his waistcoat, pulled it off, and tossed it on the bed. "It isn't my custom to knock when about to enter my own room," he said dryly. "Have I time for a bath before we eat?"

"The—" She averted her face as he began to remove his breeches. "The water was lukewarm to begin with. 'Twill be cold by now."

"It could not rival your heart, my love."

With a tight smile of satisfaction, Juliana heard the involuntary yelp he gave as he lowered himself into the copper-rimmed tub. "Enjoying your bath, Adam?" she asked innocently, her shoulders shaking with silent laughter.

"Immensely. But then, it would appear I've developed a fondness for self-torture of late." His voice was deceptively smooth. "Join me, Juliana. Perhaps together we wouldn't feel the cold."

She stiffened at the implication in his voice. "I've already bathed and washed my hair. Besides, supper should arrive at any—"

He cut her off abruptly. "Juliana, I was only joking. All I ready want you to do is hand me the soap."

"It's on the chair behind you. Under the towel."

"It was. I dropped it."

She turned and braved a cursory glance in his direction, spotted the bar of hard-milled soap lying behind the tub. As she darted forward to retrieve it, she became conscious of his eyes moving over her, burning through the diaphanous batiste of her nightdress. Damn Louisa for packing this silly thing anyway, she thought angrily. She could have been a little more subtle.

"Here." She held the soap out behind her, fixing her gaze on the door.

"I can't reach that far, Juliana. Would you mind coming closer? Or does the sight of a naked man frighten you that much?"

"Oh, for heaven's sake!" She stepped around to the side of the tub and looked him in the face with a boldness it took considerable effort to maintain. The firelight had bestowed a deep burnished polish on the skin of his shoulders and chest, accentuating the muscles gleaming beneath the fine matting of brownish hair. More than once Juliana felt—and fought—the temptation to lower her gaze.

"I wasn't raised in a house with two brothers without becoming somewhat accustomed to the male anatomy, Adam."

Adam's teeth flashed in a disarming grin. "Then you won't mind washing me, will you?"

Before she could retreat, he grasped her wrist and pulled her hand down into the water, forcing her onto her knees beside the tub.

Juliana gasped as her fingers brushed the growth of hair between his thighs, the shaft of flesh that leaped and hardened at her mere touch. "Oh, you idiot!" she hissed at him. Wrenching her hand loose, she jumped to her feet. "Now look what you've done. I've nothing else to wear to bed!"

One finely boned hand fluttered up and down to indicate the patches of dampness on her nightgown.

"Stand by the fire. 'Twill be dry before we sit down to eat." Leaning back into the tub, Adam allowed his eyes to roam appreciatively over the slender figure silhouetted against the amber-gold flames. He could barely make out the outline of one firm pointed breast, the rose-brown nipple thrusting through the clinging fabric. Dismayed to feel himself becoming aroused again, he forced his attention downward, noting the taut incurving abdomen, the prominence of hipbone from softly rounded flesh, and the long, lithe flanks that tapered into shapely calves and delicate ankles. Oh, God, how wrong he'd been. Nothing could subdue his desire for her. No amount of discomfort, no—

Juliana's scornful voice interrupted his pleasant musings. "This damned thing will take an hour to dry! I told you I had a cold."

"And I didn't believe you. However, you're welcome to wear one of my shirts." He stood and began lathering himself with vigorous abandon.

Juliana turned her head. "First, he soaks me," she muttered. "Then he offers me his shirt." She raised her voice. "Haven't we played this scene before, Adam? Is this some peculiar method of seduction you learned in the colonies?"

He chuckled richly. "It worked, didn't it? You fought me every step of the way, but you married me. I must have done something right."

"You give yourself more credit than you're due." Against her will she looked around just as Adam stepped out of the tub, a towel secured about his waist.

"Where are the other towels?"

She stepped back as he moved to the fireplace. "I put them on the floor beside the tub to keep the floor dry."

"And what am I supposed to dry my hair with?"

She allowed herself a smile. "Use the towel you're wearing."

"Very well." Placing one foot on the hearthstone, he yanked off the towel and proceeded to rub his hair dry.

"Really, Adam!" She whirled away at the sight of his lean hard buttocks facing straight toward her. "Must you be so vulgar? What if a servant were to arrive with supper?"

"Good servants, unlike husbands, are supposed to knock. If they do not, then they deserve to be shocked." He straightened, knotting the towel around his hips, and continued in a cheerful tone. "A good wife, on the other hand, is supposed to enjoy and not recoil from her husband's body."

Juliana snorted derisively. "Listen to Harry the Eighth here prattle on, spouting pearls of wisdom he probably picked up from dockside harlots. What makes you any more an expert on marriage than I am?"

Adam looked up slowly, his smile vanishing as he vainly searched his memory for one conversation between them during which Lucy's name had been mentioned. Was it possible she knew nothing of his previous marriage? Why hadn't her father told her?

"Don't you know, Juliana?"

She frowned. "Know what?"

There was a clattering of dishes and cutlery in the hallway, a timid rapping at the door. Relieved at the interruption, Adam turned and strode across the room to answer.

"Adam! You're not going to answer the door like that?"

"Why not?"

She hurried to the chair against which he'd laid the saddlebags. "At least put on a nightshirt."

"A nightshirt?"

"Which bag is it in?" she asked, kneeling.

"It isn't. I never wear one. I sleep in the nude. Have done ever since I can remember."

"You *what?*" She clutched the back of the chair and rose slowly, staring at him as though she'd just realized she had wed a lunatic.

There was another knock at the door. "Yer supper's getting cold, sir!"

"Just a minute!" Cursing under his breath, Adam struggled into the pair of breeches Juliana had just flung in his face. He could hear her laughing at him as he stumbled and banged his knee against the table. Regaining his balance, he opened the door and ordered the two wide-eyed maidservants inside.

"Leave the trays on the table, and go." He sat down on a chair, one hand rubbing his bruised kneecap, the other waving the girls away. "That will be all. Thank you."

Mary hovered uncertainly in the doorway. "The bathtub, sir. We're to drag it out of the room."

"Then be quick about it."

A few moments later the door closed with a gentle click, and Adam leaned forward to uncover one by one the steaming platters set before him. "You must have made a good impression downstairs, Juliana. This food looks quite appetizing."

"I don't want any. I refuse to eat with a half-naked man."

He uncorked the large bottle of wine, pouring a full-bodied burgundy into his goblet. "Suit yourself."

But in time the savory fragrance of well-seasoned roast beef lured Juliana to the table. Without remarking on her change of mind, Adam carved off two more slices of tasty meat and laid them on her plate beside a generous portion of onions, carrots, and potatoes smothered in rich brown gravy. In silence they finished the bottle of wine and shared a half-wheel of ripe yellow cheese and a juicy peach tartlet.

"We should sleep well after that." Adam stretched his arms above his head and yawned. "Settle into bed while I put the trays outside the door. We don't want to be disturbed again tonight."

As he pushed his chair from the table, he felt her watching him, her eyes wide and brimming with apprehension. "I want to get a full night's sleep tonight," he said wearily. "We have a long day of traveling tomorrow if we hope to reach Helston before nightfall."

"You mean, we're not—" She rose, glancing meaningfully at the bed before returning her gaze to his face.

His gray eyes glistened with amusement. "Not tonight. I'd prefer waiting until we reach Mentreath and are alone in the intimacy of our own bedchamber." He stepped around the chair and pulled her into his arms, the indulgent humor leaving his face as he bent his head to kiss her. "Unless of course you're impatient. . . ."

"You must be joking." But even as she spoke, she tilted her head back and parted her lips in unconscious anticipation, relieved and yet strangely disappointed at his announcement. Had marriage made her somehow less desirable? A melting warmth radiated through her body as he intensified his kiss, sliding his hands down her spine to clench her buttocks and mold her to his hardening maleness.

She had a sudden sensation of vertigo, the same dizzying excitement she'd experienced as a child standing at the precipice of a cliff and staring down at the sea.

Adam released her suddenly, turning away from the temptation of her delicately flushed face and moist, trembling mouth. "You'll make a liar of me yet," he said hoarsely. "Get into bed. Perhaps my self-control will prove to you that I'm not entirely crude and insensitive."

"I fear it's too late for that," she said bitterly.

He shot her a quick look from the corner of his eye, his rough-hewn face betraying the strain of the past few days. "For both our sakes, I pray you don't believe that. You can't expect either of us to find happiness in this marriage if you're determined it will fail."

"Don't forget to put the trays out, Adam."

"To hell with the bloody trays!"

Welcoming the return of her composure, Juliana climbed into the heavy carved bed and drew the eiderdown quilt up to her chin. "Snuff out the candles, Adam, and do stop staring at me. You can't say I didn't warn you."

There was a long silence before he responded. "No. I can't."

He extinguished the candles on the bedside table and slid into bed beside her, feeling her stiffen as his hand negligently brushed her shoulder. Was he handling this the wrong way? he wondered. Maybe he should just assert himself as her lord and master and hope to God that everything else fell into place afterward. But almost immediately he rejected the notion as one destined to fail. Any attempts to subjugate Juliana through force would serve only to alienate her further.

An hour passed, then another, and still sleep eluded him. To occupy his mind he began concentrating on the sounds coming from below, listening intently until he could name each one. The clip-clopping of ponies through the stable yard. The creaking of wheels and leather harnesses. The groaning hinges of a trapdoor to the cellar. He grinned at a sudden loud thud followed by a muffled curse. A keg dropped on someone's toe?

"Juliana?" He turned his head on the pillow to look at her. Her eyes were closed, and though she might not answer him, he sensed that she had awakened.

"What?"

He winced at the raw hostility she'd injected into the single word. Did she hate him even in her sleep? Watching her face for a key to her feelings, he found he could no longer hold back the question that had been gnawing at him. "The morning of our wedding, Juliana, you had every intention of running away. Who were you planning to run to?"

Her eyes flew open. "Do I really need to tell you? Haven't you guessed by now?"

"I wanted to hear it from you," he said quietly.

She sat suddenly bolt upright, glaring down into his face as she fought to restrain her raging emotions. "It was Graham, as you damn well know!" she cried, losing the battle for control. "By all rights I should be with him at this very moment, lying in his bed in an elegant Bath lodging-house instead of this—this shilling-a-night hovel!"

Adam felt something savage and ugly stirring inside him, straining at his self-imposed bonds of patience and understanding, clawing at him to be unleashed. Jealousy, he realized, in disbelief. The little bitch has made me jealous of her painted Cornish coxcomb.

"What the hell stopped you from going to him, anyway?"

"Concern for my father," she snapped back. " 'Twas certainly not because I felt anything for you, Adam."

"If I were to judge by your obnoxious behavior the past two days, I might be inclined to believe you. Fortunately, I know you better."

Juliana twisted onto her knees, clenching the pillow to her chest like a shield. "How could I have forgotten?" she shouted. "You know me better than I know myself, don't you? You're able to read my most secret thoughts, anticipate my every action!"

"Go back to sleep, Juliana. I'm aware you've been spoiling for a fight all day, but I'm not about to let you goad me into one at three o'clock in the morning."

He thumped onto his side, expecting her to lash out with threats or more verbal assaults and insults. But what he didn't expect was the forceful descent of her pillow upon his head before she wrapped herself up cocoonlike in the quilt and burrowed to the bottom of the bed, leaving him to pass the remaining hours of the night cold and frustrated, longing to turn her over his knee and give her the spanking she deserved.

Chapter Fifteen

They set out before eight the following morning, Juliana sullen and withdrawn, stubbornly resisting Adam's attempts to engage her in casual conversation. *As if ours were the most normal marriage in the world,* she sneered inwardly. *How long will it take the pompous bastard to admit he made a mistake?*

Just before reaching the mining district of Germoe, Adam decided to abandon the ancient coastal trade route and make a slight detour northward around the Godolphin hills. Not only did he want to avoid the tinners, who had a reputation for violence, but he wanted badly to escape the bustling fisheries at this the start of pilchard season when the stink of fish in the air was strong enough to make one's head reel.

And so for the next twelve miles they traveled the barren landscape of the interior, sharing narrow lanes with farmers on the way to market and packhorses transporting tin to blowing-houses. Following the steep, twisting steps of scattered hillside hamlets, they climbed higher and higher until finally, at sunset, they broke onto moorland.

As if by unspoken agreement they halted their horses and stared down at the windswept expanse of hollows and hillocks covered with waist-high tufts of gorse and heather that formed a patchwork of gold and violet against the bleak setting. Lichen-speckled tumuli, the forgotten tombs of the Druids, rose from the ground at irregular intervals. Pools of fresh rainwater shimmered in the gathering twilight, reflecting the granite boulders that were strewn across the moors as though flung from a giant's hand like so many pebbles.

Silence reigned, relieved only by the brief cawing of a crow perched on a tumulus before it took to the sky with a powerful flapping of glossy black wings. Adam looked up, following its flight with a frown.

"Damn it. It's going to rain again." His eyes scanned the brooding mass of clouds that darkened the horizon. "We'll have to find shelter for the night."

Juliana uptilted her face and sniffed delicately, inhaling the moist heather-scented air. "We could still make it to Helston tonight," she said, giving Adam a fleeting look of disdain. "I don't become hysterical in thunderstorms, if that's what you're afraid of."

"Actually, Juliana, I was thinking more of the horses. The last ten miles have been particularly hard on them."

Unable to argue the point, Juliana rode on ahead, guiding her mount down the hillside around clumps of broom and coarse dry grass that concealed stones and treacherous holes. At the bottom of the slope she felt a raindrop splash down upon her face, and she slowed to raise the silk-lined snood of her cloak.

"There's a cottage a quarter-mile to your left!" Adam shouted behind her. "Ride for it but be careful."

It had been unnervingly still all afternoon, and now suddenly, as Adam caught up with his wife, that stillness was broken by a sinister rumble of thunder and a violent eruption of rain from the bruise-colored clouds. Chins tucked into their chests, eyes blinded by the stinging pellets of rain, they rode straight for the isolated cottage-holding, a crude moor-granite structure thatched with late-blooming heather and attached to a lopsided mud-walled cowshed into which a stooped old woman was herding two milch cows.

At the sight of the two approaching riders, she slammed the cowshed door shut, then scurried into her cottage, emerging onto the crumbling stone doorstep seconds later with a pitchfork ominously held aloft.

"Typical Cornish hospitality," Adam commented under his breath. "Wait here while I attempt to reassure the old crone that I haven't come to rob her." Handing Juliana his reins, he dismounted and jogged the several muddy yards to the cottage.

Juliana eased both horses as far back as possible into the recessed doorway of the cowshed and watched dispassionately as her husband pleaded and argued with the stony-faced cottager only to have a few words of Cornish hissed at him and the pitchfork leveled at his throat. Finally, he backed off in vexation and returned to Juliana, his hair gleaming darkly with rain and slicked back against his scalp.

"I can't get one bloody word of sense out of or into her," he said furiously. "It figures that this would be the one cottage we happened upon. It couldn't have waited another hour to rain. We had to be thrown at the mercy of an hysterical old hag who's probably old enough to remember the Druids. She must be the only living soul left in Cornwall who doesn't speak English."

Juliana stirred, her lips curling into the hint of a smile. "There's another old woman over in Mousehole who speaks fluent Cornish. She's something of a legend. Martin and I saw her once—"

"My dear wife, would you kindly save the local history lesson for another time? I'm far more concerned with where we'll spend the night."

"I though you were supposed to be a dauntless settler," Juliana said, her gold-flecked eyes taunting. "Why don't you rig us shelter from the resources at hand? Furze makes excellent kindling, and if you could push a few boulders around and find us a nice dry spot under a hill, I'm sure we'd manage for the night."

Adam drew a deep calming breath, wondering how long he could keep his temper under control. "Need I remind you we're on high, open ground in the middle of a storm? I've no intention of getting struck by lightning—not even to impress you. Now, instead of constantly baiting me, why don't you put that devious little mind to work figuring out how to win over that witch inside?" He glanced over the rump of her stallion, eyeing the unattractive but warm interior of the cowshed. "I'd even settle for the use of her cowshed for the night."

Suddenly a door banged open behind him, and he turned to see a heavy-set man exiting the cottage. Adam's attention focused immediately on the pick resting on one massive shoulder. Instinctively, he slipped his right hand inside his cloak to feel for his pistol, a reflexive movement so smooth and practiced even Juliana didn't notice it.

"By the look of him, I'd say he works in the mine we passed on the moor," Juliana murmured.

Adam signaled her to silence. Miners had a dangerous distrust of outsiders, and he had no desire to provoke a fight with some burly oaf who probably wrestled for sport in county fairs. As the man neared the cowshed, he swung his pick down to his side. The gesture clearly warned he would use it as a weapon if necessary.

"Good evening," Juliana ventured. "I hope we've not upset the old woman. We were on our way to Helston when the storm broke, and we saw your cottage. . . ."

The man rudely ignored her and stared at Adam with suspicion on his lumpish features. "She be yer wife?"

Adam cleared his throat. "Well, yes, of course. We're recently married, in fact. You see, we'd hoped for shelter for the night. The use of your cowshed, perhaps."

" 'Twouldn't hurt nothing, I reckon," the miner said slowly. "But mind yer gone first thing in the morning. And I won't tolerate any unnatural acts or such during the night. I'll not have my cows giving sour milk."

"No, of course not," Adam said. "Thank you." But it was only after he and Juliana had settled into the cowshed with the horses that he paused to consider the miner's warning. " 'Unnatural acts'? What in God's name do you suppose he meant by that?"

Juliana's amused voice drifted up to him from the corner where she sat propped against Ajax's saddle. "I'm not sure. He probably sensed there was something animalistic about you."

Utterly disgusted with her after that, Adam did his best to ignore Juliana until darkness fell, when she roused herself from the corner to rifle through their saddlebags. "I'm starving, Adam. Where did you hide the food we bought this afternoon?"

He stretched forward to rescue the saddlebags from her searching hands. "I'll find it," he said, "though God knows how we're to taste anything through this perfume of manure and mildewed straw."

"Again you surprise me, Adam. I'd not have thought a big, rugged man like you would be oversensitive as to where he takes his meals."

"I'm not entirely the unsophisticated clod you make me out to be, Juliana." He regarded her over the rim of the wine bottle he had just uncorked. "As a matter of fact, I've heard

it said before that in another area related to sensual enjoyment, I possess a certain refinement.'' His voice vibrated
through the close atmosphere. ''Correct me if I'm mistaken,
but you didn't seem to find my lovemaking gauche or un-
skillful. Or did you?''

Juliana accepted the pasty he handed her, deliberately mute
in response to his question. As if he needed to remind her of her
response to him that night! Scarcely had an hour passed since
then that the memory of it didn't surface to her thoughts. Even
now, remembering, her skin tingled with pleasurable sensations, and as she had done so often since their wedding, she
wondered why he had made no further claims on her body. I
should be grateful, she decided suddenly, and bit into the folds
of flaky, golden-brown crust. But part of her could not help
wishing that he would find a way to breach the invisible barrier
that seemed to loom between them.

Her hunger satisfied by the generous portion of meat and
vegetables wrapped in pastry, Juliana lay back against the saddle with her cloak pulled up to her chin. From time to time
Adam passed her the bottle, and presently the hearty red wine
worked its relaxing magic on her body and mind. It was impossible to avoid physical contact with Adam, and she didn't try
to. As it was they could barely stretch out full-length in the
cramped low-roofed structure with its rough stone walls and
tilting hard-packed earthen floor littered with bits of mildewed,
moss-flecked straw. Across from them the two cows were enclosed behind what looked like a gate fashioned from table
planks and chair legs. Adam had tethered the horses inside the
door so that they were sheltered from the storm but unable to
eat and sicken on the befouled straw.

She had almost drifted off to sleep when she felt Adam's
hand on her shoulder, gently tipping her forward to place his
cloak across her saddle. ''You'll take a cramp in your neck
if you sleep like that,'' he whispered. ''Rest your head on
my chest while I spread the cloak out.''

She nodded drowsily, too exhausted to protest. There was
something comforting in the way Adam drew her against
him, his arm curved round her shoulders. And within moments she had slipped into a dreamless sleep, lulled by the
rhythm of his heartbeat.

Adam wondered if she had felt the sudden quickening of

his heartbeat, his body's reaction to the nearness of her. He lay motionless and tried to concentrate on sleep, but he could sense his resolve weakening. She was his wife. He wanted her.

He withdrew his hand from her shoulder and gently lowered her onto his cloak. How lovely she was in sleep. Without thinking, he shifted onto his side and pressed his mouth to hers. The delicate scent of lavender tantalized his nostrils. He squeezed his eyes shut against a violent pang of longing. Not here, he told himself urgently. For the love of God not in a byre, or she'll surely have justification for her sad opinion of you! But the constriction in his loins persisted, and suddenly he found himself kissing her again, savoring the ambrosia of her mouth with his tongue.

"Adam?"

He pulled back instantly. She had moaned his name so softly that at first he wondered if he'd imagined it. And then he heard it again.

"Adam . . . what were you doing?"

"I was easing you down onto your back. I thought you looked uncomfortable."

"Oh. Is that all?"

He could see her eyes gleaming up at him now, and the glint of moisture on her lips from his kiss. "Yes, that's all. Try to get some rest."

He felt her lift her hand, watched her touch it to her mouth. "How odd. I could have sworn—I thought you were kissing me."

"Perhaps you were dreaming."

"Mmm. I suppose."

He turned away from her, hoping she wouldn't pursue the subject. It was clear from her tone of voice that she didn't quite believe him, but under the circumstances he felt it would be an intolerable affront to his dignity to elaborate on his lie. He had enough pride left to keep him from confessing he'd had to steal a kiss from his own wife.

It took him almost two hours to fall asleep, and even then Juliana dominated his dreams. Outside the wind had faded to a whisper, but the rain continued through the night, easing to a drizzle just before dawn when Adam woke. He opened his eyes and blinked, disoriented by the unfamiliar surroundings. He was getting used to Cornwall, he realized. The perpetual moisture in the air, the wildly beautiful land and its enigmatic people. His wildly beautiful and enigmatic wife.

"Juliana?"

He sat up stiffly to discover she was gone from his side. He rose and yawned, rubbing his unshaven jaw. Less than two days ago he had bragged to her that he awakened at the slightest noise, his subconscious mind trained to protect him from a hostile environment. Yet already it seemed he had acquired the deadened awareness of a pampered gentleman, his senses dull from lack of use.

He met Juliana outside the door, returning from the cottage with a half-dozen fragrant oat scones bundled in her cloak. He stared at her as she moved past him into the shed. She looked indecently well-rested, her fine ivory skin translucent, her eyes as clear as pools of rainwater on the moor. Suddenly he felt dirty and stale, unfit to touch her.

"How did you come by the food?"

"I went outside for a breath of air and met the old woman's son coming back from the mine. They must have felt sorry for us."

He frowned, picking a scone from her cloak as he joined her on the floor. "Do you always rise at such an ungodly hour?"

"No." She brushed her mouth free of crumbs. "But then, I'm not used to sleeping with someone who tosses and turns all night, either."

Adam looked up. "It's your fault if I did."

"What do you mean?"

"Never mind. It's not a topic I care to start the day off with." He finished his second scone and got to his feet. " 'Twould help if you'd lead the horses outside for me to saddle them. We need to make Helston before evening."

Outside, the predawn mist swirled about them in ghostly tendrils, casting an eerie glow upon everything it touched. As Adam saddled the horses, he watched Juliana walk restlessly up the hillside and pause at the crumbling remains of a granite dolmen, the burial chamber of some ancient queen or chieftain. Staring at her he felt a sense of unreality possess his imagination. It was as though the auburn-haired figure rising out of the mist was not his wife but the spirit of a Druid priestess. Did the bones of one of Juliana's ancestors lie beneath those very stones? Was she descended from a pagan queen?

One of the horses threw its head and whickered, bursting

Adam's fanciful musings. But from that moment on, a shadow of the illusion remained somewhere in the back of his consciousness. And more than once during the ride into Helston, he wondered if he was the victim of sorcery.

The early start enabled them to reach Helston at a leisurely pace. At six o'clock they rode into the popular market town and, after wandering through the winding streets, finally found the old stone inn that Mr. Samuel Treffrey—Adam's solicitor—had recommended.

The chamber allotted them appeared clean and comfortable, the common room below frequented by respectable, well-heeled customers. At any rate, after a bottle of claret and a warm scented bath by the fire, neither Adam nor Juliana felt any desire to seek lodgings elsewhere.

"I feel human again," Adam remarked as he finished shaving at the washstand. "An hour ago I'd have been too embarrassed to greet Mr. Treffrey on the street, let alone sup with him."

Juliana, flung out on the bed with her face pressed into a pillow, rolled onto her back to look at him. "Sup . . . down below?"

"No. In his home." Adam held a towel to the nick on his chin and glanced down at her. "It's almost eight. I hope you're not one of those women who takes ages to dress, because we're expected in half an hour."

"Oh, God, Adam. Not tonight. I couldn't possibly."

"Are you feeling unwell, my dear?" he asked, coming to the side of the bed.

"No. Just exhausted. My limbs feel leaden. And—" She stopped herself, not about to admit she suspected her malaise had something to do with the lateness of her monthly flow.

"And?" Adam prompted.

"And I'd probably shame us both horribly by falling asleep during the second course."

"Then by all means, stay here. I daresay 'twill be a boring evening anyway, with all the business we have to discuss." At Juliana's expression of childlike relief, Adam smiled and moved from the bed to don a fresh ruffled shirt and silk-faced waistcoat. "I'll order a tray sent up to the room for you."

"Good. I'm ravenous."

He smiled again, readjusted his linen neckcloth before the washstand mirror, and went to the door. "Don't expect me back before midnight. And draw the bolt behind me."

She did not obey him, not out of defiance, but because she simply could not rouse herself from the depths of the comfortable bed. For a minute she stared at the door, visualizing Adam as he had stood there, disturbingly attractive in his velvet suit with the candlelight casting his rugged features into relief. And then, closing her eyes, she fell asleep.

She didn't awaken until a serving girl knocked at the door twenty minutes later with her supper. Adam had ordered well. The tray held a small tureen of leek soup, half a roasted hen, fresh fruit in clotted cream, and a flagon of dry white wine.

"Will ee be wantin' anything else, madam?" asked the girl after unloading the tray on the table. "A warming pan fer the bed, p'rhaps?"

"Not y—" The conclusion of Juliana's sentence was lost in the sudden explosion of laughter and high-spirited conversation outside in the hallway.

"Zounds, Belstow!" exclaimed a peevish male voice. " 'Twas me the wench took a shine to first. Isn't that so, Delphina?"

"We'll toss a coin for her, Basil," a second man replied.

Harry, Lord Belstow? and Basil Andrews? Juliana knew those names, and she knew those voices, voices which belonged to two of the most disreputable and amusing young rakes in Graham's circle of friends. Intrigued, she followed the serving girl out into the hallway to find the lively pair fumbling to open the door to the adjacent chamber. A buxom strawberry-blonde woman—most likely a prostitute—stood behind them, giggling at Harry's every word.

"Well, we'll never get back into the confounded room now," Harry announced finally. "I've just broke the blasted handle off!" At that the blonde dissolved into helpless giggles, and then Harry turned, his eyes lighting appreciatively on Juliana before recognition struck.

"By Saint George, look who it is, Basil!" Disengaging himself from his clinging female companion, he strode across the hallway to Juliana. "What a nice surprise this is! I take it you and Venetia are in town for Lady Quinceburten's anniversary ball."

Juliana shook her head wistfully. "Unfortunately not."

"Graham?" Harry's protuberant brown eyes widened. "The naughty lad's spirited you away for an illicit encounter, is that it?"

Juliana grinned, more amused than offended. "What a wicked mind you have, Harry. I hate to disappoint you, but actually, I've just gotten married."

"Married?" Harry repeated, incredulous. "So there *was* something to the rumor of Graham's elopment." He grabbed her and planted a hearty kiss on her mouth. "Congratulations, sweetheart. Now step aside and let us in to toast the groom."

Juliana, turning around after him, said, "Harry, wait—"

But he had already made his way into the room, and behind her Basil had sent the serving girl downstairs with a smack on the bottom and a request for wine to celebrate the occasion.

"There's something peculiar about this." Harry circled the room, halting at the table where Juliana's supper had been spread. "Supper for one. No sign of the groom." He snapped his fingers. "You've had a quarrel."

"No, Harry. I didn't marry Graham." That said, Juliana sat down at the table and poured herself a glass of wine. To be honest, she hadn't even given Graham much thought since her wedding. She wondered if he had gotten the letter of apologetic explanation she had sent him through Venetia. She wondered if he'd understand.

Harry took the chair beside her, his cherubic painted face alight with curiosity. "Well, well. Who did you marry, then?"

"His name is A-Ad—" She broke off, absurdly close to tears. It wasn't real. It was a nightmare! "His name's Adam Tremayne," she said quickly, recovering her self-possession. "He was a friend of my father's. Neither of you know him. He's from the Virginia colony."

"Ye gods." Harry ran a hand through his heavily powdered hair, and Basil, seating himself on the bed with Delphina on his lap, clucked his tongue in sympathy. "One of them plantation owners, is he? I expect he's very rich."

"No, he isn't," Juliana said, indulging in a moment of self-pity. "And he's taking me to live in some creaking old house on the Lizard. I shall have no friends whatsoever to comfort me, no social life to speak of."

"Why, you poor thing" Delphina blurted out. "I do hope he's at least young and 'andsome."

"He isn't," Juliana said emphatically, her resentment toward Adam growing as she sensed a sympathetic audience. "He's old—almost forty—and he has a disgusting paunch, and a huge brown wart right in the middle of his forehead like a—a third eye. Worse, he refuses to wear a wig or powder his hair."

"Shocking," Basil said, shaking his head.

Harry leaned across the table to pat her hand. "It's during times like these that you need your friends the most. Dearest Juliana, have I ever confessed how profoundly I worship your great beauty?"

With the help of Harry's irrepressible wit and ample supply of wine, Juliana managed to forget her intolerable situation with Adam for the next few hours. This is how life would have been with Graham, she thought resentfully. Good friends dropping in day and night. Nothing more pressing to worry about than what to wear to the next assembly. No problems that money and title couldn't overcome. When Harry sent word down to the innkeeper that he fancied some music to enliven the evening, a local fiddler was summoned from the taproom and promptly presented for the task.

"Dance with me, Juliana," Harry urged and boldly pulled her from the chair and into his arms. "Enjoy the short time you have left in civilized company before this Cyclops you have married returns."

Taking his cue, the fiddler straightened on his stool and launched into the opening strains of a gavotte. Across the room Basil began leading Delphina through the movements of the dance. Still, Juliana hesitated. It was the height of impropriety for her to be entertaining two inebriated young rogues and a harlot in her room during Adam's absence. To dance with Harry would be flirting with danger, inviting it.

Her lips settled into an unconscious smile. The clock in the hallway had just chimed half-past eleven, and at any moment Adam might return. How would he react to discovering his bride in the arms of another man? He claimed he understood her, pretended to applaud her unbridled conduct. Would he be angry or amused? Suddenly it seemed worth risking a scandal to find out.

Chapter Sixteen

Adam's first thought was that he had entered the wrong chamber. He stood in the doorway, staring into the intimate scene he had intruded upon. His gaze took in the empty wine bottles littering the table, the rumpled quilt on the bed, his lovely young wife in lavender silk dancing with a doting partner. She had not noticed him yet, and the sight of her face, glowing with pleasure and lifted to another man, sparked something violent within him.

"What is this?" He forced the question out between lips that had suddenly gone stiff with fury. And then, when he realized that his voice couldn't be heard over the lively music, he turned and glared at the source of the sound until the fiddler wisely slid off the stool and escaped into the hall.

"I say, don't s-shtop yet," Basil began, but his protestation ended on a drunken hiccup as Delphina elbowed him in the side with a meaningful look in Adam's direction.

Only then did Juliana finally glance up and acknowledge him. "Why, it's Adam! What time is it? I didn't expect you back this soon."

"Obviously."

He stared down into her flushed face and felt a muscle working violently under his right cheekbone. How dare she greet him with that air of brazen innocence. How dare she pretend nothing were the matter.

"It's the most wonderful coincidence, Adam," she went on brightly, making no attempt to move away from Harry's side. "Lord Belstow and his companions are staying right across the hall from us. Harry wanted to celebrate our marriage."

Adam strode into the room, glowering at the full-faced

125

man standing next to his wife. "Get out." He removed his jacket and waistcoat and flung them on the bed. "Or shall I throw you out? At the moment nothing would bring me greater satisfaction."

For a second Harry hesitated, seemingly torn between his loyalty to Juliana and his sense of self-preservation. Then he noticed Basil and Delphina were stealing out of the room behind Adam.

"No need for that, sir," he said, edging around the table and toward the door. "I'm not a man who overstays his welcome." At the threshold he glanced back at Juliana, opened his mouth to speak, then abruptly closed it, bowed, and hurried out into the hall.

"Good night, Harry!" Juliana called after his retreating figure. "Remember me to Lord and Lady Quinceburten!"

Throwing her a look of disgust, Adam went to the door and slammed it shut with a thundering bang. When he turned around, he saw that she had drawn a chair to the fire and was sitting contemplating the flames. The imperturbable detachment of her posture fanned his rage until he feared he could not control it. She had pushed him too far.

He walked to her chair, bent, and hauled her onto her feet. "Explain yourself, Juliana!" His fingers tightened around her shoulders, and he felt a stab of satisfaction at the soft involuntary gasp she gave.

"Y-you're hurting me, Adam! I can feel your fingers bruising my skin."

"Oh, I should like to do far worse than that," he said softly. "We both know you deserve it."

A flicker of uncertainty passed across her face. "All I know is that you're making a horrid fuss over nothing."

"You suggest that I shouldn't care whether you entertain men in our room?"

"How was I to know it took so little to make you erupt into a jealous rage? You'd always led me to believe you were more liberal-minded."

He loosened his fingers, allowing her to pull away from him and retreat to the foot of the bed. "Only a fool would tolerate that sort of behavior in his wife. No matter how much I condone your rebellion toward convention as a whole, I will not be made a cuckold of."

Juliana disappeared behind the dressing screen to change into her nightgown. "I danced with Lord Belstow, Adam. I sipped wine with him and laughed at the outrageous compliments he paid me. 'Twas no worse than I might have done right under your nose in any public assembly room."

"There's a world of difference, as you damn well know."

She emerged from behind the screen and sat down on the bed to brush out her hair. "How was your supper with Mr. Treffrey?"

"Don't change the subject."

"Don't be a prude."

He came to the bed and sat down beside her. It was then he caught the faint gleam of amusement in her eye. Could the bold little baggage actually be enjoying this? he wondered. He looked around the room again, noting the evidence of revelry and disorder. She had known when he was to return. She had known he would walk into a situation that might have provoked another man to murder. He glanced at her sharply as the disjointed thoughts and suspicions in his head snapped into place. So, she'd been testing him, and his every instinct shouted that he had to assert himself *now,* or forever relinquish any authority he had in their relationship.

"Put the brush down, Juliana."

She looked up. "I'm not finished yet. I still have thirty strokes left."

"Damn you!" He reached across the bed and knocked the brush from her hand, his strong fingers snapping around her wrist before she could pull away.

Juliana's eyes widened. "What on earth has come over you?"

A cold smile flattened his lips. "You're determined to brazen this out, aren't you?"

"I've no idea—"

"Be quiet!"

His fingers stole up the silken flesh of her arm, curled around her elbow and drew her resistant body toward his. "For over a week I have suppressed my desire for you, Juliana. I restrained myself believing beneath your stoic facade you were overcome with grief for your father. But tonight, by behaving like a common strumpet, you have shown me that I need no longer fear offending you with my baser urges.

"Your heart is not made of crystal, my love, but of granite. From this evening on I shall not treat you like a delicate hothouse orchid, but rather like the resilient wild heather that flourishes on the moors."

A dusky blush stained her cheekbones. "If you think—"

Those were the last words she uttered before Adam turned swiftly and wrenched her onto his lap, pinioning her arms behind her back. His left hand lifted to touch her face, to upturn her stubborn chin. She could feel his hard-muscled thighs supporting her weight, the prominent bulge of his manhood burning into her thinly covered buttocks.

"Adam," she whispered, her voice shaking. "It's very late—"

His mouth claimed hers with fierce possession. His arm tightened, shifting her weight forward so that her soft breasts rubbed his chest. He longed to push her onto her back and thrust inside her. Instead, he thrust his tongue deeper into her mouth and kissed her passionately.

Tremor after tremor jolted through Juliana's body. She had ordered herself to offer a token resistance to Adam's kiss, to appear unmoved at the very least. But from the moment she felt his tongue dart into her mouth like a searing flame, she had known she was lost.

I am his wife, she thought. Though I may despise him until the very day I die, I cannot continue fighting him.

"I should stop right now," he growled suddenly, dragging his mouth from hers. "To deny your body the pleasure it seeks would be a fitting punishment for your conduct tonight."

"But 'twas you who initiated our lovemaking, Adam," she taunted, managing to loosen her hands from his grasp. "My body seeks only to rest."

"I think not," he murmured.

Then he hooked his right arm around her waist and skillfully maneuvered her backward into the mattress. Balanced on one elbow, he dipped his head and kissed her again. This time her lips parted eagerly, welcoming his questing tongue. As he tasted and savored her surrender, Adam's eyes clouded with passion beneath the half-lowered lids. He wanted to draw her to an aching peak. Slowly he worked his left hand under the ruffled hem of her nightgown and inched it upward along her bare calf, her inner thigh, his callused fingertips scorching a sensual path.

Juliana shivered, wrenching her mouth from his to catch her breath. "Adam," she whispered hoarsely. "Please . . . I want . . ."

He smiled down at her, his heart hammering with excitement. "What do you want, love?" He moved his hand higher still, the fingers splayed, and rotated his palm over the fleshy mound above her thighs. "Shall I touch you here?"

"No!" She bit the inside of her cheek to suppress a whimper. "Oh, yes!"

She felt his fingers crawling downward, seeking, finding, stroking that secret bud of sensation that blossomed at his touch. She quivered with pleasure, parting her legs shamelessly to encourage him. Soon her body ached for relief from the delicious torture. But just as she felt herself sliding over the edge of fulfillment, Adam drew back suddenly and rolled off the bed. Juliana opened her tightly closed eyelids to see him standing before her, stripping off his clothing.

He gazed at her as he unbuttoned his shirt. "Are you ready for me, Juliana? Do you want me now?"

She turned her face to the side. Suddenly she felt uncertain and afraid—perhaps more of her own burning needs than of Adam. Her body was flushed and trembling with the passion he'd aroused within her. Heaven above, it was so clear that she wanted him! Why must he prolong her embarrassment?

"Look at me."

Slowly she returned her regard to him. Her lips parted with a bewildered gasp as her wide luminous eyes took in his broad, darkly furred chest, his narrow waist, and the large proudly erect shaft between his thighs. To her utter humiliation, she found herself unable to stop staring at him . . . unable to stop imagining the pleasure he could give her.

His eyes met hers. "I'm going to teach you a lesson, Juliana. I'm going to make you beg me to love you."

Anger filled her eyes, dimming the gleam of seductive passion which had lit them seconds before. "I will not." Her mouth, still tender from his kisses, hardened into a straight, indignant line. Wasn't it bad enough that she'd admitted she desired him? Did he need to degrade her further?

"Never, Adam. Never."

She thought herself safe, that he'd decided not to pursue his arrogant male threat until suddenly she saw him drop to his knees before her. Slipping his hands under her buttocks, he pulled her toward him so that her calves draped over his powerful shoulders. Confused, she half rose to question him, then collapsed onto the bed with a whimper as she felt his mouth touch the vulnerable spot above her thighs. His darting tongue thrust boldly within her, and Juliana's nerve endings leaped in shocked delight. Slowly, tortuously, he tasted and teased her with his mouth until she felt as if his tongue were a spark that scorched and ignited wildfire inside her belly. Her back arched convulsively; the blood poured through her veins like heated brandy. Never in her most private fantasies had she dreamed such erotic pleasure existed. Oh, God! Never had she dreamed *she* would respond to a man with such feverish abandon.

"Adam," she cried, her body shuddering, her eyes closing as her senses fluttered and rose in rapturous confusion. "Oh, I can't bear another moment of this. Love me now!"

He looked up at her briefly, smiling. "Beg me, Juliana."

She turned her head. She scarcely realized that her hands were clawing at the quilt, her fingers twisting and untwisting the heavy fabric in frustration. Damn him! To reduce her to this . . .

"All right," she whispered. "Adam, I'm . . . begging you. . . ."

The words had barely left her lips before Adam was on his feet, bending over her with one hand outstretched. "Forgive me for being impatient, my love," he said softly.

His fingers fluttered over the gleaming swell of her breasts in a lingering caress, then curled around the collar of her nightgown and tore it from her trembling body. With a smile of satisfaction, he tossed the shredded garment behind him and leaned forward.

An unexpected wave of coolness brushed Juliana's skin, raising goose bumps, and she shivered. Then Adam was on top of her, plunging his turgid organ deep into her softness. A sob of pleasure broke in her throat. Her hands lifted to his shoulders, then wandered down his muscle-ridged back, and boldly she rocked her hips forward to answer his hungry thrusting. She could feel the tip of his engorged manhood pressing against her womb, and she tightened her muscles, urging him deeper. A red haze filled her mind. Then suddenly tremors of intense pleasure ripped through her, culminating in a climax so powerful she feared her heart would explode in her chest. She stiffened, her legs locked over Adam's hips. And as she gave herself up to the sweet, melting warmth that seemed to fill her, she felt him tense and then shudder violently, taking his own release.

Moments later, he rolled onto his side, his arms crossed beneath his head, his eyes open but unblinking. Juliana lay quietly beside him, her body humming with fulfillment. She didn't know how many minutes passed before either of them finally moved.

"I hope this ends the game-playing between us, Juliana," Adam said, sliding his hand intimately between her legs. "If I had accepted your feeble explanation of your conduct tonight without a fuss, you'd never have respected me again. I'm a tolerant man, but I do have my limits. I suppose you needed to find out exactly how far those limits extended." He squeezed her kneecap, grinning. "You also needed a way to make me prove how very desirable I find you. Quite simply put, you wanted me to make love to you, but your silly pride wouldn't let you admit it."

She pushed his hand away. "What—what utter nonsense!"

His eyes glistened wickedly. "I was only restraining myself out of respect for you."

"I'm going to sleep, Adam. You're disgusting!"

"We shan't have a repeat of tonight's performance, my dear," he told her softly. "You see, from now on, as is my right, I intend to enjoy your body whenever it pleases me to do so. Naturally, I will allow you to make similar demands on me."

"What a conceited ass you are," she said furiously. And flinging him an indignant scowl, she flipped over onto her stomach to crawl under the bedclothes.

Adam chuckled quietly, his eyes following her shapely white bottom as it disappeared under the quilt. "Don't be afraid to wake me if I can be of service again tonight, my love," he whispered tauntingly. "We've no reason to get up early in the morning."

Chapter Seventeen

The following morning they set out southwest, traveling along the borders of the windswept Goonhilly Downs, skirting the ruins of several abandoned tin mines overgrown with fragrant golden gorse. They rode at an unhurried pace, talking only when necessary. Juliana, not wanting to think about the humiliation of the previous evening, concentrated instead on the austere beauty of the scenery unfolding before her. Still, every so often she caught her mind drifting back pleasurably to the moments of exquisite passion she and Adam had experienced together. In a strange way the tempestuous scene last night had been a relief—a release of the electric tension that had been building between them since their wedding. Perhaps she *had* taunted him—perhaps she'd even gotten exactly what she wanted! Sweet heaven, how was she to make any sense out of her chaotic feelings and the erratic behavior they provoked?

She slanted Adam a long pensive glance, feeling her face grow hot as she recalled how ardently she had responded to his lovemaking last night. Oh, Lord, the way he'd pleasured her with his mouth, and—Clenching her jaw, she forced herself to stare straight ahead at the surrounding hills. Would she ever regain control of her life? she wondered wretchedly. Would she always be at the mercy of her traitorous desires?

From the corner of his eye, Adam had felt her watching him. Was she thinking about last night? Noting the tension that tightened her jawline, he decided she was. The provocative little minx! How long would it take before her struggles became surrender? How many obstacles would he have

132

to surmount before he won her stubborn heart? Sighing in frustration, he reminded himself to be patient, that time was on his side. His face softened as he studied her. Oh, yes. He was willing to wait.

Just before dusk they passed through a narrow winding valley and reached Penlyn, a seaside hamlet which lay a mile northeast of Mentreath. Tiny stone cottages with thatched roofs and adjoining pigsties hugged the hillside. On boulders between them, fishing nets had been stretched out to dry.

At the heart of the hamlet sat a weathered Tudor church, encircled by a ring of wind-stunted hawthorn trees. In its graveyard huge unhewn tombstones with moss-stained epitaphs jutted from the earth in crooked rows. Riding by, Juliana glimpsed the vast ancestral vaults, almost hidden beneath the foliage of chokeweed and hart's-tongue ferns. The scent of humus hung in the air and mingled with the elusive sweetness of peppermint and evening primrose. She raised her eyes to the granite tower arch of the church and wondered if the thick vines of ivy covering it had silenced its bells. Then, through the deepening twilight, she heard the mellow notes of a skylark as it soared heavenward, and after its song ended, the tinkling of a little stream which tumbled down the hillside into the sea.

"We're almost home," Adam remarked, his voice breaking her peaceful mood.

Home. Juliana stiffened in the saddle. How could he expect her to call Mentreath home when she had visited it once only ten years ago?

Adam spoke again as they continued up the hillside. "We'll soon have workmen in to fix up the place, so don't be put off by the exterior. I haven't seen much of the inside, but what I saw looked fairly comfortable. My uncle was an odd man. Didn't your father ever discuss him with you?"

Juliana did not answer. They had crested the hill, and now, across the stark, undulating landscape, she had a clear view of Mentreath.

The grand Elizabethan manor stood on a headland of serpentine rock and sheer cliff that plunged down three hundred feet into the boiling sea. Its many rooms included a pantry, a buttery, and a chapel, and were situated around an interior court. From each of its four corners rose pepperpot-domed turrets, and on the roof between them, chimneys twisted upward to create an irregular silhouette against the darkening sky.

From a distance the house appeared untouched by the centuries. Yet Juliana soon detected the peeling paintwork between the old-fashioned leaded casement windows, the crumbling masonry of the gabled porch. The once-imposing gatehouse that had guarded the estate during more turbulent times now served as a roost for raucous jackdaws. The ornate rust-stained iron gates protecting the drive swung open on groaning hinges.

"It's hideous," Juliana mused aloud. "Like the home of an ogre in a fairy tale."

Adam reined in his horse beside her. "I'm sorry you don't like it. Perhaps you'll feel differently after the repairs are begun."

"I never said I didn't like it," she retorted, not looking at him. "I merely commented on its ugliness."

She pressed her horse forward. To her right she could see patches of the pebbly scallop-shaped cove below. Now, at high tide, the gigantic breakers thundered onshore, pouring into the hidden network of caverns that pierced the cliffside. A jagged reef of three-cornered black rocks rose from the foam-hemmed surf like the back of a sleeping dragon.

Her eyes moved slowly to the left, widening in surprise. A rough stone wall enclosed an incongruously well tended garden situated off the southeast corner of the estate. Juliana spotted musk roses and orange-scarlet trumpet honeysuckle clinging, intertwined, to a trellis archway. Here, as at Rosmorna, greenery thrived on the perpetual moisture in the air.

She was still examining her surroundings when two men came out of the stables at the rear of the house. The first, a redheaded giant whose massive chest strained the seams of his leather jerkin, eyed her warily while greeting Adam with a welcoming gap-toothed grin. The second man, greatly aged since she last saw him, had a thin, wiry body and an overlarge head covered with unruly shoulder-length silver hair. His snapping currant-black eyes brightened at the sight of her.

"Miss Juliana!" he cried, holding out his arms to help her

dismount. "You've grown so, I hardly recognized ee. I don't suppose ye'll be remembering old Jack Chenwiddy."

Juliana slid down onto the graveled drive, her aching body gratefully accepting his assistance. "Of course I remember you. And Doris too. I'm eager to see her."

"She's in the house with Mrs. Simpson readying yer chamber. We were none of us sure when ye'd arrive."

Juliana noticed Adam's head turn with sudden interest. "Did you say my sister was here, Jack?"

"Yes, sir. Arrived yestermorn with her husband." Jack took hold of Ajax's reins and directed a black look at the flame-haired Hercules standing behind Adam. "Both the groom and his stableboy are in bed with the bloody flux, Robbie. If it's not beneath yer dignity, ee might stable the master's horse."

To Juliana's surprise, the towering bodyservant flushed a fiery red, then turned clumsily and led Adam's horse away. Jack stood watching him with affectionate exasperation.

Juliana would have tarried and talked with Jack further, but suddenly she felt Adam's hand on her elbow, gently propelling her toward the front entrance porch. "You look tired, Juliana. Come inside, and let Barbara make a fuss over you. I think you'll like her."

This Juliana doubted with all her heart. In fact, the very last thing she needed in her life was another damned Tremayne ordering her about. One was enough to contend with, as the events of the previous evening had so effectively demonstrated. She simply felt too weary to wage another contest of wills tonight.

Her mood lifted as she and Adam moved through the screens passage into the great hall. Unlike Jack Chenwiddy, Mentreath's loyal steward, this cavernous oak-paneled chamber had remained true to her vivid childhood memory of it. The sooted hammer-beam roof seemed every inch as lofty as she recalled. The huge stone fireplace with the grotesque gargoyles carved into its chimneypiece still conjured up the image of a private passageway into hell as she stood before the crackling flames, swaying with fatigue.

"For God's sake, sit down, Juliana." Adam gently pushed her down onto one of two grandfather wing chairs flanking the hearth. "I'll see if I can find Doris and my sister somewhere in the maze of chambers upstairs."

Just as he turned from the chair, a woman appeared on the top of the wooden staircase which ascended from the far end of the hall. "Adam!" She glanced back over her shoulder excitedly. "Keith, do hurry! They're here."

Juliana looked up to see an attractive brunette in a gold silk gown rushing down the staircase. Following at a more restrained pace was a tall, lanky man with a boyish face and thinning blond hair. Juliana forced herself to stand while Adam embraced his sister, then warmly greeted the other man.

Barbara, Adam's sister, was the first to move toward her. "Oh, Adam, she's lovely! But how bad of you not to invite us to the wedding. I hardly know how Mother will take the news when she gets my letter." She interrupted her scolding to bestow a light kiss on Juliana's cheek. "My dear, you look awfully flushed," she whispered. "Has Adam not been taking proper care of you?"

Juliana smiled despite herself. Yes, Barbara bore a strong resemblance to Adam; and yet with her, the dominant Tremayne features—the square-cut jaw, the clear gray eyes, and softly waving air were pleasingly muted, creating an impression of elegance instead of Adam's reckless arrogance. She found Barbara's husband, Keith, equally agreeable.

"I hope you'll have enough influence over Adam to make sure he keeps in touch with us from now on," he said after they'd been introduced. "Devon isn't so far away that we couldn't manage an occasional visit."

A courteous rejoiner formed in Juliana's mind but abandoned her before she could express it. A wave of sudden dizziness swept over her, and as if from a great distance she watched Keith's smiling expression shift to baffled concern.

"Juliana, what is it? Are you ill?"

She was trying to answer no when the heavy curtain of darkness descended and she pitched forward into his arms.

An hour later, sitting down to supper in the winter parlor, Juliana scoffed at Barbara's suggestion that she summon a doctor.

"It's travel weariness, Barbara. We've been riding for days."

Adam, fingering the stem of a Venetian goblet, studied her thoughtfully. "Possibly she was hungry. She hasn't eaten a thing all day. Still, an examination couldn't hurt her."

"There you have it," Juliana said, pouncing on his explanation. "I hadn't eaten for eight hours. No wonder I fainted."

Another possibility entered her mind, but she refused to consider it. It was easier to attribute her fainting spell to nerves. The thought of living as Adam's wife in this strange old house was unsettling.

"More wine, Juliana?" Barbara asked, breaking her train of thought.

"Oh, no. Not another drop. I can barely keep my eyes open as it is."

"Then you should go to bed. I hope you'll find your room comfortable. It's the best Doris and I could do for now. With all his money, Uncle Logan refused to let her order repairs done on the house. He claimed he liked it just as it was." She flashed Adam a grin. "Do you know what I found out today, Adam? Uncle Logan didn't have a bedchamber of his own, or even a bed. He slept in the library—on the billiard table."

"Claimed it was good for his spine or some such nonsense," Keith added, his mustache twitching with a smile.

Adam laughed. "He was a peculiar fellow, no doubt about it. He also owned one of the finest private libraries I've ever seen."

Keith put down his glass. "So Barbara told me. You don't suppose we could sneak in and take a quick look around it, do you?"

"That's a splendid idea," Barbara said, pushing her chair back from the table. "Juliana and I will have time for a nice little chat before we go to bed."

Juliana snuck a covert glance toward Adam as she rose to follow Barbara from the room. Their eyes met briefly. What was he thinking when he looked at her that way? His angular face, glowing bronze in the firelight, revealed nothing of his thoughts.

Barbara turned to face her outside in the hall. "My dear, if you'd prefer to go straight to bed, I'll understand. Your eyes are drooping. Adam, on the other hand, has never looked better. I can't tell you how relieved Keith and I both are that he's remarried. We never thought he would."

Juliana stared, stunned by Barbara's careless revelation. The muffled crashing of the waves below seemed to fade into silence. "What do you mean, Barbara?"

"Well, so many years have passed since he lost Lucy and the baby—" Comprehension flickered in Barbara's crystalline gray eyes. "My God. He didn't tell you."

Juliana managed a smile. "No, he didn't. But I shouldn't be surprised. Ours is hardly a close relationship, Barbara. My dowry appealed more to Adam than I did."

"I can't deny I sensed a tension between the pair of you at supper," Barbara said, her expression softening. "However, I do feel obligated to set your mind at ease on one point: Adam couldn't have possibly married you for your money. Along with his house, he inherited sixty thousand pounds."

They resumed walking down the long gallery, Juliana's mind whirling with the startling information. Adam was rich! Perhaps—oh, perhaps he *did* love her! She wished she could be certain. She wished she knew him better. But she didn't know him at all, she realized that more now than ever before. He had penetrated her soul, and yet he was as much an enigma to her as the night she met him. She hadn't even known he'd been married before. She felt a sharp, unwelcome prickle of jealousy to think another woman had shared his name.

At last they stopped before a heavy oaken door. "This was the most presentable chamber in the house," Barbara said. "It's still quite bare, but the bed linens are freshly laundered. I hope you'll not mind sleeping without curtains. The ones Doris and I took down to beat were so moldy and moth-eaten we couldn't stand to hang them back up."

The chamber contained only a chest, a chair, and a monstrous four-poster bed with faded silk hangings and a floridly carved headboard. A fireplace of imported green marble dominated the center of one wall, and in it a fire smoldered and cast wavering shadows on the painted ceiling.

"You'll need more wood on that fire soon," Barbara observed, turning back to the door. "I'll see if I can find Jack to tell him. The dampness here seeps to the very core of the house."

Juliana roused herself from her trance. "Barbara, there's no need for that. I'm used to the sea air. I-I'd rather you stayed to talk awhile."

Barbara wavered. "I'm afraid I've talked too much as it is. I should never forgive myself if I caused trouble between you and Adam. As much as I love him, I'm well aware he's a difficult person to live with."

"He told me the same thing once himself," Juliana reflected. "At the time I didn't quite understand what he meant. I still don't." She perched on the edge of the bed, her shoulders drooping. "Our marriage was a mistake, Barbara. If only your brother would admit it."

"That isn't Adam's way. It never has been. From what I can make of the situation, I don't think he'll give up on you that easily."

Juliana rebelled at the other woman's words. "He couldn't stop me if I chose to leave him. I wouldn't be the first woman to flee an unhappy marriage."

Barbara shrugged, her face concerned but not condemning. "No. I suppose you wouldn't. But let us both hope you'll never feel the need for such drastic action. Perhaps, in a few months, after you've settled into this house, the situation will look brighter.

Juliana nodded, doubtful.

"I'm sorry Keith and I have to leave in the morning, but he has so many cases coming to trial next month. He's a criminal attorney," Barbara explained at Juliana's puzzled expression. "Didn't Adam tell you they studied law together at the Inns of Court?"

"No," Juliana said dryly. "He didn't."

Barbara smiled. "Well, I can't say I blame him. He was expelled for dueling. It was a silly affair, really, but again I'll have to let him tell you about it himself. It would never do for him to walk in here right now and find me revealing the details of his colorful past."

Barbara left her several minutes later, urging her to get a decent night's sleep. But while Juliana's body was numb with exhaustion, her mind seethed with thoughts of helpless anger. How could she sleep knowing that at any time Adam would come striding into the room? She dreaded the moment of his arrival, and yet, without him she felt strangely bereft, incomplete.

'Tis only habit, she thought. She was used to having her father and brothers around to keep her company. Adam had nothing to do with the odd loneliness she felt as she lay between the lavender-scented sheets, staring out the window over the restless sea. Yet when the door opened, and she glanced around to see him standing beside the bed, she couldn't control the sudden wild thumping of her heart.

"I thought you would've been asleep by now. Dare I hope you were waiting up for me?"

He didn't wait for an answer, but turned and began undressing with that total absence of inhibition she still found so unnerving.

Naked, he slipped into bed beside her and pulled her into his arms. Feeling the heat of his body burning through her thin lawn shift, Juliana could not repress a shiver. She prayed Adam wouldn't notice it, but he did.

"Are you cold, or do you find my presence suddenly exciting?" he asked teasingly.

She rose on her elbow to turn over only to learn he had no intention of releasing her. "I'm cold," she replied. "Had you not torn my only nightgown off me last night, I'd have had something warmer to sleep in. I can only hope my belongings arrive here soon."

Smiling lazily, he placed his left hand on the inside of her thigh and gently stroked her skin with his fingertips. "I'd buy you a hundred nightgowns for the same purpose if it relieves your conscience having me take you that way."

"Relieves my conscience?"

"Mmm. Apparently you still have a problem admitting to yourself that you desire me. By forcing me to always act as the aggressor, your passion is satisfied while your conscience and pride are appeased."

She stared up into his dark, grinning face, her eyes blazing with hostility. His arrogance infuriated her. How could he know she ached for his touch when she strived so desperately to conceal it? It was humiliating to know he could so easily strip away her veneer of protective indifference. It was humiliating to realize he knew how badly she needed him. Unthinkingly, she searched her mind for words to retaliate with.

"Is that how it was with your first wife, Adam? Did you have to force yourself on her, too?"

The sudden tightening of his features warned her she had touched upon a vulnerable area. "Damn Barbara," he muttered. "She couldn't let me tell you myself." His eyes held hers captive with their intensity. "I assumed your father had discussed my previous marriage with you. When I realized he hadn't . . . well, it seemed the wrong time to bring it up. It's not something that should affect us."

"I want to know about her. I have a right."

He drew a deep breath. "Not now. Don't spoil the present for us by forcing me to relive unhappy memories. It should be enough for you to know that she's dead."

Juliana didn't want to drop the subject, but Adam had deftly untied the ribbons of her shift and was tugging it down over her hips. Then his hands were caressing her firm white breasts, cupping them gently as his mouth descended to tease first one nipple and then the other.

"Barbara—Barbara also mentioned you were a very rich man," she whispered, unaware of the huskiness in her voice.

Adam glanced up at her briefly, his eyes glittering with amusement. "Very rich. Does that make me more attractive to you?"

When she didn't reply, he wedged a knee between her legs, forcing them apart. "I only want to please you, my love," he whispered.

Juliana's thoughts raged like a maelstrom as she felt her body answering his seduction. Was this horrible confusion that had ensnared her thoughts the first stirring of love for him? No! her mind rebelled. Don't trust him. He'd kept his previous marriage a secret—why? Had he loved his first wife so deeply that even now he couldn't bear to speak of her? She was dead, yes, but were his feelings for her still alive in his heart?

An unexpected jolt of misery rocked through Juliana, shocking her with its force. Does he think of her when he's making love to me? she wondered in anguish. Oh, if she only understood him! So many times in the past she had misjudged his motives. Maybe . . . maybe it was better not to analyze their relationship too deeply. Maybe . . . Chills of delight rippled down her spine as his hand began stroking her belly. Her thoughts scattering dizzily, she closed her eyes and let the delirium of desire overwhelm her.

She could feel his manhood pressing against her thigh, searing her flesh like a brand. What would happen if she were to touch it? she wondered. Would it bring Adam the same intense pleasure she experienced when he touched her? The question tantalized her . . . compelled her to inch her hand downward and tentatively brush her fingers across his engorged member. He didn't object, and she became bolder, allowing her hand to stroke and enclose him until he grew too large to hold.

Adam sucked in his breath, releasing it with ripple of low soft laughter. "You're learning, my love."

His praise had the unexpected effect of arousing Juliana, and intuition told her he could sense her excitement. He dragged his mouth slowly downward, his tongue teasing her navel, and just when she thought he would repeat the delicious torment of the previous night, he raised himself above her.

She looked up into his face, her eyes luminous with desire. "Adam," she breathed. "Don't tease me any longer."

He smiled and carefully lowered himself between her legs. Without hesitation she arched her back and opened her thighs in invitation, eagerly awaiting his entry. And then finally she felt him sinking inside her, his movements slow and deliberate. She flung her arms around his neck, her breathing ragged, her hips writhing. The muscles of Adam's back strained beneath her fingers, and she could feel his passion mounting in the sudden quickening of his thrusts. Unashamed, she lowered her hands to clasp his buttocks, pressing him against her, willing him to penetrate deeper and deeper still.

"Adam," she panted as he drove into her. "Oh, love me harder!" And he did, like a mighty ocean wave pounding into a fragile shell, carrying her away on a cresting pleasure and submerging her in swirling sensation as together they peaked and crashed upon the shore. Then slowly the thundering of her senses quieted, leaving her conscious of only a sweet satisfied throbbing.

She awakened the next morning to find hazy sunshine flooding the chamber, revealing the imperfections she had been too tired to notice the night before. The wooden crossbars on the old casement windows were warped and splintered. Numerous cracks cobwebbed the mantelpiece above the fireplace, and a greenish tinge discoloring the plaster cornices which edged the wall gave evidence of water damage.

She turned her head, realizing she was alone in the bed. Memories of her last waking moments bombarded her consciousness; resolutely she forced them from her mind. She had nothing to gain by dwelling on the details of her humiliation! Adam, with his usual gloating conceit, would probably remind her soon enough as it was.

Adam. With her newly gained perspective on his character, she was even more at a loss than before to understand him. His brashness enraged her; his tenderness devastated her. There were moments when she ached to claw the smile from his face, moments when that same smile nearly sent her to her knees with longing. At one time during the night, she'd realized that she had gone beyond the point of withholding any part of herself from him, no matter how frantically she might continue to deny it. And the realization had brought her both pain and an unexpected sense of peace, the peace that comes with the grim acceptance that one is probably going to lose a battle.

Where had he gone? Restlessly, she glanced out the window, thinking how clearly she could see the ocean, how it seemed to stretch out forever like an unrolled bolt of emerald silk. It was late. She had never been a slugabed before. Why hadn't she woken earlier?

She started to slide her legs over the bed, then stopped, gripped by a sudden attack of nausea that receded before she could reach for the chamber pot. It was then she remembered her nakedness, and as she groped behind her for her shift, she noticed her traveling gown lying over the back of the chair, brushed free of dust and painstakingly pressed.

A quiet knock at the door sent her back under the bed-clothes and struggling into her shift. "Who is it?"

"Doris Chenwiddy, madam. I've brought yer breakfast tray up like the master ordered."

Juliana yanked the covers up to her neck. "Could you bring it in, please. I'm not quite dressed."

The door opened to admit a diminutive woman in her fifties with gray-streaked brown hair pulled into a severe bun. "Shall I put this on top of the chest, or will ee 'ave it in bed, madam?" she asked, holding out the covered silver tray she carried.

"Oh, Doris, don't you dare be so stuffy and formal! Please, sit down beside me."

With a pleased smile, Doris obeyed, balancing the tray on her knees. "Yer every bit as lovely as yer mother was. What a shame Master Logan couldn't have lived to see ee wed his favorite nephew."

"The house has changed since I was here last," Juliana said, deliberately steering conversation away from the subject of Adam.

Doris nodded. "Aye. Fallen into a terrible state, and I had to sit back and watch it happen at Mr. Tremayne's request. Of course, that'll change now that you and yer husband are here." She shifted the tray onto Juliana's lap. "Tea, toast, bacon and eggs. Eat it while it's warm, and I'll fetch some fresh water and a washbasin for ee. I've pressed yer gown, too. Did ee notice? Yer husband brought it downstairs this morning and sneaked it back into the room before he left."

Juliana put down the rasher of bacon she was nibbling. "He didn't mention where he was going, did he?"

"He's down to the village with Jack so far as I know," Doris answered from the doorway. "There's a rendezvous scheduled with an East Indiaman at the end of the week. The men have been eager to find out whether we'd meet 'er. No one was sure what would happen to the trade after the old master died."

Damn Adam! Juliana thought. He might at least have asked her to accompany him.

"I don't suppose my husband left any suggestions as to how I should spend my day?"

"As a matter of fact, he did, madam. He thought you might like to 'ave me show ee around the 'ouse. He asked that ee make a list of any improvements needed."

"How thrilling. Have Mr. and Mrs. Simpson left yet?" At the housekeeper's nod, she vented a loud sigh. "Very well. We'll start the grand tour after I'm washed and dressed."

They spent the remainder of the morning and most of the afternoon exploring the closed upstairs chambers. As the dinner hour approached, Juliana, her head aching from Doris's well-intended suggestions and unsolicited housekeeping hints, called a halt to the inspection.

"That's all I can stand today, Doris. If I look at another crumbling ceiling or smell one more mildewed carpet, I'll scream."

"But surely ye'll want to inspect the kitchen, madam. Mrs. Runporth, our cook, planned to discuss tonight's menu with ee. She'll be terribly disappointed if ee don't come down."

Juliana patted the housekeeper's arm. "Tell her she has my permission to prepare boiled boots and shoelaces if she likes. I wouldn't dream of interfering."

"Well, as ee wish, madam," Mrs. Chenwiddy said, looking bemused. "But ee do want to meet the rest of the staff today, don't ee? 'Tis important to establish a firm relationship with them from the start."

"I suppose I must. But not until after my husband and I have eaten. I'm feeling rather tired, and I wouldn't want to greet the staff in an irritable mood. I might scare them off."

Doris smiled. " 'Tisn't likely. We've most of us been here too many years to find employment elsewhere. Of course there 'ave been a few what 'ave come and gone. Especially after Mr. Tremayne took it into 'is head to dabble in necromancy."

"Necrowhat?"

Doris continued in obvious embarrassment. "Necromancy, ma'am. The art of communicatin' with the dead. Oh, he didn't mean no 'arm. 'Twas grief over yer dear mother's death what drove 'im to it. Poor old man loved 'er

like a sister.'' She shook her head sadly. ''Caused quite a
stir around here with 'im wanderin' through the graveyard at
night, chantin' his nonsense to the long-departed. Course
there are some who swear to 'ave seen 'is ghost standin' on
the cliffs, so who's to say?''

''My uncle did *what?*''

Juliana grinned. ''You heard me. You'll have to use your
imagination to live up to his reputation around the village.''

Adam pushed his chair back from the table. ''I shouldn't
doubt it. All my life I've heard tales of his various eccentricities. I only wish I'd met the man.''

''I spent so little time with him,'' she remarked. ''He was
wonderful—like a wizard.'' Fondly her mind slipped backward in time to the summer when she and her mother had
visited Logan here. ''It's funny,'' she said, almost to herself. ''As a child I remember thinking that I wanted to live in
a house exactly like this when I grew up. I told myself that I
would fall asleep every night listening to the sounds of the
sea.''

''And now,'' Adam prompted gently. ''How does it feel
now that you are actually living your dream?''

''My dream?'' She shrugged, suddenly embarrassed by
her confession. ''Oh, I've had many different dreams since
then. Anyway, it's not at all the way I imagined it would be.
Sometimes, when we fight, I feel as though I were a captive
in an ancient castle. Other times, well, take this moment for
instance, I-I almost enjoy it. What about you, Adam? How
are you adjusting to being lord of the manor?''

He sighed quietly, enjoying their conversation, wondering how long it would last. ''It's still too new for me to decide how well I fit the role. I never really had any roots
before I came to Mentreath.''

She glanced away uncomfortably. ''Perhaps you'll grow
tired of staying in one place before long. Perhaps you'll start
craving adventure again.''

''Juliana,'' he said softly. ''You are all the adventure any
one man could possibly want.'' His eyes warmed with approval. ''I must confess I felt uneasy about leaving you
alone on your first day as mistress of the house. I should've
known you were capable of handling the situation.''

Something in his tone—perhaps a thread of condescension—irked Juliana, spoiling the pleasure she had experienced sharing her thoughts with him. She inhaled a deep breath. "You should also know that I'm not about to rot away in a decrepit old house." She set her goblet on the table, regarding him with a cool, unwavering gaze. "I want to help with the smuggling."

"No."

"Why not?" she demanded. "I know more about it than you do! I watched my father do everything from establishing contacts to—"

"Absolutely not!" He lifted his head, his strong features hardening. "I won't have it."

Juliana jumped up. "And what do you propose I do with my time?"

"Supervise the running of this household, for one thing."

"That certainly won't occupy me morning, noon, and night. Anyway, I don't know how to manage household matters. No one ever taught me."

Adam seemed to grow calmer as Juliana's temper flared. "Ask Doris to teach you. She's in her glory now that she's finally been permitted to show what she knows about domestic affairs."

"Then why should she not handle them by herself?" Juliana challenged.

"Because she is not the mistress of this house, madam, and you are."

Juliana fought against a rising panic. "If you're suggesting that I spend my days embroidering tea cosies and poring through recipe books, then you can go straight to the devil!" She glared at him through a sudden haze of tears. "You promised you wouldn't try to change me! I should've known not to believe you."

Adam swung out of his chair and swiftly moved around the table to where she stood. "Juliana, I don't want to change you. A woman who embroiders tea cosies holds no special fascination for me, I assure you. However, I do need your help setting this house in order."

He took her into his arms, staring down at her stubbornly averted face. "I want to make this rotting old house a home for us,'' he said softly. "I want to make it a proper home for our children.''

She twisted halfheartedly, feeling her face grow warm at his words. "Don't be silly, Adam. We have no children yet."

"No. Not yet." He slipped one hand down her back to settle beneath the curve of her bottom. "But we could concentrate on making a child tonight," he whispered. "Would rearing a son or daughter not be a suitable way to pass your days?"

"Stop—stop fondling me that way! I'm supposed to be meeting the staff in a minute. What if Doris comes in to remind me?"

His eyes glinted with mischievous humor. "Then I'll tell her you have a previous appointment with your husband. I guarantee she'll understand.''

Much later, as Juliana lay in Adam's arms, her body limp with satisfaction, she reflected on the peculiar malaise she had been suffering from the past week or so. Should she share her suspicions with Adam? Should she let him know she might even now be carrying his child?

She shifted her head on the pillow to study him as he slept. Sighing, she thought how handsome he was with the firelight gilding his chiseled features and accentuating the bold planes of his face. Her hand slipped down her chest and rested on her abdomen. Theirs would be a beautiful child. Tall, dark-haired, undoubtedly strong-willed.

I won't tell him yet, she decided suddenly. *Not until I'm positive.* Why should she? It would only give him another hold on her, and the sexual power he exerted over her now was frighteningly strong enough on its own. She could already feel her freedom slipping away after less than only a fortnight of marriage. A child would provide him with the perfect excuse to restrict her activities.

A single tear rolled down her cheek, and turning onto her side, she curled into a ball and closed her mind against the endless unhappy possibilities of what the future held for her.

Chapter Eighteen

It was expected to be a lucrative run, the largest single crop of goods expected until spring came with calmer seas. The *Juno,* an East Indiaman on her voyage home from China, had come off the cove shortly after twilight. Hovering just outside territorial waters, she and her crew lay in wait for the clandestine rendezvous that would unburden her of seventy chests of high-grade Hyson tea. Tonight Adam was sailing out on his uncle's small sloop to meet the broad-hulled ship in the hope of establishing an ongoing business relationship with the *Juno*'s captain. Increasingly high duties had made the nation's favorite beverage the most profitable black-market article in existence.

Layers of mist rolling onshore obscured the coastline as Juliana stood with her forehead pressed to the cool mullioned windowpane. It would serve Adam right if he were to run aground in the fog, she thought bitterly. He could have changed his mind about insisting she stay home tonight. Yet even in her anger, she heard a small voice within whispering that he did have justification in leaving her behind. How he conducted himself on his first run would set the tone for his future enterprises. A band of seasoned smugglers could hardly be expected to respect a man who could not control his own wife.

"Come away from the window, madam. Ye'll take a chill in the draft."

Juliana spun about in surprise. "What a start you gave me, Doris. I never even heard you open the door."

"Aye. I noticed," Doris said, a smile relaxing the austere lines of her face. "Don't ee worry about the master,

149

madam. My Jack'll take care of 'im. He could sail the cove in 'is sleep.''

Juliana moved away from the window, resisting the urge to laugh. What would Doris think if she knew I'd been willing Adam to run aground?

''When do you expect they'll return, Doris?''

''Can't say, madam. You being Sir Walter's daughter ought to know better than to ask.'' She swept open the bed curtains to turn down the quilt and give the pillows an expert thumping. ''Into bed wi' ee. I brought up a nice brandy syllabub to help ee sleep. 'Tain't easy to do wi' all the banging about the men'll be doing downstairs.''

Juliana got into bed. At the base of the cliff supporting most of the estate was a cave that could only be reached from the sea or through a subterranean passageway below the library. Cargo intended to be dispatched at a later date would be hidden there until it could be moved.

''I should like to explore the caves one day,'' she said. ''Perhaps I'll take out a boat and go sailing. 'Twould give me something to do.''

Doris handed her the posset cup, frowning. ''The sea 'ere is terrible dangerous, madam. Not like where ee come from. Even the strongest swimmer can drown in a riptide or an undertow. Anyway, we've enough to do inside this 'ouse to keep us busy for another century. Don't forget the glaziers and the plasterers are comin' next week.''

Juliana nodded absently, sipping the sweet, thick beverage and soon feeling the brandy's warming effect. What did she care if the whole house crumbled to dust and dropped into the sea? Her own world had collapsed. She had no heart for putting faith and effort into a new one.

Doris stirred the fire and checked under the bed for mice, seeking excuses to remain in the room until satisfied Juliana had finished the syllabub.

''That'll help ee sleep,'' she said, taking the empty cup. ''And don't worry no more about the master. I know 'tis 'ard, being newly married and deep in love, but he'll come 'ome safe.''

Juliana snuggled under the covers as the door closed behind the housekeeper's back. Silly woman, she thought with a mixture of affection and annoyance. Can't she tell I don't give a damn whether Adam returns or falls off a cliff? Why must she assume I love the man because I married him? Perhaps Adam has won Doris over to his side, persuaded her to help him influence me.

"It won't work," she muttered into the pillow. She'd fight their conspiracy!

Sleep came, ending her silent tirade but bringing her closer to Adam in an unexpected dream. Stripped of her inhibitions, she felt free to respond to him as never before, her mouth seeking his with hungry urgency, her body burning for his. Oh, if only it could always be this way between them! If only she could trust him as completely as she trusted this gentle lover of her dreams!

"What a sweet welcome this is."

The dark velvet voice penetrated the depths of her dream, disturbing the sensual illusion.

Juliana roused, reluctant to surface from sleep. Foggily she became aware that her nightgown had been pushed up over her hips, that the naked male body positioned above her belonged to reality.

"Oh, Adam," she whispered. "Why did you have to wake me?"

"I couldn't resist you," he said simply, staring down at her. "Doris said you missed me. Could it be true?"

She closed her eyes. She didn't want to think. It was so much easier not to, and as she felt Adam plunge inside her, her back arched in response and she strained upward, eager to recapture the magically tranquil mood of love and trust that had pervaded her dream.

Chapter Nineteen

Juliana managed to hide her distress from the somberly attired physician walking beside her down the long gallery to the main staircase. She saw no reason to confess her true feelings; he would only think her reaction unnatural.

"Your husband will be greatly relieved to learn the nature of your malady, Mrs. Tremayne. I shall have to stop by the orchard to congratulate him. He and the gardener were in conference there when I arrived. If the winter isn't too severe, this old house should be in fine condition for the birth of your child."

She nodded, the condition of Mentreath the furthest thing from her mind. "Fortunately, most of the damage was superficial and easily enough repaired. Still, we're far from finished."

They walked in silence for a few more moments. Then, as they were turning the corner to the staircase, Juliana stopped, her voice low and confidential. On the wall beside her hung a gilt-framed oil portrait of Logan Tremayne.

"Dr. Carew, call it woman's foolishness, but I really would prefer to break the news to my husband myself." She faltered slightly, fancying that the shrewd gray eyes in the portrait came to life at her words. "If you don't object—"

"Object? Well, no. How could I? Informing him is your duty and privilege. Now, don't come down the stairs again, Mrs. Tremayne. It's not too early to start limiting your activities. A stroll along the long gallery, or a walk through the garden once a day should suffice."

"Thank you, doctor. I'll keep that in mind."

What utter nonsense, she thought as she watched his dark

figure disappear, step by step, down the curving staircase. Her mother had gone hunting the week before Martin was born. Why should she favor the advice of some pompous old charlatan over her own more reliable instincts?

She roused herself, dismissing the doctor from her thoughts. It was Adam who posed the greatest threat to her welfare, anyway. Once he discovered the fact of her pregnancy, he would become more tyrannical than ever in his efforts to control her.

"Madam, Doris says there's a gentleman 'ere askin' to see ee. She says 'e drove up in a fancy coach-and-four, so she showed 'im into the parlor, thinkin' 'e be quality."

Juliana put down the quill with a sigh of irritation. She had spent the entire morning reviewing household ledgers, between bouts of nausea, and she was in no mood to receive the local gentry. Her frown eased as she glanced up at the sweetly composed face of the young amber-haired girl standing in the doorway. Phoebe, Jack Chenwiddy's niece, was the only member of the household to share her secret, to understand her misery.

"Ask my husband to receive him, Phoebe. I'll make a poor impression if I have to run from the room every five minutes to heave into a chamber pot."

"The master's still down at the cove with my uncle. Shall I tell the gent ye're indisposed?"

Juliana stood with another sigh. "No, no. It wouldn't do to offend the neighbors. But for heaven's sake, don't bring us tea unless I ring for it. I don't want to give the man an excuse to linger."

The uninvited caller was not a neighbor but Graham, the last person on earth Juliana ever expected to receive in her parlor. Facing him now, after all that had happened, came as a shock, caused not so much by her emotional reaction to the sight of him, but rather by the utter lack of it. She could never have loved him; in that sage observation Adam had been right. The realization struck her instantly as Graham turned upon hearing her enter the room.

He removed his frockcoat and sword, dropping them carelessly on the chair behind the door. "Juliana!"

He started toward her, and instinctively she stepped backward, shaken by the change in his appearance. Purplish half-moons of fatigue showed beneath his bloodshot eyes, and deeply etched creases hinting of strain and dissipation marred the youthful attractiveness of his aristocratic face. His long dark hair, unpowdered for the first time in Juliana's memory, fell in lank, greasy waves to his shoulders. He had lost weight, and his satin suit hung loosely, wrinkled and smelling of stale liquor and acrid perspiration.

"Graham, this is a—a surprise." Sinking gracefully to the sofa, she managed to avoid his intended embrace. "Did you get my letter? I realize it probably didn't make any sense, but had you understood my dilemma—"

He sat down beside her, interrupting with a sudden passionate outburst. "But I do understand, darling! You were *forced* into this wretched *mésalliance*. It took me days and days to realize you hadn't jilted me. Scold me for my lack of faith—admittedly, I deserve it! You see, I began drinking after I read your letter. Only after Venetia finally convinced me that your family pressured you into this marriage did it occur to me I must rescue you."

"It's too late now, Graham," she said quietly, staring into his white anguished face. "I hadn't the courage to carry through with our elopement, and now I have to pay the consequences."

"It isn't too late," he said fiercely. He grasped her hand and lifted it to his mouth to press burning kisses on her palm. "You forget who I am, Juliana. You forget I have friends in political circles who can arrange for you to get an annulment."

Juliana pulled her hand back into her lap, sadness and an echo of her former affection for him weighting down her heart. "Not even the power of your family name can help me now, Graham. My marriage has been consummated."

"Then you and he are . . . are lovers." At her answering silence, he swung away from her, burying his face in his hands.

After a time he looked up and spoke again, his voice flat, though Juliana thought she detected in it a dangerous undercurrent of suppressed rage.

"It makes no difference. I'd have preferred no other man had touched you, but it makes no difference now. You'll lie to the authorities, of course. No one will take the word of some upstart colonial.'' He smiled again, a tight cold smile that didn't reach his eyes. ''No one would not notice his disappearance, for that matter. Perhaps *that* would be the easiest solution, after all. If I spared my father a scandal, he might be less inclined to disinherit me.''

''You musn't talk like that, Graham. You know you don't mean it.'' She glanced away, so disturbed by the hatred in his eyes that she blurted out, ''I'm carrying his child. I just found out myself yesterday morning. Surely you can understand why I'm trapped in this marriage.''

He continued to stare at her, never once blinking. ''You little slut,'' he said softly. ''You were wed less than a month ago. How would you know you were pregnant unless you'd been lying with him behind my back?''

''I'm sorry, Graham. I wish I could explain how it happened.''

''Oh, you needn't explain. You're every inch the low-born whore my parents warned you were. All these months leading me on, never allowing me more than a kiss or two, and even those I had to beg for.''

She rose quickly and glanced at the door, his words justifying the initial unease she had felt when he touched her. It was too late to make him understand. Her only wish now was to bring this confrontation to a close without involving anyone else.

''I didn't mean to hurt you, Graham, but perhaps this has worked out for the best, after all. I doubt that I could ever have lived up to your parents' standards, and I don't think I'd want to. I'll ring for Phoebe to show you out.''

She had barely turned when she felt his hand clamp down on her shoulder. Fingers biting into her muscles with paralyzing cruelty, he spun her around and shoved her down onto the sofa. Slowly she sat up, her eyes never leaving his face.

''Don't make me call the servants, Graham. For the sake of the affection we shared this past year—''

He leaned over her, anger and thwarted passion thickening his voice. ''To think that I would have sullied my family's name by marrying you. I should've taken you long ago, gotten you out of my blood—''

''That's enough,'' she said, shrinking back. ''I realize you're upset, but—''

He fell upon her then, silencing the remainder of her sentence with a savage, hurting kiss. Revulsion swept through her as she felt his hot moist tongue poking between her lips and deep into her mouth, smothering her outraged cries. Frantic, she grasped a fistful of his hair and jerked his head backward, tearing her mouth free. Gasping, she twisted to dislodge him from the sofa, to throw off his crushing weight. She could understand his pain, his anger, even his hatred. But not this. Not brutal insensate lust as a vehicle for revenge.

"Hold still, you bitch," he growled. He slammed her back against the sofa, one hand covering her mouth, his arm flung across her chest. "I'll teach you to make a fool of me. This is how I should've treated you all along."

She bit his hand. She pounded his back with her fists. She could feel his free hand clumsily groping to fondle her breasts, and then he began whispering the vilest obscenities in her ear. Suddenly the scope of her danger jolted her into action: She forced herself to relax, to harness her dwindling strength. Then, rolling swiftly onto her side, she bucked upward against him with her entire weight and sent him tumbling over the edge of the sofa and to the floor.

Trembling, sick inside at what had almost happened, she sprang to her feet. "Take your coat and sword, and get out of here! Consider yourself fortunate my husband isn't home, or I—I'd have him throw you out."

"But your husband is home," a voice announced from behind them. "And he will throw the swine out after he's thrashed the life out of him."

Juliana whirled and saw Adam standing in the doorway, his face suffused with rage. Apparently he had just returned from the cove. His white linen shirt was unlaced and damp with sweat. A fine sprinkling of sand clung to his jackboots and surf-soaked breeches. At any other time she would have scolded him for not brushing himself off outside.

"It's over now, Adam." She stepped in front of Graham as though her physical presence alone could prevent a fight. "Let him leave. Nothing . . . nothing happened."

"Nothing happened?"

He pushed the door open and strode into the room, his eyes studying first her, then Graham, who by now had risen to his feet. "Your mouth is bruised, your gown disarrayed, and yet you dare to protect this swaggering monkey from the punishment he so justly deserves?''

She laid her hand on his arm. "Adam, please. It's not worth it.''

He brushed off her hand and roughly pushed past her. Juliana knew better than to try to stop him again. Her expression resigned, she moved behind the sofa, where, from the corner of her eye, she spied Robbie hovering in the doorway. Adam and Graham stood facing each other, their mutual hostility charging the air.

"Move aside, man," Graham said, straightening to his full height. "She isn't worth the time it would take to make formal arrangements for a duel. I for one have no intention of spilling blood over the deceitful little piece.''

Adam showed his teeth in a sinister grin. "Nor do I fancy a duel. For one thing, my anger demands an immediate outlet. For another, a ball fired from my pistol would surely find its way into your heart, and so swift an end to your miserable existence would leave me feeling cheated.''

"Then it's to be a brawl." Graham threw down his coat and sword. "I'm not surprised. One can inherit wealth, but not breeding—''

Adam hit him square in the jaw. Stunned, Graham staggered back, his fall broken by a sturdy cherrywood card table that scraped across the floor with his weight.

"Come on, you fancy scum," Adam said between his teeth. "Or does your courage only extend to attacking women?''

Blood trickling from the side of his mouth, Graham gripped the edge of the table and lunged forward. A crystal figurine tottered and crashed behind him. Its musical shattering could barely be heard over the sounds of heavy breathing and the surprised grunt of pain Adam gave as he felt a kneecap slam into his groin.

"You gutless worm!''

He shot out his hand to grab Graham by the ruffles of his shirtfront. Anticipating the assault, Graham jumped to the side, triumph flaring in his eyes.

The control Adam had managed to maintain over his boiling fury erupted like a volcano within him. Dispassionately, he discarded the hope he'd held for a clean fair fight. With a sharp glance he sized up his opponent. Years of tutelage under a fencing master. Riding to the hounds and shooting matches. A dirty fighter but not a faintheart, for all his foppish airs.

He began circling Graham, feet apart, knees slightly bent, his relaxed stance deceptive. Every muscle in his body had tightened, coiled and waiting to spring into service. Beneath the veneer of civilization, was this any different than facing an enemy in the forest? A faint movement behind the sofa drew his attention. Juliana. *She* made the difference.

He was ready when Graham sprang at him again, fists jabbing. Pivoting on the balls of his feet, he raised one forearm to shield his face, dropped the other to protect his throbbing groin. An ill-thrown punch glanced off his chin and grazed his cheek. In frustration, Graham lowered his head and charged him, knocking them both to the floor with a thud. Before Adam could throw him off, Graham smashed a fist into the side of his head.

White stars popped behind Adam's eyes. Blinking to clear his vision, he locked the heel of his right palm under Graham's chin and forced him backward, at the same time twisting onto his side. With minimum effort he could break Graham's neck. Instead, he pushed back only far enough to free himself. Graham landed within an inch of the fireplace, and Adam scrambled to his feet, head ringing.

"Get up," he hissed.

Face averted, Graham slid his hands behind him, bracing himself against the hearth to rise. Adam stared down at him in disgust, then glanced back at the towering figure in the doorway.

"Robbie, see that he gets into his coach and off my land."

"Aye," the big Scotsman answered. "Wi' pleasure, sir."

Adam's gaze veered to his wife, who stood watching him from behind the sofa with great distressed eyes. Her face, with its sudden delicate pallor, reminded him of the first snowdrop in February, a promise of spring to melt the cold rage inside him. In contrast to other young women of her station, she hadn't swooned or gone into hysterics at the sight of two men fighting over her. Nor, did he think, had she even secretly enjoyed it.

"Are you sure you're all right?"

She nodded, opened her mouth to answer, but was distracted by a sudden flash of movement as Graham angrily shook off the large callused hand Robbie had planted on his shoulder to hasten his exit.

"I'll thank you to keep your filthy hands off me, you hulking oaf." He collected his coat and sword and paused at the door, his face contorted into an ugly sneer. "I'll ruin you for this, Tremayne."

Robbie shoved him into the hallway. Moments later the clatter of hoofbeats and coach wheels rattling over the cobbled yard drifted through the parlor window.

Adam collapsed onto the sofa, grinning up at Juliana with devilish jubilation in his eyes. "Sit down, my love."

She started to obey, then froze, her face pinched with concern. "Oh, Adam, your jaw is beginning to swell up on one side. You'll have to come upstairs and let me rub it with ground-ivy ointment."

"Juliana, it's nothing. A little bruise. Sit down beside me."

"I can't," she cried. "I'm too upset to sit! Thank God he didn't seriously hurt you. I can't believe he behaved like such a barbarian. I don't know what I'd have done if you hadn't shown up when you did."

Adam's eyes grew stormy. "You'd have had a lifetime of his drunken abuse if you had eloped with him."

"Yes, Adam," she said quietly. "I see that now." She looked away, her mind in agitation. It was true, painfully true. Life with Graham would have been pure hell. She shivered lightly, her skin chilling as she recalled the repugnance of his touch. She would never have willingly involved Adam in a fight, but, oh, God, had she been relieved to see him in that doorway! She glanced at him again, reassuring herself that he wasn't hurt.

Another grin split his face. "I think it's safe to say that's the last you'll hear from Viscount Avonston."

Juliana looked out the window in time to see the elegant crested coach rounding the drive. She had heard that during pregnancy some women were prone to fanciful notions, to strange moods and baseless imaginings. Was that why she felt so strongly that their troubles with Graham had only begun?

Chapter Twenty

"Oh, madam, I d'wish ye'd change yer mind about tonight. The cove ain't safe even on a fair summer day. An' at night, in this weather, in yer condition . . ." Phoebe's voice trailed off on a tremulous note at the quelling glance her mistress threw her from the darkened corner of the library where she stood struggling into a pair of breeches.

"God's bones," Juliana muttered, leaning against the bookcase. "The lad who owned these must be built like a hoe. I can barely tuck the shirt in."

" 'Tis yer condition, ma'am," Phoebe ventured knowingly. "Pretty soon ye'll puff up like a woodcock."

"One more word about my condition, Phoebe, and I'll march straight to your uncle and let him know you and Robbie have been meeting in the gatehouse every evening."

"Oh, no, ma'am! Ee wouldn't!"

"Probably not. But I would box your ears. Now show me again how to open this passageway."

Withing minutes Juliana found herself squeezing behind one of the Doric columns flanking the fireplace. As she stared down the series of damp rough-hewn stone stairs, her thoughts centered on what she remembered of Mentreath's history. During Elizabeth's reign, Jesuit priests had been hidden in this same passageway and smuggled across the Channel to safety in France. Later, a little over a century ago during the civil war, Cavaliers hunted by Roundhead soldiers had also taken shelter here. The occupants of Mentreath have always been rebels, she reflected with a smile.

"I'll wait up 'ere for ee, madam," Phoebe whispered,

her face small and tense beneath the frilled mobcap. ''D'be careful.''

The column swung back into place with an echoing rumble, and then there was darkness. Juliana descended cautiously. She could hear the moisture dripping off the walls, could feel it as she extended her hand to guide her. She hadn't dared bring a candle or an oil lantern to light her way. No one must suspect that the lady of the manor had been at the cove tonight helping to land smuggled brandy.

Adam doesn't understand, she mused. He thinks my interest in the smuggling is a mere act of defiance. He doesn't realize that I want to help him, and his damned male pride won't admit I know more about the business than he ever will.

Presently she entered a low-ceilinged tunnel. Taller than the average Cornishwoman, she had to stoop to pass through it. Now she could hear the muffled clamor of the sea, waves bubbling into connecting caves, crashing and frothing against the cliffs. The air cooled, and at the end of the tunnel she saw a vast clammy cave whose entrance was well concealed, but not blocked, by a mass of upward-thrusting rock formation.

She stumbled over a coil of rope, slammed painfully into a shovel propped against the wall as she regained her balance. Suddenly a gigantic figure appeared at the mouth of the cave, holding aloft a leather-shielded lantern. Robbie!

''What the devil are ye aboot?'' he demanded.

''I—I had to relieve myself,'' she muttered in as deep a voice as she could manage.

''Ye could've done that in the water,'' he said gruffly. ''We've nae got all night.''

Satisfied that he had accepted her as one of the village lads, she followed him out of the cave through a shadowy indentation between the cliffs and toward the shoreline. Darkly clad shapes hurried past them, some shouldering brass-banded casks, others plunging into the surf to unload the small boats bumping the beach.

A French lugger, rigged fore-and-aft, lay anchored in the narrow entrance of the cove. Juliana felt a momentary stab of admiration for the captain who had the skill and daring to guide his ship between the treacherous reefs that had snared so many others before.

"Look sharp, lad!" Robbie gave her a light shove that sent her stumbling into the water. "That's Cap'n Delisle and Mr. Tremayne approaching now."

Clamping her mouth shut to keep from shivering, she waded out to meet the boat that bobbed toward her. A well-built blond man in a double-breasted navy serge coat sat in the bow.

"Give us a hand in!" he called to her in pleasantly accented English.

"Yes, sir," she cried, and as she hastened to obey, she fought the urge to sneak a glance at Adam.

And then she heard his voice, its rich familiar resonance warming her though she stood hip-deep in the icy pulsing surf.

"Help the lad, Robbie, before he capsizes the boat! The current's too strong for him."

Robbie ploughed through the waves toward the boat, glowering fiercely at Juliana. "Make yerself useful up on the beach loading the carts, runt! Ye'll nae get paid yer guinea if I catch ye dawdling again."

She scrambled onto the beach and strode across the pebble-littered cove, face hot with embarrassment. Bloody impertinent ape! She'd make him eat his words.

But her resolve shriveled as she lifted her head to watch the steady formation of smugglers, casks slung over their shoulders, ascending the steep pathway worn in a cleft in the cliffside. Hidden from view on the promontory above were a dozen heavy carts, some destined for public houses and warehouses as far away as London.

She stared up broodingly. Five months ago she'd not have given a second thought to making that climb. But now, with a child growing inside her, she simply couldn't take the risk. It had been a mistake to come here, attempting to recapture the freedom she had enjoyed at Rosmorna. First marriage and now impending motherhood had clipped her wings. Her only hope now was to return to the house unnoticed.

Adam jumped out of the boat as soon as he felt the bottom scraping sand. He strode in the direction of the cliffside pathway, his gaze scouring the beach for the supple, long-legged figure. Did she take him for such a dunce he couldn't recognize his own wife? To be sure, she had fooled him once with a similar disguise. But that had been a lifetime ago. Before he'd spent hours enjoying her lovely body, listening to her voice, studying her unconscious mannerisms.

"*Morbleu, mon ami!* What is the matter with you, Tremayne? Is there trouble? Have we been spotted?"

Adam turned to face the broad-shouldered French captain who had followed him from the boat. "There's trouble, yes, but not the kind you need worry about, Paul. It's the infuriating brat I married. She can't have gone far."

Astonishment spread across the Frenchman's craggy face. "Your wife is here? *Diable!* This is no place for a woman! I should take a hand to her, *mon ami.* If only for her own good."

"Don't think it hasn't crossed my mind," Adam said with a caustic smile. "Unfortunately, it wouldn't help. Cunning seems to be far more effective."

Paul chuckled. "Outfox the vixen, eh?"

"Precisely."

Suddenly Adam spotted a slender form skulking through the shadows cast by the overhanging cliffs. It had to be Juliana. But where the blazes was she going? Was it possible she'd tired of her game and wanted to return to the house?

"Paul, I want you to do me a favor. Run find me two men to bring me some brandy. Four casks will do. Have them deposit it outside the Priest's Cave."

Adam jogged toward the cave, reaching it a good thirty seconds before Juliana. Concealing himself behind the rock formation at the entrance, he waited until he heard her light, cautious tread on the pathway below.

"Where d'you think you're going?" he demanded, jumping out in front of her.

Juliana froze and smothered a scream, her mind and heart racing in unison. "I . . . I 'ave to relieve myself, sir," she said lamely.

"Very well. Go ahead."

"H-here? I'd hoped for a little privacy. Inside the cave, sir."

Adam smiled to himself. He knew why she wanted to get

into the cave. Well, he wasn't going to make it that easy for her. He would literally force her to reveal her identity.

"We're both men, aren't we? Pull down your breeches and get on with it. I need a hand carrying some brandy up to the house. My wife enjoys the occasional nip."

Juliana's fingernails dug into her palms as her mind spun in helpless circles. How was she to extricate herself from the situation without arousing his suspicion? How would she escape him?

A noise behind her diverted Adam's attention. Glancing back briefly, she noticed the tall, fair-haired captain coming toward them.

"Guess it must've been a false alarm, sir," she said quickly. "Where are them casks ee want me to carry?"

"Here." He walked down the pathway to the spot a few yards behind her where the porters had just dropped four six-gallon casks. "You're sure you've the strength to take the stairs with two of these?"

Juliana ignored the question. Keeping her chin tucked low, she rushed past him to lift the casks and sling them over her shoulder, one on her chest, the other behind her. Without looking back, she climbed the pathway into the cave. She prayed he wouldn't follow her; she'd have the devil's time shaking him if he did. And there was Phoebe to worry about now, too. The timid goose would confess to everything if Adam so much as blinked at her.

But Adam fully intended to finish what he had started. Hoisting the remaining casks over his shoulder, he gestured to Paul to follow him into the cave. He almost laughed at the Frenchman's bewildered expression. He was no doubt wondering what this unexplained turn of events had to do with finding the errant Mrs. Tremayne.

Juliana had just reached the foot of the stairs when she heard their footsteps behind her. Damn Adam and his whims! she thought savagely. Why did he have to interrupt the run for four casks of brandy?

"My wife enjoys the occasional nip," he'd said. What other insulting falsehoods had he spread about her?

She could hear his voice distinctly now, his footsteps coming nearer as though he was trying to catch up with her. She quickened her pace, but halfway up the stairs a cramp twisted her abdomen, the pain so severe she had to lower the casks and lean against the wall until it passed. Another cramp followed. Swallowing a groan, she realized she would have to leave the casks if she hoped to make it into the library and up to her bedroom before Adam could detain her again.

She turned to climb the remaining steps. A hand caught her elbow, whirled her around so forcefully she almost lost her footing.

"Not so fast, my lad," Adam said, nudging the casks with his foot. "You've forgotten these."

She bent, straightened swiftly with an involuntary gasp. "I can't," she said hoarsely. "It . . . it hurts—"

It was too dark for Adam to see her face, to see the genuine pain darkening her eyes. "Rubbish. A strong healthy lad like you has plenty of muscle for the job." He bent on one knee to lift the casks, stepped up beside her to hand them over her shoulder.

"Don't," she whimpered, pulling away from him as agony tore across her lower adbomen. "Oh, please don't—"

Chapter Twenty-one

Had it been a nightmare? She struggled to surface through the layers of drug-induced unconsciousness, disjointed images flitting through her mind, eluding her before she could bring them into focus. The cave. Robbie shoving her into the surf. Adam jumping out in front of her, ordering her to carry the casks up to the house. His cold glistening gray eyes.

She had to climb the stairs, warn Phoebe to hold her tongue. Something stopped her. Pain . . . shooting across her belly. And Adam again. Why did he want to hurt her?

"Why, Adam?" she moaned. "Why are you trying to hurt me?"

A low sympathetic voice answered her as if from a great distance. A hand touched her forehead, and she whimpered, fighting the darkness, frightened it would claim her again.

The stairs. Her mind seemed to balk at revealing what had happened after Adam caught up with her. Something horrible, she knew. Had he pushed her? Had she fallen?

Images swirled out of the blackness, beckoning her. She remembered a large man bending over her, whispering words she barely understood, gathering her gently into his arms. She could smell spindrift and sandalwood soap on his clothes. She felt safe in his arms. And then she felt nothing.

She opened her eyes and blinked against the unexpected early-morning brightness. Her tongue felt thick and swollen. Her temples throbbed. Gingerly she raised herself up on her elbows, anticipating pain, feeling only a cold emptiness inside her. She sank back into the pillows in dry-eyed grief. She had lost the baby.

"I think she's wakin', sir," a woman's voice whispered from across the room.

Juliana, drifting on the tide of her thoughts, only then realized she was not alone. Doris. Phoebe. Adam. She turned her head, as if by not seeing them, she could make them disappear.

"Go away," she said dully.

She heard a chair scrape, then footsteps, and she knew without looking that Adam had come to the bedside.

"How do you feel, my love?"

Grudgingly turning her head, she stared up at his tired, unshaven face. "You pushed me."

"No! How could you think such a thing?" He sat down on the edge of the bed, taking her hand. "You need to rest. Try not to think about it. It's all over."

She snatched her hand away, a tremor of hysteria in her voice. "You pushed me down the stairs!"

"He didn't, madam," Phoebe spoke up. "God's own truth."

"You collapsed in the library, Mrs. Tremayne." A man's voice, vaguely familiar to Juliana, addressed her from the doorway. "I carried you upstairs while your husband went to fetch the doctor. All the other male servants were on the beach at the time."

She moistened her lips. "Who . . . who are you?"

"Captain Paul Delisle, madame," he replied and bowed. "Forgive me for intruding. I was on my way downstairs when I heard voices coming from the room. I couldn't resist inquiring after your health."

She closed her eyes for several seconds. She remembered Adam dropping the casks over her shoulder, prodding her up the stairs. She must have made it to the library—she could visualize herself standing in front of the unlit fireplace. Phoebe had been curled up in a chair, snoring softly. Then the pain had returned and instinctively, she'd clutched her stomach and folded to her knees. The casks had rolled across the floor, and as she stared down at the carpet, she'd noticed a small puddle of bright red blood.

When her eyelids lifted, she saw that everyone except Adam had left the room. Emotion tightened her throat.

"It's your fault," she whispered savagely. "You made me lose that baby as surely as if you had pushed me down the stairs!"

He flinched at her outburst. "I didn't even know you were pregnant, Juliana. You never told me."

"I told you I was in pain!" She could tell by his face that she'd hurt him to the quick, and the knowledge filled her with bittersweet satisfaction, even though deep in her heart she realized that Adam had not deliberately played a part in causing her miscarriage, that he was wholly incapable of such cold-blooded malevolence. But as her own anguish and guilt mounted inside her with unbearable intensity, she couldn't seem to control the vicious words that sprang unbidden from her lips.

"You were determined to teach me another lesson, weren't you, Adam? What does it matter that it cost the life of our child?"

"That's cruel, Juliana. . . ."

Her chin trembled. "What happened was cruel."

Sorrow engulfed him. "It was my loss, too. Yours is not the only heart to grieve."

Sudden tears filled her eyes and spilled helplessly down her cheeks. His expression softening, Adam drew a handkerchief from his pocket and passed it to her, leaning forward to take her into his arms.

"Hold me tightly, darling. We can console each other."

She shrank from his touch. "Stay away from me. I don't want any consolation from you!"

She crawled to the opposite side of the bed, trembling, sobbing painfully. She felt the mattress lift as her husband rose and a sudden tide of desolation swept over her. *Don't leave me, Adam*, she implored him silently. *I didn't know what I was saying! Stay with me!* Seconds later she heard the door close quietly behind him.

Phoebe shook her head in disapproval at the barely touched breakfast tray Juliana had set on the floor. "The doctor said ye've to eat to build yer strength up, ma'am. Ee ain't eatin' enough to keep a chaffinch alive."

"You don't mean that Adam no longer cares for you because you lost his child?" Martin asked incredulously. "Did he actually say that?"

She shook her head, tears trembling on her eyelashes. "No. It's what I said that finished it. I . . . I accused him of pushing me down the stairs and causing the miscarriage." Her voice subsided to a whisper. "I practically called him a murderer."

"Good God, Juliana. How could you?"

"At the time I believed it was true. I was upset, Martin. I knew nothing of his past."

"You're referring to his first wife and their child?"

"Yes." Her head snapped up. "But how did you know?"

"Father told me a long time ago. He was afraid I'd keep hounding Adam about his past, and so he told me to shut me up. I swore I'd never breathe a word of it."

"Damnation, Martin! I thought we shared everything."

He hung his head, staring down at the carpet. "I know, I know. I shouldn't have kept it from you."

Silence stretched between them, then finally the bitterness faded from Juliana's face, and she reached out to take his hand.

"Enough about me for now. You haven't said a word about what happened to you in London. Couldn't you find work on stage?"

"I ran out of money before I had a decent chance to look. Stephen has control of my inheritance until I come of age, and he refused to give me a penny of it. London's unbelievably expensive. I barely had enough left for the coach fare here."

"What will you do with yourself now?" she asked gently.

"I'm not going back to Rosmorna to serve as Stephen's lackey," he said, his voice rising. "I . . . I've been considering taking Adam up on his offer to stay on here as his secretary."

Juliana sat up in surprise. "When did this happen?"

"Right before I came up to see you. I was just as taken aback as you are now. You wouldn't mind, would you, Juliana?"

She squeezed his hand. "Don't be silly. It's a marvelous

idea. I only wonder why Adam never broached the subject with me before.''

''That might have been difficult considering the fact that you're hiding yourself away in this room. Don't shut him out, Juliana. He is your husband. For both your sakes, you should give this marriage a chance.''

She lifted her hand free and got up from the windowseat, standing with her back toward him. ''It's not entirely up to me, Martin. Adam—Adam may have decided he doesn't want me anymore.''

''At least talk to him, Juliana. Let him know you don't blame him for the miscarriage.''

She turned to face him, the corner of her lower lip caught between her teeth. ''All right. I'll try. But, Martin, I'm so afraid. I'm so afraid nothing I say will do any good.''

Chapter Twenty-two

She stood outside the closed library door with her hand hovering an inch from the heavy brass knob. Approaching Adam to apologize had proven a frustrating task. In the past week she hadn't found a single opportunity to speak to him alone. She suspected he was avoiding her.

But there was only one way to know for certain. Drawing in a deep breath, she opened the door and entered the room. Before she could say a word, Adam spotted her and stood up behind his desk, almost guiltily, she noted.

She glanced around the room, self-conscious in the decidedly masculine atmosphere. Bookshelves crammed tight with leather-and-silk-bound volumes lined two entire walls. A billiard table stood before the brocade-curtained windows which looked out onto the garden. She hadn't realized it the night of her miscarriage, but of all the rooms in the house, this was the most comfortable, saturated with the previous owner's personality.

"Juliana?" Adam was watching her guardedly. "Is something the matter?"

Her courage faltering, she shook her head. If only he would smile at her, or even tease her with one of his silly little jokes. Anything to break the tension . . .

"I . . . thought I might look for a book to read in the evenings."

"Please do," he said politely. "My uncle accumulated a splendid library during his lifetime. I'm sure he would want us to appreciate it."

He sat down and returned his attention to the account book he had been working in. If he sensed that she had just made up an excuse to see him, his face betrayed no suspicion. In fact, the only hint of emotion Juliana interpreted in his blandly courteous demeanor was a faint annoyance that she had disturbed him. Studying him openly, she stepped away from the door.

"We can't continue to live this way, Adam. It's ridiculous."

He glanced up at her, his brow furrowing. "The repairs are being made as fast as possible, Juliana. The entire east wing should be finished by—"

"Damn you, don't play games with me, Adam! I wasn't referring to the house, and you know it."

He closed the book, finally granting her his full attention. "Yes," he said quietly.

"You've been avoiding me," she continued.

"Yes."

"May I ask why?"

He hesitated. "I thought it best under the circumstances." His voice cracked slightly. "My presence seems to upset you."

She clasped her hands together and walked to the side of his desk. "This isn't easy for me, Adam. I've come here to ask your forgiveness. The accusations I made that morning were cruel, and—"

"You were understandably distressed," he broke in, staring down at the stacks of paper on his desk. "There's no need to apologize."

"I disagree."

He looked up suddenly, pain darkening his eyes. "But it *was* my fault you lost the child, Juliana. I knew who you were the moment I saw you in the water. You were right. I wanted to teach you a lesson."

"Adam, if anyone is to blame—"

A knock sounded at the door, interrupting her carefully rehearsed speech.

"Adam, please tell whoever it is to go away. We have to talk."

But he was already out of his chair and crossing to the door, brushing past her as though she didn't exist. To be honest, he was relieved at the interruption. He wanted to believe Juliana, but he was suspicious of this abrupt reversal in

her attitude toward him. Had Martin put her up to this? he
wondered cynically. Had her brother played on her conscience, perhaps urged her to take pity on her poor suffering
husband? Well, it simply wasn't good enough. Juliana had
to change of her own free will. His pride wouldn't tolerate it
otherwise.

"I'm expecting an important letter," he told her. "I'm
afraid this discussion will have to wait."

Juliana leaned back against the desk, her heart aching for
him. In the course of their stormy relationship, he had always counseled her to face her feelings, to share with him
her deepest joys and sorrows. His love had cleansed her,
healed her, given her strength. And no matter how strongly
she resented having to marry him, she couldn't stand watching him suffer. Yet how could she help him, caught in his
dark lonely void of guilt and grief?

His voice penetrated her reverie. "That was Phoebe at the
door, Juliana. She said there's a Miss Polgarth here to see
you."

Juliana turned from the desk in surprise, inadvertently
knocking Adam's account book and a sheaf of papers onto
the floor. Embarrassed by her clumsiness, she knelt and
hastily began to retrieve what had fallen. As she picked up
the account book, a letter wedged between its pages, written
in a feminine hand, caught her eye. She only had time to
read the signature before Adam came forward to assist her.
Leigh Spencer.

"I'll take that," he said curtly, not giving her the chance
to protest. "You see to your caller. Miss Polgarth is Graham's cousin, isn't she?"

Juliana straightened, noticing that he had pocketed the
letter. "Yes. I can't imagine what she wants."

Adam frowned. "Would you like me to send Robbie in
with you?"

"Whatever for? Venetia isn't a vindictive person. If anything, she's come to beg forgiveness for Graham's behavior. I'm sure he's told her everything by now."

There was an uncomfortable silence. Juliana hated to go
with so much left unsaid between them.

"Adam, what we were discussing—"

"Not now, Juliana," he said tiredly. "You've a guest

waiting in the parlor, and I have important business on my mind. We have a prospective tenant for the old cottage on the cliffside road, and I'm working on the lease.''

"But you hired Martin to help. . . .''

"Another time, Juliana."

He sat down heavily at his desk, deliberately avoiding her probing gaze. He wasn't ready for another confrontation between them. Didn't she realize that he also grieved for the child they had lost? Didn't she realize that there was a limit to the hurt he could endure? He loved her more than ever, but was his love alone powerful enough to salvage the fragments of their shattered relationship? He just didn't know.

Tears pricked Juliana's eyelids as she left the library. Another time. But the longer this continued, the wider the gap between them would grow.

Twenty minutes later, she was serving Venetia tea and buttered scones in the parlor. After the first moment of awkwardness between them had passed, Venetia made it clear that Juliana's decision to marry Adam had not damaged their friendship.

"Oh, yes, Juliana. I can understand now why you married the man. I caught a glimpse of him from the hallway, and he's damnably attractive.'' Venetia shivered deliciously, then glanced out the window and grimaced. "But how you can live in such a *desolate* place is beyond my comprehension.''

Juliana took a sip of tea and smiled. "It's nice of you to come, Venetia. I know we're a bit isolated.''

"*Isolated?* Do you know there isn't a decent coaching road within miles of here?''

"It does take getting used to,'' Juliana admitted. "But I'm glad you came. I was afraid you wouldn't forgive me for not going through with the elopement. And, of course, there was that dreadful incident between Graham and Adam right here in this very room—''

"To hear Graham explain it, you'd think your husband had assaulted him without the least provocation.''

"It wasn't that way at all, Venetia.''

Venetia laid her head back against the armchair with a sigh. "I never thought it was. No, I know my cousin far too well.'' She leaned forward suddenly, her face losing its pleasantness. ''That's really why I'm here, Juliana. I think Graham's up to something.''

''I don't understand.''

''Neither do I exactly,'' Venetia went on. ''But lately he's been associating with the most unsavory characters, and I'm convinced he means your husband harm.''

''Has he told you this?''

''Well, not in so many words. But he has promised that Adam will rue the day he left America. And he's spending quite a lot of time in Helston. I'm sure it's only to keep an eye on you.''

Juliana finished her tea in silence, remembering Graham's parting words. She had often suspected a violent streak in his nature, lurking beneath the layers of breeding and refinement. And she knew him to be capable of surprising brutality. But what would he have to gain by pursuing his threat of revenge?

''Venetia, maybe we're making too much of this. After all, I did promise to elope with Graham. Jilted lovers have been known to fly into passionate rages before. He'll soon meet another girl and forget all about me.''

''I hope so. He's causing quite a stir in our set with his unsociable behavior.'' Venetia leaned across the table for her gloves, rising as she put them on. ''I've stayed longer than I intended. My poor coachman will probably never find his way back into town.''

''Then stay the night,'' Juliana said impulsively. ''I'd love to have you.''

''Can't. Graham's supposed to escort me to a wedding tomorrow afternoon. God willing, he'll stay sober until after the ceremony.''

''Venetia, I'm sorry—''

''But you shouldn't be,'' Venetia said. ''My reasons for wanting you to marry him were purely selfish. You see, Juliana, you're not like the other girls Graham has courted. You're natural and unspoiled, and most importantly, you're strong-willed enough to stand up to him. The truth is, I thought you could change him. I thought that once he married you, he'd stop drinking and gaming and settle down. Quite honestly, I'm fed up with looking after him and apologizing for his vulgar behavior.''

Juliana shook her head ruefully. ''He wouldn't have changed for me, Venetia.''

''No. I suppose he was bound to end up a drunkard sooner or later. Anyway, you're far better off with your colonial. At least you're leading a peaceful life.''

Juliana might have burst into laughter had she not felt so miserable over her unfruitful interview with Adam. A peaceful life? The words were still echoing a mocking refrain inside her head as she saw her friend to the door. Oh, Venetia, she longed to say, you couldn't possibly have been further from the truth!

Chapter Twenty-three

Winter was creeping up on the peninsula. Juliana noticed the change in the weather one afternoon during her first walk along the beach since the night of her miscarriage. Restless, bored with roaming the halls of Mentreath, she had escaped Mrs. Chenwiddy's guard and ventured out despite Phoebe's vehement warning that the ocean mists would ruin her health.

She smiled at the thought and raised her face to the sky, her nostrils quivering. Where in Cornwall did the sea dampness not penetrate?

A robust southwest wind had risen suddenly, and the sea churned restlessly against the rock-scarred shore, rushing in and drawing back with a bubbling hiss. Swollen cumulus clouds gathered on the horizon. Juliana studied them briefly and walked on, uncaring, the wind stinging her cheeks, whipping her clothing.

The weather matched her mood, she thought, or more precisely, the atmosphere within Mentreath these days. Gray, cold, the very air chilled with angry thoughts and suppressed emotions. She and Adam at the heart of an impending storm.

Adam was still avoiding her. It wasn't her imagination. Two weeks had passed since she'd tried to confront him in the library, and still she woke alone in their bed every morning. She rarely saw him during the day unless he needed her opinion on some aspect of the repairs in progress. More often than not she supped with her brother, and she had enough pride to prevent herself from inquiring of anyone where and how her husband spent his time. He had moved into the newly remodeled east wing and once, out of curiosity, she paid a late-night visit to his bedchamber only to discover the room empty. She might have suspected him of infidelity had they lived elsewhere. But it seemed unlikely that he'd taken to tumbling a shepherd's daughter in the village.

She stopped suddenly and stared up in dismay. Thirty paces or so from where she stood loomed the rock formation that concealed the Priest's Cave, the smuggler's shelter which housed the hidden staircase into the library. How had she come here of all places? She'd meant to walk in the opposite direction.

She squeezed her eyes shut as if she could blot out all the horror of her miscarriage and the soul-wrenching anguish she had suffered afterward. Why? her heart cried. Why did it have to happen? Adam's child—oh, she would have loved that baby fiercely, no matter what her relationship with its father!

She opened her eyes and turned her face to stare out across the sea, allowing the pain to flow through her as the tears trickled down her cheeks. It had been difficult to forgive Adam for what had happened that night. It was impossible to forgive herself.

Captain Paul Delisle had almost reached the end of the cliff path when, on impulse, he swiveled his head and glanced along the beach. Out of habit he lifted his gaze and searched the horizon for revenue cutters. There was no activity in the cove. The few fishermen about had brought in their boats at the first sign of the storm.

He yawned, raising a hand to rub across his eyes. He was tired. He'd been awake since before dawn evading a revenuer who had spotted him halfway across the Channel. He wanted a shave and a pot of strong coffee laced with brandy, preferably his own Norman Calvados.

He drew his thick serge coat up over his neck, half turning. And then he saw the graceful figure standing near the cave. Veiled in sea mist, with her rich auburn hair unbound, she was even more lovely than he remembered.

He hesitated, his body pleading for rest, his heart constricting with an unfamiliar longing. What right had he to disturb her grief? Obviously that was why she had returned to the cave. The sight of him would do nothing to ease her sadness.

And yet all of a sudden he found himself retracing his path, long, firm-muscled legs cutting down the cliff and carrying him across the beach with rolling catlike steps until he stood several feet behind Juliana. She had not noticed him, and for over a minute he wavered, torn between announcing himself and slipping away undetected.

I want her, he thought incredulously, and then he almost laughed aloud at his schoolboyish timidity. During his brief naval career he had fought greater battles than the conquest of a woman's heart; he had overcome more formidable foes than a possessive husband. And how could he forget that through his veins flowed the blood of Viking ancestors, the ruthless warriors who had invaded his native Normandy centuries ago?

He saw Juliana turn then and notice him, and he acknowledged her with a self-conscious smile. He did not consider himself a handsome man. His coarse mane of tawny gold hair framed a craggy face devoid of a single refined feature. Thick golden eyebrows shaded the deeply indented sockets of his dark blue eyes. Above the squarish jaw and full-lipped mouth, his prominent nose, broken during a dockside scuffle, dominated the rugged terrain of his face. And yet women found him attractive. At thirty-seven he had come to accept the peculiar fascination of his ugliness without any compulsion to analyze it.

"Captain Delisle?"

He started, his heart accelerating as he watched her approach him. "I didn't want to disturb you," he began. "I was on the way to your house when I spotted you. Perhaps you could help me locate your husband."

"That I doubt, captain. However, I will walk you to the house and offer you supper." Summoning a smile, she linked her arm through his, furtively raising her free hand to brush away the evidence of her tears.

"I hope this doesn't mean that you've urgent business with Adam. I haven't a clue where he is or when he'll return. You've probably seen more of him than I have lately."

"Actually, I've seen him only once," Paul said. "I assumed he was busy renovating the old house."

Juliana shrugged. "Adam's relegated most of the responsibility for that to my brother. Whatever it is that claims his time doesn't concern Mentreath. But of course, there are other properties along the coast.''

Paul nodded courteously. ''*Bien sûr.* That must be it.''

They continued across the cove in silence, Juliana leaning lightly against Paul's arm. The tension in her voice, on her face, when she discussed Adam had not escaped his notice, and he had to exercise restraint not to probe further. Was her marriage deteriorating? Was she unhappy? He dared not pose such personal questions on the strength of their short acquaintance.

''I admit it surprised me to see you here this soon after the—the unfortunate accident,'' he remarked delicately.

''I'm not one to make an invalid of myself, captain.'' She stopped and looked up at him. ''I never have thanked you for helping me that night, have I? It all must have seemed very strange to you—''

Suddenly Paul felt Juliana stiffen and break away from him. Following the direction of her gaze, he turned his head and saw Adam striding down the cliff path toward them.

Masking his disappointment, he raised an arm in greeting. ''Adam!'' he shouted. ''Your wife and I were just looking for you.''

Adam reached them moments later, acknowledging Paul with a curt nod of his head before he brought his attention to Juliana. What was she doing alone on the beach with the Frenchman? he wondered. What had they been discussing so intently before he interrupted them?

''You've walked a considerable distance from the house, Juliana,'' he said crisply, making no attempt to hide his disapproval. ''You shouldn't overexert yourself so soon after—''

''I'm perfectly well now, Adam,'' she inserted firmly. ''In fact, I've worked up quite an appetite.'' Her eyes glossed over him with a chilly glance that signaled how strongly she resented his attitude. She wondered if he was trying to embarrass her in front of Paul. She wondered where *he* had been all morning. ''What brings *you* this far from the house, Adam?'' she asked, overcome with curiosity.

''I had business to attend to.''

''Smuggling business?'' Paul inquired, his interest roused.

Adam frowned. ''No. It was . . . I paid a visit to the new

tenant in the cliffside cottage. She's an ailing widow living all alone, and I wanted to check that the roof had been repaired for the winter. I was on my way back to Mentreath when I saw you walking. I thought I might ask Doris if she knows of a reliable maidservant for hire in Penlyn.'' He leveled his gaze on Paul, his frown deepening. He was coming to like the man less and less, annoyed at the immediate interest Paul and Juliana had taken in each other. And what was he doing back at Mentreath this soon? he wondered, fanning the flames of his own jealousy.

''You've come at an awkward time, Paul,'' he said, not caring if he sounded rude, thinking that perhaps the man needed to be told outright that his presence wasn't particularly wanted. ''I have a hectic week ahead. I didn't expect you for at least another fortnight.''

Paul shrugged, his expression remaining blandly pleasant. The conversation so far had confirmed his suspicions of trouble in this marriage. Perhaps he had come into Juliana's life at precisely the right time, after all.

''The weather is changing, *mon ami*. I thought you'd like to know well in advance what was planned for the next run. And I, too, needed to settle a few business arrangements in the village. But if my presence inconveniences you, I could easily find lodgings elsewhere.''

''You'll do nothing of the sort,'' Juliana said. ''Doris can ready a room for you while we have supper.''

''Only if it's not an imposition,'' Paul said cautiously. ''I'll have to return to my ship to inform my crew of my whereabouts.''

Juliana nodded, satisfied. ''Adam and I will walk on ahead to the house. I'd like to bathe before supper.''

The moment Paul was out of earshot, Adam gave vent to his poorly concealed irritation. ''Why did you do that?'' he demanded. ''You heard me say I had a busy week ahead. I don't have time to entertain guests.''

''Well, I do,'' she retorted, smiling coldly. ''As a matter of fact, I've more time on my hands than I know what to do with.''

He turned away, scowling into the distance. ''I have to go into Helston the day after tomorrow for a meeting with my banker. He'll have to be gone by then.''

"As you wish, Adam."

He started to walk away and then stopped and turned, slowly extending his arm to her. "Hold on to me until we're up the path," he told her gruffly. "This is no place for you to be walking alone." His eyes met hers. "But then you weren't alone, were you? For all I know, your meeting with Captain Delisle was planned."

"Planned?" she echoed. And then, as understanding blossomed, she gave a short burst of laughter at the absurdity of his suspicions. "This is only the second time in my life I've even seen the man, Adam. How on earth could I possibly have arranged a rendezvous with him?"

He shifted his gaze uncomfortably. "I suppose I did jump to conclusions. But there is something predatory about the way he looks at you."

"I hadn't noticed." A faintly derisive smile lifted her lips. "Maybe he senses that I'm a neglected wife. Some men have an uncanny intuition about women who are susceptible to romantic entanglements."

Adam's head lifted sharply, his eyes searching her face. "And are you susceptible, my dear?"

"I didn't say that."

"You bloody well hinted at it."

"Would it surprise you if I was?" she asked. "This is the most intimate conversation we've had in weeks. The servants are starting to gossip about us."

"Then let them," Adam said wearily. "I've more pressing matters to consider than wagging tongues. My uncle's fortune is going fast to pay off an incredible collection of debts he managed to accumulate and then ignore. I'd never have ordered the repairs on Mentreath had I known how much he owed."

Juliana took his arm as he outstretched it again, and carefully they completed the steep pathway ascent. Brooding over what Adam had told her, Juliana did not speak again until they were on the outskirts of the estate.

"You should've told me this before, Adam," she said. "I have a right to know."

He sighed. "I saw no reason to worry you. You've been through enough lately."

"But perhaps I could have helped. We still have the money from my dowry."

"A trifling sum," he muttered. "Besides, I wouldn't touch a halfpenny of your cursed money after all the fuss you made over it. No, I'll work things out in my own fashion, thank you."

He pivoted and strode off in the direction of the house, his boots crunching on the freshly graveled drive. Curbing the urge to curse aloud in frustration, Juliana hurried after him. Then as she reached him, he turned and stared at her, his impatience waning.

"I don't want you to worry," he said in a clipped voice. "If I can arrange to mortgage some of the properties my uncle left me, we won't end up in debtor's prison. Now kindly forget the matter. Your brother and I are supposed to go over the accounts this evening, and I'd like a clear mind."

Falling into step with him, Juliana felt an unexpected response of compassion aroused inside her. So, now they had financial troubles on top of their marital discord. It shed light on a few things—why Adam spent hours in the library examining ledgers, why he'd hired Martin to help in handling the estate. Unfortunately, it didn't explain where he had been spending his nights of late, and that weighed far more heavily on her mind than the prospect of landing in any debtor's prison.

During supper that evening, Juliana found herself relaxing for the first time in over a month. Paul Delisle proved a splendid conversationalist, entertaining her with tales of his career as a naval officer. Unlike Adam, he hadn't received a formal education, but he was well-read and surprisingly conversant on a number of subjects. But more importantly, he didn't exclude her when the talk turned to smuggling.

"The weather will more or less decide how much trade we'll do this winter," he was telling Adam. "We'll make one last run at the end of the month, but after that, well, we'll see."

Juliana smiled at him across the table. "You don't strike me as the type of seaman afraid of sailing through a storm, captain."

"In Cornwall it's almost a necessity, madame," he said with an eloquent shrug of his shoulders. "*Malheureusement,* I had to learn to navigate these waters from experience. I lost my first ship during a storm to the rocks near the smugglers' cave where we met on the beach today. Were it not for your husband's uncle, my men and I might have lost our lives as well."

"You're lucky the wreckers didn't get to you first, captain," Juliana said.

Annoyed at his wife's rapt expression, Adam deliberately changed the subject. "You wanted to discuss the next run with me, Paul."

The Frenchman dragged his attention away from Juliana to reply. "Yes. Brandy from Calais. But I think I should warn you that the King's cutters have been unusually active in this area lately. I can't understand it. It's almost as though they've been tipped off."

Adam frowned thoughtfully. "This is the worst possible time for me to become embroiled in controversy. I'm trying to impress a certain prominent banker. I doubt he'd consider me a sound financial risk if my name were published for smuggling in the *London Gazette.*"

For a moment no one spoke. Then Paul leaned forward, bracing his large elbows on the table.

"Of course, it's not necessary for you to take part personally in the venture. Old Jack knows how to run the operation. You could hardly be held accountable for what your servants do behind your back."

"We could give a party that same night, Adam," Juliana suggested. "A ball to introduce ourselves to our neighbors. With so many witnesses present, no one would be able to associate you with the activity at the cove."

Paul nodded approvingly. "That should help divert suspicion from you until your legitimate business transactions have been finalized."

Adam's face relaxed. "It couldn't hurt. But are you certain you feel up to it, Juliana? I'm afraid we'll have to invite all the local gentry."

"Doris will help. And with the ballroom just finished—" She stopped as the door behind her opened and Jack Chenwiddy shuffled into the room.

" 'Scuse me all," he said, bowing. "There be a bit of trouble down at the cliffside cottage, sir. Seems the wind is howlin' as to snatch the roof off. The widow's worried she'll be blowed into the sea."

"What does she expect us to do?" Juliana asked, amused.

Jack shrugged. "Dunno, ma'am."

"Send my brother over to talk to her then. He has a way with old ladies."

"Martin has enough to do with the accounts," Adam said, rising. "I'll take care of this. Jack, send word to Mr. Pendarvis in the library that our work is to be postponed until the morning."

He left the room before Juliana had a chance to detain him, his face grim and preoccupied.

"Well, I never guessed my husband had such a gallant side to his nature," Juliana joked, in an unsuccessful attempt to hide her embarrassment at Adam's hasty departure.

Paul merely smiled, not daring to comment. Earlier this morning he had walked past the cliffside cottage and had noticed a lovely young woman gathering herbs in the garden. Could that be the ailing widow Adam referred to? If so, she appeared the very picture of robust health, her face luminous, her long silver-blonde hair flowing over her plump rounded shoulders.

"You're daydreaming, captain."

"What?" The golden lion's head lifted. "Forgive me, madame. How rude of me."

"Not nearly as rude as my husband leaving us the way he did," Juliana said with a lightheartedness she didn't feel. "I see you've finished your Madeira, captain. Are you up to a walk around the garden before you retire?"

"But the wind—and it's going to rain any minute now."

"So much the better. Wait here while I get my cloak."

They strolled in the garden for only minutes before the rain sent them dashing back to the shelter of the house. Like children they stood in the entrance porch and laughed helplessly while Doris scolded and clucked over their dripping hair and soggy clothes.

"Into the great hall to dry off before the fire," she ordered.

There, basking in the warmth of the blazing flames, they drank more Madeira and recited poetry until the grandfather clock in the long gallery upstairs chimed one.

Suddenly self-conscious, Juliana got up from her chair. "I didn't realize it was this late. The rain must've stopped, or we'd never had heard the clock."

Paul stood, feeling deflated. The spell had been broken. He knew that her mind had turned inevitably to Adam, wondering where he was, why he hadn't returned.

"I'll have Phoebe show you upstairs," she said. "I hope you don't mind staying in Adam's room tonight. It's our only other serviceable chamber at the moment."

Color stung Juliana's cheeks as she noticed Paul's eyes widen. Without intending to, she had just informed him—a casual acquaintance—that she and Adam kept separate beds. She tried not to think about where Adam would sleep tonight.

Adam waited alone in the library until he could no longer hear the voices in the great hall. Wearily he made his way around the room, extinguishing the candles in the gilt wall sconces. It seemed that his wife had enjoyed herself during his absence. Bitterly he realized that they had never spent an evening together drinking and reciting poetry.

He was in a black mood. As if the unhappy state of his marriage and the prospect of financial ruin weren't enough to drag him down, he had recently been shouldered with an additional burden in the person of Leigh Spencer, his late wife Lucy's seventeen-year-old sister. Unwed, entering her fourth month of pregnancy, she had risked sailing all the way from the Virginia colony to beg his protection.

"My father's disowned me, Adam." She had wept in his arms. "And you were always so kind to me. I—I had no one else to turn to."

"What about the child's father, Leigh? He has a moral obligation to take care of you." But even as he asked, he had guessed the answer.

Her sobbing loudened. "A married man, Adam. My father almost killed me when I told him. He was terrified someone else would find out. He has his practice to consider. Adultery is an unpardonable sin in Williamsburg society."

Perhaps it was guilt, a sense of obligation to Lucy's memory, but he couldn't turn Leigh away—at least not until she'd delivered her bastard and he had figured out how to send her back to America. Till then he agreed she could live in the old cottage where she would pose as the bereaved widow of a sailor recently drowned at sea. Intensely private themselves, the villagers of Penlyn weren't likely to question her story.

As if I don't have enough to worry about, he thought disgustedly. But what else could he have done? By the time he received her last letter, she had already set sail for Cornwall, confident he would befriend her. How could he refuse to help her after she'd crossed an ocean to find him?

He sat down on the edge of the desk and listened. Outdoors all was quiet, recovering after the storm. Inside, the only sound was the inevitable creaking and settling of the old house. It was late. In only a few hours he and Martin would confer in this very room, and he was tired.

But Delisle was no doubt using his room, and he couldn't bring himself to climb the stairs and enter the bedchamber he and Juliana once shared. Impossible to lie beside her, burning with longing but not touching her. For despite her apologies, he was afraid that she still hadn't forgiven him for the part he played in her miscarriage, that she wasn't ready to welcome his lovemaking. Why else hadn't she asked him to return to their chamber? His heart chilled with sudden suspicion. Could she be contemplating taking Delisle as a lover? Was her friendship with the bold Frenchman leading up to an affair? The ugliness of his doubts slowly subsided as his instincts reassured him of her fidelity. Anyway, with no evidence to the contrary, he had little choice but to trust her.

Loosening his neckcloth, he swung to the floor and lowered himself into a chair with his legs propped upon the desktop. His muscles tightened, his spine stiffened in protest, but he ignored the discomfort. He had once spent twenty-four hours hidden in a tree during a blizzard in New France. He wouldn't seek his wife's bed again without an invitation.

Juliana lay awake, staring out the window at the moon until it disappeared from the heavens and ribbons of golden dawn streaked the sky. Why had she expected Adam to come to her tonight? Why had she even wanted him to?

Refusing to wonder where he'd spent the night, she closed her eyes as watery morning light dispelled shadows around the room. Captain Delisle had asked to escort her into Lizard Town today for the country fair. She hadn't given him an answer, half hoping that Adam would offer to take her. Of course, he wouldn't. There seemed to be no room in their relationship for simple pleasures.

Well, he can't complain if I succumb to the attentions of a charming man who's already half in love with me, she thought defensively. But it wasn't Paul's touch her body ached for; it wasn't his company that her heart craved.

How could she even think of another man when she was just beginning to realize that she had fallen in love with her own husband?

It was still early. Unable to remain alone with her tortured thoughts a minute longer, Juliana had dressed in a bright yellow silk gown and left the bedchamber. From the depths of the house she heard the sounds of the servants engaged in their morning chores—pots and pans clattering in the kitchen, the old wagon rumbling across the courtyard on its way to market. She'd decided she would go to the fair today—with or without an escort. She felt she needed a frivolous diversion to take her mind off her problems.

She had just started to descend the staircase when she spotted Adam crossing the great hall. His head was bent, his expression so dispirited that her heart ached in sympathy for whatever burdened him. Then, as he walked toward the stairs, she noticed that his clothes were wrinkled, his neckcloth hanging loosely around his strong brown throat. He must have stayed out all night, she realized sickly. But where could he have gone after he visited the cliffside cottage? She still refused to consider the possibility that he'd found someone else. No, she wouldn't believe it! Their relationship couldn't have deteriorated to that point yet.

"Juliana—I didn't notice you there."

Adam looked up and stared, startled to discover her standing only four steps above him. Massaging his forehead wearily, he blinked against the sunlight that broke through the windows in the upper hallway. "I guess my mind isn't functioning properly yet. I didn't sleep much last night."

"So I gathered," she said, her lips firming with unconscious disapproval. Pride overrode suspicion to keep her from asking him where he'd spent the night.

Adam was too tired to try to figure out what she meant by the clipped remark. He was too tired to figure anything out. Quelling the urge to interrogate her about the evening she had passed with Delisle, he groped for a neutral topic.

"I didn't expect to find you about this early. Couldn't you sleep through all the din in the courtyard?"

"No." She shook her head, relieved and at the same time disturbed by the way he had manipulated their conversation into meaningless chatter. Was he trying to prevent her from asking where he'd been all night, or was this his way of skirting confrontation?

"I didn't sleep well either," she admitted. "I just kept thinking. . . ."

"About what?" Concern for her crept unbidden into his voice, mellowing its deep-toned roughness. "Oh, Lord, Juliana, is it the baby again? Are you still torturing yourself over the miscarriage?"

"No. No, it wasn't that," she said quickly, pushing away the hurting thoughts that leaped into her mind. "I'm trying not to think about it anymore. I told you I don't hold you responsible, and I believe it's best if we just leave it at that. In fact, I'd prefer we didn't discuss it again."

"But we never really did discuss it, Juliana. Not in terms of how we felt inside, or of how it affected our lives . . . our marriage. The kind of grief we experienced is too profound to simply fade away with time."

She shut her eyes tightly, feeling a lone warm tear trickling down the side of her nose. It was cruel of him to press her into dredging up those painful emotions. What good would it do? What could it possibly change? "It hurts," she whispered thickly. "Oh, God, Adam, you can't know how much it hurts to think of that innocent little soul— To think that I never even had a . . . c-chance to-to hold—"

He scaled the few steps that separated them and crushed her against his chest as great uncontrollable sobs tore through her slender frame. "This is the second child I've lost, Juliana,'' he said quietly, his voice lowering with emotion. ''Just because I'm a man doesn't mean that I can't share your sorrow.''

Juliana scarcely heard his softly spoken words, so upset that she wished only to escape him and the terrible pain he was forcing her to relive. What did he hope to accomplish? No amount of discussion or soul-searching would bring their baby back. But Adam refused to release her, and so finally she surrendered to the pain, weeping piteously against his chest until she was utterly spent.

There was silence then, and a healing current flowed through them as together their hearts mourned and absorbed each other's pain. Hope for a new beginning stirred faintly inside Adam. Despite whatever else lay unresolved between them, they had begun to accept and to console each other over their mutual loss. Perhaps one day soon they would even be able to discuss their feelings easily, to give and to receive the balm of forgiveness and understanding. Could this moment be a critical point in their relationship?

''That's just fine for the time being,'' he said gently, holding her away from him so that he could look down into her face. ''Now then. It appears to be a lovely day outside. What had you planned for yourself that you're wearing that fetching yellow dress?''

Her guard lowered, Juliana answered him honestly without any thought to his reaction. ''Paul invited me to go to the fair today. I hadn't planned on attending, but then I decided it might do me good. To get my mind off . . . everything.''

''I see.'' Adam slowly released her from his hold, his face stiff as resentment stealthily spread through him. The Frenchman again. She must have enjoyed his company so immensely that she couldn't wait to spend an entire day with him. Heaven help him, was there never to be harmony between them? It seemed as if they conquered one obstacle only to encounter a larger one looming on the horizon.

''You could come with us, Adam,'' she said awkwardly, wishing he would say something to explain his abrupt withdrawal.

He smiled coolly, taking his time before he answered her. He couldn't help wondering how disappointed she'd be if he agreed to go. ''Your brother and I have to work on drawing up my financial statement today, Juliana. I believe I've explained to you how important it is to straighten out our business affairs.''

"Yes. I—I understand."

She dropped her gaze confusedly, unwilling for him to read the anguished longing in her eyes. *Stop me, Adam,* she begged him silently. *Tell me you want me to stay home with you today. Forbid me to go—at least give me some indication that you still care about me!*

Adam's mind festered with doubt. Was she testing him? Did she expect him to forbid her to go so that she could rail at him for restricting her freedom? It would be so characteristic of Juliana to defy him for the sheer hell of it. But if she had it in her heart to betray him, he certainly couldn't stop her.

"I hope you have a pleasant day together," he drawled finally, turning to finish climbing the staircase.

"Adam—" She called his name in unthinking supplication, still hoping somehow to elicit the smallest sign that she hadn't lost him totally. "Are you sure—well, you're certain that you don't mind if Paul takes me?"

Mind? his heart echoed jealously. Of course, he minded! But why was she even bothering to ask? A guilty conscience over whatever sins she planned to commit? Or was it a tactic to allay his suspicions? And even if at this moment she had the most innocent intentions, he wasn't convinced that her commitment to their marriage was strong enough to fight off any future temptation of infidelity.

"No, Juliana," he said after another short silence. "I don't mind at all."

"Fine," she heard herself respond, forcing a shaky smile to hide her hurt disappointment. "I'm glad," she lied. "To tell the truth, I really had my heart set on going."

"Oh, I've no doubt of that, my dear," Adam said, staring at her over his shoulder. And with a smile that chilled her like a blast of winter wind, he turned and left her standing alone on the staircase, hopeless despair benumbing her entire being.

Chapter Twenty-four

Warm topaz firelight cast a cozy glow around the bedchamber as Juliana studied her reflection in the yellowed looking glass. It was almost time to go downstairs. Thank heaven the tension of the past few months didn't seem to show in her appearance on this the evening of her social debut as Mrs. Adam Tremayne of Mentreath.

Of course, the skillfully designed clothes that Adam had bought her in Helston certainly didn't hurt. Over her chemise and snugly laced corset, she wore a hyacinth-blue damask gown with ruffled three-quarter-length sleeves and a low, square neckline embroidered with miniature gold butterflies. Its stomacher was made of white satin; the gossamer-sheer gold silk overskirt was panniered at each side and split in front to display her quilted cream-colored petticoats.

"Ye're absolutely lovely, ma'am," Phoebe announced from beside the bed, where she'd laid out Juliana's painted ivory fan and stockings. " 'Tis a shame ee don't dress up more often."

Frowning critically, Juliana flicked a hare's foot dipped in rice powder across her nose, chin, and cheeks. As a rule she didn't use cosmetics, but for the party she'd lightly rouged her cheekbones, applied a trace of walnut oil to her eyebrows and lashes, and dabbed red alkanet-root balm on her lips. Her luxuriant auburn hair was arranged in a loose chignon with tiers of curls falling from each temple. Strategically positioned pearl-knobbed bodkins held the elegant coiffure in place.

"You don't think I'm overdressed, do you? After all, the invitations did say this was a 'Come as you fancy' party."

194

"And ee can wager the local gentry'll be dressed to the teeth in all their moth-eaten finery and imitation jewels. No, ma'am, 'tis more like ye'll be underdressed . . . especially if ee go downstairs without yer shoes and stockings."

"Oh, Lord." Juliana glanced down in dismay at her bare toes peeping out from beneath the petticoats. "I almost forgot."

Skirts rustling, she picked a careful path to the bed around the piles of boxes and rumpled tissue paper covering the bare wood floor.

"This chamber is a disgrace, Phoebe. We'll have to do something about it in the morning."

"Well, it don't 'elp havin' all this ugly old furniture about the place, ma'am. Dunno why ee wanted it brung in 'ere anyway."

"Because the room was as stark and depressing as a monk's cell."

And because it gave me something to do to keep my mind off Adam, she finished to herself. She sat down on the bed and felt a reluctant smile forming on her lips as her gaze wandered about the room. The latest furnishings were what she and Phoebe had discovered in the solar one day under musty old muslin sheets.

On one side of the room was a Queen Anne satinwood dressing-table mounted on a base of tiny drawers. Before it was a heavily carved Elizabethan joined chair. A functional oaken clothes press relieved the bareness of the wall opposite the fireplace. An uncomfortable settle, also of oak, sat beneath the window. And then there was the lidded mule chest, a cumbersome walnut piece from the Stuart period that she and Phoebe had dragged into the corner behind the door. Ruefully she concluded that the furnishings in the room were as mismatched as the master and mistress of the house.

She peeled on her patterned stockings and lace garters, then stepped into a pair of blue leather dancing pumps. Reaching behind her for the fan, she slid off the bed and went to the looking glass for a final inspection.

"It doesn't look at all like me, Phoebe," she said, shaking her head. "This glass is so old, it hides all my imperfections."

"Ee ain't got none, ma'am. Now, what about jewels?

Ye'll 'ave to wear somethin' with yer bosoms so bare.''
Phoebe snapped open the teakwood jewelry coffer on the
dressing table, her eyes widening in astonishment. ''Lord,
ma'am,'' she breathed. ''Where did this come from? The
colors go perfect with yer gown.''

Juliana looked down, a tiny frown etched between her
brows. Nestled in Phoebe's palm was a solid gold necklace
set with sapphires and amethysts. Paul Delisle had sent it to
her the day before yesterday with a note enclosed telling her
how much he'd enjoyed their day together at the fair. She
couldn't keep the necklace, of course. She'd have to return
it the next time she saw him.

''It belonged to Captain Delisle's mother. Hold it up to
my neck a moment so that I can compare the colors.''

''Captian Delisle, ma'am? Uh-huh. I see.''

''Do I detect a note of disapproval in your voice,
Phoebe?'' Juliana laughed softly. ''No. I won't wear it.
'Twould be wrong, considering I have to give it back. Find
my pearl choker and fasten it on instead. And hurry. I think I
can already hear a coach in the drive.''

The evening began on a pleasant note, Juliana losing
count of the many compliments she received. The atmosphere was of relaxed gentility, the guests including a local
magistrate, a prosperous farmer, several country squires and
their wives, and a few businessmen from Helston and Lizard
Point. She had thought it a worthwhile extravagance to offer
a sumptuous buffet that featured ham, fish, goose, mutton,
turkey, venison, and assorted vegetables in season. For dessert there were sweetmeats, lemon-hazelnut torte, custard-
filled pastries, and apple and gooseberry pies. The
Wedgwood plates had been piled high and wiped clean, and
even now as the guests assembled in the ballroom, strong
beer, punch, and burgundy flowed liberally.

She surveyed the ballroom with a sense of satisfaction.
The cut-glass chandeliers had been dismantled and reassem-
bled, the imported German drops and prisms soaked in vinegar and buffed to sparkle like stars against the recently
plastered ceiling. The wall sconces and the fireplace's brass
grate, screen, and andirons had been polished to a brilliant
gloss with ashes and mutton fat. Modern sash windows had
been installed in place of the outdated casements, the wood-

work freshly gilded. Plush red brocade hangings covered the walls, and in the corner niches sat baskets of the garden's last golden winter daffodils.

Adam had escorted a small group of gentlemen into the parlor, where thin-legged card tables had been placed, and brandy and cigars supplied. In the great hall, under Mrs. Chenwiddy's watchful eye, two gypsy fortune-tellers summoned from the woods fringing the estate read palms as entertainment for the female guests. Their escort, a male gypsy guitarist, provided soft background music.

"Allow me to congratulate you on your success as a hostess, ma'am."

Juliana turned, her eyes lighting up. It seemed that by tacit accord she and Adam had called a truce for the evening. With the run already under way, they dared not draw any undue attention to themselves by quarreling in public. Even so, Adam's praise took her by surprise.

"And you, sir, make a most attractive host."

"I do?" His gray eyes sparkled at her. "I don't look silly?"

"Well—" She pretended to regard him through narrowed eyelids.

He wore a suit of fashionable crimson velvet with an eggshell-white silk shirt and a short flared coat garnished with silver buttons. The snowy whiteness of his linen cravat showed up his dark complexion. His tightly molded breeches and black silk stockings emphasized his powerful thighs and muscular calves.

"Not even a little silly, " she said with a smile. "In fact, you look quite handsome. But don't expect me to repeat that tomorrow."

His face shuttered, as if she had reminded him that their closeness tonight was just another charade. Juliana could have kicked herself for spoiling the moment.

"I've come to expect nothing from you, Juliana," he said flatly.

Neither spoke again for several moments. Desperately trying to think of a neutral topic, Juliana lifted her chin and watched the activity on the dance floor.

"This banker you want to impress, Adam. He must have arrived late. I don't recall meeting him in the lobby. Point him out to me. I'll put on my best manners."

His expression soured. "He begged off at the last minute. You may as well relax and try to enjoy yourself. We spent enough for the food and drink."

"I thought you wanted me to spare no expense."

"Look, don't fret over it." He dredged up a smile. "What's spent on pleasure is never wasted. Consider that gown I bought you. It pleases me to see you wear it, and I don't begrudge a farthing of what it cost."

"Nor should you," admonished a gruff voice from behind them. "If my wife had a figger like that, I'd want to show it off, too."

Juliana turned and smiled warmly at the voice's owner, a stout little red-faced squire named Leonard Duncastle who raised sheep on the outskirts of Penlyn.

"Are you enjoying yourself, sir?" she asked. "We've plenty of food left if you've worked up an appetite dancing."

"Good God, no. I'm stuffed as a Michaelmas goose as 'tis." He offered her his elbow, his moist eyes twinkling. "Haven't forgotten this dance was promised to me, have ya?"

"Of course I haven't." She brushed past Adam, noting the glimmer of amusement in his eye to see her partnered with a man she towered over by a half-foot. Impulsively she said, "It seems only fitting that Adam dance with your wife, squire. She doesn't have a partner, does she?"

The squire turned his head. "No. She's standing over there by the window fanning herself, Tremayne. Can't miss her with those parrot feathers sticking out of that mountain of blue-powdered horsehair she calls a wig."

Juliana smiled inwardly at the expression of mild distaste that crossed Adam's face. He still balked at following the rules of polite society, but at least he made an effort. Wistfully she realized how enjoyable it was to behave as though they were any other normal married couple. Of course, it was all for appearances only. After the evening ended, she fully expected him to revert to his coldly courteous ways.

"I've been hoping for a word alone with you all evening, Mrs. Tremayne," the squire said as soon as they found a spot on the floor.

Juliana's face clouded in dismay. She'd not have pegged the squire for a lecher, and now she was obligated to suffer through an entire dance with him. She snapped her fan together. A rap across the knuckles usually kept straying hands at bay.

"It—it's about two of my neighbors, ma'am," he continued in a quietly confidential tone. "Tenant farmers who lease acreage from your husband. They're concerned for their futures, you see. One can barely make a decent living from the land these days."

Relief followed by bafflement overcame Juliana. "I don't quite understand, Squire Duncastle. As far as I know, my husband hasn't raised the rents since he took over title of the properties."

"Oh, no, ma'am. I'm aware of that. But it's the rumors one hears—"

Juliana's skin tingled. "What rumors, squire?"

The squire moved away from her in the movements of the dance, and she awaited his response with mounting unease.

"Well, ma'am, there is talk that old Logan left behind a swarm of creditors. 'Twouldn't surprise anyone were your husband to sell off his lesser holdings in order to save his home. The fear is that because he's a foreigner, he won't take into consideration the families whose very livelihood depends on that land."

"Why have you brought this concern to my attention, squire? My husband isn't a monster. He'll at least hear you out."

She had scarcely finished speaking than she realized the import of what she'd said. She was defending Adam! More remarkable still was the fact that the words had sprung from her unthinkingly—from a previously unrealized loyalty to her husband. She strained her ears to catch the squire's answer.

"Well, ma'am, you're a Cornishwoman," he said, as if that would explain everything.

She nodded, understanding the fears of his neighbors. "I'll talk to my husband, squire. Anyway, I'm hopeful we'll have our finances straightened out by the beginning of the next quarter."

He beamed at her in approval. "A few good runs can't hurt matters, eh? I've heard tonight's a grand one. Hope your husband still has Logan's list of customers. I received my brandy regular from him."

"My husband has nothing to do with smuggling, squire,"

she said crisply, inclining her head to indicate there were other people within earshot.

"What?" The squire's look of confusion vanished as he finally caught her warning. "No need to worry about that, dear lady. There isn't a man in this room who'd turn evidence against a fair-trader, and that includes the magistrate."

"Still, squire, one can't be too careful."

Juliana danced continuously with different partners until the musicians broke for an intermission. As a fresh round of drinks and light refreshments was served, she realized that Adam had left the ballroom. She dared not ask if anyone knew his whereabouts. It was possible he'd snuck down to the cove to lend Paul a hand. *I'll be furious with him if he has,* she thought.

She excused herself from her guests and made her way to the parlor, wondering whether Adam had decided to try his luck at cards. But outside the door she met Phoebe, carrying a tray of brandy and clean glasses for the players inside.

"Phoebe, have you seen my husband? I'm afraid he may have gone down to the cove."

"I 'eard the butler say 'e was wanted in the lobby, ma'am. Seems one of the guests arrived late and wouldn't come inside alone."

"How odd. Perhaps it was that banker Adam expected."

But when she reached the entrance lobby moments later, it was to find Adam seated on the marble bench in the alcove, deep in conversation with one of the most stunning women she'd ever seen. She was wearing a black satin gown with a scooped neckline that displayed a modest expanse of her large breasts and the creamy gardenia-whiteness of her throat and shoulders. Fine silver-blonde hair spilled down her back in enticing disarray. Her face was lifted to Adam, like a lush flower to the sun, and even in the candlelight, Juliana was struck by the chiseled perfection of her features. Then suddenly she noticed Juliana, and her sweet expression hardened into one of petulant annoyance.

"Adam," she whispered loudly. "Who is that?"

Juliana moved out of the shadows, determined not to let her feelings show. "I've been looking everywhere for you, Adam," she said coolly.

He looked up at her without a trace of the guilt she'd expected to read in his eyes. "I didn't mean to be gone this long," he said. "I've been trying to convince this young lady that there's absolutely no reason for her not to mingle with our guests. Just because she's in mourning doesn't mean she has to ostracize herself from people."

Juliana's eyebrows lifted. "Oh."

Adam stood then, beginning to look flustered. "I'm forgetting my manners. Leigh Spencer, this is my wife, Juliana. Leigh's originally from the Virginia colony like me, Juliana. She's been recently widowed."

"How do you do?" Leigh asked in a tone of bored indifference.

Juliana didn't trust herself to speak. A thick knot had formed in her throat, obstructing her breath. Leigh Spencer of the letter in the library? The ailing *Widow* Spencer? God, what a fool she'd been. So this was whom Adam had spent all those unexplained nights with. Oh, it was clear to her now. And to think he had the gall to bring her here, to flaunt her before everyone in the district.

She had no idea how long she stood there, numb with hurt, tortured by her own suspicions. Something of her anguish must have shown on her face, for suddenly, she felt Adam's hand on her arm, shaking her out of her trance.

"Juliana, what on earth is the matter with you? Have you had too much to drink?" He lowered his voice, mindful of the occasional guest wandering past them. "She's my late wife's sister, Juliana. Her father threw her out of his house, and she set sail for Cornwall before I could talk her out of it. She has no friends, no money. I couldn't turn her away."

Juliana glanced over at Leigh. "She looks capable enough of shifting for herself. Why should you be responsible for her?"

"Look, it's damned awkward discussing this right here. I'll explain it later." He sighed. "I had little choice, Juliana. You'll just have to accept it for now."

Juliana stiffened as her deepest fear seemed to have been realized. Accept what? her shocked mind wondered. Accept the fact that her husband had moved his mistress into a cottage barely a half-mile from their home?

Adam's voice penetrated the haze of her anger. "It's not what you're thinking."

"No?" The word seemed to stumble out over her thinned lips. "Then what's she doing at our party? She hasn't even an escort—unless, of course, you've assumed the role."

"She wanted to come," Adam said, looking increasingly tense and uncomfortable. "I suppose she was lonely. Damn, I don't know why! Does it really matter?"

"Perhaps I ought to return to the cottage, Adam," Leigh offered meekly. "I surely didn't mean to upset your wife."

For the past several minutes the subject of the heated discussion hadn't stirred, but now slowly, Leigh rose from the bench, her head bowed in a gesture of embarrassed bewilderment. Juliana stared at her with unabashed disgust, thinking that the glassy depths of those wide lime-green eyes belied the innocent face and submissive pose.

Adam leveled his gaze at Juliana. "My wife isn't upset, Leigh, merely annoyed with me for not mentioning you to her before—and rightly so. Now that you've been introduced, I'm sure she'll have no objections if you stay and enjoy the party."

Juliana froze, torn between wanting to believe him and the dark doubts gnawing at her mind. What should she do? Then somewhere behind her, a door opened and closed, footfalls sounded, and a woman's voice called out from the end of the lobby.

"Mrs. Tremayne! Diane and I are dying to have our fortunes read. Won't you accompany us?"

She hesitated. The voice belonged to Lady Hazelhurst, the wife of another wealthy landowner who'd expressed an interest in buying some of Adam's uncultivated acreage further inland for experimental farming purposes. Lady Hazelhurst and her husband were both overbearing snobs, but firmly established in society, the type of people she would neither want to offend or befriend.

She lifted her skirts, her mouth set tersely. She could either chose to trust her husband or to throw a jealous tantrum in front of everyone.

"I'm sure you'll both excuse me," she said stiffly to Adam and Leigh. "I have to return to my guests."

Without awaiting a response, she swirled around and walked toward the two matronly women at the end of the lobby. Her heart felt like a brick of ice, slowly, painfully, melting inside her, numbing her raw emotions. Then half-way to her destination, she heard Leigh laugh delicately, and the sound burned away the coldness within her, replacing it with white-hot rage.

She stopped, gripped by a sudden childish impulse to run back and slap the smile from that porcelain face. What's happened to me? she wondered miserably. Why should I give a tuppenny damn what boring old Lady Hazelhurst thinks of me? What do I care if Adam loses this morbid old house and everything else he inherited? None of it should matter to me!

Then from the corner of her eye, she noticed her reflection in the round mirror hanging on the wall. The sophisticated image took her by surprise, a mocking reminder of the subtle changes she had undergone since coming to Mentreath. With a sinking sense of destiny, she realized—and accepted—that everything that affected Adam also affected her, that she could no more disentangle her life from his than she could return to the past.

She resumed walking at a sedate pace, a practiced smile concealing her distress. Had she discovered how much Adam meant to her only to lose him? Could she blame anyone but herself if he had turned to someone else?

The two plumpish women waiting for her put an end to her self-tormenting thoughts, ushering her into the great hall with coy giggles and feigned shivers of apprehension.

"Last year at the fair, a brazen gypsy wench told me I'd have a liaison with a handsome politician," Lady Hazelhurst whispered behind her fan to her two female companions. "Well, what can I tell you, my dears, but that I'm *still* waiting!"

Juliana summoned an obligatory smile, wishing she could tune out the inane chatter. It was unpleasantly close in the great hall with the fire blazing, gilding the ugly gargoyles on the chimneypiece. Two gypsy women were holding court on a dais placed before the screens passage. A third gypsy, a young man with blackberry-dark curls spilling over his shoulders, was sprawled out at the foot of the staircase, strumming a guitar. Juliana noted with amusement that Doris stood against one of the mullioned windows, a wooden rolling pin held tightly in one hand.

Suddenly one of the gypsy women, a voluptuous raven-haired beauty with black flashing eyes, stood and pointed to Juliana. "Yehwah will read your palm, lady."

This is foolish, Juliana thought self-consciously as she walked forward to kneel before the woman. What can this unwashed peasant know of my future? She didn't put a grain of faith in these country superstitions. Still, a twinge of curiosity got the better of her practical nature.

"Give me your left hand first, lady."

Juliana obeyed, sighing as she noticed that the woman sat with her filthy bare feet curled beneath her on one of the newly upholstered wing chairs.

"O Del, lady!" the gypsy exclaimed softly, bending over Juliana's oustretched palm with a serious frown. "I see shadows in your past. . . . Death has taken loved ones away from you. A baby snatched from your womb—that is this tiny broken branch above your heart-line." She shook her head mournfully. "Yehwah lost four of her own before her two sons were born, the last delivered only two weeks ago."

Juliana jerked her hand away, her heart pounding wildly. She was still sick inside from her confrontation with Adam, and now to be reminded of her miscarriage—

"No more, gypsy. It's time I returned to my party."

But her protest was useless, for Yehwah had already reached down and taken Juliana's right hand, lifting the palm to the window to examine it in the moonlight.

"There is a cross on the Mount of Venus, lady. There will be only one love for you until you die, but with it, alas, I see tears and suffering. Ah! Another child. That is happy news, eh? But wait—this grille, marking the Mount of Jupiter, indicates a stubborn pride that could destroy your marriage." The gypsy pressed her face closer to Juliana's, whispering fiercely, "You must entice your husband back into your bed, lady, or the silver-haired one will steal him away from you. The base of your hand is highly padded, indicating a passionate nature. Use that passion to win your husband back!"

Juliana pulled her hand free indignantly. "You've said enough. You were hired to entertain the guests, not to offend them with tidbits of gossip you've picked up from the servants."

Yehwah's black eyes shone cruelly. "You know what

I've told you is true. Your husband is with this woman even as we speak.''

"I know that you didn't read all that in my palm!''

The gypsy shrugged her coppery shoulders and smiled. "Why should you care how I obtain my knowledge if I seek only to spare you pain? Bah! I don't know why I bother. You *gorgio* women are all the same. You only want to hear—''

Just at that moment an angry shout thundered from outside the door, and a footman burst into the room, holding by the scruff of the neck a scrawny young gypsy boy dressed in an oversized shirt and tattered breeches.

'' 'Ere, madam!'' he cried triumphantly to Juliana. "Look what I found sneakin' out of the kitchen with its pockets full of cheese an' biscuits!''

Lady Hazelhurst and her companion rose from the opposite end of the dais, where they had also been having their palms read. "A thief in our very midst,'' Angela Hazelhurst said disgustedly. '' 'Tis fortunate we've a magistrate here tonight to see that justice is swiftly administered.''

The gypsy woman Yehwah jumped up from the chair, her eyes glittering dangerously. At the staircase the guitarist had also uncoiled and risen, his instrument suddenly silent. Juliana guessed that the child in the doorway was the fortune-teller's son. She got up slowly, wondering how she could best handle the situation. She couldn't find it in herself to punish a hungry child for pinching a bit of cheese when she had so much food left over from the buffet.

"Doris, take the child to the kitchen and let him eat his fill. You might pack some pie and venison for him to take when he leaves.''

"Mrs. Tremayne, really!'' Lady Hazelhurst said in shocked stentorian tones. "To let this dirty little beggar go would be to condone criminal behavior in your own home. Think of the example you'd be setting before your servants. Why, there wouldn't be a menial in the house who'd hesitate to steal if your foolish leniency became known.''

Juliana glanced helplessly at Doris, but the housekeeper averted her gaze, leaving her to make her own decision.

"Doris, I repeat my instructions: Take this boy to the kitchen and feed him. And you—'' She paused, staring down at the expressionless middle-aged footman, who'd been in Logan Tremayne's employ long enough to know better than to question the eccentricities of the gentry. "I'd like you to bring me a glass of sherry," she finished lamely.

"Well, I never!" Lady Hazelhurst and her friend sailed past Juliana and out the door like twin battleships, firing off snide remarks between themselves.

"A sad example of what the *nouveau riche* have done to the quality of society."

"Hard to believe she almost snared herself a viscount."

"Sour old bitches!" Yehwah shouted after them. "May you swallow your vicious tongues and choke to death!"

Juliana watched them go with a sinking heart. Well, that brought her evening of triumph to a crashing finish. The one woman she'd intended to impress would probably never speak to her again. As if that weren't bad enough, this wild-eyed gypsy had to scream curses at her.

"Follow my housekeeper to the kitchen, and she'll see you're paid for tonight. You may cross the courtyard and leave through the garden."

"I know the way out, lady," Yehwah said. "Many a stormy winter evening the old master allowed our people to sleep in the stables."

Juliana nodded in dismissal and turned to get down from the dais, but Yehwah boldly sidestepped her, blocking her progress.

"It's not too late to lure him back, lady," she said slyly. "Come to our camp, and the *phuri dai* will blend a love philter to help you."

Juliana pushed around the woman. "Don't be absurd. I don't believe in your pagan spells and potions."

"On the outskirts of the village, lady," Yehwah called softly. "Ride past the graveyard and toward the hill until you reach the old monastery. But don't leave it too long!"

The moment the hall had cleared and the footman had delivered her sherry, Juliana collapsed into a chair and closed her eyes. She wanted to wait for the liquor to calm her nerves before she braved returning to the ballroom. Was Adam dancing with Leigh? she wondered. Had Lady Hazelhurst left in a huff, or was she gleefully spreading gossip behind her fan about her socially inept hostess?

"Thank God I found ee alone, ma'am."

Juliana opened her eyes reluctantly and looked up into Phoebe's small, worried face. "Whatever it is, Phoebe, I don't want to hear about it."

"Yes, ee do, ma'am."

"No, I don't! Find my husband and have him handle it."

"Robbie's out lookin' for 'im now, ma'am. 'Tis yer brother. Seems there was a bit of trouble down at the cove tonight."

The run! Juliana sprang out of the chair. She'd put so much effort into making the party a success that she had almost forgotten the original reason for having it.

"What's happened to my brother, Phoebe? Did he run into revenuers?"

"I dunno for sure, ma'am. I think ye'd best come to the library with me to find out what 'appened. P'rhaps we'd be wiser goin' through the screens passage and around the 'ou... So no one'll follow us."

"You're right," Juliana murmured. "Oh, what a horrid night!"

Then, as she and the girl stood outside the library, she turned suddenly, her thoughts colliding. "Did—did you say that Robbie had gone out to find my husband? Are you telling me that he *left* the house in the middle of the party?"

"I—uh—I believe one of the guests felt unwell, ma'am, and 'e felt obligated to see 'er safely 'ome."

Juliana's heart twisted. How could he do this to her? How could he leave her alone with all these people? A taunting image of him lying with Leigh in his arms flashed across her mind, but she banished it and steeled herself for whatever awaited her in the library.

She opened the door and slipped into the room. To assure secrecy, no candles or a fire had been lit, so it took her several moments for her eyes to adjust to the darkness.

"Over here, Juliana. Bolt the door behind you, and make as little noise as possible."

She moved over to the desk, so relieved to hear Martin's voice that she stumbled over a figure stretched out on the floor. The man groaned and then cursed as she trod down on his hand with the heel of her pump.

"Thank God, Martin," she whispered, crouching down

beside him. "I thought you'd been injured. What happened?
Excisemen?"

"No—no. It was smugglers, we think. A rival gang." He
turned his head to speak, and it was then she saw the large
bloody bruise coming out on his cheekbone.

She swallowed over the lump in her windpipe. "Your
face—"

"Yes. It got in the way of a swinging cudgel. Gave me
quite a bad headache, but I'm all right now. Poor fellow on
the floor behind you got beat up trying to help me."

Satisfied his injury wasn't serious, she began to think
more rationally. "A rival smuggling gang doesn't make
sense, Martin. I understood that Logan was on friendly
terms with the men from Mullion and Poldhu Cove."

" 'Tweren't none of them," a scratchy voice spoke up
from behind the desk. "They got plenty of their own business without murderin' for more."

Juliana straightened, recognizing Jack Chenwiddy by his
long silver hair. "Murder, Jack? Surely not—"

"Aye, ma'am. Sadly so. They was armed with blunder-
busses and shot one of the porters from the cliff path. 'Tis
my unfortunate duty to inform 'is wife she's a widow."

A low rumbling noise from across the room diverted Juliana's attention to the fireplace, where the hidden doorway
had just swung open. A tall, light-haired man stepped into
view, and Juliana hurried forward to greet him.

"Paul! I've just heard what happened. Who'd do such a
senseless thing? Do you think a new gang has moved into
the area to challenge Adam's authority?"

He took her hand and drew her over to the window so that
they wouldn't block the passage. "I wish I had the answers,
chérie, but I don't. All I can say for certain is that the attack
was very well planned. As to motive—" He shrugged. "Whoever it was didn't bother to steal even a single cask of brandy.
Perhaps it was staged to frighten us into retirement."

She lapsed into troubled silence, her temples pulsing.
God, what a night! If she could only go to bed and pretend
none of it ever happened. But how could she sleep with the
twin horrors of a man's murder and her husband's infidelity
on her mind?

"Shouldn't you return to your guests?" Paul asked

gently. "There's nothing you can do here, and your prolonged absence will only serve to arouse curiosity."

"Yes. I don't want to give the gossipmongers anything else to talk about."

Paul's eyes lingered on her face, then slowly lowered to her throat. "You're not wearing my necklace, *chérie.*"

She looked away, taken aback by the scorching lust in his gaze. "I couldn't, Paul. It didn't seem proper. I intend to return it to you."

"Then I'll keep it for you until the day comes when you accept it."

Her face grew warm. It was a potentially dangerous moment, fraught with temptation, and to her bewilderment, she felt a foolish impulse to encourage him.

"I think I should say good night now," she said quietly and turned away.

But just as Paul stepped aside to allow her past him, she spotted the powerfully built figure standing by the fireplace. Adam. She had no idea how long he'd been standing there watching her. She fiercely hoped he'd seen her with Paul. A dose of his own medicine might do him good, she thought. But for all her anger, her heartbeat still quickened as he started toward her.

"How good of you to return home before dawn tonight, Adam," she said. "If your moral obligations to the widow are fulfilled, perhaps you could spare a minute or two to socialize with your guests."

"Is that what you were doing just now with Paul, Juliana?" he asked coldly. He gripped her arm and steered her to the door, unbolting it to usher her into the hallway. "Leigh felt ill and I merely saw her home."

"You've been gone almost an hour."

"I noticed the excitement at the cove on the way back and stopped to investigate. That's all there was to it."

They walked down the hallway in silence, and as they neared the ballroom, Adam stopped and turned to face her. Muted strains of music and laughter drifted out through the opened double doors.

"Damn it, this has been a night, hasn't it?"

"You don't know the half of it, Adam," she said, thinking of Lady Hazelhurst and the scene in the great hall.

He stared at her in mock horror. "Judging by the look on your face, I don't think I want to."

She couldn't help laughing. "I fear I may have damaged your reputation."

"My reputation?" he said lightly. "Impossible. 'Tis already tarnished beyond redemption. Don't you know that's why I married you? No other woman would have me."

What about Leigh? she longed to ask, but she swallowed the words, determined not to start another quarrel. She and Adam spent too little time together these days to waste it fighting.

Perhaps the evening hadn't been such a disaster after all, she mused much later. Yes, there was still the unsavory incident at the cove to investigate. And, yes, Lady Hazelhurst had left the party early with her patrician nose out of joint, but the remainder of the guests had lingered on until the wee hours of the morning.

And she had actually ended up enjoying herself, somehow managing to push all the unpleasantness from her mind. Adam scarcely left her side after they rejoined the party, unless it was to fetch her a drink or to make a discreet trip to the library to confer with Jack. They even matched up with Squire Duncastle and his wife to form a square and dance a quadrille. Then, when the last guest had left, they mounted the staircase together, Juliana's heart racing with hope that he would stay with her all night.

At the top of the staircase, he paused, and Juliana waited in aching suspense, wishing she had a clue to the thoughts behind his dark face.

Then slowly he touched her cheek with the back of his hand, sending fire and ice throughout her. She couldn't move, hypnotized by his smoky eyes.

"You must be tired," he said after an endless moment. "Yes."

But it was a lie! The nearness of him shocked every fiber of her being into vibrant awareness.

And then he drew his hand back, his voice husky. "I won't keep you up any longer. It's almost dawn now."

She bit her lip as she watched him turn and walk away. His one tender gesture had filled her with such unbearable longing that it took all her will not to beg him to stay. And then finally she also turned and sought the lonely comfort of her bed.

Chapter Twenty-five

Juliana snuggled deeper into the recesses of her favorite cloak. It was of quilted royal-blue velvet, lined from the loose French hood to the hem with long-haired fox, a boon on a foggy winter afternoon. She and Phoebe had spent the morning in Penlyn, distributing food to the needy, paying a special call to the widow and five children of the porter who'd been killed at the cove.

"We're done now, ma'am, ain't we?" Phoebe asked in a hopeful voice, kicking vigorously at her dobbin to catch up with Juliana's Ajax. "That were the last cottage ee wanted to stop at."

Juliana smiled with the sheer pleasure of being outdoors after a week of inclement weather had kept her housebound. Wisps of sea mist edged the stone hedgerows which enclosed their path. Blackbirds darted back and forth between the naked dripping branches of the trees on the surrounding hillside. The air was invigorating, sharp and moist.

"What's wrong, Phoebe? Afraid of a little cold weather? 'Tis good for your complexion. Brings out the roses in your cheeks."

"Brings out the chilblains, too," Phoebe grumbled discontentedly. "I ain't wearin' an 'eavy cloak like ee, ma'am."

"That's your own fault. I offered to lend you my woolen one. Anyway, we've only got one more stop to make at the gypsy encampment. We'll have a pot of hot tea and some of Cook's scones when we get home."

"Gypsies? But they be 'eathens, ma'am. Just the other day I 'eard of a farmer up in Gweek who died one hour after

211

a gypsy horse-dealer 'ad been seen givin' 'im the evil eye! Oh, please, ma'am, don't make me go up there."

"All right. I'll go by myself. Just stop fussing."

"But why do ee 'ave to go, ma'am? Leave the food for 'em at the bottom of the hill. That way they can't put their dirty 'ands on ee."

Juliana guided her horse past the village graveyard and up around the bare wind-deformed trees that clung to the hillside. A dozen four-wheeled wagons sat in a crescent formation on the summit of the hill, painted in gay colors that mocked the mist-shrouded landscape. Farther back, thin whorls of smoke from the gypsy campfires curled into the gray sky above the crumbling ruins of the abandoned monastery.

"Oh, ma'am, ye're not goin' up there! The mists are comin' in bad. I'll be chilled to the bone waitin' 'ere for ee."

"Put this on." Juliana unfastened her cloak and threw it to the girl, dismounting with a frown. "Now pass me that last bundle of food, and lead the horses into the churchyard. I won't be long."

Juliana shivered lightly, her golden-green eyes lifting to the gypsy encampment. What am I doing here? she wondered in amused disbelief. Her mouth tightened determinedly. She was fighting for her husband, fighting to rekindle the flames of their relationship before he cut her out of his heart completely, and even though she wasn't convinced she'd come to the right place for assistance, she knew she had to take the chance.

She climbed the hill slowly, aware that a group of dark-eyed children had gathered around the wagons to watch her. As she reached the summit, she could smell the pungent odors of fish and onions frying in oil. She followed the aroma past the ancient stone tower to the campfires. In the shelter of what remained of the rectory, the gypsy Yehwah sat on a pile of old carpets, nursing a baby at her breast. Her black hair was loosely bound in a red kerchief, and she wore a necklace of foreign silver and gold coins. The air throbbed with the sounds of children playing and the Romany copper-smiths banging at their forges.

Yehwah gave her a languid smile. "So you have come, lady." She didn't get up. "Auntie has your philter ready.

You'll find her sitting right behind you. I told her to expect you."

Juliana moved away self-consciously. To her relief, the men seemed to have congregated at the far end of the camp, and the women were preoccupied with minding the children and preparing dinner. She found the old wisewoman easily, sitting against a wagon wheel with her eyes half-closed, her light brown face like a wrinkled walnut shell. Encircling her creased neck was an amulet of chitons, wolves' teeth, and the bones of something that looked horrifyingly like human infants' fingers.

"I've come for—"

"I know what you want." The coal-black eyes opened unexpectedly, and the woman leaned forward like an eager child. "Have you brought me a present?"

Juliana held out her offering of cold meats and cheese. "Yes, this."

The woman ignored the food. "Those are pretty earrings. Auntie loves pretty jewels."

"My—my diamonds?"

A minute later the transaction was completed, Juliana wending her way through the camp minus her earrings and carrying a phial of foul-looking greenish substance.

The old Romany had warned her that the philter would lose its potency unless she used it in exactly seven days' time—on the night of the new moon. She wondered how in heaven's name she'd induce Adam to consume the stuff without arousing his suspicion. It didn't look at all appetizing; supposedly its ingredients were wild thyme, extract of vervain, female mandrake root, and powdered snail shells.

Part of her dismissed the very notion of it working as preposterous, but a deeper, less rational part was willing to try anything to win her husband back.

"Madam! Oh, madam, I've 'ad such an 'orrible fright!"

Juliana looked down to see Phoebe scrambling up the hillside to reach her, feet sliding on the muddied slope, her lace cap ridiculously squashed under the hood of Juliana's cloak.

"What happened to you, Phoebe? And where are the horses?" she demanded, glancing behind the girl.

"The damn 'orses are tethered in the churchyard now, ma'am, but I almost got myself killed walking 'em across the road."

"You're not making a bit of sense, Phoebe. Slow down."

"There was this coach, see, what stopped in the front of the churchyard. I'd noticed it earlier while we was in the village, but I didn't think nothin' of it. Well, anyway, ma'am, I decided to visit the graves . . . to pay my respects to my poor dead grannie, and as I was walking the 'orses over, this coach comes chargin' out of the mist right toward me."

" 'Tis difficult to make out figures at a distance in this fog. The driver couldn't have seen you."

"Oh, no, ma'am, he did," Phoebe insisted, her voice rising. "He was whippin' 'is 'orses and lookin' right at me! 'Twas lucky I 'ad the presence of mind to shoo off our mounts and tumble to the side, or he'd 'ave run me down for certain."

"This coach, Phoebe . . . could you describe it or its occupants?"

Phoebe sniffed, a little calmer now that her mistress was taking her seriously. "Lord, ma'am, there could've been twenty Chinamen in that coach for all I could tell in the fog. 'Twas a fancy one, though . . . shiny with some sort of crest on the door."

The fine hairs lifted on the nape of Juliana's neck. A crested coach . . . no, it couldn't be. It was a coincidence. The girl was imagining things. Only an irrational person would use his own, well-marked coach to deliberately run someone over, but then Graham had already proven himself unbalanced, hadn't he?

"We'd best start 'ome now, ma'am," Phoebe urged. "When the fog rolls in off the sea like this, 'tis easy to ride off a cliff and fall straight down to yer death."

Juliana nodded, feeling the dampness saturate her gown. "My cloak please, Phoebe."

"Oh, ma'am, about your cloak . . . It got a bit muddy when I jumped to the side. There was this big puddle—"

"Never mind."

And as Phoebe began to unfasten the cloak, Juliana was struck by another unpleasant thought. In that cloak with her reddish-brown hair showing around her face, Phoebe could have easily been mistaken for her mistress in the dense sea mists. If the driver had purposefully steered his coach astray, Juliana had been his intended victim.

* * *

Juliana felt lost as she stood in the middle of the vast old kitchen. To be sure, the room was immaculate, a housewife's dream. The shelves were orderly. The uneven stone floor was scrubbed faithfully each morning. The copper pots and pans gleamed on the butcher hooks that hung from the smoke-darkened beams between bunches of fragrant herbs. But where should she begin?

She wished now that she'd had the foresight to pay closer attention to Evelyn's cooking lessons. She hadn't the vaguest notion where to find the spices, or even the baking utensils. Perhaps she'd been too hasty in ordering Mrs. Runporth and her two scullery maids off to the still-room to brew cough syrup and cordial waters for the winter months.

Her features set resolutely, she rolled up her sleeves and tied a plain muslin apron around her slender waist. She'd have to manage alone. The scullery maids were a pair of magpies who loved nothing more than to gossip about their betters. She couldn't risk having them discover her secret.

With renewed determination, she stared down at the recipe book that lay open on the immense worktable. The philter seemed too chalky and pungent to dissolve in wine, so she'd decided to bake it into something which would disguise its flavor and texture . . . the recipe for wheaten cakes looked simple enough.

It took her almost an hour of experimenting with her keys to unlock the store cupboards and assemble what the recipe called for: eggs, mace, honey, butter, nutmeg, almonds, currants, rose water, and wheaten flour. She couldn't find any leavening, but as she'd never heard of it before, she figured it couldn't be so important that a little extra nutmeg wouldn't compensate for its absence.

Afraid of being caught with the phial, she quickly dumped its contents and all the cake ingredients into an earthen bowl and beat the mixture furiously. Something told her that the dough shouldn't have been so coarse and heavy. And she was even less pleased twenty minutes later when she removed the cakes from the brick oven beside the fireplace. They looked like lumpy pieces of coal, charred on the tops and bottoms, the insides like runny pudding. She broke one in half and nibbled the corner, its scorched flavor tempting her to toss the whole pan into the fire.

Then the door behind her opened, and she jumped guiltily. Slipping the empty phial into her apron pocket, she turned and tried to assume an air of innocence as Mrs. Runporth approached her, the keys she wore at her ample waist jingling with her steps.

"Just checkin' to see if ee needed anything, mistress. I forgot to unlock the cupboards in my 'aste."

"I'm doing fine, thank you. In fact, I'm all finished in here, Mrs. Runporth. You may have your kitchen back."

The stout woman shuffled around the table, eyeing the pan of blackened cakes with sympathetic understanding. "Recipe didn't quite turn out, I see. Well, not to worry. I'll cook up another pan afore supper. The master'll never know who made 'em if ee want to take credit." She patted Juliana's arm, smiling conspiratorially. "Our little secret, ma'am."

"Mrs. Runporth, you may cook any' 'ng you like for supper, but I want *these* cakes served after rd—with the strongest wine we have. Is that understood?"

"Well, yes, ma'am, but I was only tryin' to be elpful."

Juliana began to untie her apron, then suddenly remembered the phial in her pocket. "Doing as I've asked will be the greatest help of all. And Mrs. Runporth, I don't want either of your girls interrupting supper. All the dishes are to be placed on the sideboard beforehand."

"Are ee and the master celebratin' something, ma'am?" the cook asked, unable to suppress her curiosity.

Juliana strode toward the door, her eyes twinkling. "I hope so, Mrs. Runporth."

Rather than dining formally in the great hall, both Adam and Juliana preferred the private atmosphere of the small winter parlor. The walls were paneled in pale oak with borders of painted Tudor roses. The original frescoed ceiling with its cavorting dolphins and mermaids had been restored, and new emerald silk damask curtains hung before the windows.

Adam glanced at his wife as he seated himself at the oval mahogany table. How long had it been since they had supped alone together? He studied her closely without seeming to, noticing the tension around the corners of her mouth, the faint smudges under her eyes. Was she still grieving over her miscarriage? What had caused the strain he detected on her face?

He ate in silence, appreciating the food. There was a thick leek-vegetable soup; bass poached in shallots, rosemary, and white wine; and mushroom caps stuffed with savory herbed sausage. Finally, he put down his fork and pushed his plate away.

"Have you something on your mind, Juliana?"

She looked up, holding a mushroom cap halfway to her mouth. "Why do you ask?"

"I don't know. I sensed something—" He broke off, leaning back in his chair with a frown. "Isn't your brother joining us tonight?"

"No. He said he had work to do and would take a tray in his study."

For a full minute Adam neither spoke nor ate, but merely sat watching her, his gray eyes glistening. That dress Juliana was wearing . . . had he seen it before? No. Surely he would have remembered how the daringly scooped silk bodice hugged her firm white breasts . . . how he could see the enticing pink rims of her nipples whenever she bent forward. A sudden spasm of desire shot through his groin as the image of her sprawled naked beneath him crept into his mind. He swallowed painfully, forcing himself back to reality.

"The meal was exceptionally well prepared, and you look exceptionally lovely tonight." He sat forward abruptly. "Good God, this isn't your birthday, is it?"

She laughed softly, warmed by the unexpected compliment. "No."

"Forgive me, but it feels—" He shrugged, his face confused. "It feels as though tonight were a special occasion. You did make a point of making sure I'd be home for supper, didn't you?"

"I knew Mrs. Runporth had planned a special meal," she said evasively. "I think she needs to feel she's appreciated."

Adam continued to stare at her, his rugged face impassive. If he didn't know better, he would have sworn she was trying to set the stage for seduction. Could it be possible? Could she actually have gone to all this trouble to create a mood conducive to romance? The thought provoked him, excited him beyond all belief. The past month had been an unbearable torture for him, living in the same house with her, but forcing himself to remain at a distance.

"I told you before that I enjoyed the meal, Juliana. Now I have to confess I've enjoyed the company more."

She lowered her eyes to break his intense gaze, her heart tripping over with excitement. Thank heaven he was in a receptive mood tonight, and to think he'd yet to taste the philter!

"Adam, won't you have one of these cakes for dessert? They're freshly baked this afternoon."

He shook his head, not even glancing down at the platter she offered him. "I'm not hungry. I ate my fill."

"But, Adam, I—I baked these myself. At least try one with a glass of wine."

He smiled to himself, willing to play her game . . . to do everything within his power to encourage her. He reached down and took a cake, biting into it before he realized how badly burned it was. He swallowed hard, quickly downing glass of wine she'd poured him. His eyes watered. His tongue curled in protest. His mouth puckered as the cake settled in the pit of his stomach with an aftertaste of charcoal.

"A most . . . unusual flavor, Juliana," he managed to say without choking.

"I made them especially for you, Adam. Have another."

"Another?" He couldn't bring himself to hurt her feelings. "Well, perhaps with a cup of coffee—"

She rose hastily. "I'll ring for some. No. Better yet, I'll fetch it myself. I told the staff we wanted to be alone tonight."

His expression warmed. "Did you now?"

Color crept into Juliana's cheeks as she realized what she had inadvertently revealed. Feeling Adam's eyes follow her, she hurried from the room. When she returned with the silver coffeepot, she found he'd left the table and was leaning against the windowsill. He turned to regard her, his eyes smoldering with such frank desire that she grew light-headed in anticipation of the pleasures the evening held.

I am lost to him forever, she thought with bittersweet resignation. To escape the mesmerizing influence of his stare, she glanced around the parlor, thinking distractedly how much it had changed since she'd come to Mentreath, how much *she* had changed. Only months ago she would have done anything to break free from this man. Now it seemed that she lived for his love.

"Shall I pour your coffee, Adam?" she asked, praying he

couldn't hear the tremor in her voice. Then, before he could answer, she looked down at the table and saw that he'd eaten not two but three of the cakes. Guilt pricked her conscience, but was soon replaced by worry that he hadn't taken the entire philter. Would it still work?

He nodded but didn't move away from the window. "Pour us each a cup with a little brandy in it. We'll have it on the settee."

She complied, placing the porcelain cups on the small tea table in front of the green brocade settee. A fire burned brightly in the fireplace, but Juliana's hands felt cold with mounting excitement. Finally, Adam sat down next to her, and as his thigh brushed hers, a wave of longing washed over her.

"You're not drinking your coffee, Juliana."

She reached out automatically and lifted the cup to her lips, feeling she needed the extra brandy she'd given herself to slow her pounding pulse. From beneath her eyelids, she peeked up at Adam. The philter must be taking effect by now.

"Did you have a special reason for wanting to be alone with me, Juliana?" he asked casually.

"Well . . . not really . . ."

"Ah. I'm disappointed. I thought perhaps you'd missed me. I must have been wrong."

"No, Adam." She wrapped her icy trembling fingers around the base of the cup. "You weren't wrong. I—I have missed you . . . desperately. . . ."

When he didn't respond to her painful admission, Juliana dropped her gaze in embarrassment, certain he would say that he no longer loved her, that he had taken Leigh as his mistress. But suddenly she felt his hand touching hers, his fingers prying the cup loose from her tense grasp.

"It's been a long time for us, hasn't it, Juliana?"

She watched him place her cup on the table, imagining how it would feel to have those strong brown fingers caressing her again. "Yes, Adam," she said huskily, slowly raising her eyes to his. "It's been too long. . . ."

He drew her roughly to him and kissed her until she crumpled back against the settee, her face hot, her senses whirling with giddy abandon. Then, to their mutual astonishment, she climbed onto his lap and draped her arms around his neck, bringing her mouth to his and kissing him until it was he who broke away, his breath coming in painful gasps, his eyes misty with passion.

"Not here, my love," he whispered, laughing excitedly.

She rounded her lips into a pout. "Why not?"

"I will not ravish my own wife on a settee when we have a large comfortable bed awaiting us in our chamber."

He caught her hand and pulled her to her feet, his eyes widening in delight as she swayed forward and pressed her body against his. He held her for a moment, breathing deeply to slow his galloping heartbeat, his free hand tangling in her sweet-smelling hair.

"Oh, Juliana," he murmured, dropping his face to her shoulder. "Why did you wait so long? I've been going out of my mind."

She shivered as she felt him nibbling at her neck and then her ear lobe. "I didn't realize, Adam," she whispered. "I didn't realize how much I love you."

Overcome with emotion, he gripped her to him. "I thought I'd never hear you say that. I almost gave up."

"And I thought I'd lost you forever—" She pulled back, laughing and weeping at the same time, her palms pressed to his chest.

"Never, my darling," he said fiercely.

"Take me to bed, Adam," she ordered softly. "I'm afraid I want you so very much that my knees are giving way."

She clung to him as they left the parlor, allowing him to kiss her once in the hallway, to unhook her bodice outside the bedchamber door. Then, the very moment they stepped inside the room, she delighted him further by unbuttoning his shirt and pressing ardent little kisses over his bare chest.

He leaned up against the door, a lazy smile curling his lips until suddenly, without warning, he scooped her up into his arms and carried her across the room to spill her on the bed. Swiftly he removed his shoes and stockings, dropping onto the side of the bed to lean over Juliana. She smiled up at him, her body melting with sensual languor. Then slowly she lifted her hand to stroke his cheek, to pull off his shirt so that her fingers could brush his crisp chest hair and explore the muscular ridges of his back and shoulders.

"Oh, God, Juliana, when you touch me like that—" He groaned as she ran her index finger down his spine, then traced it around his narrow waist and over the hard bulge of his manhood, imprisoned in his breeches.

"Damn these clothes!" he muttered with feverish impatience.

"Wait," she said silkily. "Let me do that."

Half rising, she brought both her hands to Adam's waist to assist him in removing his breeches. When at last he lay naked beside her, he rose to his knees to finish undressing her, quickly helping her off with her chemise and frothy petticoats, which foamed about them like an ocean of lace. With tantalizing skill he unfastened her garters and peeled off her stockings, his big thumbs rasping against the flawless velvet of her flesh, arousing countless pinpoints of glorious sensation. Then, after he'd drawn off the last stocking, he paused for a long time to stare at her, admiring her sweet rounded breasts and supple white body.

"You excite me so much, Juliana. This past month has been agony for me."

"And for me," she whispered.

"Why didn't you tell me?"

"I tried, Adam. Don't you remember that day in the library? I—I tried to apologize."

He caught her hand, lifting it to his mouth to kiss her fingers and the sensitive skin of her inner wrist. "Yes, you did. But I thought it was for the wrong reason. I thought Martin had put you up to it. I guess I was offended that another man had to intervene on my behalf. And on the staircase that day, I wanted to stop you from seeing Paul, but I just wouldn't let myself—"

"Foolish pride," she said with a rueful smile. " 'Tis a sin we'll both have to overcome."

He leaned over her, his face suddenly dark with long-suppressed passion. "If I believed you loved me, Juliana, I think I could overcome almost anything."

Even the past? she wondered. Would the ghosts of his wife and daughter always stand between them?

"I do love you, Adam," she whispered.

His hand stole up the inside of her arm to touch her face, gently flicking back a stray tendril of hair that curled across her cheek. "I'm sorry about our baby, Juliana. I swear I didn't realize—"

"I know," she soothed, her heart aching as she saw tears

glistening in his eyes. "I always knew." She raised her hand to trace a finger around the outline of his wide sensual mouth. "Enough talking for now, Adam. I don't want to be sad tonight. I don't want to think about the past."

"Then let me make you forget everything."

"Oh!"

Juliana's spine arched in pleasure as she felt his hand caress her breasts, then slide down to stroke her quivering belly. Hooking her arms around his shoulders, she lifted her face to his and kissed him hungrily. Almost immediately she felt him stiffen with excitement against the softness of her thigh.

"Ah, Juliana," he groaned against her lips. "It's been so long. I fear I'm too impatient—"

She laughed huskily, entwining her fingers in the crisp, dark hair at the nape of his neck. "So am I, Adam."

Lovingly he kissed the tip of her stubborn chin, her long graceful throat, the rose-tinted crests of her soft breasts. His fingers brushed over the silky thatch of her womanhood, then lower where they tickled and skillfully rubbed until her thighs opened eagerly to allow him entry. In an instant he was inside her, filling her with the heat of his desire.

A moan of ecstasy burst from Juliana's lips as honey melted through her veins. How good it felt to have him inside her! Feverishly she dug her nails into his back, urging him to penetrate deeper. Burning with need for him, she raised her pelvis higher. His hands slid under her buttocks to cradle her closer, to position her so that he could tease her with his slow, controlled thrusting. Juliana's head thrashed wildly against the pillow, her entire body taut with building pleasure.

Then gradually his movements quickened, and she felt herself teetering dangerously on the edge of bliss, every inch of her body straining into him, her nerve endings clamoring for release from the exquisite mounting torment. And then at last fulfillment claimed them, binding them together in a blaze of golden sweetness that lingered long after the flames of their passion had subsided.

Reluctantly Adam loosened his hold on Juliana and nimbly sprang off the bed to toss another log on the fire. With wry good humor, he reflected that it would take more than the heat of desire to counteract the damp Cornish air.

Propped up on one elbow, Juliana watched him longingly from the bed with the quilt flung carelessly over her hips. "Come back to bed, Adam. It's lonely here without you."

"Cold too," he teased. He turned from the fireplace and returned to the bed, rubbing his arms briskly. "Damn, can you hear that wind? We're in for a gale or two this winter."

He dove under the quilt and curled up against her languidly relaxed body. "Oh, no, Adam!" she cried. "Go away! Your feet are freezing."

Ignoring her objections, he locked his arms around her waist and snuggled contentedly into the curve of her back until she ceased squirming. Too exhilarated from their lovemaking to sleep, they lay quietly under the rumpled quilt and listened to the wind rattling the windowpanes.

"It must be around eleven o'clock," Juliana commented idly. She twisted around to stare up into Adam's face. "You don't know how many nights I've stayed awake wondering where you were, Adam. And then when I found you with Leigh the evening of the party, I thought—"

"No." He shook his head, his arms tightening around her. "I don't care for deception, Juliana. Had I decided to take a mistress, you could be sure I'd have told you about it first."

"Then where . . . where did you sleep on those nights I found your chamber empty?"

He gazed down at her in surprise. "I thought you knew. I had a sofa moved into the library to sleep on. The springs in the mattress in the guest chamber are gone, and I—well, to be honest, it was too hard to sleep there knowing you were so close and yet inaccessible to me. I'm afraid you are my one weakness, Juliana."

She closed her eyes, resting her head on his collarbone. "I'm so glad, Adam."

"What about you and Paul Delisle?" He shook her gently so that her head lolled back and she had to look at him again. "It infuriated me that he took you to the fair that day. Did you know I had Robbie following you?"

"You didn't! Oh, Adam, what a horrid thing to do. I'd have died of humiliation had Paul found out. Anyway, you're a fine one to talk about deception. You should've told me about your first marriage."

"I suppose I didn't want to frighten you off. So many

people have blamed me for what happened to Lucy and Anne that I've come to believe it was my fault.''

"You judge yourself too harshly, Adam. You couldn't have foreseen or prevented that massacre.''

He squeezed her gently, his hand resting on the curve of her hipbone. "You're right about one thing, my love. I should have confided in you. From now on there must be no more secrets between us.'' He prodded her in the ribs. "Have you nothing to confess?''

A smile played on her lips. "In fact, I do. Those cakes you ate at supper—'' She stopped, overcome with embarrassed laughter. "I—I fed you a love philter, Adam. I . . . was unsure how to approach you, and this gypsy—''

"I threw the wretched things down into the courtyard to Robbie's pups when you left the room.''

"You didn't!''

"I wasn't sure whether you were trying to poison me or to impress me with your culinary skills. I didn't want to hurt your feelings.''

"Oh, Adam, I feel so incredibly stupid.''

"And I feel incredibly flattered that you'd go to such trouble to seduce me. I hope you're aware it was totally unnecessary. Knowing you want me is the most effective aphrodisiac I can imagine.''

His lips brushed her temple with a kiss, and Juliana could feel his body shaking with subdued laughter. Suddenly she, too, began to laugh, unable to stop until tears filled her eyes.

"It—it really isn't that funny, Adam. I gave away my diamond earrings for that stupid philter, and—''

"And what?''

The amusement drained from her voice. "I'd forgotten,'' she said dully. "A coachman tried to run Phoebe down that same afternoon. I think—I suspect it was Graham's coach. I'd lent her my cloak—''

She didn't need to say more. Adam released her and swung upward into a sitting position, his face drawn into a mask of dark rage. "Damn that bastard! I've had enough.''

She sat up beside him, placing her hand on his arm. "We can't prove it was Graham. Besides, I've only Phoebe's word that it wasn't an accident.''

"And I've only Jack's word that a nobleman was behind the attack on the cove the night of the last run."

"What—what are you saying?"

"Those weren't smugglers who attacked our men, Juliana. They were ruffians recruited from Helston. Graham must have paid them handsomely. I couldn't find one of them willing to talk. I'll never be able to prove it, but I'll bet your mincing viscount also alerted the revenue cruisers to watch us."

Anxiety swelled in her chest. "I'm frightened for you, Adam. If Graham finds out you're trying to expose him, he might panic—"

He turned his head to look at her, the cold murderous fury in his eyes chilling her into silence. "I'm aware you think I am brutal and lack refinement, Juliana, but there are limits to what a man can endure. If Graham causes any more trouble for us, I'll kill him. I swear it on my little Anne's grave."

Chapter Twenty-six

At the escritoire in the parlor Juliana had spent an entire afternoon catching up on her correspondences: a friendly note to Keith and Barbara, the perfunctory letter to Stephen and Louisa, a few lighthearted lines to Venetia.

"Finally. That's the last one finished." She laid down her quill with a relieved sigh and rose to warm herself by the fire.

Phoebe glanced up from the hearthstone, where she knelt buffing Juliana's boots with a chamois cloth. "Did ee remember to answer Squire Duncastle's invite to tea?"

"Lord, I didn't. But the last thing I want to do is spend an afternoon discussing sheep breeding. Adam will have to help me think up an excuse." She wandered over to the window, pulling the curtains apart to gaze out at the melancholy slate-gray sky. "I hope he returns before evening. It looks like another storm. He didn't happen to mention where he was going today, did he?"

"No, ma'am, 'e didn't, but—"

Juliana turned, noting that the girl had lowered her head and was buffing the boots with unwonted vigor. "But what, Phoebe?"

"Nothin', ma'am. Ain't my place to go about repeatin' gossip. Ain't nothin' ee want to 'ear."

"Probably not, but I should like to judge for myself. Go on. What have you heard?" Juliana returned to the fireplace, her voice hardening. "Phoebe?"

The girl shrugged, not looking up. "Well, 'tis just a rumor, ma'am, but Sally, one of the scullery maids, 'as a cousin who's a barkeep in Penlyn, and 'e told 'er that the master had called the village midwife to the widow's cottage. Seems she was 'aving these queer pains, and that ain't right with 'er baby not due yet. I believe—I believe he's gone to visit 'er today, ma'am, to calm 'er down.''

Pregnant? Leigh was pregnant? Juliana's heart seemed to turn to stone. "Am I correct in assuming that Adam is rumored to be the child's father, Phoebe?''

Phoebe hung her head. "As ee say, 'tis just a rumor, ma'am.''

Juliana turned back to the window, her rigid features concealing her emotional turmoil. So much for the pact of honesty between them, she thought bitterly. It seemed Adam was allowed to play by a different set of rules.

"Give me my boots, Phoebe.''

"But, ma'am, they ain't done—''

"Do as I ask.'' Juliana bent to wrench off her satin slippers. "Go to the kitchen and have Cook pack me a basket of cheese, scones, and apples.''

"Ee can't go out in this cold, ma'am. Why ee just said yerself there's a storm brewin' and 'tis gettin' dark—''

Yet fifteen minutes later, Juliana was marching through the courtyard, oblivious to the rising wind. On the pretext of paying a social visit, she would call at the cliffside cottage and, if she found Adam in Leigh's company, then so much the better. A confrontation between the three of them was definitely in order . . . if the rumors around the village were to be believed.

Rumors. She hesitated, wondering if she was overreacting. She hadn't even given Adam the chance to defend himself. On the other hand, she hadn't questioned him in detail about his relationship with Leigh, past and present, not wanting to shatter their newfound intimacy. Now she wondered whether she had become too trusting since their reconciliation, too eager to believe his evasive explanations.

I'll have to find out for myself, she decided. Visiting the cottage, talking to Leigh would give her a keener feel for the situation. It wouldn't be fair to judge Adam until then.

She walked briskly against the strong breeze. Not caring to meet anyone she knew, she took the steep cliff path to the beach. From her vantage point, she could look out at the ocean. White horses covered the surface of the water, their foamy peaks snatched up by the wind and blown across the sea in streaks. To her surprise, she spotted Paul's lugger harbored in the cove. She could see no sign of him or his crew, and she thought it likely that they'd gone below to take shelter from the wind. Common sense warned her that she should probably turn back, but she ignored it and continued on.

Midway down the path she heard what sounded like light running footfalls following her. Turning, she saw Robbie's pair of Skye terrier pups bounding toward her, barking joyously to be free in the brisk fresh air.

"Down, Ben . . . Alfie!" she scolded, shaking sand from her skirts.

The puppies sat simultaneously and stared up at her with beseeching brown eyes, long shaggy bodies trembling with excitement, their tails thumping the ground.

"I should take both of you straight back to the house," she said sternly. "You're going to be a nuisance following me." But she didn't want to waste the time returning to Mentreath, and she suspected she was the one who'd left the gate open for their escape.

"All right. Come along."

Alfie jumped up with a jubilant yelp and took off down the path. Ben followed, but was soon sidetracked by an abandoned gull's nest that the wind had blown down from the clifftop. On the beach the pups waited briefly for Juliana before running off to chase the waves that were breaking against the shore.

As she walked, Juliana regretted having come along the beach. In order to reach the path to the cottage, she would have to work her way through the tangle of jagged rocks that pitted the shore line. And now, as the tide was rushing in, it meant that she'd probably get her boots and skirts soaked.

"Oh, no! Alfie, you naughty boy, come back here! Ben, stop—"

In dismay she stood and watched as the two pups squeezed between a crop of tricornered serpentine rocks to avoid a wave, and disappeared into the dark interior of a behemoth cave that the pounding sea had worn into the face of the cliff.

"Come back, you two! Come back here!"

But the pups didn't reappear, leaving her with no choice but to splash through the surf and climb the rocks so that she could enter the cave. Then just as she was about to step inside, a darkly clad figure on the adjacent clifftop caught her eye. Was he trying to tell her something? He seemed to be waving her away from the cave, or perhaps he thought he knew her.

A bark distracted her. Peering into the blackness, she saw Ben sitting in the shadows at the end of the cave.

"What is it? Where's your brother? Alfie?"

A plaintive howl answered her from what sounded like the bowels of the earth. Gathering up her skirts, she proceeded carefully along the rugged wall of the cave. Clusters of slippery bladder seaweed hung from its rough surface, and the steady, monotonous dripping of moisture competed with the churning waves outside. The sea had scoured a deep indentation in the floor of the cave, and shallow pockets of water surrounded it.

As she reached Ben, Juliana realized that the cave didn't end, but sloped down into a network of chambers connected by dark twisting tunnels. Cautiously, she continued down into the depths of the cave, Ben at her heels. Now and then a miserable shaft of daylight trickled down through a crack in the cliffside, piercing the dark gloom.

"Alfie?"

She heard another pitiful whine. Tracing the sound, she turned into a black airless tunnel and emerged into a lofty chamber. Delicate marine ferns flourished on its high ceiling, mirrored in the still pools of water that dotted the floor below. For several moments she gazed around the cave in delight, feeling as though she'd entered an underground fairy palace.

Suddenly Ben broke away from her and started barking at a small crevice cut into the wall.

"What—Oh, you stupid, stupid dog!" To her utter disgust, she discovered that Alfie had somehow forced his way into the crevice, and was unable—or unwilling—to get himself out. She knelt impatiently and stuck her hand into the opening.

"Come out here, Alfie!" The dog sniffed tentatively at

her fingertips, then backed deeper into the crevice beyond her reach with a playful growl.

"All right, then! Stay, you stubborn mutt." She stood, wondering if she might tempt him out with a piece of cheese from her basket, which she vaguely remembered leaving outside the cave.

But all thoughts of retrieving the food were driven from her mind as she attempted to retrace her steps. Wending her way back through the dank passageways, she felt water bubbling over her feet. Seconds later she discovered she'd been trapped by the incoming tide. Huge breakers crashed wildly into the cliffside, boiling over and spurting between the rocks outside, flooding the entrance of the cave.

In disbelieving shock she pressed back into the tunnel, clinging to the ledge. As the waves receded, she observed that the sea beyond the shoreline had heaped up beneath a rapidly darkening sky. It was a gale, she realized, its powerful winds whipping the sea into a frenzy. Why hadn't she heeded the numerous warnings given her in the past? Why was she so prone to acting on impulse, always to her sorrow afterward?

She heard whimpering below her, felt Ben jumping up and pawing at her leg. Without thinking she scooped him up into her arms. What could she do? Retreat into the cave, praying the tide would recede before it reached her? Or should she risk swimming out? After all, she'd learned to swim as a toddler almost before she could walk.

She dropped the squirming pup to the ledge and swiftly stripped off her boots and petticoats, afraid their weight would drag her under. The water was freezing—a brutal shock to her system—and she let out an involuntary shriek as she grabbed Ben and dove awkwardly from the ledge.

Nothing in her past experience as a swimmer prepared her for the unexpected strength of the invisible current sweeping through the cave. Myriad unseen fingers clutched at her lower body, sucking her under, knocking her legs out from beneath her. Too late she realized that a natural underground channel, active only at high tide, must have created the floor indentation she'd noticed earlier.

Terrified, the pup twisted out of the crook of her arm. For a pathetic moment, he flailed wildly, struggling to stay afloat. Then just as he bobbed under, Juliana flung out an arm to rescue him. But the distance between them was too great, and he didn't resurface. Muscles screaming with effort, Juliana propelled herself sideways and swam for the cave wall. Normally she'd let the current drag her out to sea where she could swim to safer waters. Here she could not chance being dashed upon the piercing rocks outside.

Shivering convulsively, she hauled herself onto the ledge and stumbled down into the tunnel. A shaggy wet object hurled itself at her legs. Alfie! With anger and relief, she bent and weakly patted his head.

"You idiot dog," she whispered. "Because of your prank, your brother drowned, and so might we."

She straightened, lifting the dog with her. Perhaps if she ventured deeper into the cave, she'd find another ledge high enough to provide refuge from the tide. She almost wept with disappointment when she returned to the fairy-palace chamber and found its only adjoining passageway was a tunnel barely large enough for her to crawl through.

And finally that was what she did, wriggling through it on her side, an inch at a time with the terrier clutched under her arm until she emerged into a chilly recess. She scrambled to her knees, shivering, feeling the cold air stinging the numerous scratches on her arms. The cold air! Sobbing with relief, she glanced around and saw a patch of stormy twilight sky revealed through a large fissure in the cliffside. After several frustrating attempts, she managed to scale the wall and drag herself out, Alfie imprisoned in her bodice.

Wind and rain pelting her mercilessly, she turned away from the sea and discovered she was standing on a ledge above the path to the cottage, separated only by a thin strip of shingle. The irony of her situation brought a bitter smile to her lips. Imagine the expression on Adam's face if he was with Leigh and she were to burst in on their amorous tryst looking like a half-drowned rat.

"Juliana?" A large shadow suddenly moved on the path, resolving into a familiar figure as it jumped down onto the shingle and strode toward her. *"Morbleu!* What happened to you?"

"Oh, Paul!" She practically fell into his arms, almost knocking them both down onto the pebbly beach. "It was so

stupid . . . the dog hid from me in the cave . . . and I—''
Her teeth chattered violently, distorting her speech. "The
p-pup drowned, P-Paul. . . ."

"Hush, hush. It's all right now. *Bon Dieu*, you're like
ice! Here, put my jacket on."

She swayed against him as he draped the heavy serge
jacket around her shoulders, too exhausted to care that her
gown clung revealingly to every curve of her body. There
was something comforting about the way Paul fussed over
her, and the sandlewood soap he used—yes, that was it, she
decided. He reminded her for all the world of her father!

"Juliana, what in the name of all that is holy—"

"It's the other pup," she said, smiling as Paul stared
down at her bodice in bewilderment. "I had to put him
some—Wait, Paul, what are you doing?"

"Carrying you to the cottage. Your husband is organizing
a search party for you from there."

"How considerate of him," she said sourly. "But—but
how did anyone know I was missing? I haven't been gone
that long."

"Apparently Adam returned to the house and found out
from your maid that you'd gone to the cottage. On the way
he'd met an old fisherman who claimed he'd seen a basket
floating out to sea. Adam feared—we all did—that you
might've slipped on the rocks and drowned."

"Put me down, Paul," she shouted to be heard over the
wind. "You're turning purple in the face. Anyway, I've
changed my mind about going to the cottage. I found out today that Mrs. Spencer, or whatever name she goes by, is
pregnant."

"And why on earth should that prevent us from seeking
shelter in her home, *chérie?*"

"Because she and Adam—oh, honestly, Paul, for a
Frenchman you're incredibly naive. Take me home."

"No. We're almost there. Besides, I could never carry
you that far. You're heavier than you look."

The cottage was in chaos when they arrived. Equipped
with oil lanterns and coils of rope, a large group of village
men stood in the tiny parlor, clustered around Adam, Martin, Robbie, and Jack, who was assigning areas of the beach
to be searched. In front of the fire, Leigh reclined on a

chaise longue. With her ripening belly prominent under a soft woolen wrapper and her long blonde hair flowing around her, she looked like a pagan goddess of fertility. Suddenly Adam swung around, throwing an annoyed glance at the figures in the doorway.

"Somebody close that blasted—Juliana?"

She wished she would shrivel up and blow away, so acute was her embarrassment. Instead, she dropped Alfie to the floor and hung back in the doorway, ignoring Adam's outstretched arms.

"Where have you been?" he demanded, pulling her resistant body against him.

"Why should you care?"

He glanced briefly at Paul, then slowly released her, an expression of puzzled concern settling on his face. "I don't understand. What has been going on?"

Paul cleared his throat, enjoying the situation more than he dared let on. "She was trapped in Satan's Maze by the tide."

"Satan's Maze?"

"A complex of caves below the cottage," Paul explained. "She's had a bad experience. One of your dogs drowned."

Adam was silent for a moment. "I see. Then it appears I must thank you for coming to my wife's assistance, captain. It's a fortunate coincidence that you were here, isn't it?"

Paul squared his shoulders, unable to miss the pointed sarcasm in Adam's voice. "I think I'd best return to my ship to alert my crew that your wife has been found. Good night, Adam. Juliana."

Juliana broke away from Adam. "Paul, wait!" she called after him as he strode off into the storm. "You've forgotten your jacket."

"Don't waste your breath," Adam drawled. "He'll use it as an excuse to visit you again."

Juliana whirled around. "He doesn't need an excuse—we're friends. And, Adam, he wouldn't have needed to come to my aid if you'd been around."

He put his hand on her shoulder to draw her away from the door. "I realize you've been through a rough time, my love, but I don't understand why you're upset with me. What were you doing in the cave anyway?''

''What were you doing here?'' she countered. Suddenly conscious that she was being overheard by the others in the room, she lowered her voice. ''We'll discuss this at home. You've put me in a humiliating enough position without forcing me to air our dirty linen in public.''

Juliana sank down lower into the large wooden tub, allowing the scented water to lap over her aching shoulders. She could sense Adam staring at her from the other side of the chamber where he half reclined on the oak settle placed beneath the window. *I will simply pretend he isn't in the room,* she thought belligerently, peeping up at him from the corner of her eye. Moonlight spilled in through the gaping curtains, etching his wavy hair and boldly cast features in silver. Even from this distance, she felt his determination, his unspoken insistence that they clear up this latest misunderstanding before it brewed into something worse. But she wasn't in an understanding mood, still recovering from her harrowing experience in the cave and the shock of discovering Leigh Spencer's secret.

''You've been soaking in that damned tub for almost an hour, Juliana,'' he commented in annoyance, springing to his feet. After the initial relief he'd felt at seeing her alive had worn off, he'd been filled with fury at Juliana for all the needless worry she had put him through. And he was even more furious at her now because she acted as though he were actually responsible for the entire silly affair. ''It's obvious you're trying to avoid talking to me.''

''We talked enough on the way home,'' she said, fresh anger surging into her voice. ''Now I need to think about what you said. Alone.''

''Unless you want to shrivel up like an old apple skin, you'll have to get out of that water soon. And I'm sleeping in *this* room tonight, so don't hope you can provoke me into storming off in a temper. You may have made me look a complete fool in front of the entire village, but I refuse to skulk around like a scolded puppy in my own house.''

''I made you look a fool?'' she echoed in disbelief. ''I

was the one who insisted we not discuss our problems in public. What exactly are you getting at, Adam?"

"I organized a search party to find you, Juliana." He snatched up the towel that was warming on a chair by the fire, and strode to the side of the tub. "I was frantic with worry. I kept picturing your body washed up on the rocks, and then you had the effrontery to turn up in the doorway with another man—and you barely spoke a civil word to me! I must be a pretty good joke around Penlyn by now."

She climbed out of the tub and yanked the towel from his hands, resenting the way he attempted to lay the blame at her feet. "Paul isn't another man, Adam. He's a friend— *our* friend, although I wouldn't be surprised if he avoided us both after your inexcusable rudeness toward him this evening. And as for looking foolish, well, you should have thought of that before you moved Leigh into the cottage." She toweled her damp skin roughly, wincing as she unwittingly exerted pressure on several stinging cuts and rising bruises. "Anyway, you have a lot of nerve to try to make me assume all the fault for this."

Anger enabled Adam to submerge the fierce desire that flooded his groin at the sight of her standing naked before him, her body tempting and pearlescent with moisture. His gray eyes like stone, he dragged his gaze up to her face and glared at her. "Should I apologize because you jumped to the wrong conclusion about Leigh's condition?"

She glared back at him, unflinching in her indignation. "How was I supposed to know that she was already pregnant before she arrived in Cornwall? You might have had the sense to forewarn me before the inevitable gossip reached my ears!"

"And you might have had the sense to trust me instead of following some childish impulse and almost getting yourself drowned!" he retorted.

"Trust!" she said bitterly, sweeping past him to reach for the white linen nightgown draped across the bed. Angrily flinging the towel aside, she turned her back to him. "Do you honestly think we'll ever put aside our differences long enough to build up any trust between us?"

"I don't know, Juliana," he replied, his tone suddenly so subdued and drained of anger that she couldn't help whirling around to stare at him again. She didn't realize how deeply her words had affected him, how close they'd come to echoing the growing despair in his heart.

She held the nightgown crushed to her chest, feeling vulnerable and inexplicably frightened. "Oh, Adam," she whispered, a catch in her voice. "What's going to happen to us?"

He shook his head slowly, his throat expanding with emotion. "I wish I knew, Juliana. We are making quite a mess of our lives, aren't we?"

"I'm scared for us," she confessed, her eyes shining with tears.

"So am I," he said softly.

She dropped the nightgown to the floor. "Oh, Adam, hold me!"

Doubts and accusations were temporarily forgotten as Adam moved toward her and roughly pulled her down beside the bed. Cradling her head in his hands, he traced the edges of her lips with his tongue, and then his mouth covered hers in urgent possession. Dimly Juliana became aware that the anger and resistance had left her body, making her pliant and feverishly responsive to his touch. Her breasts heaved with the excited quickening of her breathing; her nipples tightened into dusky points of sensation that ached for his attention. Then suddenly Adam broke the kiss and gently released her from his grasp, easing off the bed to shed his clothing.

Juliana watched him languidly through half-closed eyelids, not wanting to speak, sensing that words would only destroy the spontaneous passion of the moment. She needed him so badly. She needed the sweet rapturous oblivion that only he could bring her. Yet even as she allowed her mind to drift in enjoyable sensual imaginings, a current of sadness flowed darkly through her thoughts. Was all loving between a man and a woman fraught with this much pain? Or was it simply a dangerous combination of their personalities that made for such a volatile union? A wistful sigh eased out between her lips. If only she'd had some past experience with love to give her insight, to help her understand the fascinating, the frustrating complexity of this man. She was afraid, so desperately afraid, that one day they would wound each other too deeply, that one day they would drive each other away with all the endless fears and misgivings that plagued their relationship.

Suddenly Adam was leaning over her and kissing her again, his long unclad body pressed intimately into hers as his tongue circled hers and penetrated deeply into the satiny warmth of her mouth, chasing all her fears away. They kissed with a passionate absence of inhibition, driven by scalding need and the devastating realization that even love might not be powerful enough to bridge the ever-widening chasm of uncertainty that separated them.

"You're so beautiful, Juliana," Adam groaned as he wrenched his mouth from hers and trailed his lips down her creamy throat in a burning path that made her senses soar in anticipation. "So beautiful, so desirable . . ."

Arousal blossomed inside Juliana, unfurling deliciously in her loins and gathering heat like a flower in the sun. *Take me out of myself, Adam,* she pleaded silently from the depths of her psyche. *Oh, love, take away all of the pain and fill me with your being,* she thought. And then her body curled into a quivering arc as she felt his mouth glide wetly over her softly swelling breasts, his skillful tongue tormenting, brushing in teasing little circles and flicking at her hardened nipples.

A tender desire raged through Adam's bloodstream, the urgency of his physical craving tempered by the gentle strength of his love. His large hands slipped down his wife's back, molding her body into his so that she could have no doubts about how much he wanted her. His mouth released her breast and traveled up to linger at the glistening hollow of her throat. His heart would break if he lost her, he realized painfully. All he had ever wanted to do was to love her, to earn her precious love. He wondered how it had happened that they'd ended up hurting each other instead. How had they become trapped inside this cruel circle of pointless suffering? Would they ever be able to break free?

"I love you," he whispered against her throat, gripping her fiercely as if to prove to himself that she still belonged to him.

His hands moved over her with possessive intimacy, stroking her softly sculpted curves, probing her silken hollows. With maddening expertise, he caressed the flat plane of her abdomen, circling her quivering navel, fluffing the soft tangle of curls as his fingers drifted lower to nestle in the moist haven between her thighs. Juliana moaned and writhed against him, the stimulating friction of his teasing fingers coaxing her to part her legs in invitation.

"I need you, Adam," she said huskily, her head thrashing in restless excitement, her hair spilling across the bed like a skein of bronze-shot satin. The pressure of his strong fingers inside her inflamed her smoldering senses, caused her to wrap her calves around him to urge him closer.

"Now, Adam," she implored him. "Oh, now!"

His rugged face intense, his eyes glazed with desire for her, he thrust into the innermost heat of her, burrowing snugly within her depths, rotating his hips in a primitive rhythm that carried them closer to the contentment they sought so desperately.

Uncontrollable excitement blazed through their straining bodies, engulfing them in swirling flames of scalding sensation. Juliana arched against her husband in complete surrender, melting into his feverish core. As if through a haze she felt Adam's lips seeking hers, his breath hot against her face. Moaning into his mouth, she locked her arms around his neck and clung to him. Oh, yes, she thought distantly, this was how it should be, their bodies fused in loving harmony, communicating without the interference of words. Deeper and faster now he drove inside her, his every thrust sparking a response in her loins until suddenly they exploded together, consumed by a fiery climax that left them both shuddering heatedly in its lingering afterglow.

His chest glistening with a fine sheen of perspiration, Adam dropped onto his back with one hand resting on Juliana's hipbone. For a long time they were content to bask in the glow of blissful silence that enveloped them. Adam's mind was empty, his thoughts so quiet that he simply ignored them. Juliana tried not to think at all, concentrating on the warm feelings that radiated throughout her.

But gradually reality intruded on her contentment, reminding her of all that remained unsettled in her marriage. From beneath her lowered eyelids, she glanced up at her husband's impassive, angular face. She loved him so! Hope lifting her heart, she wondered if perhaps everything could work out for them, after all. Perhaps their lovemaking had served to clear the air of the awful emotional strain they'd been living under lately. Surely now Adam would be in a more receptive mood to understand her viewpoint.

"Adam?"

"Hmm?" He turned his head to stare down at her, a drowsy smile curving his mouth. "What, love?"

"About Leigh." She hurried on before he could interrupt, noting with unease that his mouth had straightened warningly. "I just don't think it's right that you have to take care of her. She's got family."

Adam laughed sourly, recalling his narrow-minded, embittered former father-in-law. "Not all families are as loving as yours, Juliana. The girl is alone and frightened. In fact, it wouldn't be a bad idea if you were to befriend her, have her here for tea—"

"Me?" She stared at him with insulted displeasure. "You expect me to start socializing with a woman the entire village thinks is your mistress?"

"It's what we think that matters, isn't it?" he said angrily. He couldn't believe she was behaving this way, like a spoiled, selfish child. He knew he was innocent of any wrongdoing where Leigh was concerned. Why did he have to defend himself to his wife? His word should have been good enough for her.

Juliana pulled away from him, hurt that he refused to consider her feelings. Why did he feel an obligation to this stupid girl? When would he ever be free of the past?

"I'm too tired to discuss this anymore," she said coldly. "In case you've forgotten, I had a wretched experience today."

And that was your own damned fault, you stubborn little cat! he almost shouted. But he didn't, not willing to feed the enmity between them. Instead, he shut his eyes and tried to empty his mind of thought, unable to understand how they could plunge from ecstasy into anguish in only a few short moments.

Bitterness surged up inside Juliana. Nothing had changed between them. Not a damned thing. Oh, God, why couldn't the rest of their relationship be even half as perfect as their lovemaking? Her eyes dark with misery, she turned onto her side and stared into the darkness until finally exhaustion overcame her, and she sank into the welcome forgetfulness of sleep.

Chapter Twenty-seven

A fortnight later Adam and Juliana traveled into Helston to attend a Twelfth Night ball-assembly given by the prominent banker Mr. Oliver Tomlin. It was an important evening for Adam. If all went well, he would informally settle the arrangements for a short-term loan which would cover his debts until he'd mortgaged or sold off his lesser holdings. The smuggling was too unstable to rely on, but the sizable investment he'd made in the shipyard was finally beginning to yield a return, and he was optimistic about his financial future.

If only his problems with Juliana could be so easily solved, he thought ruefully. To his dismay, they seemed to have drifted even further apart since the incident in the cave. They continued to sleep together. They dined together. But Juliana's obstinate refusal to try to understand the responsibility he felt toward Leigh was a source of bitter dissension between them, and he suspected she still harbored doubts about the nature of his relationship with the younger woman. Her unfounded lack of trust in him bothered him deeply, and he felt a wave of depression engulf him as he gazed at her across the interior of the hired coach. One day they ascended the heights of heaven together, the next they were pitching into hell. How much longer could they cling to the tenuous threads that held them together?

"You're unusually subdued, Juliana. Have I done something wrong again? If so, I wish you'd tell me so we can discuss it before it builds inside you and erupts like a storm."

She flushed lightly at his words. Why did he make her feel as though *she* were always at the root of the disharmony between them? Feeling compelled to defend herself, her

eyes glittering with golden-jade sparks, she addressed him
in acrid tones. "You're a fine one to talk. We might not
have fought over this if you'd told me about Leigh's condition in the first place."

He tilted his head back against the padded leather seat, a
slow smile stretching his lips. "I've been accused of many sins
in my day, but never of fathering a child across an ocean."

"Very amusing," Juliana snapped, unable to find the
slightest bit of humor in the situation. "I still don't understand why you don't send her back to her father."

"He wants nothing to do with her."

And neither should you, Juliana countered silently, annoyance flaring up inside her. As if they had room in their lives for
Leigh Spencer's troubles! But her irritation was short-lived,
displaced by a quiet burst of happiness as she contemplated the
subtle physical and emotional changes she had noticed in herself lately. Although it was too soon to be positive, she suspected she was pregnant again. Still, she wouldn't raise
Adam's hopes until the doctor examined her. A baby might be
just what they needed to dissolve the resentment between them
and draw them closer together. Perhaps having to raise a family
would force them to put aside their personal conflicts long
enough to achieve a lasting peace.

"Damnation," Adam said suddenly. "I must have left
those papers back in our room at the inn."

"Good. This isn't the proper time to discuss business."

The coach rounded a corner and slowed before an elegant
red-brick townhouse. Juliana suffered a pang of nervous excitement as she and Adam alit from the vehicle to climb the marble
entrance steps. She had missed socializing and dancing, having
the chance to show off the pretty clothes she owned. Or had
she? She sent Adam a searching look, her fingers tightening
around his muscular forearm. She would've gladly given up a
month of parties just to stay home alone with him tonight,
drinking brandy by the fire, or curled up on the sofa in the library while he worked on his account books. *Oh, stop deluding
yourself, Juliana,* a voice within her warned harshly. *Adam
probably wouldn't spend the entire evening alone with you if he
had the chance.* He'd rather waste his time discussing business
matters with Martin, or running down to the cottage to cater to
one of Leigh's latest whims.

"Nervous, my dear?" Adam whispered as he felt the pressure of her slender fingers on his arm. "You needn't be. You'll be the loveliest woman here by far."

Tonight she wore a silver brocade gown, the boned bodice stitched with tiny florets of seed pearls, the pale-rose lace overskirt flowing over hooped petticoats. Adam had also dressed for the occasion, wearing a tailored suit of claret-colored superfine with a ruffled white silk shirt and a cambric cravat secured with an onyx clasp. With a curious mixture of pride and jealousy, Juliana noticed that more than one female head swiveled at his entrance.

The majordomo ushered them through the paneled receiving vestibule and past the dining room, where liveried footmen scurried to and fro putting the finishing touches on the rectangular banquet table. A midnight supper was planned, and afterward the guests would share a traditional Twelfth Night cake containing a thimble, a sixpence, and a gold wedding-band.

The ballroom had just been opened. The orchestra musicians were tuning up behind a carved cherrywood screen, but the majority of guests had congregated in the upstairs state apartment and gaming room, where several intense card games were already under way. Others took advantage of the crisp starry night to stroll in the pleasure gardens, or to indulge in lighthearted flirtations on the terrace.

Mr. and Mrs. Tomlin greeted Adam and Juliana on the second-floor landing of the top-lit staircase to the circular state apartment.

"My dear, I'm so glad to meet you," Mrs. Tomlin said, squeezing Juliana's hand. "I've been meaning to send you an invitation to one of our monthly tea parties. Adam's uncle used to enjoy them, when we could talk him into coming."

Juliana looked puzzled. "I had the impression he was . . . well, antisocial."

"Oh, he was. But he liked our broad-minded group." She pulled Juliana toward her so that they were practically leaning over the wrought-iron balustrade. "He told the most fascinating stories, my dear. He was experimenting with magic, trying to contact the dead. It came as no shock to us to hear that his ghost had been sighted. You haven't seen him, have you?"

"No, I—" Juliana felt goose bumps pricking her arms as

she remembered the mysterious figure warning her away from the cave.

"I thought so," Mrs. Tomlin said with quiet triumph in her voice. "I can't imagine Logan not wanting to make a special appearance for Marie Pendarvis's daughter."

Adam was soon lured away to discuss business, and Juliana found herself being introduced to a long stream of local personages, some of whom fondly recalled the days when her mother had reigned over Helston society. Others were politically motivated landowners eager to buy up Adam's freehold estates to extend their voting power.

An hour passed pleasantly, Juliana sipping lamb's wool from a pewter goblet in the spirit of the evening. And then she looked up and noticed a tall young man dressed in a heavily embroidered gold satin suit with an amber-headed cane dangling from his wrist. For a moment she didn't recognize the face under the high powdered wig and coatings of rouge. Then he began to approach her with his mouth slowly curling into a sly mocking smile that made her shiver as she sensed the danger lurking behind it. Graham . . . more like the vain young fop she had known. God forbid that he pick a fight with Adam tonight of all nights.

"So the ill-bred colonial has allowed you out for an evening in refined society," he said quietly, his gaze raking her with insulting intimacy: "You're looking remarkably trim for a bitch that's supposed to be breeding, or was that a lie, too?"

She saw that he was quite drunk, that the layers of paint and powder only emphasized the lines of debauchery on his once-handsome face. "Don't start, Graham," she said under her breath as a footman strolled by them. "For the love of God, get on with your life, and let me do the same."

"But you've destroyed my life, Juliana. I have nothing to live for without you. I want you to suffer with me."

"Oh, I'm doing that," she said. "But you're a fool if you can't see what a full, prosperous future you could—" She stopped short as a moon-faced young man swaggered into the room, glancing around to see if his entry had been noticed. "Harry!" she cried, beckoning him over.

Relieved, she watched Lord Belstow swerve toward them, a pleased grin crossing his face. "Well, well. So the infamous couple are reunited." His merry brown eyes darted from Graham to Juliana. "Planning a liaison for this evening, are we?"

"No, Harry, we are not." Juliana laughed.

Harry insinuated his way between them, his voice conspiratorial. "In that case, why don't the three of us try our luck in the gaming room? One of us is bound to walk out a winner."

Some of the tension seemed to drain from Graham. "Good idea, Harry. Juliana, will you join us? You can just watch if you like."

She froze, unable to think up an excuse to refuse. The last thing she wanted was to antagonize him tonight, and with Harry to act as a buffer between them, she felt reasonably safe, if not comfortable, in Graham's company. Taking into consideration his potential for irrational violence, she finally decided he'd be less tempted to instigate a fight with Adam if she placated him.

Her attempt was in vain. Just as they were about to enter the gaming room, Adam turned into the hallway, flanked by two elderly gentlemen. His eyebrows lifted when he spotted her, but he maintained his self-control as he excused himself from his companions to join her.

"I was looking for you, Juliana," he said evenly, taking her arm. "I don't believe you've met our solicitor."

"A solicitor?" Graham repeated jeeringly. "Did you hear that, Harry? Smuggling must indeed be a profitable business if he can afford to keep a solicitor on retainer."

"And murder is a dirty business," Adam said quietly, "even when a man hires someone else to commit it."

Harry glanced around uneasily. "I say, Graham, I just heard someone say there's a place at the hazard table."

"If anyone else in my employ is harmed, I'll know who to come after," Adam continued, his eyes like shards of glass. "And if you ever lay a finger on my wife again, I'll kill you."

A dangerous silence ensued. Juliana could feel waves of animosity radiating from Graham, just as she felt the involuntary stiffening of Adam's body. Please, God, she prayed, don't let either of them challenge the other to a duel.

Apparently Lord Belstow shared her fear. Placing a hand on Graham's shoulder, he gently directed him toward the gaming room while affecting an authoritative man-to-man tone. "Now listen to me, you two. I've always held that there are no differences so great they can't be fought out over a card table. It's the civilized way, don't you know? No bloodshed, no broken bones—everything neatly decided by an impartial fate.''

''I'm not averse to the idea,'' Graham said tightly. ''What about you, Tremayne? How d'you think you'll fare when you can't resort to the use of your fists to gain the advantage?''

He didn't wait for a reply, but shrugged off Harry's arm and opened the door to the gaming room. The odor of cigar smoke wafted into the hallway, and Juliana caught a glimpse of tables crowded with men so engrossed in their cards, they wouldn't have looked up had a naked woman entered the room executing somersaults. Some had turned their coats inside out for luck; others wore broad-brimmed straw hats to hide their emotions from their opponents. Professional operators and croupiers had been hired for the evening, and at the back of the room, where the ladies played whist, the atmosphere was equally competitive.

''Adam, don't!'' she whispered as she felt him break away. ''Let's go back to the inn and order supper in bed. We'll tell Mrs. Tomlin I'm starting a vile headache, which, God only knows, seems to be true enough—''

He cut her off, his voice crisp with anger. ''You expect me to just calmly walk away, pretending not to care that he almost raped you—almost ran over your maid—and caused an innocent man to be murdered?''

''Yes. Yes . . . I do.''

''In the name of heaven, Juliana, you ask too much!''

''What do you hope to prove, Adam?'' she asked him bitterly. ''You thrashed the daylights out of him once, and we both know he'd be no match for you in a duel. If he causes us any more trouble, we'll—we'll notify the authorities.''

Adam's mouth twisted wryly at her naivete. ''Really, Juliana. And what do you suppose the authorities would do if I complained that the son of a prominent nobleman is disrupting my illicit smuggling activities? Grow up, my dear. We aren't living in a fairy-tale world.''

Juliana felt her own temper rising dangerously at his reckless disregard of her advice, but she restrained it, determined that they wouldn't create a humiliating scene in front of everyone.

''Then at least consider what Mr. Tomlin will do if he

sees you gambling away money you can't afford to lose. He'd think twice about extending you that loan.''

"But I won't lose, Juliana."

"Oh, damn you and your stupid male pride!" she cried out in frustration. "What good do you think it'll do you to stoop down to Graham's level?" She dropped her voice an octave, heedful of the people around them. "Maybe you don't really care what happens to you and me, Adam, but you should have some consideration for your child. What kind of future will he have if you gamble away everything we own? That's what this will lead to. One game, then another—''

"My child?" The mask of mocking anger slipped from his face, to be replaced by a slow incredulous grin. A child. Would it strengthen their marriage, or would it place another wedge between them? He wondered why she hadn't told him before. Was she keeping it a secret out of some superstitious fear that she might suffer another miscarriage? Would she ever learn to trust him?

"This is the damndest time to break the news to me, Juliana."

"Oh! I—I shouldn't have said anything. It's too early to be sure." Confused, still furious at him, she pushed his hands away as he put them out to encircle her waist. "To be honest, Adam. I almost hope it isn't true."

His smile had become brittle. "Go on."

"Well, I—Oh, life with you is just too . . . unstable to raise children." She paused, wishing she could take the words back, knowing they weren't true, but she couldn't seem to bring her emotions under control. "God, I don't even know what I'm saying! All I know is that it'll be over between us if you enter that room, Adam. That's all. I'll go back to Rosmorna to live with Stephen and Louisa."

Without giving him a chance to respond, she wheeled and hurried down the hallway, helpless tears filling her eyes. Belatedly she wondered if it had been she who'd acted rashly, allowing the mood swings of her pregnancy to sway her feelings. No. She inhaled a steadying breath. She was right, and if Adam couldn't admit that, their marriage had no future.

"My goodness, Mrs. Tremayne! Whatever is the matter?"

Juliana lifted her hand from her eyes to see her hostess walking toward her, concern stamped on her pleasant features. "Oh, it's nothing, Mrs. Tomlin. Just the start of a frightful headache. I never get them, but tonight—"

"La! I hope it's not from the lamb's wool. I told Oliver we should have served a light punch instead." She placed her arm around Juliana's shoulders, enveloping her in a maternal embrace. "Come into the bedchamber and lie down, dear girl. I'll open the windows, and have my maid bring you a cup of chamomile tea and a cool vinegar compress to lay upon your forehead."

The traditional remedies worked wonders, and within minutes after drinking the tea, Juliana stretched out on the comfortable tent bed and found herself drifting off to sleep. Another symptom of early pregnancy, she thought drowsily. Already the babe saps my strength.

To her utter amazement she didn't awaken for hours; possibly she would have slept even longer had voices from the terrace below not interrupted her dream. Disoriented to find herself in a strange bed, her mind still foggy from sleep, she lay unmoving for several moments, listening to the disjointed snatches of conversation.

"Ha! Thirty thousand pounds, and his coach and horses. Serves the little drunkard right if you ask me. Always looking down that aristocratic nose of his. Does my old heart good to see him lose his shirt to someone of middle-class origins."

"Avonston no longer owns even that shirt if the rumors about 'im are to be believed," an amused masculine voice rejoined. "He's already signed away everything but his firstborn to the usurers as 'tis. Word has it he pays them twenty thousand pounds per annum in interest on his debts alone."

A third male voice entered the conversation. "Wait till the earl catches wind of this. Wouldn't be surprised if he cuts him out of his will once and for all. Disgrace to the family name."

Juliana rose slowly from the bed, cold fear uncoiling in her belly and spreading its numbing poison through her. Oh, God! What price had Adam paid to feed his pride? Didn't he realize that ruining Graham, humiliating him in public would only provoke him to further violence? And what did it bode for her marriage that he'd ignored her ultimatum, knowing she'd threatened to leave him?

Her temples throbbed fiercely as she made her way into the candlelit hallway. By the number of guests assembling downstairs, she guessed that it was approaching midnight. She wouldn't stay for supper. She'd return to the inn discreetly, perhaps seek out the innkeeper and have him make arrangements for her to travel to Rosmorna first thing in the morning. Adam probably wouldn't try to stop her, she thought, her heart aching with unhappiness. As a matter of fact, he might be relieved to have her removed from his life. Obviously he didn't care enough for her to curb his rash inclinations to save their marriage. Obviously, appeasing his pride meant more that appeasing his wife.

"Graham!" She shrank back against the wall in alarm as she recognized him climbing the stairs, his lean face haggard.

He stared at her for so long she feared he intended to attack her again. And when he finally stepped toward her, his left hand reaching for her face, she gasped and flung out her arm to ward him off.

"You could have saved me, Juliana," he said, his voice breaking on a pathetic sob. "You alone . . ."

Before she even lowered her arm, he was gone, disappearing into the antechamber that adjoined the bedroom at the end of the hallway. Juliana stared after him, unable to move. She knew she should despise him, but she couldn't. Oh, why couldn't Adam have left well enough alone?

"Where the hell is he?" Adam appeared at the top of the staircase, his chest heaving with exertion. "Juliana, answer me! Did you see which way Graham went?"

She glared at her husband with blazing eyes, torn between loving the man she thought she had come to know and the cruel stranger who stood before her. Part of her seemed frozen in disbelief, unwilling to accept this merciless facet of his character. "Haven't you done enough damage already, Adam? Are you afraid he'll run off without signing your note?"

"I'm afraid the bloody fool is going to take his own life!" he shouted, not bothering to respond to her taunting, even though he felt the contempt in her voice like the laceration of a whip. "I heard a footman say that Mr. Tomlin's study had been broken into and a dueling pistol was missing."

"Dear God." She gestured frantically to the antechamber. "In there. Oh, be careful, Adam!"

She rushed after him, her progress impeded by her hooped petticoats. She found the antechamber in darkness, the doors to the dressing room and two connecting chambers flung open. A muffled whisper escaped from the depths of the dressing room, and she started toward it, freezing as she noticed two figures embracing in the shadows, a silver-haired woman with diamonds at her throat and her bodice unlaced, and a man who appeared several years her junior.

"Adam?" she called out, backing away from the amorous scene she'd intruded upon. She turned, and then she heard a man's voice cry out. Adam? She couldn't tell, for his next words were blurred by the sharp report of a pistol.

Her stomach lurched with fear. She whirled clumsily and raced toward the second bedroom, colliding in the doorway with a wide-eyed chambermaid who was carrying a bundle of soiled linen.

"My husband," Juliana gasped. "He was trying . . . to prevent the viscount—"

"Too late, ma'am," the girl whispered, edging away.

Juliana caught the girl's arm, her heart thudding with dread. "Go downstairs and summon your master. Be as discreet as possible."

"Yes, ma'am." The girl clutched the bundle to her scrawny chest and sidled away. "Right now, ma'am."

Juliana slowly stepped into the room, her eyes gradually perceiving details in the moonlight. Graham's body sprawled out across the bed, the side of his face unrecognizable pulp. The ebony-inlaid pistol on the floor. Adam sitting rigid and expressionless in a cane-bottomed chair, his ruffled shirtfront splattered with a few dark droplets of blood.

"Stupid little bastard," he said softly, slowly lifting his gaze to his wife's shocked face. "To blow out his brains over a card game."

Juliana averted her head, feeling hot bile bubbling in her throat. The tragic ugliness of Graham's death seemed to seep into her very soul—to think that Adam had been responsible for such senseless horror! "I hope you're content now, Adam," she said, shuddering violently as her eyes strayed once again to the viscount's lifeless form. "I hope you'll sleep well tonight knowing you brought a man to his destruction."

"I brought—" He shook his head in utter disgust. So it had come to this—his own wife condemning him as so many others had done in the past. With her heart full of that much mistrust and bitterness toward him, had there ever been any room for love? He shouldn't have been surprised that she would turn against him now, but he was. And it hurt, God how it hurt.

"Why don't you just come right out and accuse me of murdering him?"

"No, Adam, I never—" But she found herself unable to finish, unable to deny that the thought had crossed her mind.

And then suddenly low speculative voices sounded from the antechamber, and candlelight flared brightly from the doorway, illuminating the grim tableau.

"Oh, my God—Somebody send for the doctor!"

"Doctor? It's a coroner the poor wretch needs. Can't you see his face? Why—by Jove, it's young Avonston! A nasty business, this."

"Smacks of foul play, it does," a third man grunted, shouldering his way past Juliana. "Wouldn't care to be in the earl's company when he hears of this."

It was almost dawn before Adam and Juliana were able to return to the inn. Mrs. Tomlin had invited them to stay over until morning, but Juliana had declined the offer, knowing Adam needed to be away from the atmosphere of suspicion building around him. Numbed by the events of the evening, they trod the creaking stairs to their room and unlocked the door without a single word passing between them. They didn't bother to undress. Adam had too much on his mind to sleep, and Juliana knew that they would be called for the morning coach shortly after daybreak.

"I want you to return to Mentreath without me, Juliana."

He was sitting at the small round table, and she was lying on the bed, fighting a surge of morning sickness.

"That's fine with me, Adam," she said, gazing up at the beamed ceiling.

He flashed her a hostile look. "I thought it might be. I was sure you wouldn't want to travel with a man you suspect is a murderer."

"Damn you, Adam! I didn't say that. Don't start a fight." She swung her feet to the floor, her stomach rolling, her emotions reeling. "I can't take much more of this," she moaned. "The lies, the secrets, the way we always seem to be hurting each other. I don't know what made us think this marriage would work out."

"I believe we'd pinned our hopes on love and understanding," he drawled.

She buried her face in her hands, too exhausted to cry, unable to blot out the gruesome vision of Graham's face. "Right now I wish we'd never met," she said softly. "I wish you'd never entered my life. There's just been too much pain since I've known you. And tonight, when you were willing to risk our future on a card game for the sake of assuaging your damned pride—"

"My loving wife, your lack of faith in me is remarkable. Didn't it once occur to you that I might have taken your advice and ignored Graham's challenge, that our marriage mattered even more to me than my honor? Graham lost to a goldsmith, Juliana, not to me."

She gasped, her head lifting. "Adam, I didn't know—"

His lips stretched into a humorless smile. "While Graham was spending his last hours at the gaming tables, I was in the library with Lord Hazelhurst. He's offered to buy all our northern arable land at a price far lower than I intended to ask. I hadn't wanted to sell so large a parcel to any one man, especially a toady of Hazelhurst's ilk, but at least I won't be displacing any tenant farmers. Anyway, I don't have much choice. I haven't time to be particular."

Juliana stood, her wavy auburn hair swaying around her face as the last of her pins slipped loose. "You're frightening me, Adam. What do you mean you have no time?"

"It's only a precaution. Just in case."

"In case what?"

"In case I'm arrested and our lands are confiscated. I'll at least have some money put aside to take care of you—and the child. There's also your dowry, and the income from the shipyard."

Juliana shook her head disbelievingly. Everything had happened so fast, their lives turned upside down in a matter of hours. Her mind simply couldn't absorb this much anguish at one time. Graham's ghastly death. Her quarrel with Adam and, now, the horrifying possibility of his imprisonment. *Oh, Adam, Adam! I'm afraid for you!* A sudden surge of love for him overwhelmed the bitter anger she'd felt toward him earlier as she realized the breadth of the danger he faced. She wanted to tell him that she believed in him, that she loved him despite what she'd said to the contrary, but the words seemed to be trapped within her heart.

"They can't arrest you, Adam. Graham committed suicide. He was despondent, mired in debt."

"He was also the sole heir to an earldom. Will his father let the matter of his only son's death rest without even an inquiry?"

She stared at him in dismay. "Adam, why did you want me to return to Mentreath alone?"

"There's bound to be a formal investigation, and I'll be called for questioning. You'll probably be wanted later on, too. Anyway, I want to close the deal with Hazelhurst and settle a few other business matters."

"Adam, about the things I said earlier—"

"We'll discuss it later. We're both tired."

"But I want you to know—"

A loud knock sounded against the door, ending the conversation, and a young boy's voice informed them: "Coach is ready to leave! Bring out yer baggage."

"I want to stay with you, Adam. I think I should be here in case anything happens."

"Juliana, please." He turned his head, and in the milky morning light, she saw the dark circles beneath his eyes, the determined thrust of his jaw. "For once trust me and do as I ask. Think of yourself, Juliana. You don't want to lose another child."

She left the inn reluctantly, aching inside as she imagined what he must be going through. Was he blaming himself for this death, too? It was more her fault than his, she thought guiltily. She should have insisted on leaving the ball the moment she saw Graham. It would have been a small sacrifice to pay to avert the evening's tragedy. She could've pretended to be ill. She should have sensed Graham wasn't in his right mind when she encountered him in the hallway. Too late for regrets now, her mind taunted, and then she wondered with sweeping dismay whether it was also too late to salvage her marriage. Would there be any chance for them after tonight, after all the hurting words she had flung at him? Around and around in endless circles her thoughts swirled until she felt her head would explode.

Chapter Twenty-eight

Adam was arrested on suspicion of murder within the week to be bound over in Helston jail until a preliminary investigation had been made. The moment the news reached Mentreath, Robbie galloped off to Devon to summon Adam's brother-in-law to defend the case. Juliana, her nerves stretched to the breaking point, would have gladly attempted the ride herself if only as an outlet for her tension. But she didn't want to risk another miscarriage. There was no longer any doubt in her mind that she was carrying Adam's child.

Keith and Barbara Simpson set out immediately in their small coach, hazarding the bumpy rain-washed roads in what the driver grumbled was the foulest winter in memory. They arrived at Mentreath a few days later at the height of a violent hailstorm.

Over a fortifying meal of rabbit stew, cold kidney pie, and spiced cider, Juliana patiently answered Keith's barrage of probing questions. Jack and Doris flitted about in the background like nervous moths, pretending to scrape plates at the sideboard or to stir the fire. Their fussing around grated on Juliana's already strained composure, but she knew it was only concern for Adam that kept them in the room. It was after one when Keith paused to organize his notes.

"That's enough for tonight," Barbara said firmly. "Juliana needs her rest. And look at her plate. Juliana, you've not taken a bite of that lovely pie."

"I can't. My stomach is tied in knots."

"Worrying isn't good for the baby, my dear."

"I know," Juliana said distractedly. "Well, what do you think, Keith? They don't have a solid case against Adam, do they? Isn't all the evidence circumstantial?"

Keith shrugged, noncommittal. "I'll be in a better position to judge after I've gone to Helston and talked to Adam myself. We'll need to get hold of that chambermaid you mentioned. Let's hope Wynherne hasn't already bought her off."

Juliana put down her fork with an uneasy smile. "That's not very encouraging, Keith. You almost make it sound as though there's a possibility that formal charges could be brought against Adam."

"Juliana, it's possible that he could face the death penalty."

Juliana's blood chilled with fear, rivulets of ice racing through her veins. The death penalty. Oh, merciful God, none of this could be happening. Did Adam have any idea of the grave implications surrounding his arrest? Yes—he must; he'd tried to warn her that wretched night in Helston, had tried to prepare her to expect just this. Was he blaming her for what had happened to him? Did he hate her? Perhaps, she answered herself, and didn't she deserve his hatred after she'd practically told him that she didn't want his child, that she wished him out of her life? Heartsick and depressed, she wondered if this dreadful experience would serve to bring them back together or push them even further apart. Her eyes clouded with worry. She was assuming, of course, that Adam would regain his freedom. Unless that happened, there was no point in looking toward the future.

"Adam *is* innocent, Keith," she said, the truth the most reassuring—the only—defense she could summon.

"Consider the case that could be built against him, Juliana. Graham visits your home, perhaps to congratulate you on your marriage, and Adam, finding you alone together, flies into a jealous rage and assaults him."

Panic clenched Juliana. "But that's not the way it happened!" she cried. "And there were no witnesses but our own servants."

"The coachman who drove his master's battered body home? The valet who ministered to him in the courtyard? Could a jury not be persuaded that Adam caught you and

Graham embracing in the hallway, chased him into the bedroom and then shot him?''

"Don't think about it anymore tonight, Juliana," Barbara said. "Keith will do everything he can to help him. We both will."

Ten agonizing days passed before Keith returned from Helston. To keep herself occupied, Juliana spent hours with Doris and Barbara preparing a room in the east wing for a nursery. But Adam never strayed from her mind for more than a few minutes at a time, and the thought of him locked away in some cold stinking cell, awaiting heaven knew what fate, dampened the joy she felt at carrying his child.

Paul returned from a recent smuggling venture in Cherbourg, pledging his support the second the situation was explained to him. In fact, Juliana found it impossible to get rid of him. He was waiting for her in the garden every morning when she woke; he walked her to the staircase in the great hall when she retired. When he told her he'd taken a room at the Gilded Swan in Penlyn, she resigned herself to his presence and decided she should be grateful for her few loyal friends. None of her neighbors—except Squire Duncastle and Leigh—had asked about Adam since his arrest. Venetia's gossipy letters had stopped suddenly, and Juliana suspected that her friend had finally broken under pressure from her family.

"Juliana, please sit down."

The ominous tone of Keith's greeting as she entered the great hall resurrected the fears she'd been trying to suppress. Nor did she find comfort in his fatigued expression, the way his slight shoulders drooped beneath his rain-bejeweled cloak.

"Come right to the point, Keith," she said in a strained voice. "I can tell you've brought bad news."

He shrugged out of his cloak and settled into a chair by the fire, taking the glass of sherry Barbara offered him. "The prosecution is building quite a case against him, Juliana. You neglected to mention that Adam threatened to kill Graham only hours before his death. A nobleman has offered to testify to the fact."

"A nobleman?" She sank into a chair. "Oh, damn you, Harry."

"Furthermore, the chambermaid we had counted on as a witness has vanished."

"With a gold purse from the earl, I suppose."

Keith shook his head. "No. With a small fortune in jewels she stole from Mrs. Tomlin on the evening of the ball. She'd only been hired a few days earlier. It seems Mrs. Tomlin was so preoccupied with her arrangements, she failed to check the girl's references. You must have intercepted her escape. She'll never come forward to testify."

"What about the couple in the adjoining bedchamber? There's a good chance they saw what happened."

"If they did, they're not talking. Believe me, Juliana, I'm investigating every angle. My assistant from Devon is working full-time on the case."

Silence descended. Juliana felt Paul come to stand behind her chair. "How is Adam?" she asked at length.

"Quite understandably in a foul humor," Keith replied. "The quarrel you two had that night hasn't helped his spirits."

"Nor mine," she said quietly. "Isn't there anything I can do, Keith? I feel so helpless. Can't I at least visit him?"

"Adam is dead against it, and so am I. A filthy jail cell is hardly the place for a pregnant woman. For the sake of your health, he wants you to remain at home."

There was another long silence. Then Paul spoke up in his roughly melodic voice. "If money proves a problem, *monsieur,* if we are forced to bribe witnesses for Adam's protection, I would be more than willing to increase the number of runs I'd planned."

"No!" Keith nearly choked on his sherry to get the single word out. "That's all we need. Adam musn't appear to have any more blemishes on his character. Anyway, you'd never raise enough funds to outbribe Wynherne. All connections with the smuggling must be severed." He looked pointedly at Juliana. "Is that agreed?"

"Of course," she said. "I'll do whatever you ask."

"Good." He stood, his scowl receding. "I'm going upstairs to rest for an hour. After that I'll probably spend the remainder of the day in the library. I need to review my briefs for the preliminary hearing before riding back to Helston.''

She followed him to the bottom of the staircase, her voice sharp with anxiety. ''If he's formally charged—''

''I don't know, Juliana. We'll do our best.''

Paul came to her side. ''If he is charged, we'll have to break him out of jail and smuggle him across the Channel. There's no other way to save him.''

Juliana was about to object when Barbara spoke. ''Where would you find men willing to take such a dangerous risk?''

''My crew. The smugglers here. Adam's manservant. What do you think, Juliana?''

''I can't think that far ahead yet. I still haven't given up hope that there won't be enough substantial evidence collected to merit a trial.''

Two weeks later Keith returned from Helston with news that destroyed her final hope. During the preliminary hearing, the prosecution had presented a witness—a guest in the Tomlin household—who swore he had seen Adam on the staircase with the missing dueling pistol.

''Who?'' Juliana demanded, her face white. ''Who would dare to perjure himself with such a brazen lie?''

''Lord Hazelhurst.''

''The unscrupulous bastard! After he practically stole our lands—'' She broke off, too distraught to continue.

''Adam's to be tried in Bodmin at the spring assizes,'' Keith went on. ''He'll be held over in Helston until he's transported at the end of the month.''

''Bodmin,'' she said bitterly. ''The earl's own town. There won't be a juror within a hundred miles that he can't buy or intimidate.''

Paul turned away from the window, his dark blue eyes reflective. He was a simple man, fond of action and not given to deep introspection. He didn't understand why he felt a compulsion to imperil his life for Juliana's husband. Maybe it arose from a previously unrecognized need to repay his debt to Logan Tremayne for rescuing him and his crew years ago. Possibly it stemmed from the begrudging respect he held for Adam, an inner conviction that Tremayne would take the same risk for him if necessary. But didn't Juliana come into his motives somewhere? Was he acting strictly out of concern for Adam? Perhaps, yes, perhaps it wasn't so much that his friendship for Adam outweighed his desire for her as it was he couldn't stand by and watch her suffer without attempting to help her. He sighed, uncomfortable with his thoughts, intuitively sensing that she would never belong to him, even if Adam were not between them.

"You know what we have to do," he said quietly, his musical voice interrupting the silence.

Keith looked up, his brow furrowed. "For God's sake, captain, whatever it is you're planning, plan it well, or you'll all hang."

"We'll overtake them on the moors," Paul said, staring at Juliana. "So long as no one panics, there won't be any lives lost. Adam will be on his way to France before the local authorities can be alerted. I'll visit him in jail myself next week."

Keith raked a hand through his sparse blond hair. "You'll lose everything, Juliana. The Crown will confiscate your properties."

"I'll lose everything if Adam is hanged," she said. "Anyway, the lands mean nothing to me. Except this old house. I can't imagine why, but I've grown quite fond of it."

"It's become your home," Barbara said gently. "I felt that way about the little country house Keith and I bought right after we were married."

Understanding passed between the two women, and suddenly Juliana found herself remembering her first evening in the house, her first conversation with Barbara. How much had happened since then! But on one point Barbara was wrong: Mentreath would be her home only as long as she shared it with Adam. She would follow him into exile without a second thought.

Chapter Twenty-nine

The anxiety was unbearable. Juliana lived in a constant state of dread that something would happen to thwart Adam's escape. The earl would pay a jailer to have him murdered in his cell. Paul's attempt to rescue him would fail. Somehow, despite all their efforts, Adam would be found guilty and hanged. She filled the letters she sent him with insignificant everyday news that wouldn't arouse suspicion if intercepted by the wrong hands. But Adam never once replied, and she feared he hadn't forgotten the bitterly unfair treatment she had meted out to him their last night together in Helston.

She forced herself to eat for the baby's sake. Nightmares invaded her few sleeping hours. More often than not she lay awake with her eyes closed, listening to the restless sea outside, which seemed to echo the rhythm of her thoughts.

Then late one night, as she was dropping off to sleep from sheer fatigue, she heard a commotion in the courtyard—Alfie barking, a door slammed.

She jumped out of bed and threw on her dressing gown, her heart knocking with fear. Before she could put on her slippers, the door opened and Phoebe shuffled into the room holding a taper, the puffs and creases from a sound sleep still evident on her face.

"Doris thought I'd better wake ee, ma'am."

"Is it word of my husband?"

"No, ma'am. 'Tis the widow at the cottage. Her maid-servant was at the door. She said her mistress has gone into an early labor. The midwife claims the master left instructions that he was to be notified in case of an emergency."

"He probably did. Set down the taper, and help me dress."

"'Tis four o'clock in the mornin', ma'am. The maidservant's on her way back to her mistress. What can ee do?"

"Probably not much. But I can't stay here now knowing the woman might die. The least I can do is offer my comfort."

Silence greeted Juliana as she pushed open the cottage door, its wooden frame warped from the recent rains. Why were there no sounds of a baby crying? she wondered, her stomach tightening. Why had the fire in the hearth been allowed to die down?

She dumped the contents of the scuttle onto the fading coals, then straightened and headed toward what she assumed was the bedroom. She heard soft whispering voices. The door was ajar, the windows shuttered against the breaking dawn.

"Mrs. Tremayne, 'tis kind of ee to come." The midwife slid off her chair at Juliana's entrance. "I 'eld off summonin' ee until the very end. But ee never know in these cases. Poor woman. Losin' 'er husband and now the child."

Juliana's gaze darted to the inert figure on the bed. "Is she going—"

"She's fine. Ought to sleep for hours," the midwife reassured. "I've had 'er in bed since yestereve, drinkin' brandy to stop the contractions. In fact, if ee don't mind stayin' awhile, Mrs. Tremayne, I'd like to pop 'ome and tend to my own young-uns."

"I can brew ee a pot of tea, ma'am," the maidservant piped up from behind the midwife.

Juliana nodded, unfastening her cloak as she settled into the chair at the bedside. Presently the maidservant returned with the tea, then excused herself to tidy the parlor. To Juliana's surprise, she dozed off. Then Leigh's voice woke her.

"What time is it?"

Juliana lifted her head to find a pair of bright green eyes studying her with cold suspicion. "It must be around seven. How do you feel?"

"Wretched." Leigh's face was sallow, her hair hanging in greasy uncombed curls. "Adam promised me he'd be here when my time came."

"He's in jail," Juliana said wryly.

"I know that." Leigh sat up against the pillows, grimacing with the pain movement caused. "Paul told me everything."

"Paul? I wasn't aware you and he were acquainted."

"I met him the night you were missing. He's come to visit me once or twice since then."

Juliana was annoyed at herself for feeling upset with Paul. She didn't have any claims on him. "I think I know how you feel, Leigh. I'm sorry you lost your child."

"I'm not. It was a horrid little maggot." Leigh's voice climbed to a quivering pitch. "It ruined my life. I hated it."

In an instinctively protective gesture, Juliana placed her hand across her own abdomen. "You're still in shock. You can't mean that."

"No." Leigh began to cry, her plump shoulders jerking convulsively. "I didn't mean it. I'm an awful person. I think God took the child to punish me for my sin."

It took several minutes before Leigh calmed down, Juliana reassuring her everything would be all right, when in her own heart she doubted. Finally, Leigh fell back against the bed, exhausted. To Juliana's amazement, she discovered that she felt more sorry for Leigh than jealous of her. And yet, she couldn't stop herself from wondering whether Leigh's lush golden beauty had tempted her husband. Had he merely taken pity on Leigh as he claimed, or had he welcomed the excuse to visit her to escape his disappointing marriage? Juliana shoved the thought to the back of her mind. This wasn't the time for condemnation or suspicion. For the moment Leigh was only a fellow human being, one who desperately needed help, and Juliana refused to allow her negative emotions to interfere with her natural instinct of compassion.

She slid forward in her chair as she heard the midwife in the parlor. "I have to go now, Leigh. I want to be back at the house in case something develops concerning Adam."

Leigh nodded tiredly. With the covers pulled up to her chin, she looked like a scared child. "Let me know the moment you hear anything. Adam was the only person who stood by me in this."

On the walk back to Mentreath, Juliana realized that most of her resentment toward Leigh was fading, leaving only a vague sense of regret for all the pain the girl's presence had caused. It was easy to see how Adam had felt constrained to befriend her. But it was impossible to imagine how she and Leigh would manage if anything were to happen to him.

Chapter Thirty

Paul Delisle was acutely conscious of the guard posted at the other side of the cell door as he presented his plan to the lean figure sprawled out the length of a horsehair-filled pallet. His eyes lifted countless times to the grille in the door.

"You take a great chance for a man you've known but a matter of months," Adam remarked dryly when the Frenchman had finished. "I'd be a fool to imagine you'd risk your life for me on the basis of our friendship alone . . . or even out of a sense of obligation to my late uncle. There must be something more."

"You're referring to Juliana," Paul said quietly.

Adam raised himself to an upright position. The mention of that name alone seemed to counteract the unsavoriness of his surroundings. "If you hope to gain her appreciation for rescuing me, you're wasting your time. The lady would undoubtedly like nothing better than to have me removed from her life."

"You have a low estimation of your own wife."

"I have a low estimation of her opinion of me," Adam retorted, the angular planes of his face softened by a growth of silky beard. "But then, you'd be in the best position to judge Juliana's current frame of mind regarding me. I don't doubt you've taken full advantage of my absence."

"You *are* a fool. I offer you freedom, and you repay me with insults."

"You offer me freedom in return for the one thing I value above all else." The anger ebbed from Adam's voice. "Still, you're mistaken if you think I'm not grateful for your

262

help. I don't want to die, especially for a murder I didn't have the satisfaction of committing.''

''The arrangements have been made,'' Paul said in an undertone. ''From France you will sail to Boston. Your partner will know to expect you.''

Adam reached for the bottle of brandy the Frenchman had smuggled into the cell. ''Has my wife mentioned what she intends to do after I leave?''

''No.'' Paul hesitated. ''But then, perhaps you could discuss the matter with her yourself.''

Adam's head lifted sharply, anger darkening his features. ''You brought Juliana *here?* God, man, have you no common sense?''

''She's a woman who follows her impulses,'' Delisle replied, unperturbed as he tapped the grille to indicate he had finished. ''It wasn't my place to try to stop her.''

The sudden sight of Juliana standing before him filled Adam with an irrational fusion of both anger and violent longing. He felt like shaking her for disobeying him in coming here; he felt like crushing her against him and savoring the sweetness of her velvet mouth and womanly flesh. Instead, he remained seated on the soiled pallet, unwashed and unshaven, disgusted by his own appearance.

Juliana's eyes widened in alarm as she studied him in the semidarkness. ''Adam, you're losing too much weight—''

''Why the hell did you come here, Juliana?'' he interrupted with harsh impatience. ''Why do you always insist on having your way?''

''I thought you—'' She shivered beneath the folds of her heavy cloak, chilled by the coldness of his reception. ''I was concerned about you, Adam. Keith is so vague whenever I ask how you are. I wanted to see for myself that you were all right.''

His face relaxed briefly. ''Now that you've seen, go home. Please, Juliana.''

''I only wanted to see you,'' she repeated, venturing several inches closer to the pallet. *He hasn't forgiven me,* she thought dully. *He's never been this cold and distant before. What should I do? I can't leave without at least trying to make amends with him.* ''I worry about you constantly, Adam.''

His eyes flickered. ''Even while you're entertaining Captain Delisle?''

She froze, her face registering genuine bafflement. "What are you talking about?"

"Damn you, Juliana, don't play the innocent with me! I know he's practically living at Mentreath. Tell me, my dear, do you and he recite poetry to each other in the great hall every night?"

Indignation swiftly replaced her confusion. "Surely you don't—you can't think that he and I have become intimate?"

"I don't know what to think," he hissed. "He makes no secret of the fact that he's in love with you. And as for you, well, perhaps this is your subtle revenge for my interfering in your life. I can't help wondering—" He stared at her unflinchingly, his gray eyes piercing with pain and misgiving. "I can't help wondering how he managed to earn your trust so easily when for me it was like fighting a bloody war."

"That isn't fair," she whispered stiffly. "Paul and I are merely friends, concerned for your well-being—"

"Oh? Was it for my benefit that he gifted you with jewelry?" Adam's lips curled into a sneer. "You might teach Phoebe the value of discretion if she's to be an accomplice in your amours."

"My amours? Oh, God, Adam! Why must you torture yourself so? Why do you torture us both?"

"Perhaps you'd be relieved if I were convicted and hanged," he continued ruthlessly. "Perhaps you and Paul could found a smuggling empire together."

Juliana's eyes fluttered and she swayed on her feet, the stifling closeness of the cell and Adam's unwarranted tirade making her feel dangerously light-headed. Then suddenly she felt a strong arm gripping her elbow, supporting her, and she opened her eyes to see Adam staring down at her, his rough face dark with conflicting emotions.

"Stubborn to the soul," he growled softly. "I told you not to come here. There's nothing wrong with the baby, is there?"

"No." She inhaled slowly and felt the faintness passing. " 'Tis normal at this stage of pregnancy. I've not been sleeping well."

"Then for God's sake, go back to Mentreath and get some rest." Satisfied she was steady on her feet, he released her arm and strode to the door to summon the jailer. "If any harm should befall you or our child—" He turned away

from her so that she couldn't see his face. "Another burden
of guilt would be more than I could bear."

Tears of frustration pooled in Juliana's eyes as she
watched him return to the pallet, dismissing her without a
single caress or affectionate word. Oh, damn him! she
thought miserably. He's every bit as stubborn as I am!

"I thought ee wanted to leave," the large, stoop-shouldered
turnkey said, jangling his keys impatiently to stir her.

She sighed, drawing her hood up over her head. It would
do her no good to stay, anyway. Adam had already closed
off his mind to anything she had wanted to say.

"Yes. I'm ready."

She threw her husband one last anguished look and quietly
followed the jailer up the worn stone steps. Adam gazed after
her hungrily, then as the door slammed shut with cruel finality,
he reached behind him for the dusty bottle of brandy.

He dropped onto his elbow, his long legs overhanging the
end of the stiff pallet. The alcohol burned into the hollow-
ness of his gut. In a little over a week he'd be on his way to
Boston, and his life in Cornwall would begin fading into
memory. He didn't expect Juliana would offer to join him in
exile, and in his heart he believed that their days together
had probably been drawing to an end anyway. They had
caused each other nothing but pain and unhappiness from
the beginning. Perhaps it was time to exchange the passion
they had shared for a well-deserved peace.

The rescue attempt was to be made shortly after daybreak. Unable to sleep, Juliana had stolen from the house in
the predawn darkness. Without thinking—perhaps because
there was nowhere else to go—she walked toward the sea. A
piercing offshore wind rose to greet her, but she welcomed
its numbing coldness, her mind detached from her body.

Paul had flatly refused to let her accompany him and
Robbie, stating that it was her part to run the estate until
Adam reached safety. The constable in charge of transporting him to Bodmin would most likely search the grounds and
interrogate her and the staff.

Emotionally she was prepared to leave her beloved Cornwall, knowing she might never return. And though the subject
hadn't come up between them at their last meeting, she assumed Adam understood she would follow him. Still, she was

upset that he hadn't sent her any messages through Paul or Keith.

Dawn broke over a choppy sea, the sun shrouded in an eerie blood-red haze. Pendulous gray clouds brewing on the horizon promised yet another day of foul weather. A gust of wind jolted Juliana from her reverie, and she started back to the house, thinking that this had been the longest winter of her life. Then all of a sudden she turned, on impulse, and looked back.

At first she saw nothing. And then something drew her gaze to the clifftop, where she spied a solitary figure staring out at the sea. Even from that far away, she couldn't mistake the arrogant stance of a Tremayne, the prominent jaw jutting from the profile. She glanced around to see if perhaps a fisherman had also sighted the apparition. But when she returned her attention to the clifftop, the lonely figure had vanished.

"Watch over Adam for me, Logan," she said softly.

Juliana hadn't put up an argument when Paul refused to let her participate in her husband's escape, but no one could have stopped her from riding to the Half Moon Inn, where she could intercept Adam before he left the country. They'd leave Cornwall tonight together if she had her way. At the very least, she wanted to make arrangements with him about when and where they were to meet in France.

"They've done it!" Martin's face was a picture of jubilant exhaustion. Dismounting, he entrusted his horse to the stableboy who came staggering across the rear courtyard of the coastal inn, buffeted by the rising wind.

Laughing with relief, Juliana hurried her brother inside, past the crowded taproom and through the timbered gallery to their first-floor chamber. The old Tudor inn was a smuggler's drop, the owner sympathetic to their plight, but Juliana knew they still had to exercise caution. Revenue officers disguised as common sailors often frequented the local seaside haunts, hoping to glean tidbits of information about a scheduled run.

"Phoebe, help him off with his coat."

"They met the post chaise carrying Adam on the moors outside Helston," Martin told her excitedly.

"No one was hurt?" Juliana asked.

"Not really. Robbie had a tussle with one of the guards. Looked like he left him with a broken arm and a couple of bruises. But nothing fatal." He paused for effect, lowering his tone. ''They'll stop here for a quick meal and be on their way to France before morning.''

Phoebe pressed a blackjack of bitter ale into his hands. ''In this gale? God's bones, I don't like the sound of that. The wind's already blown the weathercock off the roof 'ere. Would it 'urt for them to wait a few hours until the storm passes?''

''Too much at risk,'' Martin replied. ''I could smell dragoons on the trail the entire ride back. Besides, they don't want to lose the tide. I'm not worried about them. If anyone can sail through a gale, Delisle can.''

Another gale. Juliana's face darkened as the memory of her mother's death crept into her mind. But she, too, had faith in Paul. He had taken his lugger through worse weather.

''Martin, did you let Adam know I was waiting for him?''

''The situation was hardly conducive to passing love messages,'' he said, scowling up at her. ''Anyway, he'll probably skin me alive when he finds out I brought you along. Not that I was given a choice in the matter.''

It seemed like forever to Juliana before she and Adam were allowed any time alone. Paul and his men had ridden ahead to ready the lugger for the crossing. Wrapped in their own intimate world, Phoebe and Robbie lingered in the chamber until finally Juliana, desperate for an excuse to spend a private moment with Adam, sent them outside to check on the horses. Apprehensive, steaming with impatience to get Adam to France, Martin also took the hint and reluctantly volunteered to wait below in the taproom.

To Juliana's astonishment, Adam hadn't lost his temper upon finding her at the inn. Perhaps he'd even half expected it, but she knew him well enough to detect the disapproval smoldering in his smoky eyes. She raised her head, her gaze meeting his. She had steeled herself to face his anger. She could face anything now that she knew his escape had been successful.

''I had to come,'' she explained simply. ''I don't care if you're angry at me.''

He embraced her with rough urgency, burying his lean, unshaven face in the satiny mass of hair coiled on her shoulder. Out of necessity, he had prepared himself to leave Cornwall without seeing her again, and the intensity of the emotions he experienced at meeting her here so unexpectedly made him struggle for self-possession. And yes, he was

angry at her for coming here, for risking her safety just so
that they could spend a few minutes together. But it seemed
pointless to quarrel over it now.

For an extended interval neither of them moved, then Juliana drew away, indicating the small table behind her as her
practical nature took over. "There's mutton and kidney pie,
and some cold roast beef on the platter," she murmured.
She paused, so relieved to see him safe that her hands were
trembling as she uncovered the dishes. "And there's ale
warming on the hearth. It's not much, but—"

"It's a banquet compared to the jail fare I've been fed
lately," he said wryly, eyeing the food with appreciation.
"Not even the rats who shared my cell had much of an appetite for it."

She repressed a shudder of distaste and sat down at the table
opposite him, waiting until he'd devoured half a pie before she
spoke. Their last meeting had left her uncertain of where she
stood with him. Had he forgiven her yet? Had he realized how
foolish he'd been to accuse her of infidelity? "I've been thinking since we last talked, Adam. Keith and Martin could handle
the business affairs at Mentreath until we find out what the
Crown intends to do with our properties. There's no reason
why I couldn't leave with you tonight."

"Isn't there?" He wiped the edges of his mouth with the
linen napkin, choosing his next words with cold deliberation. "I've been thinking, too, Juliana. Less than a month
ago, you told me that you wished we'd never met, that you
hoped you weren't carrying my child. Considering your
feelings, I assumed you'd be happy to get rid of me."

She cringed at the pain in his eyes as he reminded her of
her cruel outburst that night in Helston. *So, he still hasn't
forgiven me,* she thought, feeling a wave of icy foreboding
wash over her. "I want to forget that night, Adam, and
everything associated with it—"

"Well, I can't forget," he said forcefully as all the anger
that had been simmering inside him over the last few weeks
suddenly exploded. "Nor can I forgive you for doubting
me, for jumping down my throat and accusing me of driving
Graham to suicide before you even knew what had happened. You couldn't wait to turn against me, could you? But
I guess I should have expected it. You were never able to

make that ultimate commitment of trust to me. You never really wanted to be my wife.''

She stared at him across the table in stunned bewilderment, unable to believe how much bitterness was pouring out of him. God, how deeply she must have wounded him.

''You're not being fair, Adam,'' she said, her voice faint. ''I never said that I—''

''I saw the look on your face, Juliana,'' he cut her off scornfully. ''Lord, I've seen it often enough in my life to recognize it by now. It accused me of murder.''

She felt her face tightening with resentment. ''The past again! Always the past. Why must I pay for what happened years before I even met you? I never accused you of murdering Graham, although yes, I admit I did misjudge you again. But, for the love of God, the guilt and condemnation are in your own mind!'' She buried her face in her hands with a frustrated moan. She couldn't reach him. He didn't want to hear her. ''Oh, I don't know why I bother! After all the worry these past weeks, I can't stand any more pain.''

''I'm sorry, Juliana,'' he said quietly, his eyes focused on the table. ''Maybe we just need time apart to think everything through.''

Her head lifted. ''Time apart?'' she echoed in a dead voice while her mind struggled to make sense out of what he was telling her. It's an excuse, she realized, stricken. He's trying to reject me as gently as he can manage. I've disappointed him, or perhaps he's grown tired of me. Oh, God, he doesn't want me anymore! She moistened her lips.

''How much time, Adam?''

The hurt disillusionment in her voice tore into Adam's heart, forcing him to question the conclusions he had drawn. Was this really what he wanted? he wondered. Hell, did it make any difference at this point what either of them claimed they wanted? They obviously couldn't get along together for even ten minutes, let alone an entire lifetime, without clashing dangerously.

''I don't know, Juliana. Time enough to examine our feelings, to decide whether or not this is worth all the pain—''

She stood slowly, anger, misery, and damaged pride raging through her in dark, uncontrollable torrents. ''What do you expect me to do, Adam? Lock myself away at Mentreath while you decide whether or not you want me?''

"Dear God, it's not an issue of wanting you, Juliana. I'm just not sure anymore if we can survive all the suffering we seem determined to inflict on each other." He rose from the table, his own pain and confusion so powerful that he gave up trying to constrain it. "Besides, I don't expect you'd wait alone for long. Captain Delisle will be on your doorstep to court you with jewelry and Gallic flattery the minute he's back from France."

Out of frustration she raised her hand to strike him, then abruptly dropped it to her side. "My God, how can you be so ungrateful? The man is only trying—"

Before she could finish, the door flew open and Martin stepped over the threshold, walking midway across the room before he sensed the tension between her and Adam. His mouth twisted in disgust.

"Goddamn it! Will you be battling him to the gallows, Juliana? I assure you that's where he'll end up if he doesn't get the hell out of the country tonight."

She turned her head to respond. Although tears glittered in the green-yellow depths of her eyes like emeralds, her chin pointed forward in defiant pride.

"He can leave whenever he likes. He entered my life without any concern for my feelings. I shouldn't be surprised that he's leaving the same way."

Adam looked at the younger man, his expression a silent plea for privacy. "We're not quite finished. Another minute—"

"What for?" Juliana asked with a mirthless laugh. She wasn't about to beg Adam to reconsider. She was done with apologies and explanations. "Take him, Martin. I never want to look at him again."

Martin vented an exasperated sigh. "Five more minutes, and I must be out of my mind to allow you that."

"Juliana," Adam said as the door closed again. "Can't you see what we're doing to each other?"

"No! Don't come near me!" As she noticed him moving toward her, she whirled to escape him and retreated to the stone hearth where the fire had burned down to ashes. All too often in the past, he had only to touch her in order to crumble her defenses. She wouldn't give him that chance now, not when he'd made it so plain that he no longer desired her as part of his life. She wanted him to leave. She wanted him to turn around and walk out of the room so that she could fall apart alone.

"I don't want to hear another word from you, Adam," she said, her entire body aching with the effort it cost to control her sick trembling. "There's nothing more to be said between us. You may as well just go. I can't imagine what you're waiting for."

Adam wondered suddenly whether he wasn't making a terrible mistake, whether he shouldn't just take her with him and risk the consequences. Which was preferable, he wondered, the pain of staying together or the pain of living apart? Time was running out for them. Indecision wrenched him apart. This wasn't the way it should be. They belonged together.

"When all the furor over my escape has died down, perhaps—perhaps you and I might . . . have another chance—"

"A chance for what?" she asked, longing to hurt him as he was hurting her. "To utterly destroy each other? No, thank you, Adam. I'm glad it's over! What a relief to end all the hurting and frustration!"

"I'll provide for you and the baby, Juliana." His voice wasn't entirely steady. "Neither of you will ever go without."

"How very generous of you, I'm sure," she said savagely. "Shall we stand in line behind Leigh for your charity?"

She stared at the wall until her vision dimmed and darkness swam before her eyes. She heard Adam walk to the door, hesitating as he turned to exit, and her heart splintered into myriad fragments at his final words.

"I loved you, Juliana, but it seemed that my love for you was never enough. I didn't mean to hurt you—despite what you may think, and if I've done nothing else to please you, at least now I can offer you a parting gift of freedom. Unless I'm mistaken, that was what you wanted all along."

There was silence. Then the door closed, and as Juliana listened to his footsteps fade away, her thoughts collided and plunged within her shocked mind, slowly centering on the horrible realization that he was actually leaving her. It didn't matter why. It didn't matter who was to blame, or even whether it had been inevitable from the start. It was over. Pain and despair filling every grain of her being, she folded slowly to her knees and wept with heartbroken abandon until Martin returned to the room to crouch down beside her and gather her into his arms.

Chapter Thirty-one

The French lugger, *Le Triton*, had limped into the ancient river harbor of Honfleur, one of her three masts missing, her sails ripped from the bolt-ropes. Gigantic waves had swept the length of the deck from bow to stern and washed a man overboard. Flying canvas had knocked a second sailor from a yardarm as the vessel lurched and labored across the English Channel. Unfamiliar with the coastline, Adam could do little to help besides reef the sails and secure cordage and rigging on deck. It was a credit to the nautical skill of the captain that more lives hadn't been lost; spindrift and driving rain had decreased visibility, leaving him to rely on instinct and past experience to keep the lugger on course.

The sky was peaceful now, and feeble glimmers of sunlight glinted off the gray-slate roofs of the tall, weathered houses lining the quayside. Seagulls wheeled and circled above the old docks, where fishermen hawked their freshly caught wares. In the center of the town, the bells of St. Catherine's church pealed the Angelus, summoning the faithful to prayer. It was here that Paul Delisle's Norse pirate ancestors had settled long ago.

Brooding, Paul gazed at his ship through the cracked windowpane of the dockside tavern where he and his two passengers had assembled. The damage sustained was heavier than expected, but not irreparable. At worst it meant that he'd be inactive until late spring.

Adam had no trouble guessing what had brought the ill-humored scowl to the Frenchman's face. "I can repay you for the repairs needed to make her seaworthy again, but not for the lives of your men. I'm sorry, Delisle."

"You're not to blame," Paul said bluntly. "I knew what kind of seas we might encounter. Anyway, the men had been drinking. They knew better."

A hush fell over the table as the three men present drank and subsided into reflective silence. At the opposite end of the taproom, the lugger's first mate flirted with the barmaid, bragging in detail of his bravery during the storm.

Robbie finally ended the lapse in conversation, turning his shaggy red head to Adam. "Are we tae spend the night here, or head straight for Le Havre, sir?"

Adam turned away from the window. "There's no reason to tarry. We'll leave after we finish the meal we ordered."

"Your ship doesn't sail for days," Paul said. "Stay the night with me, and get a fresh start in the morning. My home isn't far from here."

Adam frowned, pushing his bullock's horn mug away. "You've done enough already. I'll not involve you further."

"Is there any message for Juliana?"

Adam's stomach clenched, and he slumped back against the hard wooden chair, his expression clouding. The question reminded him that Paul could hardly wait to take advantage of Juliana's sudden vulnerability. Juliana—oh, God! Memories of her rose painfully to his fatigued mind, her lovely eyes crinkling with laughter as he teased her, the fragrance of her like sun-warmed lavender as she lay naked beneath him. What had made him think that by leaving her he would find the peace he longed for? Already she haunted him. Already he regretted his decision not to bring her with him. And yet even if things had been different for them, if he'd thought they could rise above the rancor of their failed expectations, would he have wanted to drag her down deeper into the hell his life had become?

He had brought misery to so many people he'd loved. Lucy and Anne had died violently because of his reckless decision to leave them at Fort William Henry. What would happen to Juliana if he asked her to leave family and homeland for an uncertain existence in America? It was possible the earl would trace him to Boston, perhaps send hired assassins after him. Was his love so selfish that he'd jeopardize her life by keeping her with him? Could he stand to have their child brought up knowing its father was an escaped criminal? No. He'd rather be dead than destroy their lives.

His lips curved into a self-deprecatory smile. There had been an instant aboard *Le Triton*—as water flooded the waist and the ship pitched sickeningly, throwing him against a bulwark—when he thought he might die. And he'd been surprised to feel more remorse than fear. Remorse that he'd hurt so many people he cared for. Remorse that he and Juliana had parted with so much unfinished between them. It wasn't the first time he'd faced death . . . but he'd never before considered it as an avenue of escape. Had Graham's disturbed soul found its peace in suicide? he wondered.

Nothing mattered now anyway. He had been unable to live in harmony with the one woman he loved, and perhaps she'd never been meant to belong to him, after all. In time, Juliana would forget him, and he'd return to the loneliness he had known before her, remembering not the pain of their relationship, but those few achingly sweet moments when they had transcended their differences to come together in love.

He looked up across the table at the craggy-faced Frenchman, wondering how he could feel such intense dislike for a man who'd just saved his neck. But it was undoubtedly for Juliana's sake that Paul had taken the risk, and it was Juliana who stood between them.

"Juliana won't expect any messages from me, captain," he said carefully. "And if you seriously hope to stay in her favor, I'd suggest you don't discuss me in her presence."

Robbie's unruly eyebrows shot up in disapproval, and Paul sat forward slowly, his large elbows jarring the table. "What—have you taken leave of your senses? Am I to assume that the separation between you is to be permanent?" Paul asked.

Adam glanced over at the raw-boned Scotsman. "You're not obligated to follow me, Robbie. I know you'd planned to wed old Jack's niece. The choice is yours."

"Aye. I'm wi ye, sir. But—"

"But what?"

"But I canna say I approve of what yer doin'," Robbie exclaimed in an uncharacteristic burst of emotion. "Och, but then, what the hell do I know aboot women, anyway? Phoebe couldna understand why I'd nae leave ye when she herself won't even consider leavin' yer wife. I only wonder, sir, well, are ye sure 'tis what ye what?"

"No, Robbie, I'm not. But it's done now. I have to live with it." Adam returned his attention to Delisle, his voice deepening in cynical tones. "Will you watch over her?"

The astonishment still hadn't faded from the coarse face. "With my very life," Paul said earnestly. "But I must confess, I still think you're an incredible fool."

Chapter Thirty-two

"Adam's portion of the income from the shipyard will be forwarded directly to the bank, Juliana. You might want to consider placing it in a trust fund for your child. The rent revenues should be kept in a separate account. The codicil to old Logan's will shouldn't have any effect at all—Juliana, have you heard *anything* I've said?"

She turned from the bookshelf with an apologetic sigh, her abdomen straining the aquamarine wool day gown. "Not really. Do you believe in ghosts, Keith?"

"Do I—" The perplexed attorney put down the sheaf of estate papers he'd been rustling through and exchanged worried looks with his wife. "Have Martin contact me when he returns from Helston, Juliana. Perhaps he'll appreciate how much effort it took to insure that the Crown wouldn't encumber your properties. I don't have time to discuss ghosts and goblins."

Barbara laid aside the baby blanket she was knitting. "Uncle Logan took all that nonsense quite seriously. What a lurid waste of his last years."

"Perhaps not, Barbara," Juliana said, her face pensive. "You see, I believe he's appeared to me twice now, the last time the morning of Adam's escape. Your uncle was looking out across the sea." She smiled self-consciously, realizing they probably thought she was out of her mind with loneliness for Adam, which sometimes she suspected wasn't far from the truth. Sometimes, oh, God, sometimes, she felt as though her heart had been wrenched from her chest and in its was place was a cold aching chasm. "I'm not the only one who claims to have seen him," she went on in an artificially casual tone, trying to surface from the despair that engulfed her whenever she thought of Adam. "The village pastor and several fishermen have sighted him, too."

"He's probably some harmless old cave hermit who imagines he's Hamlet or King George," Keith said, shoving papers into his leather portmanteau. "I wouldn't get too near him, just in case. Barbara, you're welcome to stay if you like. I'm going home."

Barbara began collecting her belongings. "So strange about that Spencer girl," she murmured. "To just disappear like that without a word. Still, I expect it's a relief to you, Juliana. She wasn't your responsibility."

Juliana's mood darkened again as she followed them out to the courtyard. She had a damned good notion why and where Leigh had gone, but her sense of self-preservation was sufficiently intact that she refused to torture herself by dwelling on her own jealous imaginings. Neither of them are part of my life now, she thought bitterly, feeling a knot of misery settling in her throat. Hurt and humiliated, she only wanted to blot out the shattering pain of Adam and everything associated with their turbulent marriage. Unfortunately, she had so far failed dismally because everything from her own swelling body to the color of Barbara's eyes seemed to mock her resolve by reminding her wrenchingly of him.

It had been a month since his escape. The shock of their separation had only recently begun to subside, ending her numbing reprieve from the clawing anguish of her mixed emotions, cutting off the short period she'd had in which to gather strength to face the emptiness that lay ahead. Disillusioned and depressed, she took one day at a time, looking forward in the future only to the birth of her child. And yet despite the intense resentment she harbored toward Adam, she still caught herself aching for his presence, especially alone at night, when she craved the comforting feel of his body next to hers. But damn it, he had left her! Why did she continue to miss him so? When would the hurting diminish? She had to forget him. Sooner or later she had to banish every memory of him from her heart.

She forced herself back to the present. "You musn't think

I don't appreciate all you've done, Keith. I feel terribly guilty about dragging you away from your practice."

He grunted ill-humoredly, struggling into his coat. "It's not finished yet. I still intend to clear Adam's name."

What did it really matter now? she wondered, watching the small coach lumber down the drive. Adam would probably never return to Cornwall, and no one in Penlyn cared whether or not he'd murdered some dissolute nobleman. Let the scandalmongers say what they pleased. It didn't bother her. Let the Crown confiscate the very ground she stood on. She and Martin would return to Rosmorna.

But as summer approached and she neared the end of her pregnancy, she changed her mind completely and decided that having a father labeled an escaped murderer might haunt her child in years to come. And then one drowsy afternoon in late August, she went into labor and by twilight had delivered a wailing dark-haired son. The moment she nursed the tiny infant at her milk-swollen breast, she felt an incredible burst of tenderness blossom inside her, and immediately knew she'd do anything to protect him.

"Dr. Carew said we could come in one at a time," Evelyn whispered as she tiptoed to the bed and gazed down in awe at the bundled baby. "Oh, good heavens, Juliana. He's so perfect, and oh, my, look! He has a cleft in his chin just like his father!"

Juliana sank back against the pillows in lassitude, tears clouding her sight as sadness and joy fought for supremacy in her heart. This baby—this precious being—would be a constant reminder of Adam, the flawless product of their stormy union, an irrefutable link to the bittersweet past. This baby would help soften the scars that had formed around her heart when Adam left.

"Would you like to hold him before Stephen and Louisa arrive, Evelyn?"

"Could I? He's so sweet, Juliana, that I'm sorely tempted to try again for one of my own."

Juliana relinquished her son with fierce pride flooding her heart. The old animosity between her and Evelyn seemed to be lifting, or perhaps, as they matured they drew closer together. At any rate, Evelyn had been a blessing the past two weeks, her no-nonsense nature preventing Juliana from sinking into a dangerous depression.

"I suppose we should name him after Father," Evelyn said, then added hastily, "unless, of course, you've already chosen a name."

"I have." Juliana closed her eyes in exhausted contentment. "His name is Logan Randall Tremayne."

In the middle of September, Keith and Barbara paid Juliana a short visit to inform her that Adam's name had been cleared. The attorney had taken painstaking measures to make certain that the fact of Adam's exoneration was widely publicized so that no shadow of scandal would darken Juliana's future. Captain Delisle was with her in the parlor when the Simpsons arrived.

"I'll leave you alone in privacy," he said, rising.

Juliana, rocking Logan to sleep in her arms, shook her head in protest. "You're practically a member of the family now, Paul. I want you to stay. You don't mind, do you, Keith?"

"I suppose not. Anyway, Juliana, it all boils down to this: The young lieutenant you spotted in the bedchamber that night suddenly came forward to verify that Adam had tried to prevent Graham's suicide."

Juliana turned the baby over her shoulder, pain flaring into her eyes. "Why? Why did he wait so long?"

Keith shrugged tiredly. "It appears he was involved with a certain married lady who was paying him for his—his services. She begged him not to involve her in his confession. He claims to have had quite a battle with his conscience over reporting what he witnessed to the authorities. The fact that the woman cut off his allowance may have decided him."

"What was the earl's reaction?" Juliana asked. "Was he willing to take this lieutenant's word?"

"Then you haven't heard," Keith said, surprised. "The earl suffered a stroke a fortnight ago. He's totally incapacitated. The countess has already made plans to have him taken to their Italian villa. You'll also be relieved to know that the authorities have agreed Adam shouldn't be prosecuted for his escape due to the special circumstances surrounding this whole sordid incident."

Juliana gasped softly. "You bribed them."

Keith sighed in pretended offense, ignoring the remark. "Adam's a very fortunate man. I warn you that should he return to Cornwall, his activities will be closely monitored."

"I don't think we need give that possibility unnecessary concern," she said in a subdued voice, her heart sinking in hopeless dejection as she thought how unlikely it was that she and Adam would meet again . . . unless he returned to seek a divorce. "Still, I'm thankful for all your hard work, Keith, especially for my son's sake."

"Well, it's all over now, praise God," Barbara said, helping herself to a cup of tea. "Perhaps Keith will stop behaving like such an ogre. I've been trying to talk him into visiting Virginia for a few months, but he has two important cases coming to trial. My father's health is declining fast, Juliana. I fear he'll die before little Logan is old enough to visit him. What a shame he and Adam couldn't have patched up the breach between them."

Juliana caught Paul and Keith exchanging uncomfortable glances, and she suspected that the emotional turn of the conversation had embarrassed them. "I'm sorry about your father, Barbara. He's been so kind, sending Logan all that money as a christening gift. We really don't need it."

"What *you* need is cheering up," Barbara said absently. "Perhaps a change of atmosphere."

Paul nodded in agreement. "Exactly what I told her this morning. I share a delightful country house with my nephew and our housekeeper. We'd enjoy having Juliana stay with us this autumn. Normandy during harvest is heaven. The ripening apple orchards, the golden woodlands at dusk—the peacefulness would do her a world of good."

Keith scowled in frank displeasure, and Barbara put down her cup, endeavoring to conceal her startled reaction to Paul's suggestion. It wasn't that she disliked the Frenchman—no, she had to admire him for the courage he'd shown in executing Adam's escape. But in her heart Barbara cradled a quiet hope that her brother and Juliana would be reunited. Of course, it wasn't her business to tell Juliana *not* to go to Normandy, and she couldn't deny that her sister-in-law seemed to be languishing away here at Mentreath since Adam's departure. And it couldn't be good for the baby to have his mother so withdrawn and self-absorbed, she thought worriedly.

She sat forward, forcing a smile, hesitant to express her reservations aloud. "Well, actually, Juliana, I was thinking that you might come to Devon for a while, but, of course, the decision is completely yours."

Juliana looked up slowly, her arms tightening around the sleeping infant. "Thank you, Barbara, but I wouldn't dare impose after all you and Keith have done for me. And anyway, if I could take Phoebe and the baby with me, I don't see that it could do any harm to go to France. Martin can certainly manage the estates without me. Yes. Perhaps I will consider your invitation, Paul."

She glanced away, too caught up in her own thoughts to notice how her announcement had been received. Maybe she did need a little time away from Mentreath, where every room held a torturous memory of Adam. In Normandy she wouldn't see him sitting across from her at the table or bent over his desk in the library. She wouldn't imagine she saw him riding into the courtyard at least once a day, or standing at the foot of the bed in the middle of the night. She had to do something to keep herself from sinking lower into her alienated state of hopelessness. Maybe this was the answer.

Chapter Thirty-three

Paul had been right. The pastoral charm of Normandy was a gentle balm to Juliana's ragged emotions. The sixteenth-century country house was built of mellowed rose-brick and located three miles inland, nestled like a jewel in the clearing of a dense woodland where royalty had once hunted. A sparkling river supplied the estate with fresh water, its fern-covered banks an idyllic picnic spot. From the dormer window of the attic bedchamber she'd chosen, Juliana looked down upon a sprawling apple orchard whose small gnarled trees sagged with rosy fruit.

Paul's nephew, Justin, lame from a childhood riding accident, and the old housekeeper, Maude, were warm, guileless souls, their mere presence dispelling Juliana's uncertainty about the propriety of her staying in the house. Of course, Phoebe had accompanied her to watch over Logan, and she had come on the unspoken condition that her relationship with Paul remain platonic. Any other arrangement was unthinkable.

For his part, Paul was willing to bide his time. He couldn't believe Juliana had actually agreed to come in the first place, and he was afraid of destroying her tentative trust in him with any crass attempts at lovemaking. But as the days passed, it became more of a temptation to touch her. In the hopes of furthering his cause, he quickly discovered a few subtle ways to take advantage of her unconscious vulnerability.

He learned that the swiftest way to her heart was through Logan, and he rarely let a day end without lavishing gifts and attention on the unwitting child. Juliana bore his efforts with tolerant amusement, unaware that he felt only the mildest affection for her son.

"Honestly, Paul, a chess set and a crossbow! It will be years and years before Logan can use either."

"True," he murmured. "But now I'll have an excuse to teach him how to shoot and how to play chess. A boy needs a man to look up to, Juliana."

It became their habit to stroll through the woods in the early-autumn twilight, when the lilting song of the nightingale haunted the sylvan shadows. During these peaceful walks, he learned that the deeper Juliana drew him into her confidence, the more she relaxed with him, and so he encouraged her to talk freely about her past, about Adam and her relationship with her father.

"Do you know, Paul, I think you remind me of Papa," she said to him once, and at his disheartened expression, she had fallen back against a chestnut tree, dissolving into laughter. "I've offended you—forgive me! I only meant that I feel safe with you, Paul, as though you wouldn't let anything harm me."

"You make me feel like a depraved old roué," he said stiffly, stung by her laughter. "But you're right, Juliana. I will take care of you—to the degree that you allow me."

Then one evening his control slipped. He and Juliana had gone boating on the river, returning to the house to find the table spread with cold chicken, crusty bread, mild white cheese, and a silver bowl brimming over with peaches, grapes, and apples. There was also a bottle of Calvados and two short crystal glasses, and Justin, Maude, and Phoebe had hidden themselves elsewhere in the house.

They ate in the long dining room with the windows opened to enjoy the view of the surrounding woodland, a blazing autumnal glory of copper and scarlet. As dusk fell, Paul rose from the table and beckoned Juliana out onto the stone-paved terrace.

"It's different from your wild storm-swept coast, isn't it?" he asked, taking her hand.

"Yes. And yet I do miss Mentreath. Don't ask me why."

He stared at her, his blood surging with excitement as he realized she hadn't pulled her hand loose. She was so lovely, it made his heart tighten with longing just to look at her. Her hair cascaded down her slender back in riotous waves, red and bronze, the hues of autumn itself. Motherhood had added an alluring maturity to her appearance, shading her face with attractive hollows, imparting a womanly softness to her figure.

Gently he gathered her into his arms. She stared up at him with uncertainty in her eyes, her body stiff but not resistant. "Paul, I don't think—"

He brought his mouth down on hers and stilled her objections with a lingering kiss. Juliana didn't respond. But Paul, just feeling her soft breasts crushed against his chest, was aroused beyond rational thought. He lowered his face to the hollow of her throat, his tongue patterning sensual circles over her warm skin. His fingers clenched her shoulders and stumbled down her back to clasp her buttocks through her gown, pressing her closer to his muscular body.

"No. Don't!" She jerked loose and withdrew into the doorway, shaking her head in hurt confusion.

He reached out to her, his breath labored and uneven. "Juliana—"

"Don't—don't touch me again, Paul, please. I value your friendship far too much to have to end it over this."

His hand dropped to his side. "I am repulsive to you."

"Repulsive? Oh, no, Paul, anything but. It's just . . . too soon." She ventured back out onto the terrace, her gaze lifting to the rising harvest moon. "I can't forget Adam. He was my first real love—perhaps my only love."

"He was mad to have left you," Paul said with vehemence.

She turned to face him, sadness flitting across her delicate face. "Mad? Maybe he and I were both mad, Paul. Why else would we ever have thought our marriage would work? And yet, there were times when we got along so well. I wonder, if circumstances had been different . . ."

She lapsed into brooding silence, and Paul cursed himself for the thoughtlessly uttered comment as he sensed her heart eluding him again. Why did she continue to allow her past with Adam to prevent her from enjoying the present with him? She wanted him—he was experienced enough to recognize desire in a woman's eyes. But how much longer must he wait? Should he cunningly seduce her, prey on her loneliness and restrained sensuality to lure her into his bed? No. He wanted so much more than her delicious body. It didn't matter that she might never be free to marry him. He would be satisfied with her love.

He sighed heavily, his composure returning. "I'm sorry. I will behave from now on."

She stared down at her hands, suddenly uneasy. "I'm sorry too. Perhaps—if this is a trial for you—I should go home."

"Not yet, Juliana. Stay at least until the end of November." A note of entreaty crept into his voice. "Don't let this spoil our friendship, *chérie.*"

She lifted her face and gave him a tremulous smile. "It's forgotten already. Come inside, Paul, and let's finish our brandy."

Juliana decided it was time she learned to accept life without Adam as she faced her last week in Normandy. She was glad she'd come; the black depression that had enveloped her since their estrangement had eased slightly. Paul had the ability to amuse her and yet make her feel acutely desirable. But she felt that she was putting a strain on their friendship, unable to commit herself to the type of relationship he craved, and she realized that it would be better for them both if she returned home. Besides, it wasn't fair to saddle Martin with all her responsibilities, and it might do her good to take more interest in running the estates. She was also considering Keith's admonition that she permanently quit the smuggling business. She grinned at the thought. Maybe a small run now and then wouldn't hurt—just to keep the village supplied with tea and brandy.

She spent her last Tuesday in France helping Paul, Justin, and Maude gather in apples from the orchard. It was a demanding job. She picked the ripened fruit from the low, twisted branches until her arms ached, the muscles quivering. At midday, they broke for luncheon. Juliana sat against the old oaken cider press and ate hungrily, watching Paul and Justin pelt each other with handfuls of fallen, rotted apples. Maude, flapping her apron, chased the brood of chickens from the barn to make storage space for the heavy barrels they had filled.

That evening she and Paul drove the apple cart into the village for harvest home, a noisy celebration of cider-drinking and dancing gay country dances on the common. During the ride home, she snuggled up next to him on the driver's bench, craving warmth and simple human contact. It was an ordeal for Paul, his defenses lowered from drinking.

"You have two left feet, Paul," she murmured. "My poor toes are bruised."

He laughed, his face relaxed under a big felt hat. "You drank so much cider, I'm surprised you felt anything at all, *chérie.*"

The cart bounced over the bumpy dirt track. A sickle moon hung low in the sky, its light barely penetrating the blue-gray vapors that veiled the woods. Juliana's eyelids drooped sleepily. Then suddenly two black-cloaked horsemen materialized from the misty shadows of the oak-hazel coppice that loomed to the left.

"Stand and deliver!" the tallest rider exclaimed, spurring his horse toward Paul. A vizard concealed his face, but it was obvious by his unsteady voice and nervous gesturing that he was a novice to the crime.

Paul laughed contemptuously. "Little boys shouldn't play in the woods at night. Go home to your *maman* before she discovers your beds are empty." He lifted the reins and clucked softly to the horse. But the cart had barely rolled forward an inch than he found himself staring into the barrel of a pistol.

"Your purse, *monsieur*," the youth demanded angrily. "I assure you, I am not playing."

Paul remained unperturbed. "My purse? Well, my young highwayman, I have no purse. Search me if you like. In fact, the only article of value I'm carrying is a harvest bottle filled with cider." He raised a hand to reach back into the cart for the wooden bottle. "Why don't you two criminals go off into the hedgerow and get drunk instead of pestering us?"

"Put your hand down, *monsieur*, unless you want it blown off!"

"We're wasting our time," the second youth hissed, backing up his horse in disgust. "I told you we should have tried the main road."

The first rider waved his pistol menacingly toward Juliana. "She has a ring. The stone is big, too."

Juliana balled her fist and buried it in her skirts. "My wedding ring? No, impossible."

The youth swung his pistol sideways to level it at her forehead. "Hand it over, you bitch."

Juliana unballed her fist and slowly began tugging off the ring until Paul stopped her, his big rough hand covering hers. "No, *chérie,*" he murmured. "Just hold still."

"Let her keep it, Jean-Pierre," the second rider whined. "It probably isn't real."

"Jean-Pierre," Paul echoed, then sat up suddenly, thrusting Juliana behind him, his massive body shielding hers. "Jean-Pierre, the miller's son! I thought I recognized that voice. Why, you little swine. Your father will wring your dirty neck when I tell him what you're up to. But first, perhaps, I should teach you to intimidate a lady—"

Juliana gave a startled gasp as Paul sprang up from the bench and dove at the youth. "Paul, be careful! It isn't worth—"

The pistol exploded with a burst of amber sparks and a muffled roar. And then everything seemed to happen in a confused blur: the boy flinging down his weapon in horror; the sound of galloping hoofbeats as he and his cohort fled into the night; Paul slumping in her arms, his blood drenching her gown.

There wasn't time for hysteria. She tore off her shawl and knotted it tightly around Paul's waist to stanch the copious outpouring of blood. She whipped the frightened cart horse into a frantic pace, her eyes fixed on Paul's unmoving body. *Why?* her dazed mind asked over and over. *Oh, God, not Paul, not like this.*

She pounded on the heavy kitchen door until Maude and Justin appeared before her. In incoherent fragments of faltering French learned from her governess, she tried to explain what had happened.

"I will fetch the doctor," Maude cried, throwing a cloak on over her nightgown. "Oh, *pauvre monsieur!* Only a monster could do such a vicious thing!"

Justin and Phoebe helped Juliana carry Paul into the house, laying him on the parlor sofa. He was a big man, awkward to move, and a few moments after they had stretched him out, he opened his eyes and began muttering about the burning pain in his side. The ball had ripped into the muscular flesh of his waist, and Juliana's stomach knotted with dread as she helped Justin cut off the blood-soaked clothes and bathe the jagged fiery wound, washing away particles of singed flesh. Why didn't I just give up the ring? she thought wretchedly. Why had Paul antagonized the boy?

The sound of Logan crying penetrated her stupor. She nursed him back to sleep, brewed tea for her and Phoebe, then brooded at Paul's side until the doctor arrived and ordered everyone but Justin from the room. A half hour dragged out, and Juliana waited outside the door in agonized suspense, flinching as she heard Paul cry out twice in pain. Then finally the door opened, and Justin emerged, his nightshirt splotched with fresh blood, the doctor following several steps behind him.

"Well, madame, it wasn't as bad as it looked, after all," he explained to her in perfect English. "I've managed to remove the ball, and I'm confident that no vital organs were affected. However, he is in a great deal of pain, and I've given him laudanum to lessen his distress. I will return in the morning to check his progress. You must summon me at once, though, if he develops a fever."

"Is it all right to see him now, doctor?" she asked haltingly, awash with gratitude and relief.

"Oh, yes. Go in and sit with him until he falls asleep. He was asking for you."

Juliana stumbled into the room, Justin and Maude following. "Paul?" She knelt beside him, gently touching his cheek with her fingers.

Countless minutes passed. Then his eyelids lifted, and he smiled, recognizing her. *"Ma belle,"* he whispered. "Don't cry. I brought you here to make you happy, remember?"

She shook her head, tears slipping down her face and throat. "How can I be happy when my closest friend is suffering so needlessly? Oh, Paul, I was so worried about you. I thought that you . . . . I feared you might—"

"Madame," Maude interrupted with a whisper. "I think

we should let *monsieur le capitaine* sleep now. You and he can talk in the morning.''

Paul grabbed Juliana's hand, his grip surprisingly powerful. "Not yet. First, I must make a confession to you, *chérie.*"

"Confession? There's no need for that, Paul. You're confused. The doctor promised you would be fine."

"Is Justin here?" he asked suddenly. "Justin! Do you remember your history books, Justin? Do you remember reading to me about the Viking funerals at sea . . . the burning ships?"

"I remember, *oncle.* But I don't know why—"

Paul laughed quietly. "None of that splendor for me, Justin. You must bury me in the village graveyard beside your mother."

"And so I will—when the time comes." Justin edged toward the sofa, sharing a tolerant smile with Juliana. "But you're not going to die, *oncle.* It was only a flesh wound."

Paul's eyes glazed over with confusion as he tried to grasp his nephew's words, then suddenly his grasp on Juliana's hand tightened. "I beg your forgiveness, Juliana. I came between you and Adam."

"It wasn't your fault, Paul. I never blamed you. Anyway, this isn't the time to discuss all that."

"You don't understand. . . . Ah, *Dieu!*" His face convulsed as a spasm of pain passed through him. "I—I sent Leigh after him. I arranged for her passage back to the colonies. I . . . I thought she could keep Adam from returning to you. I knew that sooner or later, he would try . . . would realize that . . .''

"No, Paul," she breathed, feeling a faint gleam of hope brighten her heart at his words. "And it doesn't matter now, anyway."

"I took advantage of the situation," he continued weakly, "all the time knowing that you and he belonged together. It was obvious I caused trouble between you. Forgive my selfishness, *chérie.* I wanted you for myself."

"There's nothing to forgive, Paul," she whispered, her voice thick with tears—tears for him, for herself, for Adam.

"He loves you, *chérie,*" he said softly. "Perhaps even more than I.''

"Oh, Paul, if only I could believe—"

"Believe, Juliana," he advised her in a strong whisper. "I saw the desolation on his face the night he left you."

Maude tapped Juliana's shoulder. "Please, madame. This conversation is obviously distressing to both you and *monsieur*. A close brush with death is sometimes a blessing in disguise, forcing us to face the truth of our own emotions, *non?* But everything will take on a different perspective in the morning. Come, madame. *Monsieur le capitaine* needs his rest, and so do you."

Paul's eyes had closed again, but as Juliana rose to exit the parlor, he called out to her in a slurred voice. "You must go to him, *chérie*. Put pride behind you and find him. Neither of you will be truly happy until you're reunited. Bring him back to Mentreath, and we will toast your reconciliation with my best brandy. It will be like old times again."

"I—all right, Paul," Juliana said numbly, more to placate him than out of agreement to take his advice. Maude was right. They could pursue the subject later when Paul had begun to recover. She couldn't bear delving deeper into it tonight.

The following morning, Jean-Pierre and his companion turned themselves in to the local magistrate, confessing to a string of petty offenses, convinced they would be hanged if Paul did not survive his injury. Juliana left Normandy almost three weeks later, in the middle of December, entrusting Paul to Maude's capable hands. He was in general good health, and his wound was healing without infection. They parted on affectionate terms. Sadly reconciled to the fact that they would forever remain only friends, Paul promised to visit Juliana at Mentreath after he had recuperated fully.

By tacit agreement, they'd never resumed the conversation Paul had initiated the night of his shooting. Juliana supposed he might be embarrassed by what he'd confessed, even though she held no grudges against him. And, of course, it was possible that a discussion held during his drugged suffering had slipped his mind entirely. But every single one of his words still haunted her, resurrecting the agonizing memories of Adam that she'd tried to deaden within her heart. Why had Paul felt so strongly that Adam had never stopped loving her? Was it possible that her husband had still truly cared for her when he left Cornwall?

For most of our marriage I was so intent on fighting him that I failed to realize how deeply, how irrevocably I'd fallen in love with him, she thought forlornly. *And then, even after I admitted my feelings for him, I never really tried to understand him. He was justified in accusing me of not trusting him.* Oh, God, how different everything looked in retrospect! How much easier it was to see her foolish mistakes long after she'd committed them. If only they had learned the value of compromise. If only they'd viewed their difficulties not as barriers but as stepping stones to a closer relationship. If only she had yielded just a little more.

It was useless to search for answers now, she decided with a heavy heart, and perhaps she should merely heed Justin's discreetly whispered advice that she not take his uncle's sickbed ramblings seriously, that the laudanum had put him into a maudlin frame of mind. *For whatever reason, Adam has put me out of his life,* she reminded herself with brutal frankness. *No matter how badly she yearned for him, shouldn't she attempt to do the same?*

She had a total change of heart the very same day she arrived back at Mentreath. Doris met her at the door with a welcoming hug and the message that Mrs. Simpson had come down from Devon a week before, and wanted to see her immediately in the parlor. Juliana braced herself for the interview. It had to be something important to bring Barbara here so unexpectedly.

She swept into the parlor, her spirits collapsing as she took in Barbara's tight, worried face and nervously clasped hands. "Oh, no. Please don't say you've brought me bad news, Barbara."

"Perhaps you ought to sit down for this, my dear." Barbara motioned Juliana to the settee, launching into her explanation without preamble. "Three weeks ago, I decided to pay Keith a surprise visit at his office. He wasn't there, which isn't unusual, but as I was leaving, the post arrived. Now, I didn't mean to pry, Juliana, and I won't go into the details, but in his mail I found a letter sent from Boston.

It—it was a plea for help from a man named Colin Bartell, Adam's partner in the shipyard venture.

"Adam is utterly miserable, Juliana, and Colin is at his wits' end. He claims Adam is drinking excessively and making so many irrational decisions that the business could go into bankruptcy. I'd hate to see the shipyard fail like that after all the work that Colin's put into it, but it's my brother I'm most concerned with—"

"Why are you telling me this?" Juliana interrupted, her eyes dark with distress. "Why should I care anymore what happens to Adam?"

Barbara lowered her voice in desperation. "Frankly, I don't understand *why* you should care, but I sense that you still do. He needs you, Juliana. He needs your love. God, you don't have any idea of how he was before he met you. I know my brother. I know he loves you. Please—give him another chance."

"I don't think so, Barbara," Juliana replied, her heart slamming painfully in her chest. "You don't know what happened between us. You don't know the terrible things that were said, that *I* said. . . ."

"Juliana, does it really matter who said or did what? It's what's in your hearts that counts. Maybe this separation has been good for both of you. You've had time to contemplate your mistakes, to gain a fresh appreciation of each other."

Juliana glanced away, fighting against the tangled feelings that surfaced at the thought of a reconciliation with Adam. Dear Lord, was it possible for them to begin again? She wondered whether Adam would even be willing to try. Could they recapture the sweet essence of their love? Was it worth the risk of making one last attempt, of throwing away her pride to find out? He might rebuff her. He might even refuse to see her. But on the other hand . . .

"I'll have to think it over, Barbara. The weather makes a lengthy sea voyage impossible right now, anyway, and I have the baby to consider now, too." She rose, suddenly needing to retreat to the privacy of her own chamber where she could confront her emotions. "I need some time to absorb this. You'll know as soon as I decide. Excuse me, Barbara. I—I just have to be by myself."

Chapter Thirty-four

Leigh Spencer had been standing in the doorway of the ship-yard office for over twenty minutes before Adam even acknowledged her presence. She had correctly interpreted his rude silence to mean that he wasn't pleased to see her. Ordinarily, she would never have deigned to visit the wharves. In fact, Adam and his partner had forbidden her to come here at all, but she'd decided tonight was an exception. She sighed impatiently, offended at having to wait about like a servant for her master's attention. She didn't dare speak first. Her relationship with Adam was too precarious to stretch its boundaries.

She sighed again, then deliberately wriggled her shoulders so that her cloak parted to reveal what she wore beneath it. There! she thought, flushing with satisfaction as Adam's head lifted a fraction of an inch. Her opulent figure showed to advantage in a red taffeta gown with a deeply scooped bodice and wide lace-ruffled skirts. She felt confident that she looked too enticing for him to continue ignoring her.

Adam glanced up at her then, flinging his quill across the desk in annoyance. He'd been hoping that she'd take the hint from his silence that he wanted to be left alone. "What the devil are you doing down here this late at night?"

Leigh closed the office door behind her, quaking inside at his hostile tone, but refusing to be deterred from her purpose. This certainly wasn't the reaction she'd hoped for, but then, lately with Adam, she never knew quite what to expect. His recent tendency to mercurial outbursts both frightened and excited her.

"I might ask you exactly the same thing, Adam Tre-

293

mayne. Did you forget we were invited to a ball this evening?''

"Yes," he said without a thread of concern in his voice. "As a matter of fact, I did." He noted her new gown with a coldly insolent gaze, wondering how much it had cost him, finding it more vulgar than appealing. "Is that what you came here to tell me?"

"Yes." Her confidence had wilted a little when he'd failed to compliment her on her appearance. "Colin allowed us the use of his coach for the evening. I believe we still could make it there for an hour or so if we left now."

"And had I promised to take you?"

"Well, not—not in so many words." She chewed the inside of her cheek, realizing what he was leading up to. She simply didn't know how to manipulate him when he was in one of these moods.

"It wouldn't hurt either of us to do a little more socializing, Adam," she said quickly. "I'm frankly sick of staying home all the time."

He grinned unpleasantly. "I don't believe I've ever stopped you from going anywhere except the shipyard, have I?"

"No," she replied, her pretty face petulant. "And perhaps I will start accepting more invitations, if that's your attitude. Do you remember Tobias Willard, that polite young sea captain from Newport? Well, he's in Boston again, and I suspect he's staying on just to court me. He always brings up the subject of marriage whenever I see him."

"Then I'm sure he'd be delighted to escort you to the ball tonight."

"Oh, I didn't mean—" She stopped short, aware that her attempt to make him jealous had backfired. Suddenly her eyes lit on the brandy decanter on his desk. "Why, you've been drinking again, haven't you? That's why you forgot about the ball tonight. That's why you're in such a stinking humor."

Adam didn't bother to respond. He'd already dismissed her from his mind, his attention returned to the contract he'd been working on before she interrupted him. In fact, he was not drunk, though it was a sure bet he would be before the night ended. Work and drink. Anything to keep him from having to deal with the gnawing emptiness inside him. Anything to keep him from thinking about Juliana and the times they'd shared . . . the times they could have shared if they had fulfilled the promise of love that had first drawn them together. The pain of their breakup should have lessened by now, but it hadn't, eating away at him until he felt as though he were utterly hollow inside. He'd given up the hope that his suffering would ease. What could a future without Juliana hold for him but a deeper descent into loneliness?

Leigh twisted her hands in vexation, trying to figure out what caused his strange behavior. Her heart contracted suddenly. It's his wife, she realized, feeling sick inside. He still hasn't gotten over Juliana. Lord, how long would it take him to forget her? She experienced a stab of guilt as she recalled the beautiful young Cornishwoman's compassion toward her. But even stronger in Leigh than conscience was the growing fear that Adam might be nurturing a secret hope of returning to his wife.

"Adam, I've been wondering, well, I—You haven't been considering returning to Cornwall, have you?"

Slowly he looked up from the desk, the anguish on his face too striking for her to miss. "Leigh, I consider returning to Cornwall practically every hour of the day. Does that answer your question?"

She glanced away, unsettled, not knowing what to say next. She hadn't been prepared for his honesty. She almost wished she hadn't indulged her curiosity.

"Do you really think that's wise, Adam?" she asked after a short hesitation. "You and she haven't seen each other for nearly a year now."

A wry smile briefly twisted his mouth. "Don't worry, Leigh. She'd never take me back. I'm not deluding myself there. But if I thought for one second that she would—" He shuffled through the papers scattered across the desk, embarrassed at the emotion he'd revealed, desperate to get off the subject.

He frowned. "Damnation, can you believe this? That odious little Philadelphian merchant and his West Indian partner intend to pay off part of their bill in rum and molasses. We should've filled the ship's seams with molasses instead of oakum. Sometimes I just can't believe the way Colin runs this business.''

Leigh relaxed, relieved that the conversation had shifted away from Juliana. ''I thought it was common practice to accept goods for partial payment. Of course, I don't know anything about business—''

''No, you don't,'' Adam said brusquely. ''And I'm beginning to wonder whether Colin does either. Take this issue of the shipyard workers demanding higher pay. Colin's afraid they'll walk out on us if he doesn't increase their wages. I say let them go. We'll soon replace them.''

''But they're some of the finest carpenters in the colonies. At least that's what Colin claims. And you have to admit that the shipyard's doing well.''

He ignored her comments, muttering angrily under his breath. ''I also think it's time we began refusing these damned merchants free tonnage.''

''But Colin said—''

''Goddamn you!'' Adam shouted, slamming his fist down on the desk. ''Who asked for your opinion anyway, you interfering little bitch? If you can't keep your stupid mouth closed, then get the hell out of my office.''

Tears sprang to her eyes. ''There's no n-need to be so abusive, Adam. I only wanted to h-help—''

''Then sit down on that bloody bench, and don't talk until I finish what I'm doing. Lord Almighty!'' He scowled in irritation as she began to sob. ''For heaven's sake, Leigh! Can't you cry a little quieter?''

''Y-you're so mean to me, Adam. You're always t-taking out your nasty moods on m-me.''

''I take them out on everyone I encounter, actually,'' he retorted quietly, sighing with a combination of impatience and self-disgust. ''Look, Leigh, if you're that miserable around me, I suggest you marry that polite captain of yours and start a new life for yourself.''

''But, Adam, I'm—I'm *soiled.* . . .''

''You are *not* soiled,'' he said, his features softening slightly. ''If he loves you, he'll understand.''

''But I . . . I don't want Tobias. I want you, Adam.'' She spoke his name in a breathless caressing whisper, gliding across the room and around the desk to sit down in his lap.

She curled her plump arms around his neck, the heady scent of her imported frangipani perfume filling his nostrils. Adam sucked in a sharp breath, his body tensing. He didn't want this woman. He wanted Juliana. God, how he wanted her! He had awakened her beautiful body to the pleasures of love. How could he forget the exquisite feel of burying himself inside her, the blazing ecstasy of their nights together?

"Don't, Leigh. I'm warning you. Don't tempt me into doing something we'll both regret."

"I wouldn't regret it, Adam," she whispered against his ear. "Anyway, you can't just order me out of your life like that. You owe it to Lucy's memory to take care of me."

The mention of his late wife's name was like a wave of cold water splashed on Adam's passion-starved senses. He reacted instantly, thrusting Leigh off his lap and back onto her feet.

"That's rich, Leigh—suggesting I bed you out of respect for your sister's memory." He sneered in disgust. "What a moving tribute."

Leigh blinked in bewilderment, wondering what was happening to him. Usually she only had to mention Lucy to rouse a response of guilt in Adam. "You've forgotten all about Lucy and Anne, haven't you?" she asked accusingly. "I'll bet you never even think of them anymore. It's Juliana again—I just know it. She's responsible for turning you into such a cold, unfeeling monster!"

Anger tautened Adam's features. "If Juliana did anything at all, my dear, it was to teach me how to feel again."

"Well, I—"

He didn't give her a chance to continue. Swinging out of his chair, he grabbed his coat from the wall peg behind him and forcefully propelled her to the door.

"Let's get out of here. It's obvious I'm not about to draw up that contract tonight."

"Does that—does that mean you've changed your mind about taking me to the ball?" she inquired in a hopeful whisper.

Adam's temper boiled. Spewing out a shower of curses, he dropped Leigh's arm and strode back into his office to extinguish the oil lamp. "It means we're going home, Leigh, where I intend to sit in peace drinking fine brandy until it's time to go to bed." He glared at her. "*Alone.* Have I made myself clear?"

She made a face at him behind his back. "Quite."

They rode home in glacial silence, both aching for the love that seemed to be denied them. It was a cold, quiet night. Gossamer clouds of fog rolled in off the sea and drifted across the wharves, reminding Adam of the Cornish mist, reminding him inevitably of Juliana. Did she ever think of him? Would she encourage their son to grow up hating him because he'd left them? Pain seared his heart as he recalled practically every word of Barbara's last letter chronicling little Logan's growth. *Oh, my boy, my son!* Every day the desire to see him became stronger, more difficult to restrain. He wanted to participate in Logan's upbringing. He wanted to share the experience with Juliana, feeling instinctively that her passion for living would make her a wonderful mother. He knew that he would never forget her; the best he could hope for was to numb the misery of missing her so that he could function normally again.

Leigh leaned forward suddenly to close the window, briefly jarring Adam's train of thought. In the darkness she reminded him of his first wife, and then guiltily he realized that he'd had an easier time facing Lucy's death than he was adjusting to living without Juliana. But then what he'd felt for Lucy had been no more than a blaze of selfish passion that had quickly burned itself out—nothing compared to the sweeping range of emotions he had experienced loving his stormy auburn-haired temptress. *I think I understand a little better now what happened to us, Juliana,* he thought with aching sadness. *It was always so much easier to blame each other than to accept responsibility for our own behavior. We wasted all our energy doubting and accusing instead of spending it on overcoming our problems. We didn't have long enough together to build a solid foundation of trust, and now . . .* He gazed out at the waterfront, his eyes dark with regret. And now it was too late. His chest tightened. He would have to learn to accept that. He was certain that Juliana had.

Chapter Thirty-five

During the six-week voyage from Falmouth into Boston Harbor, Juliana had a surfeit of time for reflection. With ruthless honesty, she reviewed every phase of her relationship with Adam, the sweet times and the bitter, the passion and the pain. And then finally she refused to think anymore. From now on she would let her instincts guide her, following them across an ocean to find her love, trusting she would know what to do when the time came.

She had her trunk sent ahead to the inn and hired a sedan-chair to convey her the short distance to the shipyard on the northeast shore, a densely populated section of shops, wharves, stone warehouses, and private residences. The unevenly cobbled streets were crowded with merchants bustling about in elegant finery, housewives running errands with their servants, and sailors gathering around benches outside the grog shops. Juliana couldn't help looking for Adam's face among the passersby.

By the time she reached Bartell's shipyard, her insides were cramping with a combination of nerves, fatigue, and excitement. She wished she had someone to talk to, to confide in, but Phoebe had refused to come, convinced savages were waiting to scalp her the minute she disembarked in the harbor.

She climbed out of the chair, her gaze drawn beyond the storehouses to the private dock where craftsmen were at work: joiners, coopers, caulkers, painters, and carpenters. A sloop was under construction, and the air rang with the sounds of shouting and caulking irons hammering oakum. A light breeze carried the strong odors of fish, pitch, and seasoned timber as it rippled through the lofty tangle of masts, spars, and rigging that cluttered the skyline.

Impervious to the interested looks she received from the workmen, she strode briskly to the front of the main building. A middle-aged clerk in the outer office told her Mr. Bartell was in conference, but she brushed him off with a haughty glance and proceeded down the corridor until she found the shipwright's private office.

The door opened before she reached it, and a well-dressed man emerged. "Unless the final order of canvas is delayed, I see no reason why she won't be completed by the end of April," a polite voice inside the room promised the departing visitor. "I assure you, we'll do our best."

Juliana made her way into the office and closed the door before she could be turned away. A bespectacled young man clad in a loose ink-stained shirt and wrinkled buff breeches stood behind an immense desk that was strewn with drafts, contracts, and unanswered correspondences.

Colin Bartell blinked, praying he hadn't forgotten another appointment. He thrust his long arms into his jacket, trying to recall whether this woman was the wife of one of the London merchants he'd met with earlier in the week to discuss financing.

"How may I help you, ma'am?" he asked, coming around the desk to show her to a chair.

"You can tell me where my husband is," she said with a coolness she didn't feel.

"Your husband?"

"Adam Tremayne. He is your partner, isn't he?"

Colin backed up to his chair and sat down heavily. He was a master shipwright who had learned his craft in a royal English shipyard on the Thames, but he'd never have gotten established without Tremayne's backing. In fact, Adam was like a brother to him. But, Lord, he didn't want to get involved in *this*.

"My appearance has come as a shock to you, Mr. Bartell," she said dryly. "Obviously you weren't aware Adam had a wife."

He sighed, removing his spectacles to rub his pointed nose. "Oh, no. I was very much aware of your existence. I know the whole pitiful story."

Uncomfortable silence mounted between them. Juliana sat stiff as a flagstaff in the chair, pinning the shipwright with a merciless stare. Finally, Colin slapped his hands down on the desk, frowned, and blew out another sigh.

"He's gone into town on business. I don't expect him back here today."

"Then I'll wait. Right here in this office—in this chair—until he returns."

"No, madam, that won't be necessary," Colin said defeatedly. "Adam is still residing with me. I'll escort you from the shipyard this very afternoon and allow you the privacy of my home for your reunion."

"Thank you, Mr. Bartell. You're most kind."

"Kind? Not at all. Living with Adam has been the most miserable experience of my life. You can barely say good day without him snapping your head off. He's rude to our customers. He drinks too much and quarrels with the workmen. Quite frankly, I've often been tempted to send for you myself. I'm delighted you're going to take him off my back."

"Well, that remains to be seen, doesn't it?"

He peered at her nearsightedly. "No. I don't think so. You must have strong feelings for the man if you came all this way to see him after what you've gone through together, and I can tell you that Adam loves you so much, he's slowly dying of it. Oh, I don't doubt you find that difficult to believe, but then you haven't known him as long as I have. No, madam. Adam is a complex man. You've no idea of the torment he's put himself through, the enormous burden of guilt he carries."

Juliana gave him a smile that pierced his heart with its poignant sadness. "Oh, but you're wrong. I know Adam loves me. I know that he's driven by inner demons that will destroy him unless he confronts them. That's why I'm here, Mr. Bartell."

Adam wasn't expected to arrive at the house until suppertime, and Juliana made good use of the long wait to soak in her first real bath since leaving Cornwall. She was determined to look her best, to face Adam with every ounce of her feminine charms. Somehow just looking nice gave her an added edge, made her feel calmer about meeting him.

Yet she was anything but calm when the time came to descend the narrow walnut staircase and enter the dining room. She balked at the last step, gripping the carved newel post until her fingers numbed. Through the half-opened door, she could see the guests gathered at the table: Colin; two of his prospective clients; Adam, his back to her; and seated next to him, Leigh, like a tawny tigress in gold satin. A sour taste filled Juliana's mouth. She wasn't really surprised. But what did startle her was the difference in Adam's appearance. He'd lost at least ten pounds, and when he turned his head to speak to Colin, she noticed how gauntly drawn his cheeks had become. But the rough profile and arrogant jawline remained unchanged, and he was still so recklessly handsome, it hurt to look at him.

She ventured away from the staircase and stood in the shadows beside the small wooden serving cart a maidservant had just wheeled out from the kitchen. Colin had refused to intervene on her behalf, insisting she confront Adam on her own. She realized now she'd have to wait a few hours longer. She couldn't possibly go in there and face him in front of all those people. What needed to be said between them was too private, too painful for anyone else to hear.

"You going in to supper, ma'am?" the maidservant asked politely, setting a tureen of steaming lobster bisque on the cart.

"No," Juliana murmured, stepping aside. She was trying to listen to the conversation inside the dining room. One of Colin's guests was laying out detailed instructions for the hull design of his vessel, and Adam drained his wine goblet to interrupt him.

"We'll need a down payment of seven hundred pounds to cover our initial expenses if you expect her to be launched on schedule," he said, his tone brusque.

Colin muttered something about not discussing money at the table, and Leigh, apparently thinking to console him, laid her hand on Adam's thigh and patted him under the table. Juliana had a wicked urge to carry the tureen of lobster bisque into the dining room and dump it on his lap, where Leigh's small white hand rested so intimately. She had the urge to, but she didn't. Instead, she turned and quietly wandered through the hallway until the glow of a dying fire beckoned her into a small drawing room. A year ago she would have given in to the impulse, the consequences be damned. But not now.

She dropped into a corner chair, watching the fire fade to smoldering embers. She hadn't prepared a speech for Adam. She'd find the appropriate words when it came time.

And it came sooner than she expected.

The door creaked open, and she peered into the darkness to see him entering the room—to be alone? she wondered. Her heartbeat accelerated, the blood singing through her veins. What an idiot she'd been to think she could face him with her emotions in check! How could she possibly hope to reason with him when the mere sight of him drove every sensible thought from her mind?

He loosened his neckcloth and strode toward the sofa. Then as he folded at the waist to sit, he glanced up and noticed the woman seated in the chair. He stood, looking surprised.

"I'm sorry, ma'am," he said, edging back to the door. "I didn't realize there was anyone else in the room. Mr. Bartell did mention he had another guest in the house. Obviously, neither of us is in the mood for socializing."

"No, Adam—don't go."

At the sound of her voice, he pivoted and stared in disbelief. *"Juliana?"* He moved haltingly toward the chair, his eyes devouring her as she rose slowly to face him.

Silence crackled between them. Then Adam drew a long, ragged breath, openly shaken. "My God, Juliana. I feel as though I'm in a dream. I—I never thought I'd see you again."

Juliana fought with all her will not to break under the force of the powerful emotions surging through her. The expression on Adam's face was all the proof she needed that he still loved her, that he had never stopped loving her.

She shook her head, struggling for composure, trying to speak past the tears that closed her throat. "You fool, Adam Tremayne. It would serve you right if I had left you alone to suffer in your own private hell. What made you think that either of us could ever find happiness apart? Or was I mistaken in coming here, Adam? Have you finally made the life you wanted for yourself?''

He flinched at her words, his eyes filled with suffering. ''When I left Cornwall, I left behind everything that gave my life meaning.''

''Then why didn't you let me go with you, Adam? You knew I was carrying your child.''

''I knew I was hurting you, that we seemed compelled for some unaccountable reason to keep hurting each other,'' he said unevenly. ''And I was always painfully aware that I made you marry me, Juliana. Yes, I was arrogant and unrefined, and perhaps I shouldn't have tried to force fate, but God knows I've been richly punished.'' He passed a hand over his face, his voice hoarse. ''You brought me the only happiness I've ever known. It broke my heart to leave you.''

''Mine too,'' she whispered. ''Oh, Adam, how could you have been so blind? You didn't force me to marry you any more than you forced Lucy to follow you into the wilderness. I made the choice, and so did she. You're no more responsible for her death that I am for Graham's. I beg you, Adam, for us—let go of the past—even our past.''

His hand lowered slowly. ''For us? After all the hurt and disappointment, you'd be willing to try again?''

She smiled through her tears, raising her hand to touch the few strands of silver at his temple. ''Willing with every particle of my stubborn Cornish soul,'' she said shakily.

He caught her hand, the warm contact of his brown tapered fingers igniting liquid flames in the pit of her abdomen. ''How much you've changed,'' he said, his voice catching. ''Still headstrong, still incredibly beautiful, but so poised and self-possessed. As a girl, you bewitched me, Juliana. As a woman, you devastate me.''

''The past year was hard on me, Adam. Loneliness changes a person, as you well know.''

A shadow crossed his face. ''Was it loneliness that lured you to Normandy?''

''Don't.'' Anger and pain darkened her golden-green eyes. ''Paul Delisle was a good friend to me when I needed one—when you left me. I haven't made an issue of the fact that you're here with Leigh.''

"She doesn't mean anything to me. I couldn't turn her away before, but there's nothing to bind me to her now."

"Or to the past?" she challenged. "Has your debt to Lucy and Anne been paid?"

He exhaled slowly, forever releasing the burden that had imprisoned his soul. "Yes."

Juliana's heart rejoiced in his freedom. "I love you, Adam."

"I love you too, Juliana."

Cupping her radiant face in his hands, he closed his eyes and kissed her with a passion that separation had not dimmed. "I'll never leave you again," he whispered against her mouth.

She clung to him, melting into the comfort of his embrace until suddenly he thrust her away from him. "My son," he exclaimed. "Is he here with you? Can I see him?"

She laughed, the tears in her eyes stemming from happiness now. "I left him at Mentreath with Barbara. He's still too young to travel this far."

He squeezed her shoulders. "Tomorrow morning we'll arrange for passage home. I want to see him, Juliana."

"Adam—" She became serious again. "Logan is still a baby. Another two months won't make that much difference to him. Your father is another matter. He's dying."

"I know." He hesitated. "He wants to see me."

"Adam, please. Make amends with him. For me."

"Yes." He smiled. "For us."

Chapter Thirty-six

Juliana stretched luxuriously beneath the covers, feeling the comforting warmth of Adam's body fitting against hers. Her eyes still closed, she remained in the same pleasurable position for several moments longer, savoring the profound bliss that filled her at being back home with her husband. It's been a week now, she mused. A week of heaven . . . How many mornings had she lain awake in this same bed, her heart as empty from loneliness as it was now brimming with joyful contentment? How many mornings had she been loathe to rise, dreading the prospect of facing another day without him?

Nothing would ever separate them again. Nothing in the past. Nothing in the future. It was a commitment they'd made to each other during their short stay at the Tremayne plantation house in Virginia, where Adam and his father had at last reconciled their differences. Determined not to interfere in Adam's relationship with his family, Juliana had spent her days there strolling along the sweeping lawns and sitting in the enclosed formal gardens that fronted the tidal river. Only she knew the tremendous effort of love and courage it had taken Adam to ask for—and to accept—his father's forgiveness. But finally forgiveness had been granted—on both sides—and William Tremayne had died at peace with his youngest son.

She opened her eyes and slowly turned her head, gasping in surprise to find Adam awake and watching her, love and passion burning in the muted gray depths of his gaze. She lifted her hand to his face, touching his mouth gently as if to reassure herself that he was really here beside her again.

"Good morning, Adam," she whispered.

"Good morning, love," he whispered back, kissing her fingers.

Easing himself up onto one elbow, he stared down into her eyes and smiled at the sheer delight he knew at awakening to find her in his arms. He, too, was glad to be back at Mentreath, although privately he'd enjoyed their lengthy voyage across the Atlantic, he and Juliana sequestered in their tiny cabin with no demands on them but that they become reacquainted. Separation had only added spice to their lovemaking. In bed together now, they exhibited no shyness, no holding back, as if they strived to make up for all the time lost between them.

"What are you thinking?" Juliana asked softly, drinking in the sight of his rough beloved face above hers.

His smile widened. "Do you really need to ask?"

Their gazes connected in the ages-old signal that passes between a man and a woman. Then Adam dipped his head and melded his mouth with her temptingly parted lips. Slowly, sensuously, he sucked her lower lip between his even white teeth, nibbling the tender flesh with an erotic tenderness that sent a shower of sparks shooting through her body. His tongue slipped into her mouth, intercepting the provocative moan of pleasure she gave. Wrapping his fingers in the luxuriant heaviness of her hair, he braced his hard, muscular body between her legs and deepened his kiss.

Wanton in her need for him, Juliana laced her delicate fingers around the nape of his neck and kissed him back until he pulled away to drag his mouth in a molten path down her throat and shoulders. She gasped with building excitement, her breath sharply drawn in and fluttering out over lips that were moist and engorged with passion. Her spine curved in unconscious anticipation. The flame in the hollow of her belly flickered and spread, filling her loins with scorching heat. Craving closer contact, she inched her fingers down the length of his back and fitted her fingers around his tight buttocks to draw him lower.

"Adam," she groaned as she felt his mouth close around her nipple, which shamelessly sprang erect beneath his teasing tongue. "I want you—I need you so!"

"I'm here for you, my love," he whispered huskily. "I'll be here for you forever. . . ."

Forever! she thought joyously. *This is the start of forever for us.* Tears of emotion filled her eyes, but before they could fall, she blinked them back, refusing to permit anything to spoil her enjoyment of the moment. They were together again. They were reunited, their hearts joined in harmony, their bodies seeking to express their love. And had it been worth all the pain? Yes . . . oh, yes!

Adam lifted his head and smiled lazily, his hand brushing her taut abdomen and wandering lower with bold intimacy. He delighted in the unflawed loveliness of her body, still firm and supple after bearing him a son. God, he thought, inhaling deeply to control his desire, she excites me more now than when I first met her. To think they'd been given another chance—a chance to spend eternity together. He worshiped her. He trusted her with the secrets of his soul. She was the center of his life. She *was* his life.

"I love you," he said fiercely. "I love you, my darling."

His fingers tangled in the dark triangle of hair between her thighs, slipping downward to caress and probe the most sensitive depths of her body. He felt the sweet fluid of her excitement as he rubbed and teased without mercy, and he knew she was more than ready to welcome him.

"Now, Adam," she urged him breathlessly, her head twisting against the pillow. "Oh, now—"

Still, he delayed, continuing his calculated sensual assault until he felt her tense and then shudder heatedly against his hand. Securing his free arm around her waist, he drew her toward him and held her tightly as the spasms of release shook her slender figure. Then suddenly he pressed her back into the mattress and maneuvered himself between her eagerly opened thighs.

Juliana shivered expectantly. She no longer fought or questioned the desires of her body. She obeyed them . . . as she had finally learned to obey the innermost urgings of her heart.

"I love you, Adam," she whispered, closing her eyes in rapture as she experienced the pleasure of his first powerful thrust. "Oh, God!"

He kissed her again and she whimpered into his mouth as

she felt him pull back—only to drive himself deeper into her accommodating warmth. Desire throbbed through her system as he repeated the teasing rhythm, each thrust leading them closer and closer to the ecstasy they sought. Then with a low fierce growl deep in his throat, he plunged into her one final time, and Juliana stiffened, her body quivering in climax. Sobbing with delight, she felt a violent tremor jolt through Adam's frame, and then the warmness of his seed foaming into her womb. Gathering her against his damp, darkly furred chest, he kissed her moist eyelids, the tip of her nose, her adorable stubborn chin.

"Juliana, my beloved," he murmured, his voice languid with satisfaction. "My wild beauty . . . I'll never hurt you again."

"We'll never hurt each other again," she corrected softly, fulfillment tranquilizing her whole being as he cradled her in his arms.

Julian stayed locked in her husband's possessive embrace for a long time before she finally disengaged herself and slid from the bed to dress. Nothing would have pleased her more than to remain beside him until he arose, but she had a busy morning ahead. In an hour she was to begin conducting interviews for a nursemaid for Logan so that Doris would be free to continue strictly as housekeeper and Phoebe as her personal maid. But first she wanted to feed and cuddle the baby, perhaps take him out to the garden for an hour in the sunshine.

"Love, it's still early," Adam said softly from the depths of the curtained four-poster. "Come back to bed."

"I've too much to do this morning," she replied absently, her mind running through the thousand questions she had prepared for the prospective nursemaid. She finished fastening the bodice of her lightweight plum silk gown and fluffed out its skirts over her petticoats. She musn't forget to insist on references.

"Go back to sleep if you want," she encouraged her husband, her thoughts circling back to him as she paused at the dressing table for a brief toilette. "Oh, by the way, Doris wondered whether you'd like breakfast in the winter parlor today, or—" She halted in amusement, turning back to the bed to discover Adam was already asleep, his sinewy brown arms wrapped lovingly around her pillow.

The old house was coming to life, heavy-eyed servants emerging from their quarters, hiding yawns behind their palms as Juliana greeted them on her way to the nursery. Phoebe met her at the door, pressing a warning finger to her lips.

"Baby cut another tooth last night, ma'am," she whispered. "He's been fed and bathed. I just rocked 'im back off to sleep."

"Oh, thank you, Phoebe," Juliana said in an undertone, feeling a little pang of disappointment to have been deprived of the pleasure.

Smiling with anticipation, she tiptoed across the room to the richly carved wooden cradle and peered down at the pink-cheeked infant sprawled out on the feather mattress.

"Oh, my little cherub," she told him softly. "Mama missed you so these past few months!"

Gently, she reached down and rearranged the blanket covering his perfect, plump body. He'd grown so much while she was gone. He had even taken his first steps! She could never bear to leave him for that long again.

"I'll be off now, ma'am, if ee don't mind," Phoebe whispered. "Robbie's takin' me and Doris into town today."

Juliana looked up from the cradle with a pleased expression. "So, you're finally speaking to him."

The girl's eyes glittered wickedly. "Only through Doris, ma'am. I want to make 'im suffer a little bit longer for runnin' off to America."

"Good for you," Juliana said, smiling. "These men need to know we won't be taken for granted."

"Poor Robbie," an amused baritone voice drawled from the doorway. "I hate to think of what gruesome punishment the pair of you are plotting for him."

"Adam!" Juliana exclaimed quietly, whirling toward him. "I thought you were going to stay in bed. Do lower your voice, or you'll wake the baby."

Adam strode into the nursery, grinning at Phoebe as she brushed past him in embarrassment. "Well, what if I do awaken him? Then I suppose I shall have to pick him up and play with him, won't I? Now, wouldn't that be a shame?''

As if on cue, Logan stretched and opened his gray-green eyes, his rosebud mouth breaking into a smile to see his mother and the big smiling man bending over his cradle.

"Mama! Mama!" he cried excitedly, lifting his pudgy arms to her. "Up, Mama!"

Juliana leaned down to lift the infant, but before she could, Adam shouldered her aside and scooped Logan up into his arms, carrying him over to the window that overlooked the garden and, just beyond, the sea.

"Daddy," he whispered coaxingly into the child's tiny ear. "Say, 'Daddy,' Logan."

Slowly, Juliana followed after them, watching father and son with proud reverence shining in her eyes. Joy flooding through her, she stopped at her husband's side and stared out the window over the stone wall that surrounded the garden. A sudden blur of movement on a distant cliff attracted her attention, and she caught her breath in wonder, releasing it with a wistful smile as a flock of seagulls took flight across the pale summer sky.

" 'Tis so quiet at the cove these days," she mused aloud. "Adam, do you think we could convince your mother to come stay with us awhile? She'll be very lonely now."

"That's a wonderful suggestion, darling. My uncle would've heartily approved.'' The baby gurgled and waved his arms playfully, swatting his father on the chin. Adam chuckled. "Our Logan here also seems to like the idea. Perhaps the little devil will help cheer up his grandmother."

Adam lifted his gaze then and followed the route of his wife's absorbed gaze, noting there were no ships on the horizon. The days of smuggling at Mentreath are over, he thought a trifle sadly. Still, he wasn't a man to sit about idle like so many of his contemporaries. While in Virginia, he had visited his brother's thriving tobacco plantation. To his surprise, Edgar had become something of a farming enthusiast over the years, having achieved great success conducting agricultural experiments with crop rotation. Adam had been sufficiently impressed by what he'd seen to decide he would investigate the feasibility of employing the revolutionary technique when he returned to Cornwall. It was obvious that improved farming methods would increase food yields. With the time, land, and money to invest in this new venture, he saw an opportunity to make a valuable contribution to the people who had given him so much.

He shifted his regard back to Juliana's pensive face, the love he felt for her overflowing his heart. "We'll make a good life together, Juliana," he promised her, his voice deepening with feeling. "We'll rise above all the sadness of the past. Our son will grow up in the happiest of homes."

She inclined her head and smiled up at him, gazing into his darkly handsome countenance and seeing there the purest reflection of her own abiding devotion. "I know, Adam," she said in a simple reaffirmation of her loving trust in him. "I know."